# MANSIONS OF MADNESS

*second edition*

## Six Classic Explorations of the Unknown, the Deserted, and the Insane

*By*

**Michael DeWolfe**
**Wesley Martin**
**Mark Morrison**
**Keith Herber**
**Fred Behrendt**
**Penny Love**
**Liam Routt**

*cover painting* **Lee Gibbons**

*interior illustrations* **David Lee Ingersoll, Janet Aulisio, Sam Inabinet**

*editorial and additional material* **David Conyers, William Dunn, Keith Herber, Charlie Krank**

*maps, plans, and scans* **David Conyers, Carol Triplett-Smith, Lydia Ortiz, our friends at Pegasus Spiele**

*additional editorial* **Matt Helm, Lynn Willis, Anne Ω. Merritt**

*layout* **Charlie Krank**

*Chaosium is* **Charlie Krank, Lynn Willis, Dustin Wright, & Fergie**

CHAOSIUM®
INC.

**New England**

**H. P. Lovecraft**
**1890-1937**

Address questions and comments concerning this book to
**Chaosium Inc.**
**22568 Mission Boulevard #423**
**Hayward CA 94541-5116**

Chaosium publication 23110. Published in May 2007.

ISBN 156882-211-1

Printed in the USA

# Contents

## Expanded Table of Contents

# Mister Corbitt

*In which the investigators get to know their neighbor and his family
a little better than they would like.*

This scenario is designed for play with one or more investigators. One investigator must live in his own home in an expensive upper middle class or better residential neighborhood. Across the street from this investigator dwells a kindly widower, Mr. Corbitt.

## Player Information

The scenario begins on a Sunday evening in the home of the selected investigator. Either he, or possibly his guests (other investigators), are sitting around the dinner table or living room. Looking out the window, one notices the neighbor, Mr. Corbitt, park his automobile in front of his house across the street. Unaware he is being watched, Corbitt exits the car and pops open the trunk, withdrawing from it two canvas wrapped objects. One of the objects is small and round, the other approximately the size and shape of a small baseball bat.

Carrying these to the front door, Corbitt holds both under one arm while struggling with the stubborn lock. The larger of the two packages slides loose and falls to the front porch with a resounding plop. The canvas folds fall open and the watching investigator glimpses something white and cylindrical lying in the gloom. If the investigator can make a successful **Spot Hidden** roll he will see at one end of the object what looks to be the hand and fingers of a small child! Lose 0/1D3 points of SAN. Glancing around quickly to assure himself no one watches, Corbitt quickly wraps up the item, then, after successfully unlocking the door, disappears into the tightly shuttered house. A moment later a light appears in a basement window, quickly blunted by a hastily drawn shade. A quiet approach to this window and a successful **Listen** roll hears gurgling noises and the crackling of electricity.

As far as the investigators know, Bernard Corbitt has always been a quiet, inoffensive, and normal man. His only oddity is a touch of absent-mindedness. As mentioned previously, he lives on a large, well-kept estate across the street from one of the investigators, with whom Corbitt has a nodding relationship. He is one of the more respected and prominent businessmen in the area and his habits and mannerisms are known to most of his neighbors.

Years ago Corbitt would often leave home for long periods of time, traveling out of the country to attend to his business. However, the last few years have seen him spending more and more time at home. He maintains regular hours, working five days a week in his downtown office.

Corbitt's membership in the local businessmen's club sometimes keeps him out late, but other than that, he seems to have very little social life, not an unusual pattern for an over forty widower. During weekends he usually stays at home quietly but he regularly goes out in the late afternoon on Sunday, usually returning home before dark. If the neighbor investigator's player can roll D100 equal to or less than POW x2 or less he has noticed that Corbitt's late-afternoon weekend excursions always take place on Sundays between the hours of five-thirty and seven or eight. Failing this, investigators will have to watch

Corbitt's comings and goings in order to recognize the pattern.

Today, the Sunday on which the adventure begins, is no different from those previous, except for the strange and sinister items Corbitt seems to have collected on this evening's excursion.

Mr. Corbitt's personal history is also well known in town. Born locally, Corbitt is the son of the late Theodore Corbitt who founded the small but very successful Corbitt Importers of America, now owned and operated by Bernard. Bernard took over the business fourteen years ago, when the elder Corbitt was accidentally killed while father and son were hiking in the mountains of India.

Once married, Corbitt is presently a widower and lives alone. His investigator neighbor knows that Corbitt's wife has been dead at least a dozen years.

Local people, including the investigators, all know Corbitt to be a kindly and gentle individual. At one time a medical student, Corbitt has often provided neighbors with small acts of medical assistance. Two years ago his timely first aid was credited with saving the life of a youngster hit by a truck. He sometimes regrets having left medical school to take over the family business but he is quick to say that he has no complaints about his life.

Corbitt is an avid gardener and the neighbors, including the investigator, are often recipients of produce from his bountiful vegetable patch. In a greenhouse off the back of the house he raises orchids and other exotic flora.

## Keeper's Summary

Corbitt, a servant of Yog Sothoth, has been indefinitely insane since witnessing the terrible death of his father on a windy mountaintop in India some fourteen years ago. This was at the hands of Ramasekva, a multi-limbed manifestation of Yog-Sothoth. The murder caused Bernard to lose a large amount of SAN and left him with a split personality and partial, somewhat selective, amnesia.

He shortly thereafter married a young girl and then allowed Yog-Sothoth (who took the form of Bernard Corbitt) to father twins upon his bride. When the children were born, the birth caused the death of his wife and the more nearly normal of the twins. The surviving son, a grotesque creature, has been kept for years in a secret basement room, fed and surgically modified by Corbitt to meet Yog-Sothoth's unfathomable demands. Growing at a progressively increasing rate, the creature will soon be ready to fulfill its destiny, to the pride of its foster father and the horror of the sane world.

The currently immature form of the creature is not hard to kill, nor is the cautious and confused Mr.

Corbitt likely to present much of an obstruction to ruthless investigators. The adventure does present a roleplaying challenge in that Corbitt is a neighbor, not a stranger, and thus might retain some right to being treated fairly and humanely.

Also, the well to do investigator who is the neighbor of Mr. Corbitt should be reminded that there might be a lot of questions if he and his friends simply blow up Corbitt's house with dynamite, or blast it with long range gunfire.

## The Yog-Sothoth Connection

Fourteen years ago Bernard Corbitt was called to India by his father, an amateur student of the occult. The elder Corbitt had happened upon a remote mountain village that worshipped Yog Sothoth in the form of a multi-legged, multi-armed Indian demon called Ramasekva. Making use of certain hallucinogenic drugs manufactured by the cultists, the father had worshipped with the tribe and seen the manifestation of the god.

Yog-Sothoth, after reaching out to read Corbitt's thoughts, commanded the man to bring his son before him, promising the elder Corbitt power beyond imagination and eternal life for father and son. Believing that he was doing something wonderful for his only child, Theodore Corbitt dispatched a telegram to America urging Bernard to immediately join him in India. Bernard left medical school, never to return.

In India, Bernard followed his father into the mountains and there, after ingesting the drug, was confronted by the Ramasekva avatar of Yog-Sothoth. Bernard's father was destroyed and consumed by the god who then reached out and touched the terrified young Corbitt. Impressed by the young man's intelligence and force of will, the god spared the youth to be his servant. Since that time Bernard, his mind warped by the god, has lived to serve Yog-Sothoth. On his chest he bears an ugly burn scar nearly two inches wide, a mark that resembles the outline of the multi-limbed Ramasekva. This sign would prove to any knowledgeable student of Indian occultism that Corbitt had been touched by the god.

Returning from the mountains, Bernard explained the disappearance of his father by telling the authorities the man had slipped and fallen into a deep ravine while the two were being pursued by bandits. The disheveled, haggard appearance of Bernard went a long way in convincing the magistrate that the tale was true. Upon his return to America, Bernard quickly made arrangements to take over the family business. His mother, broken by the death of her husband, soon lapsed into early senility and was supported by Bernard in a New York nursing home until her death three years later. Since the demise of his mother, Bernard has been sole owner of the firm.

Less than a year after his experience in the Punjab, Corbitt met and married the young Lynn Meyers. Yog-Sothoth soon reached out to Corbitt's mind and demanded the right to father children upon the woman. Using his own supply of the drug, distilled from the hallucinogenic plants now cultivated in his greenhouse, Corbitt called forth Yog-Sothoth. While the young man cowered in the basement, an avatar of the Outer God in the perfect semblance of her husband, bedded Corbitt's wife.

Mrs. Corbitt, unaware that her pregnancy was caused by something not human, went the full nine-month term before delivering, at Corbitt's insistence, in their own home. Corbitt was the only attendant at the birth, but a private nurse, Mona Dunlap, hired by Corbitt to help care for his wife, was attracted by the shrieks of the delivering woman. Opening the door to the room, she was unfortunate enough to witness the birth of the horrible second twin. Driven permanently insane by the sight of the thing, she was hospitalized in a near comatose state in the local public sanitarium. She died eight years later.

Corbitt hurriedly hid the surviving twin in a specially prepared room in the basement, then notified the authorities of the death of his wife and infant son. The condition of the nurse he was unable to explain, theorizing the poor woman must have suffered an untimely stroke while attempting to deliver the child. He himself — as Corbitt was quick to explain to the police — was not present at the time of the birth and had only just returned home from his office to make the grisly discovery. The police, unable to see any reason for foul play, believed the story.

At the urgings of Yog-Sothoth, Corbitt began preparing to equip the creature in his basement for life on this plane of existence. As it lacked limbs as well as lungs and other organs, Corbitt acquired the necessary parts through the agency of an unscrupulous hospital orderly named Randolph Tomaszewski. Tomaszewski, bribed with drugs supplied by Corbitt, saves certain desirable body parts from incineration and puts them with the regular hospital trash, which is eventually hauled away to the town dump. Corbitt makes twice-weekly trips to this dump, Wednesday and Sunday evenings, and searches the fresh trash for any treasures sent his way by Tomaszewski.

## LOCAL BUSINESSMAN KILLED IN ACCIDENT

It was learned today that Theodore Corbitt, owner of Corbitt Importers of America, is dead, victim of a tragic accident while vacationing in India. Corbitt, while in the company of his son Bernard, died in a fall while the two were traveling through the high mountains of the Punjab.

According to authorities, the two men were on a hiking trip when they were set upon by a group of bandits known to frequent the area. While being pursued down the mountainside the elder Corbitt apparently lost his footing and fell to his death. His son managed to escape, eventually making it to safety. The elder Corbitt's body has not yet been located and authorities fear that it may be lost, possibly consumed by wild dogs that roam the mountain.

Theodore Corbitt is survived by his wife, Elaine, and one son, Bernard. At this time it is not known if Bernard Corbitt will take over management of Corbitt Enterprises.

*(dated 14 years ago)*

*The Corbitt Papers #1*

In order to perfect the techniques needed to modify the child, it was necessary for Corbitt to spend many years experimenting with the organs and limbs sent his way. Using a combination of modern surgery and arcane magic, he created a number of living and semi-living experiments, most of which can be found buried in his vegetable garden. Once sure of his procedures, he began by grafting lungs to the incomplete creature. Other organs were later added and then came the limbs — many limbs.

The child is to be called Man-Bagari, a grotesque parody of the multi-limbed Ramasekva. It is destined to become the Bridge, a necessary part of The Opening of the Way. After many experiments, Corbitt has recently begun attaching numerous arms and legs to the child thing, with excellent success. Parts deemed unsuitable have been used in other experiments or fed to the ever hungry Man-Bagari, who eats only uncooked flesh. Parts that are totally unusable are buried, along with Corbitt's many dead experiments, in his vegetable garden. They fertilize the ripe, red summer tomatoes the neighborhood so much enjoys.

Corbitt presently finds the nearly matured Man-Bagari's growth increasing at a disturbing rate, necessitating more and more small limbs. Also, its appetite has become almost insatiable. Corbitt, a good foster father to the child thing, has pressed Tomaszewski to provide him with more and more parts. Tonight, Corbitt will feed a partially decayed spleen to the growing creature and will add the near perfectly preserved left arm of a young girl to Man-Bagari's ever growing collection of appendages.

Corbitt goes about his life, respected by his neighbor and giving no outward sign of his connections with Yog-Sothoth or with the horrors he keeps in his basement. Care must be taken by the keeper so that Corbitt does not expose himself. He will not reveal his magic abilities unless he is in fear of his life or is sure there will be no surviving witnesses. Yog-Sothoth takes little interest in the situation and if the Outer God senses that the investigators are interfering with his needs, he will rely on Corbitt to take action against the characters rather than taking any action himself.

Corbitt is likely to regard any threat to his pampered child thing as an attack on his "family". He is loyal to Yog-Sothoth and solicitous of the thing's welfare, and will do

*Mr. Corbitt*

whatever is necessary to preserve the creature's life. But he will refrain from using more force or violence than necessary; he actually is a gentle man (remember that so far, he has neither wounded or killed anyone, though he certainly has accepted several killings by Yog-Sothoth without question). One obvious tactic for Corbitt is simply moving to another quiet residential neighborhood in another town. Calling the police on the investigators is more risky, but possible. His experiments with exotic hallucinogens have brought him knowledge of obscure plant-derived toxins and hallucinogens which can be used as indirect attacks against the investigators. Some of these substances must be ingested and Corbitt will inject them in food or use them to lace a drink. Others are airborne at Corbitt might apply these to a dusty rug that he beats when the investigators walk by. His compounds cause the victims to experience intense hallucinations. Anyone failing a resistance check against Corbitt's hallucinogens suffers illusions of horrifying monsters, cataclysms, etc. The effects last 2D4 hours and cost the victim 1D4 SAN points. Corbitt's poisons are unusual and so subtle that current forensic science is unlikely to detect their presence (25% chance of success).

As a last resort, Corbitt will call upon Yog-Sothoth himself to destroy the investigators. Yog-Sothoth, should he condescend to respond, will then attack the player characters with his bolts of silvery fluid energy. The keeper is warned against bringing such an awesome being as Yog-Sothoth directly into the adventure without proper ritual and pressing need.

Corbitt's damaged mind retains little or no memory of day-to-day events, especially if they are Mythos related. Since becoming aware of this problem, Corbitt has kept a daily journal (see below). Even so, only if cured of his insanity will Corbitt be able to fully comprehend all of the unspeakable acts he has committed or allowed to happen in the last fourteen years.

## Bernard Corbitt, a quiet neighbor

| STR 10 | CON 12 | SIZ 12 | INT 17 | POW 19 |
|--------|--------|--------|--------|--------|
| DEX 13 | APP 15 | EDU 15 | SAN 22 | HP 12 |

**Damage Bonus:** none

**Weapons:** none

**Spells:** Call Ramasekva, Contact Ramasekva, Dread Curse of Azathoth.

**Skills:** Anthropology 70%, Astronomy 90%, Botany 97%, Chemistry 80%, Concoct Untraceable Poison 75%, Cthulhu Mythos 13%, Drive Automobile 55%, Fast Talk 55%, First Aid 60%, Geology 45%, History 70%, Occult 45%, Pharmacy 85%, Spot Hidden 80%, Unorthodox Surgery 87%, Zoology 60%.

**Languages:** French 60%, Punjabi 30%, Spanish 35%, Mandarin Chinese 55%, Sanskrit 40%.

# Investigations

## Local Newspaper Stories

If the investigators check the back issues of the local news¬paper, either at the newspaper's offices or at the local library, they may find several stories of interest. see **The Corbitt Papers 1**, **2**, and **3**. A successful **Library Use** roll is necessary to find each entry, and in the case of the Tomaszewski story, they must know of his existence in order to notice the article.

## The Hospital Connection

Corbitt was directed to seek out someone who could procure the necessary limbs and organs. Contemporary medical procedure calls for removed body parts to be first wrapped in canvas, to keep anyone from seeing what they are. They then are disposed of in the hospital incinerator. Occasionally, specimens are saved for hospital and medical school experiments.

Corbitt has found an orderly, Randolph Tomaszewski, who is willing to select and save certain items he is in need of. Tomaszewski has the unpopular assignment of cleaning up operating rooms and disposing of the rubbish therein. Instead of following normal procedure, he simply puts some of the organs in with the unburnables and lets them be hauled away to the dump. The dump site itself is mainly unsupervised and located in an uninhabited area.

### LOCAL MAN ARRESTED IN ANIMAL SLAYINGS

Police today announced that a suspect has been arrested in connection with the recent rash of pet kidnappings in the southwest part of town. Although released later for lack of evidence, Randolph Tomaszewski is considered the prime suspect in the recent disappearances of nearly a dozen dogs and cats from the homes and yards of the neighborhood surrounding Central Hospital. Tomaszewski is employed at the hospital as an orderly.

It will be remembered that many of the missing pets have been discovered later in parks, usually mutilated or partially eaten. Public outcry over the atrocities has been strong and police hope that they have uncovered a lead that will eventually allow them to close this case.

*(dated 3 months ago)*

*The Corbitt Papers #2*

When dealing with Tomaszewski, Corbitt is in his near-possessed state and most of the time remembers almost nothing of his relationship with the orderly. Traveling to the hospital during his lunch hour, Corbitt usually takes Tomaszewski groceries, vegetables from his garden, and hallucinogens from his greenhouse. All of these Tomaszewski greatly appreciates.

Tomaszewski is a deranged, deluded worshipper of Satan who uses the mild drugs supplied him by Corbitt in fruitless attempts to "contact the dark master." He believes the organs are being fed to wild animals so they can develop a taste for the flesh of children. He expects these beasts will then be possessed by his evil lord, and go on a rampage. Tomaszewski is paranoid, sadistic, and masochistic. He lives in a one-room apartment on the fourth floor of a downtown building. The place is filled with the paraphernalia of his misguided beliefs. If the characters are able to track down Tomaszewski and confront him, he'll panic, attacking the nearest character and then attempting to escape by running through the halls. The encounter likely takes place in the hospital — or his home — and several floors up. Tomaszewski climbs out of the nearest window to attempt an escape, only to fall screaming to his death. A search of his body, his apartment, or his locker at the hospital turns up samples of Corbitt's drug as well as objects used in the man's satanic worship.

### Randolph Tomaszewski, hospital orderly

| | | | | |
|---|---|---|---|---|
| SIR 14 | CON 15 | SIZ 14 | INT 11 | POW 10 |
| DEX 13 | APP 08 | EDU 08 | SAN 15 | HP 15 |

**Damage Bonus:** +1D4

**Weapons:** Fist/Punch 60%, damage 1D3
Kick 40%, damage 1D6
Grapple 75%, damage special
Switchblade 45%, damage 1D4

**Spells:** none.

**Skills:** Dodge 40%, Hide 50%, Occult 65%, Sneak 30%.

## The Sanitarium

If the investigators learn of the existence of the nurse, Mona Dunlap, and track her down to the local sanitarium, they will be told the woman died six years ago without ever regaining consciousness. The attending

physician still works at the facility and with a successful **Credit Rating or Fast Talk** roll, the doctor will be willing to talk with them. He can tell them little new about the woman's case. He will reveal that, just moments before her death, she did regain consciousness. Her last words were: "It was awful! It didn't have arms or legs or hardly a face! It should have died! It should have died along with the other one!"

## Garbage Hunts

If the investigators follow Corbitt on one of his garbage hunts they need two **Drive Automobile** rolls to keep sight of their quarry while lagging far enough behind to keep from alerting the suspect. If either roll fails, the wary Corbitt detects them and turns down an alternate road leading them on a merry but slow chase that lasts almost three hours. The trip is more like a Sunday drive through town than an evasion.

If the investigators escape detection, the unsuspecting Corbitt leads them to the city dump. Birds circle the closed up place, and the investigators may watch while Corbitt slips through a hole in the chain link fence. Inside, Corbitt makes his way to one or two specific piles of junk and from them extracts several canvas-wrapped objects. He opens each and discards the object if the part is too mutilated or decayed, or keeps it if it seems whole and useful. When he has one or two bags, he will sneak back out. Investigators watching him from the fence need two successful **Hide** rolls to avoid being seen while those following him into the dump will have to make two **Sneak** rolls. Modify these according to the investigators' actions, but any unsuccessful roll will indicate that Corbitt has spotted someone. It is probable that Corbitt will ignore the investigators' presence, pretending he has not seen them. However, he will now suspect the group and begin laying plans to distract or mislead them.

*Mr. Tomaszewski*

## Confronting Corbitt

If the investigators later visit Corbitt and question him about these happenings, he discloses only that he has been gathering bark and foliage samples for his studies. If his frequent trips to the garbage dump are mentioned he explains that the dump is the best place to gather certain mold specimens important in his research into special plant fertilizers. He will go so far as to offer to give the questioners a tour of his greenhouse should they express any interest in "the gentle science of botany". See "The Greenhouse", below.

If the characters choose to confront Corbitt at the dump, he quails at their approach. He will not willingly reveal the contents of his packages and fumblingly claims they are tree branches bearing certain types of fungi he has been searching for. If the investigators take the packages by force Corbitt will try to escape to his automobile and drive home. Corbitt only reveals his magical abilities if faced with death or immediate incarceration. One of Corbitt's packages contains a human liver (0/1 SAN loss) and the other the mangled leg of a ten year old boy, 1/1D3 SAN loss to see.

## Corbitt's Trip

If Corbitt's actions fail to arouse the interest of the investigators, he one day comes to the neighboring investigator's home and knocks on the door. When the investigator appears, Corbitt explains he is going on a week-long business trip to New York and asks if the investigator would mind keeping an eye on his place and collecting his mail. In return, Corbitt offers the investigator a basket of fruit and vegetables freshly picked from his garden — a token of his appreciation. The gift is benign and delicious, or at least previous such gifts from the genial Corbitt have proven to be so.

If the investigator asks what type of business trip, Corbitt replies, "Oh, don't you remember? I'm in the importing business, Corbitt Importers of America. I have to make arrangements with the Customs Dept. regarding the quarantine of a special shipment I'm expecting soon."

If the investigators have had past dealings with Corbitt, he asks, "Anything you want? Anything I can hunt up for you? I expect to be in contact with some associates just returned from the Orient." If the investigators make a request, Corbitt says he'll try his best. After the investigator agrees, Corbitt gives his thanks and departs.

If Corbitt suspects the investigators have been watching him, the gift he offers will be laced with a hallucinogen POT 16. If an investigator's player can succeed with a **Spot Hidden** roll at −10% he will notice the small needle holes in the bottoms of the fruits and probably avoid ingesting the drug. If the fruit is consumed, the investigator needs a successful **Resistance Table roll** or will suffer the effects of the drug. These effects include hallucinations of monsters, fits of screaming, profuse sweating, and loss of control of bodily functions.

If the neighbors have any question about an investigator's current state of mind, seeing him running down the street in soiled trousers, screaming at the top of his lungs about horrible monsters chasing him, ought to convince them the character is in need of a long rest.

# Corbitt's House

In the following section the yard and interior of Corbitt's house is described. This is an expensive and respectable neighborhood, and if the investigators are spotted breaking and entering by a neighbor or a passing motorist, it is likely that the police will be called.

## The Greenhouse

Toward the back of Corbitt's extensive grounds is his greenhouse. Here he raises a number of dangerous and exotic plants along with a few harmless orchids. If Corbitt is giving a tour, he will allow the investigators only a few minutes in the greenhouse, explaining that the plants are very delicate and sensitive to the slightest change in their environment. The investigators are allowed no more than fifteen minutes in the building. If the investigators enter on their own they can of course spend as much time as they like. Every fifteen minutes of investigation, allow one **Botany** roll. Each roll reveals one of the following (in this order):

☀ many of the plants are unusual specimens found only in the remotest parts of Asia, Africa and South America;

☀ aside from Corbitt's orchids, most of the plants contain powerful narcotic chemicals or toxins, and the collection includes such things as coca and cannabis bushes, foxglove and fly agaric plants, and deadly nightshade.

☀ Two of the plants show no resemblance to any earthly species. They are of unimaginable origin.

**The Orange Vine:** One of the dangerous alien growths in the greenhouse is a vine sporting large orange and blue leaves. If one of these waxy, bitter tasting leaves is thoroughly chewed, the chemicals it contains stimulate the pineal gland allowing a character to see objects outside of this reality. Unfortunately it also allows the character to be seen by the creatures who inhabit this "outside world". It can happen randomly (roll **POW x1** or less) or be brought on with concentration (roll **POW + INT** or less) any time within three hours after ingesting the chemicals.

Such delvings into another reality last POW + 1D10 minutes and reveal to the investigator a dark, rock-strewn landscape decorated with crystalline growths and occasionally lit by flashes of rose-colored lightning. An investigator can explore this new world, moving about simply by exerting his will. Anyone who explores this new world for at least ten minutes increases his or her **Cthulhu Mythos** score by 1D4%. For every ten minutes spent exploring there is a 50% chance of being noticed by one of the denizens of this world. The first intimation of this an investigator receives is the sight of a scuttling spider-like form advancing across the landscape directly toward him. Seven feet tall and emaciated looking, the scuttling thing hungers for human blood. It will attack without hesitation.

Unless the character can escape this alien dimension with a successful **POW x3** roll, he will have to fight with the creature. Investigators who have not chewed the leaves are unable to see the monster and must watch helplessly as their companion's clothing and flesh are torn away and large quantities of the victim's spurting blood sucked away into nothingness. Seeing this event provokes a SAN loss of 1/1D6.

**Dimensional Being**

| STR 18 | CON 16 | SIZ 19 | INT 07 | POW 10 |
| DEX 16 | Move 10 | | | HP 17 |

**Weapons:** Claws (x2) 65%, damage 1D8+1D6

**Sanity loss:** 1/1D8 SAN

**The Purple Flower:** The second alien plant in the greenhouse has spiky blue green leaves and a large, fleshy, white and purple flower. Sensing mobile life forms by their vital energies, the plant attempts to kill the life form and turn it into fertilizer for itself. After an investigator has been in the greenhouse for minutes equal to 40 minus POW+CON, the plant turns silently toward the character. He or she can detect the slow movement of the plant with a **Spot Hidden** roll. If the investigator remains unaware of the menace, it attacks by emitting a cold, cloudy gas that does not immediately kill the target but rather sets in motion a rapid decomposition of the victim's flesh.

Should the investigator inhale the gas before managing to flee the greenhouse (by failing a CON x4 roll), he will, within sixty seconds, begin to rot, losing 1D3 hit points every round thereafter. The victim suffers intolerable pain as his flesh blackens and splits open like rotting fruit. This process continues until there is nothing left but a brown mush along with whatever metal objects the investigator may have been carrying at the time. Witnesses lose 1/1D6 SAN.

## The Vegetable Garden

Should the investigators hit on the idea of digging up Corbitt's large vegetable patch, they are quickly rewarded

with the discovery of grisly remains of the madman's many experiments. Rotting ribcages, decaying heads, and, most frightening, the grafted atrocities created by the insane Corbitt can be found here. Headless corpses with legs where arms should be, a human trunk with six human feet growing from the ribs, numerous limbs and other indefinable lumps of mud-coated human anatomy cost the diggers a cumulative 0/1D4 SAN.

## Entering the House

Eventually, investigators should get around to peeking into the house itself. At the very least they will have to visit it in order to collect the absent importer's mail. When nearing the house, the investigators hear the crash of breaking glass and the rattle of furniture coming from the front basement window. If they look through the window into the basement work room, they see something vaguely man-like flash into view for a split-second, before jumping into the shadows. To all appearances it seems as though a burglar is afoot. If the players think to call the police, suggest they may not arrive in time to apprehend the thief before he makes his getaway.

### Corbitt's Early Experiment

In order to perfect his strange surgical/magical arts, Corbitt practiced for years on early collections of finds. Some of his experiments died and others eventually had

## CORBITT'S PROPERTY

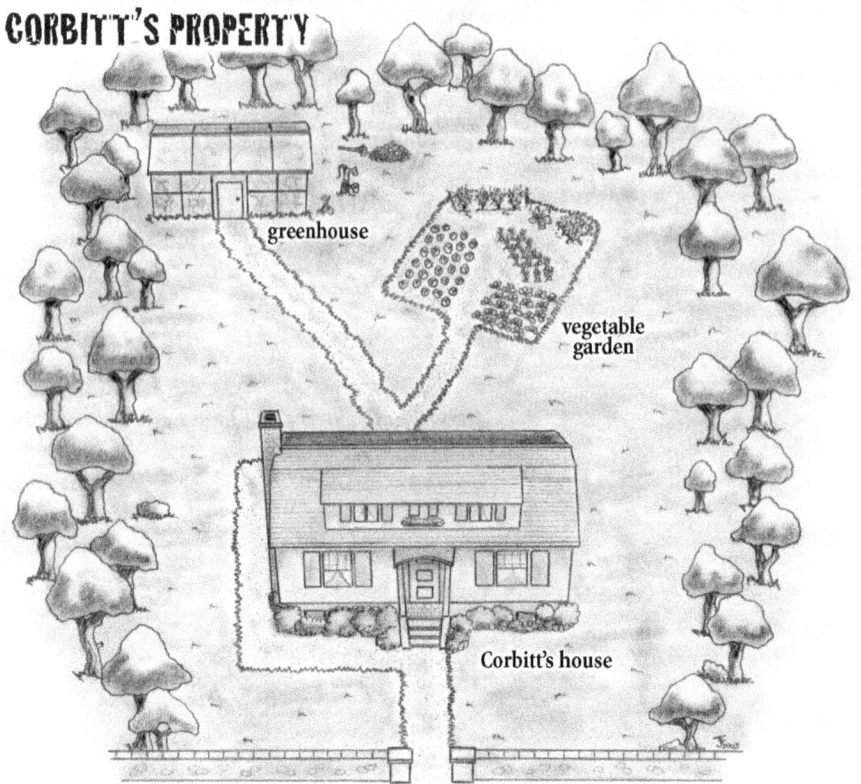

greenhouse

vegetable garden

Corbitt's house

to be killed. One that he's found particularly amusing for years, Corbitt has kept around the house. The thing made from discarded parts of humans and consists of a woman's head with two arms sprouting from where there would normally be ears and a single human leg attached to the neck. The thing is nearly mindless, its brains replaced by a rudimentary digestive system. The experiment, allowed the run of the basement while Corbitt is at work, hops and scampers about, behaving for all the world like a housebound cat

The basement windows are shut but not locked; a **STR vs. STR of 8** will open any of them. As the investigators crawl into the house, the door to the next room slams shut, as if the thief has just fled. If the investigators pursue, the experiment, terrified by the intruders, makes its way up the stairs and attempt to bash in the lightly latched door (STR 5). If successful, the thing flees to the upper floors of the home, leading the investigators on a merry chase. If cornered, the thing hisses and spits in a threatening way, its semi-human face twisted with fear

### Scampering Woman-Thing, early Corbitt experiment

| STR 09 | CON 09 | SIZ 05 | INT 05 | POW 05 |
|--------|--------|--------|--------|--------|
| DEX 09 | Move 9 | | | HP 07 |

**Weapons:** Charge 30%, damage special. The creature can charge people it scared and trapped. If it succeeds with its attack, match its STR versus the target's DEX. If the creature succeeds, the investigator falls and takes 1D3–1 dam-

age. With the scampering thing kicking and charging at him, the investigator needs 1D3 rounds to stand up.
**Armor, Spells, Skills:** none.
**Sanity Cost:** 1/1D6.

### The Ground Floor

On the ground floor, only the front room contains important items.

**Front Room:** Corbitt uses this room as his study. Above the desk is a collection of books standing on a single shelf. The four most interesting books include an Arabic copy of the Koran, a copy of *Twenty Experiments in the Occult* by the charlatan Dr. Arthur Tumley (no Mythos or spell bonus), and a wellworn copy of *True Magick* by Theophilus Wenn (*Sanity loss 1D4/1D8; Cthulhu Mythos +6 percentiles: average 24 weeks to study and comprehend.* **Spells:** Contact Deity/Nyogtha, Summon/Bind Byakhee, Summon/Bind Servitor of the Outer Gods, Summon/Bind Star Vampire. There is also a large, crudely fashioned book bound in cobra skin, called *The Key and the Gate*, written in Sanskrit. There are also fourteen leather bound annual journals dating back to Corbitt's first encounter with Yog-Sothoth, and complete to the current year. A black loose-leaf binder holds Corbitt's notes regarding his botanical experiments.

If an investigator can read *The Key and the Gate* he will learn about Yog-Sothoth and his manifestation as the multi limbed demon Ramasekva, who splits worlds apart and devours the survivors. Reading this book adds 5 points to an investigator's **Cthulhu Mythos**, but costs him 1D6 SAN. It contains the spell Call/Dismiss Ramasekva. The spell is fairly complete and can be learned with an **INT x3** roll. Casting this peculiar version of the Call/Dismiss Yog Sothoth spell does not involve building a stone tower, but does require the use of a drug Corbitt manufactures.

The journals describe the life of Bernard Corbitt since India. It will take ten minutes to leaf through a single volume; in-depth reading makes for boring fare and takes a half hour per journal: see the boxed section "Corbitt's Journals" nearby (see ***The Corbitt Papers #4***).

Corbitt's complicated botanical notes, somewhat soiled and faded, can be comprehended with a **Botany** or **Biology** roll and will tell about Corbitt's experiments with drugs derived from the plants growing in his greenhouse. Investigators will learn that Corbitt uses fly agaric, along with extracts from several other of his plants, to produce the drug he calls "Soma," a necessary ingredient in the calling of Ramasekva. Using this drug to elevate his state of mind, Corbitt can then successfully contact Yog-Sothoth in his Ramasekva guise.

With a successful **Pharmacy** roll, this potent drug can be correctly compounded by an investigator. A supply of the drug is hidden in a carved Indian box under a sofa in this room. The drug can be identified as a hallucinogenic by a competent analyst, and if ingested costs the user 1D4 SAN from the cosmic visions it reveals.

A second successful **Botany or Biology** roll will allow the investigator to learn about the two alien plant species kept by Corbitt and perhaps allow them to avoid their respective dangers. The plants' true origin is obscure but Corbitt claims the seeds were gifts from Ramasekva.

Elsewhere in and around the desk there is nothing of particular importance. Four expensive dictionaries sit in a drawer: Classical Greek to English, Sanskrit to English, Chinese to English, and Russian to English. The other drawers contain envelopes, paper, pens, ink bottles and a supply of paper clips and elastic bands.

## The Second Floor
**Master Bedroom:** This is the room of Bernard Corbitt; it is relatively well kept, the closet only a third full of clothing. A framed photograph of Corbitt's late wife has a prominent place atop the nightstand next to Corbitt's bed. There is nothing of special importance here unless the characters enter at night while Corbitt is asleep.

**Nursery:** This room was intended for Corbitt's child; it now sits empty but for a dusty crib. Nothing out of the ordinary will be found here.

**Empty Bedrooms:** Spare bedrooms used by previous generations of Corbitts. They sit unfurnished and empty.

## The Basement
**Laboratory:** One end of the lab is filled with various chemicals stored in jars. There are numerous beakers, retorts, mortars and pestles, and balances. Several dried plant specimens litter the table. On the other side of the room can be found Corbitt's surgery. Scalpels, catgut, needles, rib spreaders, clamps and other implements are all stored in a large metal cabinet.

When nearing this cabinet, the faint sound of an electric compressor can be heard and it might be noticed that the lowest drawer gives off a faint draft of cold air. If opened, the investigators discover a host of refrigerated human nerves, tendons and blood vessels, all carefully stored for what looks like future use (lose 0/1 SAN). In another part of the lab are bottles of glucose and saline solutions. The place is confusing: it seems to serve a surgeon, a chemical manufacturer, and a plant breeder. The investigators may wonder at the cost of all this equipment; several thousand dollars is more than most men are able to spend on their hobby.

**The Creature's Room:** The closet in the south of the lab is empty, but anyone opening this door will immediately notice the fetid, unidentifiable smell that pervades the closed space. Anyone who investigates and makes a successful **Spot Hidden** roll will see that the back wall is a false panel, easily removed. If this panel is disturbed, the investigators hear a faint, plaintive, gurgling from the other side. When opened and light is produced, the investigators can see the "child." The horror stumbles out of the room, making its way toward the investigators. Thinking they are his father come to add more limbs and organs, the-as-yet undeveloped Man-Bagari reaches for the characters with its multiple little arms, whimpering for food.

## CORBITT'S HOUSE

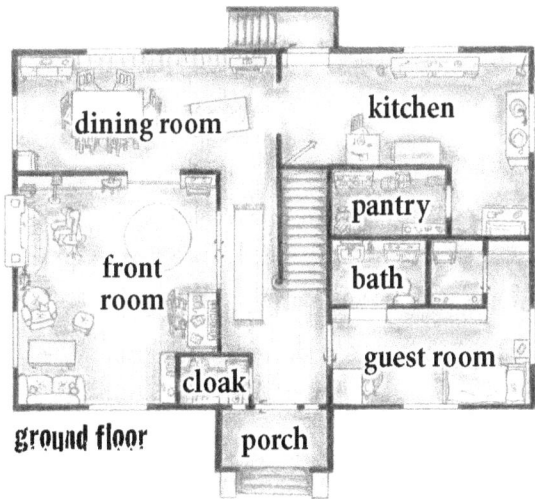

ground floor

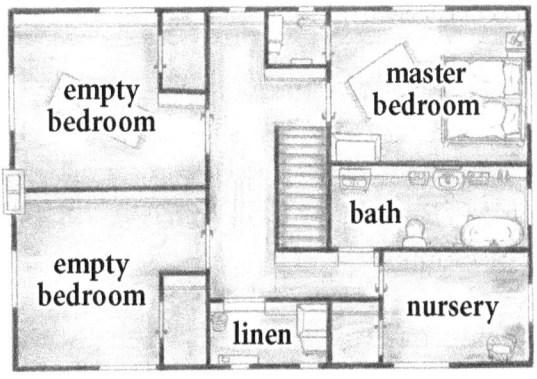

second floor

# CORBITT'S JOURNALS

Some notable excerpts are listed below; Journal One is from fourteen years ago and Journal Fourteen is for the present year. Entries not listed are very mundane, with statements like "Nothing occurred today," or "Purchased new suit in my afternoon off."

## Journal One

**September 10:** Another embarrassing memory lapse today. This journal should help me deal with the problem.

**September 13:** I have had Mother sign the last of the legal papers that transfer ownership of Corbitt Importers of America from her to myself. She seems to be doing well in the new nursing home and I hope they can give her the treatment and attention she needs. I'm afraid her condition continues to decline rapidly. The death of Father seems to have unhinged her mind. If she knew my role in his death, although I don't in the least feel responsible, I'm sure it would kill her. She would never understand the power of my new lord, Ramasekva. Could she have but experienced those moments on the mountain when HE appeared in all his terrible magnificence! He spoke with me and left his mark upon my breast. Then he took hold of my father and the two became one with each other. Before devouring him,

Ramasekva tore my father's head from his shoulders . . . .

**October 29:** Have met a charming young woman at a social gathering, her name is Lynn Meyers. I have arranged to take her to the pictures next week. My lord, I think, would approve of her.

**December 12:** Spent thirty hours in ceremony, have located Ramasekva. He wants a bridge to the world, and needs my help. I have agreed. My studies have shown that Ramasekva is an obscure Asura, an East Indian demon. The Asura are said to be older gods, the ones who ruled before the coming of Shiva. Certain things spoken of in Wenn's book lead me to believe there may be a link to a being called Yog-Sothoth.

## Journal Two

**January 10:** I found myself wanting to make Lynn my wife and have sealed the thought by proposing to her. She accepted and we have set the date of marriage for March 9 of this year. Ramasekva assures me the time is right.

**March 13:** Have returned from our honeymoon. Lynn and I have decided to keep the family place as it is excellent for raising children. In May, all being well, Lynn will accompany me on my trip to Ceylon for a new herbal tea supply. This may be my last trip out of the country for a while. A man who plans a family must be willing to settle down a bit.

**April 1:** Had to send Lynn to visit her mother while I cast the ceremony. I don't believe she is ready to understand yet. Ramasekva has told me he wants a union of flesh. He demands the union be made with my wife. I am to await thirteen days, cast another, easier ceremony, and then wait. Ramasekva is to take my place.

**April 14:** Cast the ceremony in the morning and Ramaseva came. I waited in the basement while he visited Lynn for several hours. She seems to suspect nothing.

**July 19:** Have told my wife to remain in bed throughout the day, as she has taken ill from her pregnancy, I took the day to contact Ramasekva. I am to deliver the child myself, at home. My master has directed me to raise this child as if it were my own.

**November 21:** Horror of horrors! My life is ashes. Poor Lynn went into labor today and in the course of giving birth to the child she expired, despite all I did to save her. Nurse Dunlap blundered into the room at the wrong moment. When she saw the child, she took leave of her senses. In trying to take care of her I may have neglected Lynn at a critical moment. At any rate, she is gone and I blame only myself. A second child, a boy, was born dead. I have turned both bodies over to the funeral home. The child of Ramasekva I have hidden in the basement. The thing is limbless and appears to have

*(continued on next page)*

---

The creature's body looks like a huge, dense mucus with the consistency of an overcooked pudding. An interior skeleton can be seen poking through the body from time to time while three great vents, closed by wrinkly lips, rhythmically aspirate the monster with puffing, wheezing sounds. Ten human legs, all children's, though of various colors and sizes, rim the lower part of the body, providing it with locomotion, while the fifteen chubby little arms encircling the upper side of its body writhe about, grasping at nothing.

The thing is quite featureless except for a wet circular mouth located on the creature's underside that gurgles and coos softly, in a way that resembles the sounds a human baby makes. The creature frequently stops to squat and scour the floor with wet sucking noises, searching for food.

The thing's waste products are passed out of its digestive system via a sphincter opening atop the center of the monster's body, much like that of a sea urchin. A stream of foul smelling brown goo issues from this hole.

The whimpering child thing will follow the intruders about the basement, looking for food. If fed (and the creature will only accept raw flesh) it will prove some-

what tractable, if clumsy. However, at its current stage of development it requires regular feedings and if denied food for more than twenty-four hours it will turn vicious and attack and eat any investigator that comes near it.

If Man-Bagari sees an open door, it attempts to escape the house, running down the street with great

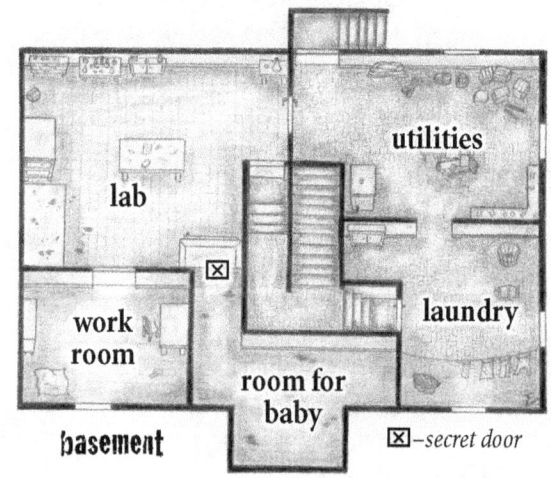

*(continued from previous page)*

trouble breathing. I don't think it can live for long.

**November 25:** The funeral of Lynn and the child was held. Her parents were heartbroken and felt pity for me. I later consoled them and promised to stay in touch.

**November 26:** The ceremony of Ramasekva brought him forth to explain the child. He said the thing would live and that I am to spend the next ten years preparing for a time when it would need me. When the time comes, I am to equip it for life on Earth. It will be given limbs and lungs. I am not to contact Ramasekva until ten years and a day have elapsed.

**December 14:** I have found someone to help me, a man named Randolph Tomaszewski. He works at the local hospital and assures me that he can supply me with the parts necessary to the experiments I need to conduct over the next few years. He is an unsavory type but I need his help. I have agreed to supply him with a small amount of the drugs he desires and he, in return, will try to fill my needs. Perhaps through association with myself, he will find a way to better himself. He seems a particularly irreligious and bitter man. Next week I will make my first trip to the dump and see what my confederate has been able to find for me. The experiments should prove a challenge, but I have every confidence that I can learn, especially with my lord Ramasekva's guidance.

## Journals Three Through Twelve

Nothing of importance to this scenario is included in this time period. The journals cover three trips to the East, acquisitions of unusual orchids and other botanical curiosities, the meeting of several old friends, work-matters and various accounts of mundane purchases and such. Experiments are occasionally mentioned but Corbitt does not elaborate.

## Journal Thirteen

**November 25:** The child grows large, and the time has come. Entered the ceremony with Ramasekva. He told me that when Spring has arrived that I am to search out fresh limbs and organs to be added to the creature — the time of experimenting is over. As the thing is still a child, I will use only the limbs and organs of children. My experiments show that youthful parts adapt much better than older ones. I am directed to feed unusable parts to the child. Ramasekva wants it to develop a taste for such things and says that it is now the time for growing.

## Journal Fourteen

**March 19:** Tomaszewski says I am asking too much of him and claims that he is having difficulty supplying me with parts. The needs of the child increase all the time and I have boosted again the strength of the drug I give the man, hoping that it will entice him to be more cooperative. I fear however that the drug simply exacerbates his derangement.

I must admit to feeling guilt — aiding and abetting his false beliefs somehow seems wrong. However, to try and tell him the truth would, I'm afraid, serve only to further unhinge his mind. I will continue the pretense of believing in his Master. I value the services Tomaszewski renders too much to risk further damage to his grasp on reality.

Most of the child's organs are now in place and a few limbs have been attached. The grafts heal nicely. My years of experimenting are paying off.

**March 28, April 8, April 11, April 19, May 14, May 25:** These dates contain similar statements to those above. The increasing growth rate of the child thing, necessitating increasingly frequent trips to the garbage dump, is a source of surprise (and pleasure) for Corbitt.

## Added Entries

If Corbitt has reason to suspect that the investigators were plotting against him, he will include his thoughts in his journal. If he knows the investigators have followed him to the dump or broken into his home, he will leave an entry that reads: "I am being followed. If I cannot find a way to deal with them myself, in the next ceremony with Ramasekva, I will be forced to ask for their destruction." Another entry mentions the possibility of sending Tomaszewski to deal with the investigators. ☼

*The Corbitt Papers #4*

---

curiosity and enthusiasm, grabbing at things and trying to evade any attackers. However, it can recognize its foster father, Mr. Corbitt, and obeys his commands as long as they are simple and clearly stated.

### Man-Bagari, the Child-thing

| STR 25 | CON 50 | SIZ 25 | INT 08 | POW 22 |
|--------|--------|--------|--------|--------|
| DEX 09 | Move 9 | | | HP 38 |

**Weapons:** Fist/Punch* 50%, damage 1D3+2D6

    Grapple 50%**, damage special

    Bite/Suck, 80%, damage 1D8 (only if victim is grappled or prone)

    *The Child-thing can make up to three Fist/Punch attacks per round, on three separate targets.*

    **The Child-thing can make only one such attack per round, and no Fist/Punch attacks that round.*

**Armor:** none

**Skills:** Dodge 20%, Sense Food 90%

**Spells:** none yet. If the investigators take too long killing the hapless creature, it might have a chance to call upon its father for help in its hour of need.

**Sanity loss:** 1/1D10

If the investigators try to keep the thing alive and happy they will find it requires at least three pounds of raw meat per day to keep it satisfied. These demands increase by 10% per week, its growth rate accelerating in a like manner. If the investigators are crazed enough to nurture the monster as it grows, they each lose 1 SAN per week of such folly. Disturbing changes take place — the creature's immature arms and legs grow larger and stronger, its size increases, and it begins to talk to them.

In only a year's time from the beginning of the adventure, the creature reaches maturity and calls itself Man-Bagari, the Bridge. All its characteristics are doubled and it possesses 10 points of armor. It cannot fly, but will be capable of jumping up to 200 feet in a single bound. In adult form it can grab hold of a life form, burning it and draining energy from it (1D4 CON per round), converting these points into hit points for itself; a side effect causes a 1D2 loss of APP for each CON loss. Seeing the thing at this stage of its development costs 1D3/1D20 SAN.

Any affection the thing may have felt for its keepers is long gone and investigators will be viewed as so much potential food. Man-Bagari will be able to summon Yog-

Sothoth simply by calling the Outer God's name (in a thunderous voice) and expending 8 magic points. It is able to leave this plane at will. The creature serves as the son of Yog-Sothoth, herald for the eventual Opening of the Way and the coming of the Outer God.

# Resolving the Adventure

There are various ways to resolve this scenario and a number of things that can happen to the investigators. If the characters are discovered meddling with Corbitt's plans he first attempts to intoxicate them with one of his hallucinogens, provoking in the victim symptoms of insanity. More drastically, he tries to separate the investigators and then murder them either with poison or magic. If the investigators have waited until the child is near maturity, Corbitt may simply sic his creature on them, knowing the time for it to leave is drawing near anyway.

If Corbitt is unsuspecting of the investigators, but they know of the monster, they have a choice of destroying it or leaving it be. Destroying the creature will bring an award of 2D6 SAN simply from the knowledge that the horrible thing is gone. If they fully understand the thing's link to Yog-Sothoth and its role in the eventual Opening of the Way, the Sanity award increases, to 2D8+2 points.

If Man-Bagari is destroyed, Corbitt's remaining shreds of sanity dissolve, leaving the man in a near hopeless condition. The investigators may turn him over to the authorities, but if they realize that Corbitt's mental state keeps him from taking responsibility for the things that have happened, they may choose to try and help him get his life back together. Successful rehabilitation of Corbitt will bring an additional SAN award of 1D4 points.

Should the investigators allow the creature to escape, they eventually hear stories of horrific sightings and people disappearing. Strangely burnt and shriveled corpses begin to turn up. These stories go on for two weeks, 1D10 stories in all, and will be broadcast over radio stations and printed in the newspapers. Each time an investigator hears one of these stories he will suffer an additional SAN loss of 0/1D2 points.

If the investigators choose to not deal with the monster themselves and instead notify the authorities, the police will arrive and enter the house. When they find the creatures, one police officer faints and another runs screaming from the basement. The police contact the United States Bureau of Investigation (renamed the FBI in 1935) who arrive on the scene, kill the creatures, confiscate Corbitt's books, notes, and medical supplies, and order the house burned to cinders. If he still lives, the Bureau tracks down Corbitt and arrests him on some obscure charge. He will not be seen or heard from again. Hint to the investigators that certain people within the government are aware of the Mythos threat and practice a policy of misinformation to avoid creating a panic among the public. A statement will be issued claiming the house was infected with a contagious disease that required immediate and drastic control. It was decided that burning the property was the most expedient method of dealing with this threat to the public well being. Allowing the police and federal government to take over the case rewards the investigators with less SAN, 1D10 if they do not understand the link to Yog-Sothoth and 1D10+3 if they do.

## THE END!

*The Child-Thing*

# The Plantation

*In which the investigators search out the secrets of a swamp in the Deep South, and descend into the lair of a being of passive disposition, but exhibiting an insatiable hunger.*

This adventure is intended for investigators who have had at least some experience with the Cthulhu Mythos. Although scholarly skills may prove helpful, violent confrontations with cultists, zombies, venomous snakes and evil serpent people should be expected. Good weapon skills are almost essential.

The beginning of the story is nominally set in Arkham but at the keeper's discretion it could begin in almost any city in the United States as long as there is a college or university nearby. One of the leading characters, Professor Albert Gist, teaches at this school. Even this may not be necessary. Gist's profession could be altered if the keeper so chooses.

## Keeper's Information

The investigators are about to become the unwitting pawns of Yig, the Great Old One and god of the serpent people. Yig has been angered by an ancient serpent-woman sorceress who for ages has been absorbing the energy of magical sacrifices and rites properly intended for Yig. This depraved and bloated snake woman dwells in an ancient underground temple beneath a backwoods swamp in South Carolina. Yig has suffered enough from this interloper and intends to use the investigators and a serpent-man sorcerer as the tools of his revenge.

The investigators will be drawn into this adventure by a young boy from South Carolina named Joe. Joe has traveled to Arkham in search of Albert Gist, brother of Caleb Gist, owner of the plantation where Joe's sharecropper family works and lives. The evil Caleb has kidnapped Joe's older sister and intends to sacrifice her in an upcoming ceremony to Yig. Caleb and his cultists disguise their Yig ceremonies as rites to Dambala, the serpent god of Obeah. The rites of Obeah are a practice which, to some degree, are tolerated in parts of the South. Caleb has so far managed to fool the local authorities but he himself has been duped by the serpent sorceress. All the energies of his rites to Yig are sucked off by the serpent woman and used by her to sustain herself. The sorceress, much like a god, has taught Caleb a number of secret magicks in exchange for the rites he performs. Caleb honestly believes he has been dealing with Yig.

Although the investigators may at first believe the solution is to do away with the nefarious Caleb and save Joe's sister, they will soon learn their task is much more difficult. Either by way of the Messengers of Yig or through the serpent man the investigators will learn the true purpose of their visit to the plantation.

The adventure is presented in five parts, as follows:

### Part I: Strangers Meet

The adventure begins with a near traffic accident: the investigators are driving in crowded afternoon traffic when a small boy (Joe) suddenly darts in front of their vehicle. The child is slightly injured (probably not seriously) and asks the investigators to help him reach the residence of one Albert Gist, who lives not far from Arkham. Helping the boy find the place, they meet the seemingly innocent Albert Gist, then become involved in a shootout when cultists trailing Joe lay siege to the house. Drawn into the story, the investigators will be led to South Carolina.

## Part II: The Journey South

Whether the investigators choose to travel by rail or auto makes no difference to the cultists on their tail. A huge zombie will be sent against them — a foe they must face and defeat.

## Part III: South Carolina

Arriving in Charleston, the investigators have at least an evening and part of a day to research local sources (libraries, newspapers) before the arrival of Professor Gist's friend, Elihu Winsworthy. Winsworthy will give them a ride to the plantation. On the way to the plantation they have time for stops in the small town of Walterboro and at the Gist country store, meeting two possible allies: Colleton County Sheriff Virgil Trucks and the Reverend Isaac Hilson.

## SOUTH CAROLINA

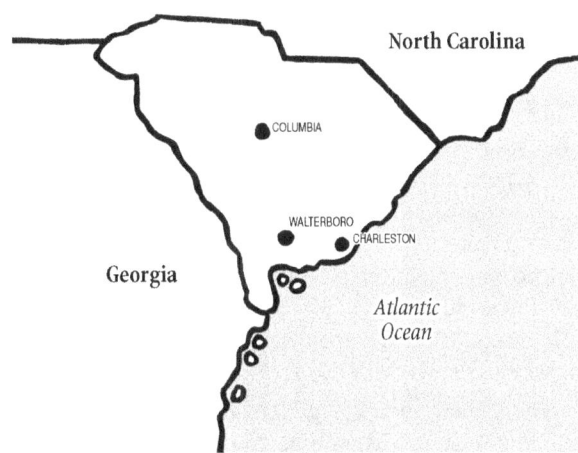

## Part IV: The Plantation

The investigators will be able to stay overnight at the decaying Gist family mansion. They will meet the owner, Caleb Gist, his mistress Elly, the evil overseer Rafe Bodeen, innocent sharecroppers, Yig cultists, and finally, an ancient and deadly serpent man sorcerer, brought here, like the investigators, to perform Yig's bidding.

## Part V: The Night of Yig

The perverted ceremony will probably be held the night after the investigators arrive. They will have a chance to witness the depraved rites and perhaps, be able to prevent the dreadful sacrifice of Joe's sister to an ancient god. During the ceremony the homunculi servants of the serpent woman sorceress appears, digging up

through their muddy tunnels to snatch unsuspecting cultists entranced by the celebrations. These filthy burrows lead back to the buried temple of the sorceress, the lair of the one that Yig has marked for revenge. Two undercover cops from Charleston might be spotted and the investigators might be able to enlist their aid.

## Cast of Important Characters

*(in order of their appearance)*

### Joe

This twelve-year-old boy has arrived in Arkham searching for help for his endangered family. Joe is seeking Albert Gist, brother of the plantation's owner, Caleb Gist, in the hope that Albert will help him. Although frightened of both Gist brothers, Joe has been unconsciously led here by Yig in order to involve both the elder Gist and the investigators. Joe will first be met when he is nearly run over by the investigator's automobile.

Joe has lately been the victim of disturbing dreams — dreams brought on by the Messengers of Yig (see p. 21 for text on Yig). Yig wants both Albert Gist and the investigators to aid him in ridding the plantation of the gigantic serpent queen. To this end he has manipulated Joe's dreams to show him the worst possible conclusion — the sacrifice of his sister during the perverted Yig rites planned by Caleb Gist. Joe bears, on his left side, the Mark of Yig and it's possible that during some point in the adventure the investigators will discover the sleeping boy being visited by one of the sacred Messengers.

### Professor Albert Gist

Gist, 44 years old, is intelligent and educated, a visiting professor of psychology at Miskatonic University. He is sane but unstable, obsessed with the mysteries of the occult and the hidden powers of the human mind. Having gained an inkling of the true situation at the plantation, he intends to use the investigators as bodyguards and assistants while he determines the facts. Believing Caleb may have made some occult breakthrough, he is both curious and jealous. Although he pretends to be interested in the welfare of the sharecroppers, they are of little importance to him. He shares the legacy of the Gist family and, like his brother Caleb, wishes deeply to make contact with what he calls "the outer forces". Albert may try to replace his brother as the leader of the upcoming Yig ceremony.

**Special Note:** Although Albert will be required to make SAN rolls and have points deducted from his SAN total, he will not be subject to insanity caused by any manifestation of Yig or his powers. His overriding obsession to make contact with Yig is practically an insanity in itself.

## Big Rafe Bodeen

He is the new overseer at the plantation, recently hired by Caleb Gist. A huge, hulking brute, the 28-year-old Bodeen first appears in Massachusetts, attempting to kidnap or kill little Joe. If Bodeen is not killed or arrested, he returns to South Carolina, showing up at the plantation to further trouble the group.

## Sheriff Virgil Trucks

The Colleton County Sheriff is headquartered in Walterboro, along the route to the plantation. Trucks is quite aware that Caleb Gist is up to no good, but hesitates to make a move against the man. Caleb is a long time landholder in a tradition bound South and wields considerable local influence. The large masses of worshippers that have lately shown up at the plantation, ostensibly to worship Dambala, also deter the sheriff from actively involving himself. His small force of men would be no match against such a large and well armed group should the cultists decide to resist. However, the recent murder of a Charleston detective has aroused the sheriff's ire. His role is undefined and he may be used as the keeper sees fit. His presence in the area will serve to prevent both the investigators and Caleb Gist from committing overt acts of violence against each other prior to the ceremony.

## Reverend Isaac Hilson

A black Baptist preacher with a strong faith and almost magical healing abilities. A strict Christian, Hilson decries all pagan religions, especially the practices that have been going on at the Gist plantation. Like the sheriff, his role is undefined and it is up to the keeper to make use of this character. He may secretly contact the investigators looking for aid, or he may show up at the last minute with a horde of torch bearing, hymn singing Christians, intent on wiping out the nest of evil. If necessary, they can arrive just in the nick of time, pulling the investigators' fat out of the fire if all seems lost.

## Caleb Gist

Albert Gist's less respectable brother and owner/operator of the plantation. Caleb, 41 years old, has, like all the Gists, been long obsessed with the mysteries of the occult. He has for many years been under the influence of the hidden serpent sorceress, mistakenly believing her to be Yig. Caleb unknowingly serves the queen and, in return, he and his mistress, Elly, benefit from what she teaches them. The sorceress greedily absorbs all the magical energies released by Caleb's celebrations of Yig.

Caleb hates his brother, Albert, and will not be happy when he shows up, especially since Albert is towing along a bunch of nosy investigators from up North. Highly suspicious of their intentions, Caleb would prefer to murder the whole bunch of them and dump the bodies in the swamp. But the time of the big ceremony draws near and Caleb doesn't wish to have the local Sheriff breathing down his neck. He will try to make the investigators as uncomfortable as his southern hospitality — and the law — allows, hoping fervently they fall afoul of some accident while prowling around the house or swamp. Caleb knows the secret of creating zombies, and both he and Elly can charm poisonous snakes. If the investigators survive these threats and still insist on staying on through the night of the Dambala ceremony, Caleb strongly warns them away from the place of the rites, claiming that white men "are not welcome there." He then sneaks out of the house and joins the cultists.

Although Caleb will be cautious about harming his guests, he makes a determined effort to eliminate little Joe as soon as the opportunity arises.

## Elly

This young black woman works as a maid at the plantation house but, more importantly, she is Caleb's mistress and high priestess of the Yig cult. She is cunning, crafty, and capable of brewing both poisons and love philters. She can charm snakes and will work with Caleb to make sure the investigators do not disrupt the upcoming ceremony. Elly, as an opponent, may prove to be more dangerous than Caleb.

## The Serpent Man

The serpent man encountered in this adventure is magically disguised as a voodoo priest and, like the investigators, has been brought here by Yig to help punish the bloated serpent queen. He knows what Yig expects of him and serves the god, but only because he feels he has little choice. It is likely the investigators find themselves in uneasy alliance with this serpent mage.

The serpent man has presented himself as a friend and ally of Caleb Gist and has helped him make "corrections" in his rites. These corrections are supposed to finally allow the calling of Yig, something the Gist family has tried to accomplish for nearly a century. He despises Caleb — as he does all humans — and is merely making use of the plantation owner to achieve Yig's demands. There never has been anything wrong with the various Gists' attempts to call Yig — only the presence of the leaching sorceress has kept the Call/Dismiss Yig from being successful.

The serpent man has included a human sacrifice in the ceremony, claiming it to be an essential part of the rite. This is a falsehood. The serpent man has included it to amuse himself. He is counting on Caleb to lead the ceremony (although either Elly or himself could suffice in a pinch), and to this end will help to protect the man against unruly strangers. Nevertheless it is likely that the serpent man will inform the investigators of what is really happening, to a degree, and recruit them in the fight against the serpent queen. He can explain to them that, like himself, they have been manipulated by Yig and that there are few alternatives to helping the Great Old One achieve his godly ends.

## The Human Cultists

The cult of Yig worshippers pose as followers of Obeah and claim to worship Dambala, the serpent god. In truth, the cultists worship Yig, a far darker being than Dambala. They have been lately holding large ceremonies at the plantation four times a year and are well organized and violent. Like Caleb and Elly, they are the dupes of the hidden serpent queen. Caleb has invited a horde of over 150 of them to attend this latest attempt to call Yig.

## The Serpent Sorceress

Unknown to anyone save the serpent man, beneath the swamp lives a great and powerful being, an ancient and gigantic sorceress of the serpent people, S'ssruxxa. This foul being, guilty of crimes too vile for even the serpent people to contemplate, has dwelt for millions of years within her ancient temple, imprisoned there eons ago by others of the serpent race. She lives eternally, half awake, half asleep, preserved by her magicks and tended to only by her servant homunculi — beaked, man-sized reptilian beings created of her own flesh and blood, and capable of burrowing to the surface to hunt food for their mistress. These homunculi are the cause of the hell holes which some locals claim open up unexpectedly to swallow dogs, livestock, and occasionally people.

Thousands of years ago the sorceress sensed the coming of sentient beings — humans — and contacted these primitives by way of their dreams. Wrongly believing her to be a god, these early humans worshipped her and eventually erected a stone altar above the ground where she was entombed. In the past century the worship of the sorceress has passed from the hands of the local Indians to the Gist-led cultists of Yig. The sorceress feeds off the magical energies generated by these rites.

## Yig's Role

Yig, offended by the sorcerous queen and her felonious leaching of the magical rites intended for him, is manipulating fate. Using his Messengers of Yig he has lured to South Carolina the serpent man sorcerer and now attempts to draw in the investigators, planning to use all of them as instruments of his revenge.

Putting self interest first, like any sentient beings, both the serpent man and the investigators may prefer not to be Yig's agents of punishment. Once in South Carolina, however, it should become evident that the investigators have but little choice. Brought here by Yig, they will be expected to fulfill their role in the Great Old One's plan. Both the serpent man and Yig's sacred snakes will work to prevent the investigators leaving the plantation before the sorceress is uncovered and punished. Yig's plan is to use his newly recruited agents to attack or somehow distract the sorceress during the ceremony. With the serpent woman's attention diverted, Yig will be able to take advantage of Call/Dismiss Yig and through it, enter this world and exact his vengeance.

## Snakes

Normal snakes, both wild and magically charmed, play a large role in this scenario. For an extensive treatment of them, see the appendix at the end of this adventure.

## PART I

# Strangers Meet

It is a sunny afternoon and the investigators are in their automobile going somewhere (library, school, work). When a small black child suddenly darts out into the street, the driver of the car will barely have time to hit the brakes. If a **Drive Automobile** roll is made the driver is able to stop the car just as it strikes the lad, knocking the boy off his feet onto the macadam for 1D2 points worth of scrapes and bruises. If the roll is failed the boy will be hit much harder and knocked flat to the ground for 1D6 points of damage (a loss of 6 HP means his arm has been fractured and requires a cast). In either case the boy will need some type of medical aid and only the most heartless of investigators will refuse to help. If they choose to ignore the child, a policeman who witnessed the event will show up on the scene. The officer starts to talk about filling out accident reports, making trips to the station, future court dates, etc. Investigators wishing to avoid long entanglements should offer to take the boy to a nearby doctor or hospital, and possibly provide some first aid on the scene. The policeman will be satisfied by these efforts and, providing they take the boy with them, allows the investigators to leave.

They will spend the next hour or so with the injured youngster, and during this time have the opportunity to learn something of why he is in Arkham. Joe has a distinctly southern accent and investigators may wonder what he is doing so far north, and by himself.

"My sister's in a peck of trouble," the boy explains. "I was hopin' to find Master Gist up here. Somehow I just know he'd be willin' to help."

As the boy's tale unfolds the investigators are amazed to learn that the boy has traveled, all alone, from his home far away in South Carolina, in search of

Albert Gist. Most remarkably, Joe has covered the 950+ miles by train, car, and on foot, in little more than a week. Investigators notice that his bare feet are torn and cut. If asked how the boy knows that Albert Gist lives in this town (Joe apparently doesn't even know the name of the town he's in) he merely shrugs and answers: "I don't know. I just sometimes get these feelin's and sometimes the feelin's come true."

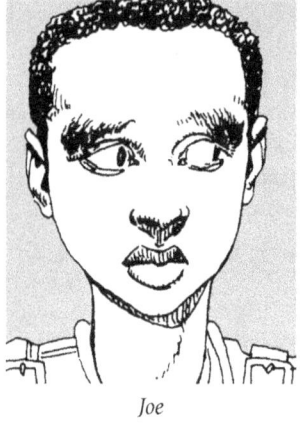

*Joe*

A **Psychology** roll allows an investigator to notice that the boy seems upset when talking about his sister. If pressed on the issue, Joe is reluctant to answer. "Somethin' bad's goin' on back home. I have to see Master Albert right away. Master Caleb's up to no good."

Further questioning brings no additional information but Joe asks if they can help him find "Master Albert Gist". The boy is distraught, almost frantic with worry.

If any of the investigators are employed by, or attending Miskatonic University, with a **Know** roll they recognize the name the boy has given them. Gist is presently in Arkham as a visiting professor at the University, where he teaches psychology. This investigator can learn where Gist lives by visiting the school's administration building. Otherwise, a quick check in the phone book will show a listing for a Professor Albert Gist. He lives a short distance southwest of town, about four miles from downtown Arkham. Only the most callous investigators would refuse to offer the injured boy a ride.

## Meet Professor Albert Gist

**Keeper's Note:** during this encounter the investigators will be given numerous opportunities to involve themselves in Joe and Albert Gist's problem. First, there is sympathy for the boy they've injured. Then, they should be intrigued by what they learn of the activities of Caleb Gist, Albert's brother. Next, the investigators will be involved in a shootout — Caleb's deranged cultists trying to kidnap Joe — an event that might make them feel a need for revenge, especially if one of them is wounded. Failing all else, Gist will offer money in an attempt to persuade them to accompany him and Joe to South Carolina.)

Finding Professor Gist's rented farmhouse would be difficult for someone not familiar with the rural area southwest of Arkham but Joe exhibits an uncanny ability to home in on the place. At least once, he is able to immediately inform the driver that he's made a wrong turn.

Following Joe's directions, the investigators soon find themselves at the modest, rented home of Albert Gist.

Gist answers the door, a look of puzzlement on his face when he sees a group of strangers standing on his front porch. Then he notices little Joe, and recognizes him instantly.

"Joe!" exclaims Gist. "What are you doing here?"

As Joe begins to spill his story, Gist gives the boy's injuries a cursory examination, questioning the investigators and learning how the boy was hurt. He accepts their explanation and asks politely: "Would you care for some coffee? Tea? It's quite a long drive out here and I want to properly thank you for helping little Joe here." The investigators notice that, although Gist's accent is more refined, it is similar to Joe's.

*Professor Gist*

The professor ushers the investigators into a large, book lined study and goes to prepare the refreshments. Any investigator who checks the bookshelves will notice among the works on Psychology are a preponderance of occult titles but nothing particularly interesting from the viewpoint of the Mythos.

After Gist returns with the coffee he asks Joe to tell them what has happened.

## Joe's Tale

Joe, standing in the center of the room, surrounded by seated white people, begins nervously: "It's Master Caleb, Sir. He's been messin' around with a new mojo man come to the plantation from down south somewhere. Master Caleb and this man been doin' somethin' secret and now there's talk of holdin' a special ceremony down in the swamp by the old Obeah stone. They got my sister, Master Albert. They came right into the house and grabbed both her and my ma. Now he's holdin' 'em prisoner. They tried to catch me, but I was too fast for 'em. I lit out across the swamp and didn't stop runnin' till I hit the highway."

Joe pauses for a minute, and the investigators notice Albert Gist's face has turned pale and tense.

"Thank you, Joe," he finally says. "Please go wait in the kitchen." Joe turns and leaves the room.

Once Joe is gone, Gist apologizes to the investigators: "I'm sorry you've had to hear about this Judging from what Joe has told me it sounds as though my younger brother, Caleb, has committed some grave errors of judgment." Gist turns thoughtful a moment and the investigators will have an opportunity to question him. If they don't, he continues.

"My brother has for a long time amused himself with the study of ancient forms of magic, a study that until recently I've not taken seriously. Caleb, although an unscrupulous sort, never seemed to show more than an amateur's interest. Now I learn this."

"The Gist plantation has been owned by my family for generations, Joe and his family work there as sharecroppers. My brother Caleb, after a dispute we had years back, lives there by himself running the plantation — at little or no profit, I might add. I visit the place usually once a year, but relations between my brother and I are, shall we say, strained, and I do not stay very long."

For the last year or so I've heard rumors about Caleb's behavior but now I'm convinced something is amiss. I don't know about the things little Joe's said — his people are a superstitious lot and you can't always believe everything they say — but certainly Caleb's foolishness and bad management have gotten entirely out of hand. It seems almost certain that Caleb is terrorizing the sharecroppers for his own amusement and, worse yet, has gotten himself involved in some sort of unsavory religious practice. I've even heard rumors of trouble with the police."

He stops and takes a deep breath. "It's time someone put a stop to Caleb and I suppose it's my responsibility."

As the sun sets, Gist stands and calls to the kitchen, telling Joe that he should be ready to leave for South Carolina in the morning. Joe peeks out the door (he's been listening the whole time) with a pitiful look in his eyes. "Are these people here gonna help us?" he asks imploringly.

Telling the boy, "No, I'm afraid not," Gist then apologizes for the boy's forwardness and again thanks them for their help. "I'm sure these nice folk don't want to get involved in our problems."

Just then there is a knock at the front door. "Probably one of my students," Gist explains. "They're in the habit of stopping by unannounced." Excusing himself, he goes to answer the door, leaving the investigators and the young boy alone in the room.

## A Vicious Attack

Meanwhile, outside the house, four cultists sent by Caleb Gist have positioned themselves to open fire on the rear of the house. These cultists are led by Caleb's brutal overseer, Big Rafe Bodeen and are here to take Joe back to South Carolina.

The cultists are not particularly effective, and the group has arrived too late to stop Joe from talking. But they do intend finish the job. They have already been paid half the fee agreed upon by Bodeen.

The keeper must make sure that events occur suddenly in this scene, without giving the players a chance to talk over their actions or tactics. It is suggested that the keeper do a countdown while the players give statements of intent. Players who hesitate too long get no action for the round.

# Yig

Although one of those referred to in ancient texts as a Great Old One, Yig is one of the least dangerous of these alien and terrible beings. For centuries, primarily in the North American southwest and the Andes region of South America, Yig has been worshipped by various Amerindian tribes going as far back as the pre Incan Huari tribes. The Toltecs, Mayans and Aztecs also paid homage to Yig (under names such as Quetzalcoatl and Kulkucan) as did many of the more primitive tribes of North America. With the coming of the white man and the destruction of Indian civilizations, Yig has been forgotten by many of the tribes and is worshipped sporadically, if at all.

Despite his semi-benevolent reputation, those few Indians who still honor Yig understand his true character. In the months of August, September, and October, Yig's reptilian hunger overcomes the god and he stalks the North American plains and desserts in search of food. It is said that during these nights certain learned members of the Pawnee, Wichita, and Caddo tribes hold nightly tomtom rituals intended to drive the ravening god away from them, keeping their people safe.

Yig is served by his Children, the sacred snakes of Yig. These large snakes, always of a poisonous variety, are indigenous to the area in which they're encountered. These specimens are always much larger than a normal member of the species and are easily identified by a white crescent on the back of the head. Their venom is far more potent than that of their kin, and a bite from one of Yig's sacred snakes always results in a swift, painful death. The sacred snakes exhibit intelligence and cunning far beyond that of normal snakes and additionally serve as Yig's Messengers. These messengers are sent directly by Yig and bring to chosen humans (and others) dreams and vague insights into future events. Messengers silently approach sleeping humans and, by inserting their tongues into the ear of the individual, induce the strange dreams. Experiencing one of these dreams costs a human 1D3 SAN and leaves the sleeper with what seems to be a certain precognition about events and people. These half-remembered dreams do not predict an exact future, but only one of many possible futures. Yig chooses a future that will most likely cause the dreamer to act in the manner Yig desires. Yig can only dispatch his Messengers from an area that is sacred to Yig, which is why he has not contacted Gist and the investigators more directly.

Occasionally, certain individuals are chosen to be blessed by Yig. These individuals bear the mark of the white crescent, usually hidden beneath an arm, and share a special rapport with Yig. Those who bear this mark are immune to normal snakebite, nor will the sacred Children of Yig, unless sent by Yig himself, attack a person bearing the mark of Yig. In return, the person becomes a servant of Yig and cannot act against the interests of the Great Old One. Yig can force these individuals to serve him anywhere or anytime, contacting the person by way of his dreams. A servant of Yig who refuses is immediately tracked down by Children of Yig and slain. ❈

The cultists' attack is a ruse intended to make little Joe panic and run. This is the plan of Bodeen who, once things are underway, will slip away from the scene to avoid arrest or danger.

Before the gunfire erupts, the investigators hear Albert Gist arguing with the caller at his front door. Gist is disputing something with his visitor. "Somethin' bad's gonna happen," Joe says softly, a look of panic creeping over his face. If anyone can make a successful **Listen** roll they will be able to hear the stranger's voice well enough to recognize the man's southern accent.

If any of the investigators peek out into the front room they see a very large, brutish looking man standing in the front doorway, arguing loudly with the professor. The man is badly dressed, and claims to be a sharecropper at the plantation. He insists Joe stole money from him and he's come "to get my due."

"Ah know he's in there," the man growls. "Bring that bo' out here now, before ah gits mad."

The man arguing with the professor is Rafe Bodeen, Caleb Gist's new overseer. He and Professor Gist have never met. Joe is innocent of any crime, but he knows the foreman's evil reputation and is justly terrified of what the brute will do to him if he should get his hands on him.

Joe makes a sudden bolt for a nearby window or door, intent on escape. The second the boy reaches the window or opens the door, gunshots ring out, bullets shattering the windows and thudding into the walls. Little Joe, by some incredible luck, avoids injury and falls back on the floor, scrambling underneath the sofa. Any investigators in the path of the bullets, including anyone who attempted to stop Joe's exit, have to make **Luck** rolls to avoid being hit by a stray shot for 1D6 points of damage.

If the investigators rush out the back door they are met by a second barrage of pistol shots. Framed in the lighted doorway they are easy targets and their assailants all fire at +20% for that round. Worse, since the investigators must go immediately from a well lighted room into darkness, they are partially blinded, and their chance to hit is halved for the first round of combat.

The cultists are about thirty yards from the door, and have clear fields of fire from their positions behind trees or shrubbery.

If the investigators extinguish the lights and/or fall to the floor rather than immediately attacking, the assailants fire for one more round then escape into the darkness, reloading as they go.

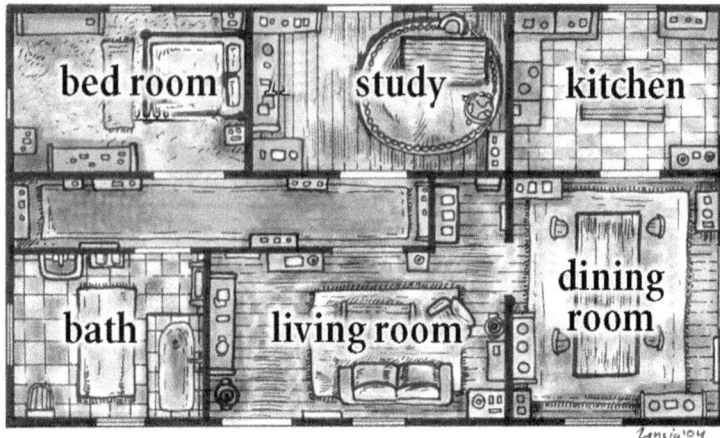

# PROFESSOR GIST'S HOUSE

bed room · study · kitchen · dining room · bath · living room

Lensig'04

There are four cultists in the backyard, each armed with concealable short barreled .38 revolvers. The leader has, in reserve, a sawed off shotgun hidden under his overcoat. Each cultist has a fresh $10 bill in his pocket, paid to them by Bodeen.

Rafe Bodeen flees the moment he hears shots, running in the opposite direction from the cultists. Professor Gist, aghast at the violence occurring in his back yard, makes no attempt to stop the fellow.

If any investigators are at the front door, they may pursue the overseer. Bodeen has the getaway car waiting for him just around the corner, loaded with three more armed cultists and a vacant eyed zombie. If he gets away, he will double around to pick up the other cultists escaping on foot. (See the statistics at the end of this adventure for information on Rafe Bodeen and the cultists.)

If the investigators wish to chase Bodeen, they will find their automobile has been tampered with. It will take ten minutes and a successful **Mechanical Repair** to get it running and Bodeen will be long gone before they ever get it started. Gist's model T is nearby but has suffered the same sabotage as the investigators' auto.

## Aftermath of the Attack

Everyone is likely to be shaken up after this scene. Gist is particularly upset, as is poor Joe. Whether or not the investigators notify the police, officers show up at the farmhouse in 3D10 minutes, called by anxious neighbors who overheard the noisy gunfire. Any cultists taken prisoner refuse to answer questions and, if possible, attempt suicide.

If asked what the man at the door wanted, Professor Gist says "He claimed little Joe stole money from him and wanted to see him. I wasn't about to let the ruffian in, of course, obviously was a part of some vile plan. Lord help poor Caleb."

Professor Gist has no idea how the man could have tracked Joe down and is very concerned that events are moving too fast for him to handle alone. "I had a feeling that I'd need help in any dealings with brother Caleb," he says quietly. "After this disaster, I'm sure of it. Thank God you were here, or we might have been killed."

The police will sooner or later arrive and reports must be written and depositions made. Injured investigators must be cared for. Asked by the police, Professor Gist describes the man at the door as best he can. Little Joe states that he is sure the man was Big Rafe Bodeen, overseer at the Gist plantation back in South Carolina.

The investigators are required to stay in Arkham overnight while the police conduct their investigation. The next morning it is learned a large group of badly dressed men with thick southern accents, one answering to Professor Gist's description of his caller, arrived at the Arkham train station the night of the attack. Apparently they were responsible for the theft of an automobile that was parked in front of the station.

## What Albert Gist Knows

If and when the investigators begin to question Professor Gist, he inquires if they are familiar with the worship of the Obeah god, Dambala. The investigators need a successful Occult roll to remember any information about this religion (see boxed text). A successful **Cthulhu Mythos** roll allows them to realize that there may be a remote connection between Dambala and the far more primitive and dangerous cult of Yig. Any investigator with actual experience involving Yig need not make a roll.

Gist will tell the investigators his brother has apparently been seduced by the primitive Dambala worship and now is driven by it to commit criminal acts.

## Further Information

The professor is happy to give a somewhat edited version (no mention of Findley Gist) of his family history and that of the plantation. The keeper should read the boxed sections nearby and give out whatever information the players request, as long as it does not reveal the full extent of occultism and insanity in the family. Albert knows full well Caleb is trying to raise Yig and, jealous of his brother's actions, would like to make the attempt himself. This he will not tell investigators.

Nor will he display, while in the investigator's presence, his prejudice against the black sharecroppers. He attempts to present himself as an unselfish scholar and libertarian, a friend to all men. Once Gist has finished answering questions, he remarks that it was surely a stroke of luck that an illiterate black child, who had

# OBEAH & DAMBALA

The beliefs and practices brought to the South by West African slaves are sometimes called Obeah and sometimes called Mojo. These beliefs are significant to the background of the adventure, although the hideous ceremonies performed herein bear little resemblance or relation to conventional Obeah rituals, and only superficial connection to normal Dambala worship.

Obeah is a general term. The worshippers of the religion are Obeah, the religion itself is Obeah, the world is Obeah. Obeah is all that is. It includes the material as well as the spiritual. Obeah has many spirit entities or gods, some good and some bad, and some both good and bad. Obeah is neither good nor evil, it is neutral or amoral. It is the person who is good or evil, depending upon the use the person makes of Obeah.

Many blacks in the South are not rigidly opposed to Obeah, unlike the Reverend Isaac Hilson (a dogmatic Christian minister encountered in the adventure): however, they know that there are dangers in Obeah that must be avoided, dangers that plantation owner Caleb Gist has ignored in his headlong pursuit of power and an escape from his poverty.

For example, they know that an Obeah spell improperly done carries a shock in return. The Obeah priest (also called a Houngan or Mojo man) who stumbles or strays is subject to painful correction by the gods. This fact may be known to any investigators familiar with Obeah.

Bad Obeah arises from an intention to do harm: to blind, deafen, paralyze, even to kill. Its rites are often conducted in cemeteries in the dead of night, attempting to attract the attention of long forgot-

ten elder gods. Bad Obeah calls up the dead to serve as zombies and summons monsters from other planes. Monsters so summoned will do the bidding of the Houngan: however, they must be fed frequently upon human flesh. If they grow too hungry, they will turn upon the Houngan and eat him.

Good Obeah is a way of ironing out the minor difficulties of life. Its spells bring love to the unloved, forgiveness to the unforgiven. Much of good Obeah is an attempt to ward off harm done by evil gods. This is accomplished by spells, amulets, charms. Such charms can be twisted to selfish ends, as the black maid and priestess, Elly, does in a later part of the adventure.

Obeah does not usually involve human sacrifice, though it frequently involves animal sacrifice.

Most Obeah people in the South regard Christianity as a part of Obeah. Christian paraphernalia — crosses, pictures of Jesus, Bibles — are often used in good Obeah.

The two aspects of Obeah, good and bad, make one whole, and it is not always easy to distinguish between them: however, in the adventure, there is no doubt that the cultists are practicing the darkest kind of Obeah. Any investigator making a successful Occult roll realizes the repulsive practices of the cultists are a loathsome perversion of Obeah.

## The Gists and Obeah

From the time he first explored his grandfather Findley Gist's books, Caleb Gist moved steadily down the dark Obeah path laid out by Findley. In the beginning, Caleb attracted many other Houngans, of both the light and the dark ways: however, the Houngans of the light quickly left him, and when the ancient serpent man showed up, even the Houngans of the dark departed in terror. ✸

# THE GIST FAMILY FORTUNES

The impoverishment of the Gists, like so many other members of the Southern cotton aristocracy, began immediately after the Civil War. The Gists lost almost everything when the Southern Rebellion (the term Professor Gist prefers to use) failed.

By the 1900's the Gists were eking out a living renting their land to sharecroppers. The house in Charleston was sold. The education of Albert and Caleb used almost the last of the family's capital.

During World War I, high prices for cotton brought a return of prosperity to the plantation. In the 1920's, however, prices for farm products plunged to all-time lows. Worse yet, the boll weevil invaded South Carolina and devastated the cotton crop. It is said in the South that "The twenties may be roaring for the rest of the country, but they are groaning for South Carolina farmers."

Since the falling out with Albert, Caleb is the only Gist now living on the family plantation. Even though life there is not prosperous, either for Caleb Gist or the sharecroppers, it is remote and provides Gist the privacy he desires.

## The Current Situation

The routine at the Gist plantation has never been as placid as that on neighboring plantations, although poverty has been, if anything, even more grievous due to the insanity of many of the sharecroppers. Long before Findley Gist's discoveries, the plantation held a reputation for having been the site of foul rites conducted by degenerate Indians. The altar to Yig in the swamp, ignored by the original Gists, has been in sporadic use lately, although local authorities have occasionally threatened to shut down the services. Most everyone in the area is well aware that dark magic and things even worse are practiced there, although educated, upper class whites consider such talk simply superstitious hysteria.

Since Caleb Gist's successes of the last year, the plantation has been dominated by terror and black magic. A few of the sharecroppers on the plantation have packed up and left, but most remain. Unable to find work elsewhere, fatalistic and superstitious, they persevere as best they can. The worst of them have become cultists. Even the white overseers, like the new foreman, Big Rate Bodeen, have been corrupted.

## Caleb Gist and Obeah

Like many farmers of the time, the twin blights of low prices and the boll weevil have brought Caleb Gist to the verge of bankruptcy. Caleb believes, however, that he can return the Gists to prestige and power through Yig worship.

While Albert, after his disagreement with Caleb, lost interest in the traditional family focus on Yig and moved north to eventually pursue other occult paths, Caleb persevered. Last year he was contacted by a strange Obeah man (the disguised serpent sorcerer) who has been helping Caleb with one of the spells in Findley's notes; the powerful ritual, Call/Dismiss Yig. Findley himself had tried this spell on several occasions, but to no avail. Now Caleb intends to attempt the rite using the modifications (including human sacrifice) taught him by the Obeah man. On the upcoming Night of Yig, Caleb will perform a human sacrifice and, with the aid of over 150 fanatical cultists, attempt to call Yig. For this feat Caleb feels sure he will receive exceedingly great rewards. The serpent man has selected a young sharecropper girl as the victim.

Even if Yig confers no heaps of gold or other special boons upon him in return for the sacrifice, Caleb hopes that the summoning of Yig will permit him to terrify and dominate all the sharecroppers in the area, increasing both his work force and the level of profits gleaned from the land. With any luck, he figures to gain enough power to extort money from other landlords, and eliminate the annoyance of the county sheriff once and for all. ☀

---

hardly ever been off the Gist plantation, should have found his way almost 1000 miles north to this backwoods farm in Massachusetts and in just a few days' time. "I can only assume that divine providence has played a hand in this meeting," he says, patting little Joe on the head. A **Psychology** roll allows investigators to notice that Joe flinches slightly when patted. He seems to instinctively distrust Albert Gist.

## What Will the Investigators Do?

If by now the investigators have still not decided to help the pair, Gist will appeal to their honor, stating that the boy's family is in grave danger and that Caleb must somehow be stopped.

Little Joe will add his tearful pleas. If necessary, the boy can ask the biggest or meanest of the investigators if he can borrow their gun. "I don't blame y'all for being scared, mister, but ah'm the only man in the family. I'm gonna get them fellas that took my sis an' my ma if it's the last thing ah do," he says, a harsh expression darkening his youthful face.

If all else fails, Gist will offer them money. His savings are meager but he is willing to give all he has

($1100) in an effort to persuade the investigators to help.

## Researching the Situation

Before leaving town, investigators may wish to do a little research. In Arkham, Miskatonic's famed Orne Library provides the most comprehensive catalogue of books and publications. A study of the history, religions, and economics of South Carolina is a possibility and information on Obeah and the cult of Dambala can confirm what Joe and Professor Gist have told them. No information on the Gist family can be found.

Asking around campus will turn up nothing unusual regarding the habits or personality of Professor Gist. He seems a typical, if somewhat reclusive scholar.

## Checking Up On Gist

If the investigators make any local inquiries into Albert Gist's character, neither the police nor the university will turn up anything negative about the man. However, at the university they may learn that Gist's psychology teachings refer often to the occult.

## PART TWO
# The Journey South

The journey to South Carolina can be made either by rail or auto but the train is quicker and far more restful than a car trip through the back roads of the South. No matter which form of transportation the investigators choose, they will find themselves harassed by the cultists.

The cultists who made the attack on Gist's house have been ordered by Caleb to delay his brother and any companions on their journey south. The survivors of the assault on the house will be aided by several additional cultists, some female, on the lookout for Gist or little Joe at the Arkham and the Boston train stations. Rafe Bodeen (or, if he is dead or jailed, another one of the cultists) is to return home immediately and report to Caleb. The remaining cultists are to telegraph the results of their encounters back to Charleston.

The harassing cultists are accompanied by a large zombie, created by Caleb Gist with magic taught to him by the serpent queen.

If the investigators go by train, the cultists and the zombie will be on it. If they go by car, the cultists will steal cars for themselves and attempt to follow them, making several night ambushes, attacking when no witnesses are around, or unleashing the zombie at an appropriate time.

In the 1920s the basic means of transportation from Boston to Charleston was the railroad. The train ride takes little more than a day and a half; by comparison, the automobile trip is much slower and more susceptible to unexpected delays. Gist informs the investigators that he has a reliable friend (named Elihu Winsworthy) in Charleston who owns his own car. He can provide transportation for the group from Charleston to the plantation itself.

If the train is taken, see "The Train" below. If they take a car or an alternate route, see "Other Routes."

## The Train

Sometime after boarding the train an investigator with a successful **Spot Hidden** roll notices a man who seems to be watching them. The man is only watching; he takes no action against the investigators. If confronted, the stranger denies everything. If the investigators make a scene or threaten him, he calls the conductor and attempts to have them put off at the next stop. (A successful **Fast Talk or Credit Rating** roll dissuades the conductor). The investigators will know that the man is a Southerner by his accent, and probably assume (rightly so) he is a cultist.

The watcher has a zombie on the train with him, hidden in a coffin that was loaded onto the baggage car. It stays hidden here until the cultist awakens it by rapping on the coffin three times in a particular rhythm. The zombie then breaks its way out of the coffin and awaits its orders. The zombie will obey any one set of simple commands given to it by the cultist. Once these orders are fulfilled the undead thing wanders away in search of its grave.

The watcher may try to lure the investigators to the baggage car or, if this fails, will send the zombie against them while they sleep. The zombie smashes its way into the investigators' compartment late at night and, after breaking out a window, begins throwing investigators from the train (windows on U.S. passenger cars do not open, but the zombie easily smashes through). The watcher's thinking is straightforward. He does not need to murder the investigators. He needs only to delay their arrival at the plantation until after Yig Night.

After completing its mission, the zombie will jump from the train and disappear into the darkness. If someone on the train thinks to pull the emergency stop cord, the train will stop and return for the investigators.

Falling from a moving train is not necessarily fatal; the territory they happen to be traveling through is soft and swampy. The investigators' clothes will certainly be soiled beyond redemption but those who make a successful **Jump** roll, lose only 1D4 hit points. A failed Jump roll (or an unexpected push from behind followed by an unprepared fall off the train) costs 1D8 hit points.

If the train does not stop, investigators who are thrown off can tramp along the railroad to the next station and catch another train south the next day — provided they are decently clothed and have money for tickets. Alternatively, they can hitch a ride on a freight train. In order to do this the investigators must wait until a train slows down (going up a hill) and then run and jump on. To succeed the investigators need a successful **Jump roll at +25** percentiles. Once one investigator is aboard he may help the others to hop on. In the freight car the investigators encounter five to ten surly hoboes. If these hoboes are antagonized — and any sort of critical remark will antagonize them — they will attempt to throw the investigators from the train. Investigators overpowered by the smelly bums must yet again successfully **Jump** or lose 1D8 hit points.

## Other Routes

An alternative to the train is private automobile and the cultists naturally attempt to follow and slow the investigators. The keeper may wish to refer to the automobile chase rules in the *Call of Cthulhu* rules. One likely event on the trip is a series of shotgun blasts from a passing car along a lonely stretch of road, directed at the tires. If the investigators stop along the route at a hotel or other rest stop, and have not lost the cultists, the zombie is released, with orders to kill. Meanwhile the cultists will take care to sabotage the investigators' vehicle(s).

# PART III
# South Carolina

## Charleston

One way or another, the investigators ought to arrive in Charleston, population 75,000. If the investigators still have an automobile, the cultists take advantage of the stop in Charleston to blow it up or set it afire, once and for all eliminating the investigators' private transportation. They do not, however, attack the investigators themselves.

While in Charleston a successful **Spot Hidden** reveals two watchers, neither of them familiar. If confronted, the watchers attempt to run away. If caught, they deny everything. They are poor, white, uneducated, and loyal to their faith. No amount of persuasion or non lethal violence will cause them to reveal anything, although their unstable behavior and fanatical religious beliefs is obvious to any observer.

Professor Gist indicates that his friend Elihu, their driver, will arrive in the morning, and so the investigators have the remainder of the day and that night in Charleston. Professor Gist at some point remarks wistfully that "once the Gists kept carriages in Charleston to drive guests out to the plantation, but no more."

## Local Rumors

If the investigators should talk to the locals they will hear that the area around the Gist plantation is "bad juju". Several people mention the hell holes which appear suddenly, dragging victims screaming into the earth, then soon after closing back up.

Research either in newspaper offices or with the police confirm that people and large animals are reported missing in the area of the Gist plantation about four times a year. The police claim this is normal for an area as extensive and poverty stricken as the Gist plantation.

### DETECTIVE MURDERED!

The mutilated body of missing Charleston Police Detective Jasper Galloway was discovered early yesterday morning by local fishermen. The body was found under a tangle of cypress roots in the Edisto river just south of the estate of Mr. Caleb Gist. Officer Galloway had been looking into rumors about a Satanist church operating in Charleston. He had been missing for several days. An inquiry by Colleton County Sheriff Virgil Trucks included a search of the Gist land but no evidence regarding the detective's death was discovered. Sheriff Trucks has stated that he believes the detective must have been murdered in Charleston and the body later dumped in the river. Officer Galloway was unmarried and is survived by his father and mother.

*The Plantation Papers #1*

"Between the snakes, the 'gators, and the quicksand, I'm surprised we don't lose more."

## Newspapers

The only newspaper in the city with files worth examining is the Charleston *News and Courier*. A search of these files produces one recent article on the Gist plantation, see **The Plantation Papers #1**). The article is dated roughly two months ago. If an Idea roll is made, the investigator may wonder, if the detective was murdered in town, why wasn't the body dumped in the convenient Charleston harbor?

If the investigators pursue their researches and make successful Library Use rolls, they may find an additional article of interest, much older than the first (see **The Plantation Papers #2**).

## The Next Day

Professor Gist's friend, Elihu Winsworthy, is late (he is a dilettante). He arrives around noon in a large new automobile, immediately suggests lunch, and will not leave without it. It is late afternoon before the party leaves Charleston. During lunch, Winsworthy comments with amusement on any unusual items of baggage that the investigators have brought, such as elephant guns, folding boats, or odd occult paraphernalia. He is not pleased to have little Joe in his fine new car, but any firm comments from the investigators will shame him into silence.

Winsworthy is a handsome, well dressed white male with refined Southern manners and expensive tastes. He is independently wealthy and a dabbler in the occult, having accompanied Albert on several of his minor endeavors. He is overbearingly chivalrous towards female investigators, considering himself to be a bit of a Casanova, but is a generally boring conversationalist.

Winsworthy assisted Professor

### Voodoo Rituals Uncovered

A raid led by Captain Pearson of the Charleston town constabulary disrupted a Voodoo Ritual being held in the swamps to the south of Walterboro on property owned by the Gist family. Interrupted was a slave ceremony involving non Christian practices of worship. All participants in the primitive ceremony, escaped into the swamp. Several of Captain Pearson's men were wounded in the assault.

The raiders discovered odd paraphernalia including swords, flags inscribed with undecipherable runes, and human skulls.

*July 6, 1825*

*The Plantation Papers #2*

Gist in earlier investigations of palmistry and witch-craft, and once, to his thrilled terror, actually saw a ghoul prowling an ancient cemetery. He is eager to assist Gist again. Albert has sworn him to secrecy regarding their previous occult investigations. How Winsworthy will react if the unbalanced Albert take over the rites to Yig, is unpredictable.

Winsworthy is particularly proud of his automobile. In the 1920's most South Carolinians who could afford a car drove a Ford Model T. Winsworthy, however, drives an Anderson, an expensive touring car manufactured right in South Carolina. He is inordinately pleased with this vehicle, and its origins, and will talk about it at length to the investigators.

### Next Stop, Walterboro

The investigators travel west from Charleston into Colleton County, either chauffeured or guided by Elihu Winsworthy, who reveals himself a slow and cautious driver. The first stop is Walterboro, the seat of Colleton county, some fifty miles away.

Once in Walterboro, Gist insists they stop and visit the county sheriff's office. Not trusting Caleb, Albert wants to make sure the local lawman, Sheriff Virgil Trucks, is aware that they are in the area and

*Mr. Elihu Winsworthy*

visiting at the Gist plantation. The investigators can meet Trucks and possibly question him. They find him to be tight lipped regarding recent events around the Gist plantation and he will not mention his suspicions about Caleb's activities. He is distrustful of northerners. If asked about the hell holes he will brush them off as "simple superstition". "More'n likely just quicksand, if you ask me," he says. If the investigators can bring him some clues regarding the murder of the Charleston police detective, Trucks proves more amenable.

### Back on the Road

Leaving Walterboro, the group finds easy traveling for about ten miles, before Winsworthy turns south onto a dirt road that seems to grow narrower by the mile. Soon after, the investigators see a vast area of swampland, the road only slightly elevated above brackish water. Giant cypress trees shrouded with gray, hairlike Spanish moss tower up out of the water to overshadow the road. The air is humid, fetid, and many soft, odd sounds can be heard over the muted rumble of Winsworthy's expensive car. Winsworthy mutters to the investigators that it

In the days before air conditioning, Low Country summers were so hot, humid, and pestilence-ridden that wealthy Charlestonians often fled the city in July and August for the milder climate of the up state. If the investigators are not accustomed to the climate, they will be most uncomfortable in South Carolina in the summertime. If the investigators insist upon prolonged physical activity during the heat of the day, heat exhaustion, heat cramps, and even heat stroke are real possibilities — depending upon the CON of the investigator. CON rolls at x5, then x4, etc., may be appropriate at the keeper's discretion, particularly if the investigators are fighting or clambering through the noisome depths of the swamp. Failure indicates significant fatigue, with reductions to skills at -10 to -20 points.

If your players are good roleplayers, the summer heat so drains the energy of the investigators that by the afternoon they will be eager to nap in the shade.

Wounds will not heal as quickly in the heat and dampness, and a greater chance of infection exists. ☀

has been years since the last time he was out here. "Blasted road sinks deeper into the swamp every year, ah swear," he says.

After roughly an hour, they come to an intersection with another dirt road. A cotton gin stands on one side of the intersection. On the other side stands a large, tin roofed building. The building is rectangular, wooden, unpainted, with a large porch. To one side of it two white men wearing overalls are playing horseshoes. In front stands a gasoline pump with a glass reservoir. On the porch there is a crank-operated kerosene pump.

"We had better stop here," says Winsworthy. "This is the last chance for gas."

"The Gist general store," explains Professor Gist. "Been here for years."

*Sheriff Trucks*

Then, turning to the investigators, he says, "And that is the Gist cotton gin. It's not far to the plantation now."

Once the car has stopped, little Joe jumps out, and nervously thanks Professor Gist and the rest of the group for their assistance. "It's best I not be seen comin' into the plantation — Master Caleb's men be looking out for me, sure enough," he tells the investigators. "Muh house, it's the one with the blue painted door. Ah '11 be lookin' out for yuh."

Unless they forcibly stop Joe, he will depart, promising to contact the investigators later this evening or tomorrow. Some sort of signal or arrangement should be agreed upon at this point. If one of the investigators offers the boy a gun or other weapon, he'll take it. "I sure hope you folks can do something to stop Master Caleb an' save Cassy — I'll help all I can," Joe whispers as he slips off into the woods.

## The Country Store

The country store in the 1920's provided "necessities and notions" to farmers. It was a combination bank, store, post office, and marketplace. The store sold everything from cradles to corsets to coffins, and had a mail order catalog from which customers could order merchandise not kept in stock. Most stores charged high prices, provided year long credit at high interest and, at harvest time, insisted that debtors pay in cotton.

After the church, the country store was the chief social center of the rural South. Since it was the only store around, it was, of necessity, racially integrated. Everyone in the area eventually stopped by the country store to gossip, whittle, chew tobacco, or play checkers and horseshoes.

Assuming the investigators decide to enter the store, they have the opportunity to purchase various useful items. Or they may wish to return here later for such things as snakebite kits, weapons, or boats. The keeper should limit the available items to what sharecroppers of the 1920's could afford and use; tools, clothing, staples, small boats, etc.

## Isaac Hilson

Inside the country store the investigators encounter a number of men and women who stare curiously at the strangers. Sitting to one side of the counter, talking quietly with several sharecroppers is a tall, cadaverous black male of indeterminate age. He is wearing overalls, a well worn but clean white shirt, steel rimmed spectacles, and a straw hat. He carries an enormous Bible. The other persons in the store, white or black, treat him with obvious respect. His name is Reverend Hilson.

Albert Gist and Isaac Hilson know each other from years back, and do not get along particularly well. Considering their respective attitudes toward magic it could hardly be otherwise. Hilson's opinion of Professor Gist's brother Caleb is, of course, even more negative.

If they meet in the country store, Professor Gist politely introduces Isaac to the investigators as "a preacher of local fame." Hilson is cordial but the investigators feel the chill in the room. The two men are obviously not close.

If Rev. Hilson realizes that the investigators are on their way to the Gist plantation, he harshly warns them about the place. "Don't go to that pit of Satan, in God's name! There are things being meddled with there that ought not to be awakened. Some powers are best left alone, should a man value his soul." His eyes flash toward Albert.

If pressed further about these things, he becomes tight-lipped and only mutters, "The things of the Evil One don't work for people. Never have and never will. Caleb Gist ought to know that." If asked, he will explain that the hell holes are just another example of what can be caused by people tampering with "evil things that should not be awakened."

Rev. Hilson knows much about Obeah, but will have nothing to do with it because he believes it is tainted by the Evil One. He is convinced that the plantation now belongs to the Evil One and will not set foot on it except in the direst of circumstances. His attitude is not the usual one.

Most Christian blacks of the time saw nothing wrong with practicing both Obeah and Christianity. Of course, Hilson is half convinced Caleb Gist is practicing something darker than simple Obeah.

Hilson is a graduate of a segregated Charleston high school and a black seminary. He is intelligent, well educated, but a proud and obsessively religious man. Over a lifetime spent in the Low Country, Hilson has seen certain things unexplainable by

*Reverend Hilson*

## REVEREND HILSON'S HEALING ABILITY

Hilson has a magic-like ability, Faith Healing. He prays, reads appropriate passages from his bible, and lays-on hands. 1D3 hit points will be restored at the cost of 1D3 magic points. Hilson knows no actual spells, nor will he use any. He feels that they are inconsistent with his religion.

Faith healing requires that the recipient, as well as the one who administers it, be of strong faith, as evidenced by previous conduct.

This ability is occasionally encountered among devout religious persons. Faith healing never works upon persons antagonistic to the religion practiced by the healer, even under duress or in life threatening situations.

A faith healer heals minor injuries through the force of his will, working in combination with the willing faith of his subject. The religious rituals appropriate for the culture are performed.

Extensive injuries or other physical problems, such as lameness, shock, broken bones, and minor diseases, may be healed after several successive treatments. The effectiveness of such treatments on investigators will have to be adjudged by the keeper but they will take at least a month of time to administer. ☼

science. These experiences have confirmed his belief in demons and the works of Satan. Hilson has no knowledge of the Cthulhu Mythos, but may be willing to help the investigators against Caleb Gist should they approach him seeking aid against Satan's works.

Hilson can be a powerful ally for the investigators. His fanaticism has given him the ability of Faith Healing. He also has great influence in the area. Finally, he has a fist like a mule's kick. It is easy to keep in communication with him, should the investigators so desire. Any of the black sharecroppers at the store can be relied upon to deliver a message. Of course, he warns the investigators that most blacks in Caleb's household are not trustworthy. Even if the investigators reject his aid, Hilson can appear at the last minute, at the head of a brave group of Christian sharecroppers, arid save the investigators.

Hilson does not use his powers casually, or upon those of little faith. Should the investigators be wounded, it may require a **Persuade or Credit Rating** roll to convince him to aid them. Fast Talk will not fool the preacher. A generous donation to his church will undoubtedly help.

If the investigators have been unsure about what to do with little Joe, and have not let the boy run off yet, then Hilson is willing to take care of him.

## Another Ambush

When the investigators resume their journey, they drive about a mile or two before they sight the broad, murky Edisto river. A large plank bridge can be seen ahead. It is wooden and crudely assembled, but quite sturdy. Professor Gist remarks quietly, "Here's the old bridge. When we cross the river, we are on the plantation. Be on your guard."

As the car approaches the bridge, Winsworthy halts. Everyone can see that several planks have been removed from the center of the short span. The planks are lying by the road on the investigators' side of the river. They look to be easily replaced.

"Why in the world . . ." Winsworthy mutters. Then he shrugs and says with an amiable smile, "The locals must have been doing some work on the bridge." Winsworthy gets out of the car. "Simple enough matter to put them back, I suppose," he says, looking around for help.

A shot suddenly rings out and slams into the side of Winsworthy's car, narrowly missing the man. Winsworthy yells: "Hell's bells!" and dives face first into the mud. The shots continue and the investigators should be allowed only a limited amount of time to decide what they wish to do.

The sniper is hiding in bushes about 25 yards off the road to the left of the car. He will fire four shots at the party before his gun goes silent. The first shot hits Winsworthy's car and the rest are aimed at random individuals and fired with a skill of 45%. The weapon is a .22 rifle, damage 1D6+2.

Regardless of investigator actions, the gunman fires no more than four shots, then goes silent. If the investigators have returned the fire they may assume that they have hit their adversary — but there is no way of telling without approaching the stand of bushes from which the sniper fired. If they check, they find the body of a lower class white man lying upon his back, his .22 fallen by his side. If the investigators reach this spot reasonably soon after the firing stops they are startled to see a very large water moccasin crawling away from the already dying man. The snake is a Child of Yig (**Cthulhu Mythos** to identify) and bears upon its head the tell-tale white crescent. If left alone the Child makes no attempt to harm the investigators and passively crawls away. Spotting a Child of Yig so suddenly, without warning, costs knowledgeable investigators 0/1D2 SAN.

If they wait longer before approaching the sniper, the Child is gone and they find only the dead man. A quick check shows no bullet wounds. It requires a **Spot Hidden or Medicine** to find the snakebite on the man's left calf, just above his boot. The virulent poison of Yig's Child will already have blackened the flesh around the wound. In 24 hours' time the entire leg will have blackened and swollen to the bursting point. Any local resident can then easily identify the cause of death as snakebite.

This ambush was not intended to be lethal to the group, even brother Albert. The gunman was ordered to fire a half dozen rounds, then flee. It was hoped the attack would slow the investigators down a bit and demonstrate to them the kind of the power Caleb wields. He does not want the visitors around and hopes that actions like this will drive them away. However, he did not count on his efforts being thwarted by the serpent man who is serving Yig.

### Ambush Aftermath

Surely one or more of the investigators notes the snake's attack on the cultist is not normal behavior, particularly for a cottonmouth, which is usually fairly cowardly (allow a **Zoology or EDU x1**). All investigators who realize the strangeness of the snake's actions lose 1 SAN if they fail a SAN roll.

Unknown to both Caleb and the investigators, this whole scene has been carefully observed by the serpent man sorcerer who has come to the plantation at the bidding of Yig. Though usually disguised as the mysterious Obeah man, the serpent man has presently dropped this illusion and appears in his true form. If any of the investigators explore past the immediate area of the body they find themselves at the edge of the swamp. Far away they see a large animal of some kind, swimming quickly away with a sinuous, serpentine motion. The serpent man is too far away to be identified without binoculars or a Spot Hidden roll. Anyone who does positively identify the creature will lose 0/1 D6 SAN points. If fired upon, the serpent man ducks under water and in any case, soon be out of sight around a nearby spit of land.

Catching him will be difficult. If the investigators bought a folding boat at the store, they may be in luck. Or they may attempt to follow him on foot across the swamp. If the keeper rules their efforts to be successful, see the section below, "The Lair of the Serpent Man."

## PART IV

# The Plantation

After the binding of any wounds — and much genteel cursing from Winsworthy — the expedition reconstructs the bridge and crosses the river. The road now bends due south, following the riverbank through even more desolate areas of swamp, occasionally inhabited by a cleared patch of farmland. The group passes several crude shacks and rotting sheds, some with a thin black woman or child sitting outside. Professor Gist comments pedantically on the unfortunate lack of attention to proper nutrition and hygiene that prevails in the South at this time.

Soon the investigators arrive at a slightly higher section of ground. Before them, the investigators see a large riverside plantation, dominated by a house on a low hill. "Here we are," says Winsworthy, slowing the car.

The house was obviously once a magnificent example of Southern plantation architecture. Two storied, a large screened porch completely surrounds the ground floor. The peeling white paint is splotched in many places with gray mold and the porch screen is riddled with holes. From the roof, several lightning rods reach toward the sky and it can be noticed that many shingles are missing. Four gigantic oaks surround the house, but they are dripping with Spanish moss and appear nearly dead.

About 200 yards downhill from the house is a small but sprawling hamlet of shanties and tin roofed farm buildings. Most are in poor repair, and some have collapsed. A cluster of sharecroppers, mostly women and children, are gathered in the hamlet, staring up at the recently arrived strangers. Most are black but a few are white. Joe's shack, with its blue painted door, can easily be seen. Four armed men guard the entrance.

## THE LAND & PEOPLE OF SOUTH CAROLINA

The southern half of South Carolina, or Low Country, is only a few feet above sea level. The rivers, navigable by small boats, flow sluggishly between low banks, or extend themselves beyond their banks into the thickly wooded swamps. The water in the swamps is generally only one to three feet deep, but certain areas, called "holes" by the locals, may drop off as much as twenty feet. These rivers and swamps extend all down the coast where they form a bewildering maze of sea islands.

In the 1920's, due to the difficulty of bridging combinations of swamps and rivers, adjacent South Carolina counties were almost like different countries. These counties were composed of farms and small communities that had little or no contact with the outside world. The majority of these populations was black — although whites owned most of the land — and they had almost no economic or political power.

Southern sharecroppers of the 1920's were usually black, but not always. Black or white, sharecroppers were not much better off than their fathers had been in the days of slavery. Sharecroppers were illiterate tenant farmers who paid as much as half their crop to the landlord. Since the soil of the Low Country had been exhausted by a generation of cotton growers, and given problems with procuring effective fertilizer, sharecroppers got little reward for their labor — even before the arrival of the boll weevil. Whole families were crowded into dilapidated shacks that leaked rain in the summer and cold air in the winter. Plumbing was little more than a rumor. It was a common saying that the sharecropper's bleak existence consisted of five "M's": meat, meal (cornmeal), molasses, mules, and monotony. Foreign visitors to the Low Country at the time reported that Southern sharecroppers lived much like serfs in Czarist Russia.

Since the landlord depended upon the sharecroppers, if all or most of the sharecroppers had a bad year, he was not much better off than they were. Moreover, many landlords were simply 'land poor." They owned large tracts of useless land from which they derived little or no income. Caleb Gist falls into this category. Of course, the trackless wetlands around his plantation have not been entirely useless, since they are sacred to Yig, the god Gist wishes to call. ☀

Little Joe (if the investigators have brought him this far), now panics and leaps out of the car, bolting toward the nearest woods.

### Meet Caleb Gist

The group arrives at the plantation late in the afternoon of a typically warm, humid summer day. Caleb, aware of their impending arrival, awaits them in the house. They are met at the front door by an aging black man dressed in antiquated butler's garb who ushers them politely into the house. "Master Caleb's waitin' fo' you folk on the back veranda. Follow me if you please," he says in his deep voice.

Caleb Gist, a tall, tanned man in somewhat worn white riding clothes, greets the group. He is handsome in a disreputable sort of way, with dark, lustrous eyes and a commanding manner. "Welcome to the plantation," he says with an elegant bow and a handshake like a dead fish. "Brother Albert, it's been a long time." Professor Gist gives a stiff little bow in return.

If the investigators are polite and look unthreatening, Caleb says, "Please introduce me to your associates, brother."

If the investigators are surly or hostile, or if anyone is displaying an obvious weapon, he bows again and says with a smile, "The police are already taking an interest in the affairs of this plantation, gentlemen, so I hope there won't be any trouble. The sheriff tends to look very harshly on unnecessary gunplay in his jurisdiction."

## Caleb's Household

Only four people occupy the rotting Gist mansion — Caleb and his three black servants. Until recently, there was a fifth member of the household, the ancient serpent man who stayed in a now locked upstairs bedroom. Aware of the investigators' impending visit, the serpent man has lately withdrawn to the swamp. But evidence of his stay in the mansion can be discovered.

The person in charge of keeping the dilapidated mansion running is old Bess, the cook, seamstress, and housekeeper. Bess is an elderly black lady who was nanny to both Albert and Caleb. She is not subservient to either one, and still regards them as the children she raised. They call her Aunt Bess. If engaged in conversation, Bess regales the group with tales of Albert and Caleb's childhood. ("Albert was quiet. Caleb was always into something.") Over the years Bess has become more loyal to Caleb than to Albert, and she reports anything she sees or hears directly to him. She is too old to engage in violence of any kind, although capable of cooking up some dangerously poisoned dishes if asked to.

The maid, Elly, is young and very pretty. She seems unusually assertive and self confident for a black woman in her position. Professor Gist remarks that she must be a recent addition to the household. Winsworthy snidely comments about "Southern gentlemen and their black mistresses."

Elly's duties as a maid are not demanding, and she accepts them until such time as the power of Yig will let all people cast off their mundane burdens, and live, love, and die as the Great Old One commands.

Caleb Gist is extremely jealous regarding the girl and has warned her not to try any of her tricks with their guests. How far

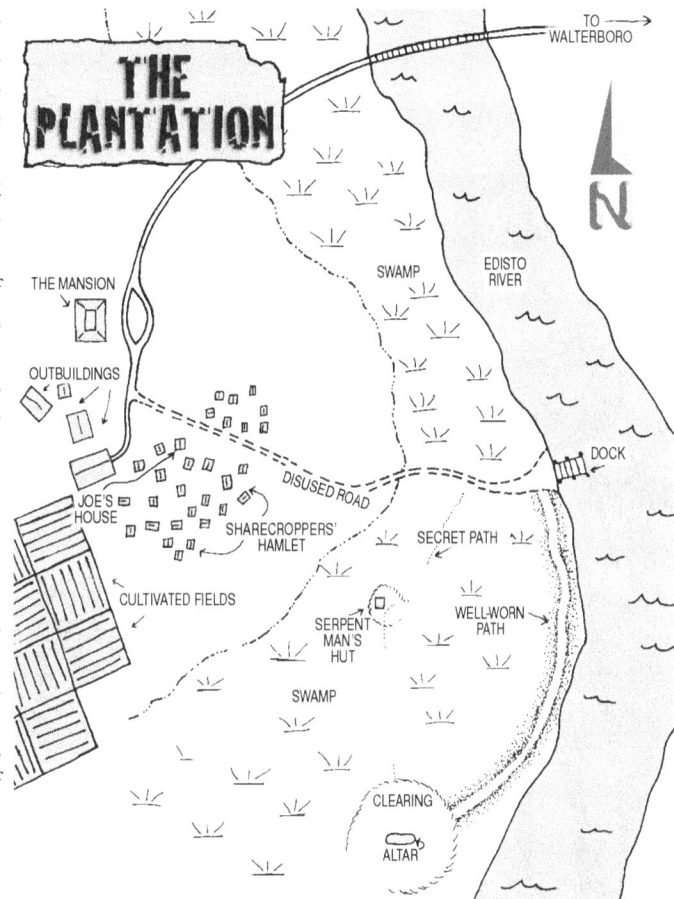

*Master Caleb*

she goes to seduce one or more of them depends on how much of a threat they seem to be, and not on Caleb's orders. She is a proud woman and a free agent, with rank in the cult equal to his. If the investigators do nothing but read books, she will consider them harmless. If they injure Caleb or any cultists, or demonstrate the ability to use magic, she will consider them a far more serious threat.

Elly is always armed with a straight razor (1D3 plus impale), and hidden somewhere in her clothing lurks a small, deadly coral snake. She also knows how to use magic. The local folk are more terrified of Elly than of either Caleb or Rafe Bodeen.

With her potions and remedies, Elly is a good healer. She can also concoct deadly poisons and powerful love philters. If convinced that a male investigator is a serious threat to the Night of Yig, she may attempt to give him one of these philters. She will attempt to befriend or seduce her victim first, then offer the brew under relaxed and unsuspicious circumstances.

The fourth member of the household is Old Ben, the elderly black butler who greeted the investigators upon their arrival. He is a quiet and dignified man, and has been with the family as long as

*Elly the Maid*

Bess has. Although sane, Old Ben is used to the occult shenanigans that go on around the plantation, and is, in fact, an initiate of the Yig cult. Should the investigators be at desperate risk, Ben might help them leave the plantation rather than allow them to be killed before his eyes. He would never defy Caleb directly, however, and he is too feeble to be of much help in combat situations.

## The Investigation Begins

The butler and the maid will deal with the group's luggage which includes Professor Gist and Winsworthy's small trunks. There are a number of bedrooms upstairs, all of them musty and badly kept up. Albert will take his usual room, to be shared by Winsworthy, leaving the investigators to choose between the two vacant ones. One bedroom is locked and unavailable to the guests.

There are a couple hours to kill before dinner and nightfall and the investigators may feel that they would like to immediately begin prying around. However, Caleb will do his best to distract them; first by playing the part of the gracious host, and then with the offer of a guided tour of the plantation.

If they turn the down the offer (or some turn it down) they will be allowed to roam pretty much where they will but the sharecropper cultists will keep a close eye on their movements.

## A Guided Tour!

Caleb Gist offers them drink — iced tea or mint julep, depending upon the visitor's preference — then begins showing the investigators around the plantation. "After all," he smiles, "you have come nearly a thousand miles just for the chance to see a real Southern plantation."

If any investigators are polite enough to agree, Caleb wastes as much of their time as he can. During the tour, Caleb explains that nearly every task on the plantation

---

## ELLY'S LOVE PHILTER

Brewing this potion costs 2 magic points and requires an hour's time. It is nearly flavorless (POW x1 to successfully notice its subtle, bitter mint flavor) and can be added to any refreshment. If drunk by a human male (no effect on females), the victim becomes susceptible to the charms of the first female he meets. She needs a roll of POW x5 or less — whether she intends to charm him or not. If a successful roll, the man will become completely enchanted with that woman for the next 1D6+1 days. For that length of time he will be so completely in love with the her that he will follow almost any demand she should make, excepting those that would cause him to leave her indefinitely or cause him do harm to himself. (*Example: "go away and die" will not be obeyed.*) If properly manipulated, the character will act against his friends. However, any sort of insanity, temporary or permanent, neutralizes the effects of the love philter. ☼

---

is still done by hand: milking cows, churning butter, picking cotton, feeding livestock, cutting wood. "We tan our own leather," he says, "shoe our own mules, grind our own cornmeal, and make our own soap. The plantation is a totally self-sufficient enterprise." He does not add that at the moment the enterprise is almost broke. He points with pride to the windmill, saying that he had it constructed during the period of prosperity of the Great War, The windmill pumps water to his house and to the barns (but not to the sharecroppers' houses). The investigators see mostly cotton fields and deteriorating farm buildings, and are mostly bored, which is Caleb's intention.

At some point during the tour the investigators notice the old dirt road leading into the swamp. If they ask about the road, which appears to be in good repair, Caleb answers: "It goes down to an old dock on the river, but it's no longer used and all grown over. The swamp quickly reclaims its own." He warns them to stay out of the swamp "Snakes and 'gators, you know."

### Private Explorations

If the investigators go off on their own they are watched at all times. In the house, the three black servants keep a constant eye on them, while outside, the sharecropper/cultists dog their footsteps. Investigators can choose to explore "The House," "The Sharecroppers Hamlet," or "The Swamp."

## The House

All the rooms downstairs are well furnished but most contain nothing of interest to the investigation. The study, however, is filled with the journals and books of generations of scholarly Gists. Many titles are difficult to read without close examination and the few the investigators can easily spot appear to be mostly about farming, hunting, and fishing. There is also a wide selection of late nineteenth century novels by notable authors.

The study is the place Professor Gist will wish to examine first. If anyone is with him they see the professor go directly to the far side of the study and begin closely examining the books contained on a particular shelf. He leafs through each page of every volume, searching carefully. Once finished, he seems disappointed and, if his brother is present, says, "Well, I see you still have our collection intact, Caleb." He sits down on one of the moldering armchairs and thinks quietly for a moment.

Professor Gist is disappointed because his expectations were raised by Joe's descriptions of the magical doings at the plantation. Professor Gist expected to find a new book or books that would account for what Joe

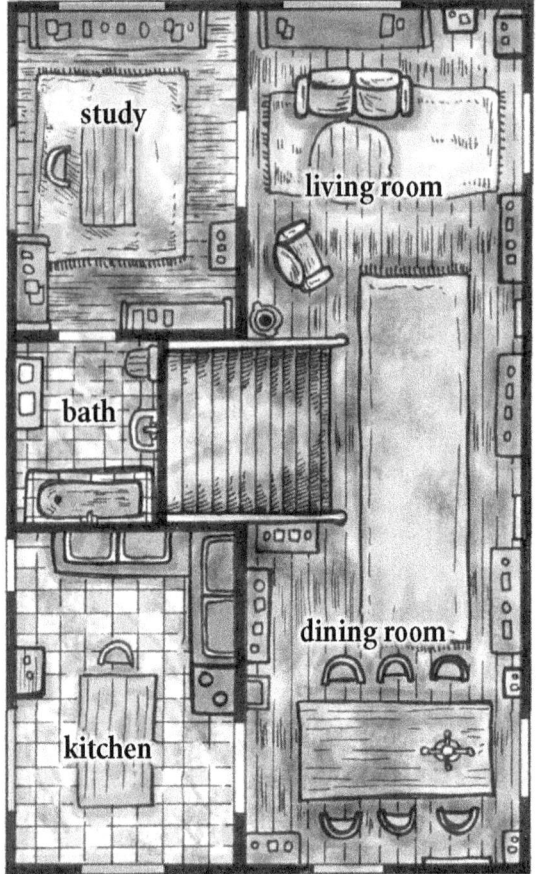

**ground floor**

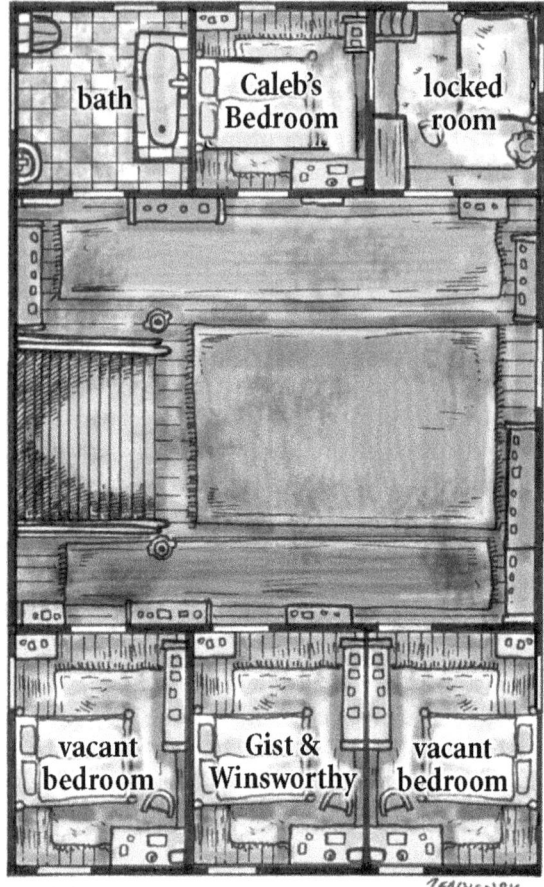

**upstairs**

seemed to be describing and is disappointed when he does not.

The books that Albert was interested in all have similar covers brightly labeled "Minutes of the Colleton County Agricultural Society", for various years. An investigator making a **Spot Hidden** notices that these covers fit their pages loosely. Looking inside, it's easy to tell that the books do not correspond to their titles.

If Albert, Winsworthy, or an investigator begins reading one of these books in Caleb's presence, Caleb will walk over and remove the other four books and place them in his room. Otherwise, Caleb remains uninterested. For further details about the tomes, see the "Gist Library", opposite.

### Findley Gist's Books:
*(spells are presented in the Gist Library box)*

❈ A translation by Findley Gist of Father Juan Martin's the *Cult of Kukulcan*.

❈ Father Martin's original work in Spanish.

❈ A brown untitled volume. On the first page is written, in Findley's large cursive, *Papa Shapo*.

❈ Also a brown untitled volume. It is volume two of *Papa Shapo*.

❈ A diary of certain experiments conducted nearly a hundred years ago by Findley Gist. The experiments are so horrible that reading the book costs the investigator 1 SAN.

### Upstairs

The only unusual room upstairs is the former quarters of the serpent man, presently unoccupied and locked. Upon learning of the approach of the investigators, Caleb asked the serpent man to temporarily move out to a remote shack in the swamp.

If the investigators attempt to enter this room they need a successful **Mechanical Repair or Locksmith** roll to open the door with minimum noise. If all else fails, the door can be broken in (STR 9).

Once inside, the investigators encounter a noxious odor; a successful **Zoology or EDU x1** roll identifies it as reptilian. The smell is disturbing and unexpectedly strong, reminiscent of the snake house at the zoo. If the investigators have entered at night, only starlight through a window illuminates the room. In one corner squats a strange, low shape, far too broad and short to be a human being (it is a wadded up bundle of bedclothes). The keeper should request **Spot Hidden** rolls. Any investigators who fail are uncertain as to what the shape is. If the

# THE GIST LIBRARY

In the mansion library can be found the following titles in disguise:

CULTU KUKULCANOS -- *in Spanish, by Father Juan Martin, sixteenth century.* A deceptive outer binding titled "Minutes of the Colleton County Agricultural Society" shields this rare volume from curious eyes. Few copies of *Cultu* survive. It faithfully describes the worship of Central American primitives. Martin was an early Franciscan missionary to the New World. In the course of his attempts to convert the primitive Indians, he made a study of the worship of their snake god Kukulcan (Yig). Though the good father dismissed the worship practices of the Indians as "the work of the devil," he was an accurate observer. The last chapter of the book is a word for word record of the liturgies of Kukulcan, *Sanity loss 1D6/1D8; Cthulhu Mythos +6 percentiles; average 23 weeks to study and comprehend.* **Spells:** Call/Dismiss Kukulcan, Chant of Warding, Command Serpent, Contact Kukulcan, Send Sacred Snake, Summon/Bind Child of Kukulcan. Minor spells such as Bless Meal are scattered through the book; some are so terse as to be not translatable.

CULT OF KUKULCAN — *in English, translated by Findley Gist very recently.* A longhand manuscript of 264 unnumbered pages, it too is bound as a "Minutes of the Colleton County Agricultural Society". Findley's literal and wooden translation is inferior to the original in every possible way. The spells are underlined, and an annotation in a margin adds "Same as Papa". *Sanity loss 1D6/1D8; Cthulhu Mythos +4 percentiles; average 22 weeks to study and comprehend.* **Spells:** Call/Dismiss Kukulcan, Chant of Warding, Command Serpent, Contact Kukulcan, Send Sacred Snake, Summon/Bind Child of Kukulcan. Possibly one spell is defective.

PAPA SHAPO — *in English, in two volumes, written by Findley Grist earlier in his life.* Both volumes are bound in brown cloth, and both volumes bear misleading new colorful covers of the "Minutes of the Colleton County Agricultural Society". *Papa Shapo* is in two volumes but treated as one work; number of pages unknown. On the first page of each volume is written in Findley's large cursive, Papa Shapo. These are Findley's transcrip-

tions of the lessons of his teacher, the West African Yoruga tribesman who was a powerful Houngan of the left hand path. This is the blackest of black magic and refers to Yig as Dambala. *Sanity loss: 1D8/1D10; Cthulhu Mythos +3 percentiles and Occult +6 percentiles; average 33 weeks to study and comprehend.* **Spells:** none.

FINDLEY GIST'S JOURNAL OF EXPERIMENTS — *in English, written by Findley Grist, datable to the early nineteenth century.* In longhand and of 311 pages, bound as "Minutes of the Colleton County Agricultural Society". Within this foul work are many entries concerning a series of ineffectual but lurid occult experiments performed upon unlucky slaves. There is no gain from reading this journal, but anyone methodically going through it loses 1 point of SAN.

## New Spells

The volumes above contain the following spells in various slightly different forms.

### Command Serpent

The caster can hypnotize any snake to do tasks that are within the reptile's ordinary physical capability, such as moving and biting. Elly uses this spell to create her charmed snakes.

To perform this spell the caster must be within sight of the snake. The caster must overcome the snake's POW with his own on the Resistance Table. Casting the spell costs 1 SAN and a number of magic points equal to twice the SIZ of the snake. Once the snake is charmed, it will follow orders given mentally by the caster, as long as the caster can see the snake. If the orders are completed, and no more are received, the snake will go back to carrying on its normal activities until new orders are received. Duration of obedience is equal to the number of magic points expended in hours. The spell may be cast several times on several different snakes, in order to prepare a group of snakes for the caster's purposes.

### Send Sacred Snake (of Yig, Dambala, Kukulcan)

This spell can only be cast in an area consecrated to Yig by a priest of Yig. The target's actions, description, and name, if known, must be repeated out loud several times during the casting process. The process costs the user 1D4 SAN and 9

magic points. Magic transports the sacred snake to very close to the target.

The snake appears and immediately strikes on its DEX rank. The victim is automatically hit unless he succeeds in a Luck roll. If the sacred snake misses, it pursues its victim, striking repeatedly. The victim must make Dodge rolls to avoid the snake's bite. The bite of a Sacred Snake is always fatal.

The sacred snake is always a huge example of whatever type of snake is dominant in the area of the victim. For example, a victim being attacked in the American West would be attacked by an enormous rattlesnake. The sacred snake always has a large white crescent on its head. Other than size, the sacred snake's only unusual feature is the virulence of its venom, which is magically powerful, enough to kill the chosen victim immediately upon being bitten.

### Call/Dismiss Yig / Dambala / Kukulcan

This dangerous and obscure spell summons Yig, Father of Serpents. The spell may only be cast in an area well suited to snakes, such as a desolate swamp, jungle, or desert. A number of snakes (or serpent men) must be present at the site, with a total combined POW of at least 100. The spell, as described, makes no mention of human sacrifice. Casting this spell costs 1 D10 SAN and 8 magic points. See the *Call of Cthulhu* rules for additional details of such spells.

### Chant of Warding

The chant described is one of a number of variations on the same spell. This one is commonly used by certain Indian tribes of the American Southwest. Properly performed, the chant protects the caster and his domicile from both Yig and Children of Yig.

The chant must be repealed thrice daily. Once at sunrise or upon awakening, once at midday, and again at sunset or before retiring. The chant must be recited for approximately three minutes and 4 magic points expended. If performed faithfully, the individual will be protected from harm caused by Yig or his sacred serpents. This spell affords no protection from normal snakes, either wild specimens or ones that have been enchanted by another sorcerer. Neither does it offer protection against serpent men. ✦

---

keeper begins a countdown at this point, one or more of the investigators, in apprehensive terror, may open fire upon it. If instead they whisper to each other, the characters who made their roll can reassure their comrades.

If the room is lit, the investigators see a double bed stripped of its covers (which are rolled into a ball in a corner), a desk and chair, and a chest.

The desk holds nothing of interest. The chest is unlocked and contains herbal remedies, several glass bottles of strange and useless potions, a human skull, a beaver hat, a long black coat, a flag covered with unidentifiable markings, a large bottle of wine, a box of cigars, and a saber (old and rusty). An **Occult** roll indicates that these items could be useful in Obeah ceremonies (this trunk belonged to the former Obeah man who was driven off by the serpent man).

On the floor, just inside the door, lies a ragged piece of what appears to be a parchment-like material roughly a square inch in size, noticeable with a **Spot Hidden** roll. It is stiff and crinkly stuff, and if bent or handled with much force, breaks and crumbles away. It is snake skin, but only a **Zoology or EDU x1** roll reveals this. A **Cthulhu Mythos** roll further identifies it as serpent man skin.

## The Sharecroppers' Hamlet

The hamlet is a sorry sight. Starved dogs and skinny, scabrous children lurk in the shadows. Questioning the inhabitants proves difficult. Many of the sharecroppers are cultists and are rightfully suspicious of the investigators. Innocent sharecroppers avoid the investigators out of fear of reprisals by the cult. It is nearly impossible for the investigators to tell innocent sharecropper from evil cultist. The most likely thing they might learn is the 'Obeah man' (the serpent man) who was former-

*Big Rafe Bodeen*

ly staying in the plantation house has recently moved out to somewhere in the swamp. It is obvious from the attitudes of those questioned that the man is deeply feared.

Guarding Joe's shack, the one with the blue door, are four surly sharecroppers, two white, two black. All have 12 gauge shotguns and plenty of ammunition. They will chat with the investigators, particularly if any are women, but not let them look inside the shack. "We got some bad folks inside, no visitors allowed." For their stats, see the section near the end of this adventure.

Inside the shack is Joe's sister, Cassy. She is guarded by three large copperhead snakes (enchanted by Elly and Caleb) that lurk under the floorboards. They have been commanded to bite any human who passes through the door. Caleb has already disposed of Joe's mother.

If Big Rafe Bodeen, Caleb's notorious overseer and right hand man, survived the first encounter with the adventurers, he lurks around the hamlet, heavily armed and ready for trouble. If none of the investigators have

actually seen Bodeen, a successful Listen or Idea roll identifies the man's voice as the one the investigators heard arguing with Professor Gist that night back in Arkham. If questioned, both Bodeen and Caleb deny that Bodeen has ever been out of the state. Albert Gist however, if he accompanies the investigators, will quickly identify Bodeen as the culprit that argued with him at his front door.

## The Swamp

If the investigators go outside the house during the day, they are allowed to roam about freely. They discover the old road leading down to the swamp. While traveling along the road or well worn path in either direction, a successful **Spot Hidden** discovers the faint trail leading to the hut of the serpent man.

### The Altar to Yig

If the investigators follow the well worn path all the way back into the swamp they will eventually be led to the ancient stone altar. A huge, table like rock almost five feet high, the altar is covered with very worn, unidentifiable symbols, carved here by the primitives who thousands of years ago gave worship to Yig. It is impossible to accurately identify or read these writings. Dried blood stains the top of the rock but whether animal or human the investigators will be unable to tell (it is animal). A **Cthulhu Mythos** roll positively identifies the altar as dedicated to Yig.

### The Lair of the Serpent Man

Deep in the swamp is the lair of the serpent man who, at Yig's bidding, has come here to seek vengeance on the serpent queen. Getting to the lair will take time and a certain willingness to suffer. Rapid movement through the swamp is impossible, except on paths and roads, due to the miry ground and thick undergrowth. Huge, misshapen trees rot amidst the treacherous pools. The odor is foul. Strange noises lurk at the edge of hearing; the buzz of huge insects, the dripping of oily water, the slither of a snake, the croaking bellow of a distant alligator. In the gloom, who knows what strange enemy lurks around the next corner?

Other problems may present themselves. The serpent queen's horrible homunculi have been keeping watch on the lone serpent man and while they hesitate to attack the sorcerer, they feel less compunction about grabbing investigators, or an accompanying non-player character. If they do, they drag him down into subterranean tunnels familiar to them.

Should this happen, the other investigators can write off their friend and continue their investigation of the serpent man lair, or they may choose to immediately follow the tunnel down into the temple/prison of the

# Denizens of the Swamp

Generally speaking, visiting the swamps of the Deep South in the summertime is not a happy experience. The investigators are made miserable by hordes of stinging, biting insects: mosquitoes, flies, fleas, ticks, mites, chiggers, lice, and scorpions. If the investigators dare to venture into the swamp's waters, they will be frightened by alligators and bitten by leeches. The most serious natural threats in the swamp, however, are bees, wasps, hornets, spiders, snapping turtles, and of course, snakes, particularly cottonmouths, which are common to the area.

The keeper may find it useful to distract the investigators with occasional minor attacks from creatures on this list, rather than constantly inflicting the investigators with snake and alligator attacks.

## Minor Denizens

Hordes of mosquitoes are a fact of life in the South Carolina Low Country. In houses where windows had to be opened to let in every breeze, screening and netting were necessities. Mosquitoes are more than an annoyance. They sometimes carry malaria and yellow fever. In the 1920's both of these diseases were treatable and death was unlikely. Malaria, however, once contracted, can be reoccurring. An individual so infected will suffer from occasional bouts of the disease, its fevers and chills, for the rest of his life.

Ticks are also a problem. Ticks sometimes transmit Rocky Mountain Spotted Fever, which can be fatal. Millions of other insects — flies and fleas and mites and lice and chiggers — combine to make life miserable for swamp dwellers.

To ward off all of the above, it is customary to wear lots of clothing in the swamps: long sleeved, cotton shirts, overalls, boots, and straw hats. If they go outside at night, swamp folk smear small amounts of kerosene on exposed skin, and sit in the smoke of campfires. Natural nostrums were also used, some of them quite effective.

If the investigators run wildly through the swamp, some small chance exists that they will encounter swarms of bees, wasps, or hornets. Multiple stings of these insects are dangerous and may be fatal.

Two types of poisonous spiders lurk in the swamp: the brown recluse and the black widow. The black widow, marked with a red hourglass, is a menace. Her bite will certainly cause sickness and perhaps death. The bite of the brown recluse, while less often fatal will still incapacitate an individual for up to two weeks.

The sting of the swamp scorpion is painful, but not fatal. Scorpions tend to hide in clothing, shoes, and bedding. Investigators should be warned to check for scorpions before getting into bed or putting on shoes and clothes. If they grow careless, they should be punished with a painful sting.

Leeches live underwater and attach themselves to the exposed skin of swimmers and waders. If an investigator tears off the leech, it will create a nasty little wound. The traditional method of removal is by applying a lighted match to the leech.

Alligators are the meanest looking denizens of the swamp, but normally they never attack adult human beings. Small children and dogs can be in some danger. The serpent man has a charmed gator that he can turn against intruders.

Snapping turtles usually have shells covered with swamp growths and are hard to see. They will bite any toes, feet, fingers, or hands that come within range of their beak. Normal snappers can easily nip off a digit, while the gigantic alligator snapper has been known to remove a hand at the wrist. ☼

---

sorcerous snake queen (see The Queen's Lair, further below). The investigators will have to act quickly as the tunnel will collapse in 1D2+1 hours (a **Geology or INT x1** roll will tell them that).

Drawing nearer to the serpent man's lair the investigators see a small hut set atop a low rocky hill rising up out of the swamp. In front of the hut, burning and smoking profusely, a small fire blazes amidst a circle of large stones. A black man, the Obeah man, sits in front of the fire, staring into the flames. He wears a black coat without shirt, a top hat, and from his belt hangs an odd metal hammer, a weapon of some sort, a serpent man club.

The man the investigators see sitting in front of the fire is merely an illusion created by the serpent sorcerer who watches from nearby, concealed behind a large cypress tree. The investigators may have good reason to suspect the Obeah man and will have to decide what to do: approach and speak with him, or simply open fire.

If the investigators choose to shoot at the Obeah man the illusionary priest will slowly look up from the fire, grin at the investigators, then dissolve into thin air (the serpent man will have collapsed his illusion). Judging the investigators' mood at this point, the serpent man may either flee through the woods to take refuge in the swamp, stay in the area to spy on the group, or attempt to approach them, seeking their aid in destroying the evil serpent queen.

If the investigators openly approach the illusion and speak to it, it will, as before, dissolve while the serpent man (in the guise of the Obeah man) appears from behind his cypress tree. He addresses the group in a commanding, but non-hostile manner. He may or may not choose at this time to reveal to the investigators what is happening at the plantation or about Yig's plans. At any rate it is unlikely that he reveals all he knows about the situation. Although he may believe the investigators' aid is essential, he neither trusts nor likes the humans. He may or may not reveal his true identity.

If the investigators have a chance to search the hut they can find a fine metal box, made of some odd and ancient material, locked by a mechanism of peculiar design. The box is about 10 inches long, and triangular in cross section. It is strong but not bullet-proof (STR 18).

Inside are a number of thick, triangular metal

*The Obeah Man*

tablets with incised writing on them. A **Cthulhu Mythos** roll identifies them as books of the serpent race. If an investigator can read the language of the serpent folk, he finds the tablets are an extensive journal of scientific observations concerning various contemporary human cultures of North America. The observations, apparently made over the last five or ten years, are in an insultingly contemptuous tone.

Should the serpent man have reason to fear for his life he can silently call upon several Children of Yig (water moccasins) that will encircle the investigators in a threatening manner. A huge alligator, charmed by the serpent man, also lurks nearby, ready to attack at the sorcerer's command. The serpent man will hesitate to kill the investigators if at all avoidable. He needs their aid. He prefers to use his reptilian helpers as a threat - an exhibition of his powers.

### The Charmed Alligator

| STR 25 | CON 20 | SIZ 24 | POW 10 | DEX 08 |
|--------|--------|--------|--------|--------|
| Move 6/8 swim | | | | HP 22 |

**Weapons:** Bite 50%, damage 1D10+2D6
　　　　　Tail Lash 35%, damage 1D6+2D6

**Armor:** 6 point hide.

**Skills:** Hide 75%, Sneak 65%.

## Caleb's Actions

If Caleb somehow discovers the investigators prying around the house, especially if they have forced their way into the serpent man's bedroom, he bursts in on them, pistol in hand, and puts on a show of moral outrage, telling the thieves that they must be off his property within the hour (or at first light) or he will send for the sheriff.

The keeper should give the investigators an opportunity to think of some appropriate excuse for their behavior. If they can think of none, Professor Gist (if present) says they heard sounds in the room and thought something was wrong. Caleb will grudgingly let the matter drop, but warn the investigators against further transgressions. Since Caleb wants no trouble with the authorities, he will not fire unless fired upon. Should, however, Caleb wound or kill an investigator, no charges will be filed against him. He is, after all, only a homeowner defending his property.

On the morning following the investigator's arrival, Caleb begins a determined effort to convince Professor Gist and the investigators to leave by peaceful means. If any investigator assures him they will be gone by nightfall, he is mollified. If not, the warmth of his Southern hospitality cools almost by the minute.

This behavior should make it clear to the investigators that the fateful night of sorcery mentioned by Joe is this very night.

At breakfast Caleb says that they will enjoy the historical sights of Charleston much more than "this swamp of a farm" and suggests that they leave shortly. If his suggestion is rebuffed, he stomps out of the house saying "Some people have work to do. Excuse me." If followed, the investigators see him march off into the swamp.

When Caleb returns at noon and finds that the investigators have failed to depart he comments pointedly upon the uselessness of wasting food and bed on "carpetbaggers". He inquires sarcastically into his visitor's sources of income, particularly those who dress stylishly or expensively. It is assumed that the investigators ignore what Professor Gist calls his brother's "boorish manners".

## Elly's Actions

If Elly accidentally discovers the investigators breaking into the serpent man's bedroom (with a **Listen** roll) she attempts to **Sneak** up on them. A successful **Listen** roll by the investigators allows them to hear Elly's footsteps on the stairs. If they ignore her requests that they desist, or threaten her, she calls out the nearest window for help, which soon arrives in the form of 1D6 nervous and unusually well armed sharecroppers. (See their statistics near the end of the adventure.) She does not hesitate to question any investigator she catches in the midst of suspicious actions.

Once suspicious of the visitors, Elly attempts to isolate a male investigator (or Winsworthy) and with erotic promises trick him into ingesting a love potion. She knows better than to try to deal with brother Albert and will attempt nothing with him.

To allay her victim's suspicions, Elly can drink the philter with her dupe, since it has no effect upon females. Alternatively, with the help of Bess, she can insinuate its ingredients into the lemonade, or some other part of the lunch. If she is successful, she commands her victim to remain inside the house that night and insists he force his friends to remain inside as well.

If an investigator avoids the philter and returns to the group, she lets him go, seeking another victim when the opportunity offers itself.

If Elly notices the investigators talking about magic or mentioning Yig by name, she becomes convinced that they are here to interfere and steps up her efforts to the maximum, regardless of Caleb's wishes. When the opportunity presents itself, she attempts to entice a male investigator into her surprisingly large and luxurious room. Once there, she does whatever is needed to get him to drink a love philter.

## The Serpent Man's Actions

The serpent man, like the investigators, has been lured here by Yig to perform a service for the Great Old One. The serpent man knows that if he, or the investigators, try to flee, Yig does everything possible to destroy them. The investigators will be forced back by Children of Yig who spring up in numbers to block the investigator's path. Alligators attack at Yig's command and even the serpent man will try and stop them. If all else fails, the escaping investigator will find himself suddenly attacked by hordes of poisonous snakes either pouring up out of the ground or from within the seats and floorboards of Winsworthy's car. Even should someone successfully escape the plantation, Yig's wrath follows them and they may find themselves forced to live in some completely snakeless part of the world (Greenland? Antarctica?).

Unless one or more of the investigators has been visited by a Messenger of Yig it is quite unlikely that they will guess why they are here. Stopping the sacrifice of a young girl is probably their main goal and the disguised serpent man will be a prime suspect. At some point the serpent man will probably be forced to meet with them and outline the situation. This could take place at the serpent man's hut or, failing this encounter, the serpent man will visit the investigators around the plantation grounds or even in the house. In any event, he does it in a way designed to keep the meeting a secret from both Caleb and Elly. Albert Gist and Winsworthy may be included among the confidantes.

Play this encounter for all it's worth. The Obeah man himself commands vast amounts of respect and if the investigators suspect he may also be a serpent man the tension should be heightened even further. Keep in mind the serpent man is, in most measurable respects, far superior to the mammalian humans he now finds himself amidst. Their odor alone offends him; a much more pungent smell than the faint reptile scent that surrounds him. He is far more intelligent, more educated, vastly older, and the product of a civilization that lasted for millions of years. His actions and attitudes toward humans are like the intolerant Winsworthy's, should he suddenly find himself forced to sit down and treat with a group of illiterate black sharecroppers.

The serpent man will tell the investigators only as much as he feels they need to know in order to accomplish the task at hand — no more. He does not trust them in the least and does not care at all what eventually happens to them. He only needs them to fulfill certain tasks required by Yig. At the first sign of treachery on the part of an investigator he kills or escapes as the opportunity presents itself. His poisonous bite is swift and deadly, and pushy investigators may need to be reminded of how dangerous this individual is. The serpent man's venom kills almost instantly and his bite is far quicker than any human drawing a gun.

Sitting across the table from the investigators, the serpent man tells them what needs to be done. At some point the investigators notice his serpent shadow, or perhaps he drops his illusion, momentarily revealing the snake man behind it. Just flicking out a long, forked, serpent tongue is enough to make his point. Any of these events, if sufficiently startling to the investigators, cost 0/1D3 SAN to witness.

The serpent man tells them that they have been lured here by Yig to accomplish a task for him. Beneath the swamps, in a long buried temple, lives an ancient sorceress, a serpent woman. For untold ages she has dwelt here in an area consecrated to Yig, and greedily devoured the magical energies from ceremonies and rituals properly intended for Yig. Yig wants this being punished and, as the serpent man sees it, the investigators have little choice but to cooperate with the god.

**The Serpent Man's Plan:** The investigators are told they will have to find the sorceress's lair and slay her. They will probably not be able to locate her until the ceremony is held. He explains that the hell holes the investigators may have heard about are caused by this being's servants who, attracted by the rhythmic poundings of the Yig ceremonies, burrow upwards to snatch unsuspecting cultists and carry them back to their evil mistress. He tells the investigators that unless they can convince Caleb they are active Yig cultists (quite unlikely by this time), they will have to sneak down to the ceremony after it has begun and observe from the sidelines. If they obtain the proper clothing, they can disguise themselves as white sharecropper observers, fringe members of the cult. There will be over 150 worshippers in attendance and the investigators should be able to melt into the background. When they see one of the hell holes open up they are to plunge below the ground, seek out the sorceress, and slay her. If the investigators express concern about the girl to be sacrificed, the serpent man assures them he will not allow it to take place. (This is a lie. He planned it and is looking forward to it as a compensation for having to spend so much time among the hated humans). He makes it very clear that escape is nearly impossible and that blocking the ceremony only serves to anger Yig — an almost certain doom.

**The Serpent Man's Secrets:** The serpent man does not tell the investigators the underground sorceress is of gigantic size, not does he give any indication of her great magical powers. Although he leads the investigators to believe they are supposed to kill the being, he is quite sure they are incapable of such a feat. The true purpose of the investigators' attack is to distract the attention of the evil sorceress allowing the magical energy of the ceremony above to be used by Yig to enter this plane. Keeping the queen distracted for three rounds will be long enough for the accumulated energy to open the door for Yig, who will not hesitate to step through into this world. Yig will then seek out the queen and take revenge into his own hands. Although the serpent man cares not one way or the other, Yig's appearance underground may be the investigators' only hope of survival.

Once the ceremony has continued for one hour, Yig can appear at any time as long as the queen's attention has been distracted away from the magic rites. Among the things Caleb has not been told is that Yig will make his appearance via Caleb's own body, a painful and debilitating experience.

With this knowledge in hand the investigators may find themselves forced to change their plans. If they are bound to fulfill Yig's wishes or suffer the consequences, they have to be sure the ceremony takes place, unless they can discover and kill the serpent sorceress ahead of time, without the help of the Great Old One. If Reverend Hilson or Sheriff Trucks should show up, intending to put a halt to the proceedings, the investigators may have to take steps to stop him.

## Albert Gist's Actions

The professor is intensely jealous of his brother's magical prowess and may, on the sly, approach the serpent man. If the keeper decides it is okay, the serpent man agrees to throw over Caleb in favor of Albert, who will then lead the ceremony and conduct the sacrifice. The serpent man may even suggest that Caleb be offered up as sacrifice in addition to, or instead of, the young girl. Albert may agree. Winsworthy may or may not be told about this change in plans. The investigators will certainly not learn of it.

## Little Joe's Actions

Little Joe has not let any of the sharecroppers know he has returned. He skulks around the outskirts of the hamlet, hoping against hope the investigators can do something. By late morning of the second day, he will get up enough nerve to try to contact someone. He knows he has to avoid Bess, old Ben, and the deadly Elly in doing so. A whisper through an investigator's window is the best tactic. See Joe's skills in the statistics near the end of the adventure.

Joe tells the investigators that although he is sure Cassy is being held prisoner in the hut, he has been unable to learn anything regarding the whereabouts of his mother. "No one's seen nothin' and no one's talkin,'" says the boy. "I'm powerful worried about my ma."

At some point during the investigator's meeting with Joe, the boy's mother does return, as a zombie. Mercilessly slain by Caleb and turned into one of the living dead, she is under orders to find and kill little Joe. The keeper must arrange this encounter. It will not occur while Caleb or Elly are present as they will wish to deny any connection with Joe's death or disappearance. The zombie may attack outdoors, from behind a tree or building, or wander right into the house in search of her prey. If the investigators destroy the zombie they save Joe and gain 1D4 points of SAN in addition to what they receive for killing the monster. Joe, confronted and

# THE SERPENT PEOPLE

The serpent men have been enemies of the human race since Pleistocene times when they actively plotted against the human kingdom of Valusia. Even then the serpent men were known to use supernatural means to disguise their true appearance, taking the form of men in order to infiltrate human society. Many of these serpent men posed as priests and used their position to try and introduce the worship of their dark snake god into mammalian culture. Although humans considered the serpent people's disguises the product of sorcery, it was a form of hypnosis natural to the serpent man species, trained to a high degree and only augmented by magic. This ability was so powerful that once a full blooded serpent man ruled over Valusia, disguised as a human king. A variety methods of casting this kind of illusion are known to exist.

In the last century and a half a great number of ancient serpent men have reemerged from their age long hibernations and now move secretly about and within human society. It is possible that their reappearance has to do with the prophecies found in the *Pnakotic Manuscripts* and repeated in the *Necronomicon*.

> *"in the time of the last troubles even the great serpents shall come forth, crawling from their resting places beneath the earth..."*

This prophecy was long interpreted by the serpent people to predict a return to power by the ophidian race. Most serpent men alive today believe in this interpretation and work toward its fulfillment.

**Serpent Man Club**

This strange weapon hangs from the belt of the Obeah man and is not disguised by the illusion. It is made of a strange alloy and is oddly curved, suited to the differently structured arm and shoulder of serpent men. Degenerate serpent men living in Britain (and perhaps elsewhere) still make use of this weapon although their cruder versions have stone heads and wooden handles.

Used properly, these hammer like weapons are capable of inflicting 1D8+2 points of damage, with the possibility of impaling. Humans who try to use this weapon will find it difficult. The strange weight and balance of the hammer requires an odd, sideways swing. The initial skill of an investigator unused to the club will be half their normal Club skill. Like any other weapon, an investigator's skill can increase with experience. ☀

attacked by his vacant eyed, undead mother loses 1D10 points of SAN.

The zombie mom tries to grapple the boy and carry him off to the swamp to drown him, after which she will return to her secret muddy grave and never be seen again. Caleb will then turn Joe himself into a zombie. Zombie Joe puts in an appearance during the ceremony to Yig, either aiding in the performance of the rites or wandering about the crowd looking for investigators to attack and kill.

## PART FIVE
# The Night of Yig

As the afternoon wears on, the homunculi below ground prepare themselves for the anticipated ceremony. The serpent sorceress, always aware of the astrological conjunctions, anticipates the festivities planned by the Yig worshippers. Like snakes, S'ssruxxa's homunculi are very sensitive to vibrations transmitted through the ground. They can accurately judge the number of people at a large gathering and choose likely victims, all while lurking in their muddy tunnels.

Farm work seems to be neglected this afternoon. As the sun sinks low, many of the sharecroppers gather in front of the mansion, and begin setting up crude tables. Old Bess and some of the sharecropper women begin setting out simple food and drink, enough for a very large group.

If little Joe is still alive and about, he may again try to contact the investigators. He has no plan, but is desperate for action.

### The Night of Yig
On the supposed night of Dambala, all the Yig cultists of the area, over 150 in all, begin to arrive. There are many women and children as well as men. They arrive by foot, or packed into beaten-up trucks, on bicycles or mule back. They are greeted boisterously by the locals, with much singing and festivity.

Given such a huge ceremony, one planned for many weeks previously, the police have had time to get going. Two of the cultists are actually Charleston police agents investigating the recent murder of the police detective. This should not be revealed to the investigators unless they are specifically looking out for such persons. If they are, a **Spot Hidden** indicates that two young white men look suspiciously well-groomed among this shabby bunch, and are wearing oddly clean ragged clothes. The two men avoid contact if the investigators approach them openly, but

they are competent and reasonably intelligent. With discretion on the part of the investigators, all agree to join forces. See the statistics section near the end of this adventure.

The cultists gather in front of the house at around sunset, light their torches, and march into the swamp, chanting and singing. Caleb tells the investigators that this is some kind of backwoods religious rite and that outsiders, himself included, are not particularly welcome. He says that they should respect the religious beliefs of others and remain inside tonight. He suggests that fearful things may happen to them if they do not. Caleb says he is going to retire early and suggests that the investigators do likewise.

Caleb retires to his bedroom, locking the door behind him. He immediately crawls out the bedroom window, and drops to the ground, following the crowd into the swamp. If the investigators are attempting to detect what Caleb does, a **Listen** roll will let them hear him scrabbling across the porch roof. A successful **Spot Hidden** allows them to see him crossing the yard, just before he disappears into the darkness of the swamp.

### The Last Ambush
An armed group waits outside, determined to keep the investigators in the house. If the investigators openly march out of the mansion armed and ready, Bodeen and his men open fire. The investigators get a hint of what's in store for them first — just before they open the door, old Ben and the housekeeper suddenly find reasons to hurry down into the cellar.

Bodeen and his men are in covered firing positions and snipe at the investigators while they are silhouetted against the lights of the mansion. Investigators will need to make **Spot Hidden** rolls in order to pinpoint a sniper's position. Investigators' return fire is at half their usual skill due to the darkness. Rafe and the boys also suffer from this penalty if the investigators turn off the lights or get away from the house.

Although the investigators may at first find themselves trapped, after a few rounds the firing stops and then frantic shouts from the snipers are heard, then silence. The ambushers are found dead of snake bites, their bodies already swelling and blackening. Atop Rafe Bodeen's chest is curled a huge copperhead with a white crescent on its head.

### The Cultists
Meanwhile, down at the dock, several boats have arrived including one filled with Charleston cultists. They are greeted by the plantation's inhabitants with handshakes, hugs, slaps on the back, and laughter. All await at the dock until Caleb arrives. When he comes down the road, a shout of exultation goes up. He leads the

group to the great clearing in the swamp. There the Obeah man awaits.

The early portions of this version of the Call/Dismiss Yig spell are performed entirely by the Obeah man and Caleb. The cultists sit or stand in small groups around the altar area. They are silent but not particularly attentive to the two in the center, knowing that their time comes later. Since all the cultists know each other and the area is ablaze with torches, an investigator attempting to slip through the crowd toward Caleb will probably be recognized.

## Balancing the Adventure

If the keeper feels that the investigators have had too easy a time up to this point, Albert Gist and Winsworthy are both available to cause trouble. They can disrupt the investigators' plans in many ways, ranging from simply making a noise at some inopportune time, all the way to actually taking over from Caleb in the ceremonies.

Also, remember that Elly, the maid and high priestess of Yig, may have secretly seduced one of the party. Perhaps Winsworthy has fallen prey to her potions and wiles.

It is possible that Sheriff Trucks in charge of a band of armed deputies, or Reverend Hilson leading a crowd of fanatic Christians, will show up, intent on stopping the rites. The investigators will be forced to find a way to neutralize this threat. Unless they have already found some way to destroy the serpent queen it is imperative that tonight's ceremony take place — it is the only way to find a path to the serpent queen's lair. If they fail, they will eventually have to face Yig's anger. Of course, it is likely that they will also be concerned for the life of Joe's sister. This is an additional wrinkle in the problem.

## The Rites of Yig

The rites begin around 10 P.M., and culminate at midnight with the sacrifice. Various rituals and ceremonies precede the sacrifice, followed by an hour and a half of chanting and orgy.

In the light of a score of smoking torches, the huge open area around the altar fills with whispering, half naked cultists, many of them armed with crude weapons such as machetes. If it is truly an Obeah ceremony, a surprising number of the cultists are white.

Many of the worshippers wear bizarre costumes, mostly made of snake skin. Some carry crude instruments, such as reed flutes, drums, or gourd rattles, with which they now begin to produce an odd, rhythmic cacophony.

Several of the women in the crowd are very beautiful, particularly a tall, laughing girl in a queenly headdress who carries, wrapped about her, two massive, sleek diamondback rattlesnakes. The girl is treated with great respect and adulation as she mingles with the crowd. It is Elly, Caleb's mistress and the high priestess of Yig.

## Strange Sights

The first unnatural thing the investigators notice is the ominous appearance of thousands of snakes, many of them rare and poisonous species, crawling out from under bushes and out of the swamp. These snakes writhe among the cultists, crawling up their legs, and coiling into heaps that are often several feet high. This sight costs 0/1D3 SAN. A different sort of shock is the sight of the ancient serpent man, now undisguised and peacefully mingling with worshipful cultists.

Neither the snakes nor the serpent man bite or annoy the cultists in any way. If anything, man and snake are excessively cozy together. Some cultists fling themselves to the ground before the ancient serpent man, begging to be blessed.

## The Rituals Begin

Caleb Gist, dressed in an odd, shimmering scarlet and green robe, begins the rites of Yig Night by lighting several small fires around the altar. The drummers set up a soft, steady beat that echoes eerily through the humid air of the swamp.

Caleb, Elly, and the ancient serpent man go to each fire, carrying between them a large caldron that contains a mixture of oil, kerosene, and stranger substances. They ladle this mixture on the fires, causing the flame to leap up, throwing off sparks high into the night. When the caldron is empty, they then walk through the flames to prove that they are true Houngan.

At the conclusion of these rites, Caleb and the ancient serpent man turn to the assembled cultists and raise their arms high in the air. The initial preparations are over. The drummers begin a new and faster beat.

As the drums thud, members of the crowd fall one by one to the ground, writhing oddly. As the investigators watch, the cultists begin to slither bonelessly about the clearing like snakes, their sweating bodies twisting and contracting in ways that no normal human being could hope to duplicate. The three high priests (Caleb, Elly, and the serpent man) begin a new chant, calling to Yig.

The sounds and smells rising from the writhing revelers during the serpent ceremony are disturbing. A waft of reptilian stench, mixed with the fumes of the torches and the odor of unwashed bodies, drifts over the swamp. Weird moanings and whisperings fill the night. Deep bellowings, alligators calling out, echo from the darkest depths of the swamp.

As the ceremony degenerates into a horrible reptilian/human orgy, the players must make SAN rolls against a loss of 1/1D6. Investigators suffering from *ophiophobia* lose 1/1D10 SAN. Witnesses to the rites will also receive 1D4 points added to their **Cthulhu Mythos** knowledge.

One possible result of temporary insanity at this point is that a mad investigator might strip off his or her garments and join the appalling rites, his body writhing like a great snake across the stained ground. Any investigator who does so adds an additional 1D2 points to his Cthulhu Mythos knowledge.

Any noise other than gunshots (screaming, etc.) during the snake ceremony goes unheard. However, an investigator who is nervous or acting with hostile intent toward the cultists is likely to be bitten by several ordinary snakes.

## The Hell Holes

At this point some of the hell holes will start to open up as the horrible homunculi of the evil queen burrow up to drag off hapless worshippers. It is up to the keeper to decide whether the investigators see a hell hole appear in the distance or have one open up under their feet. Winsworthy, standing just a few yards away, is a good potential victim; one of the young detectives is another possibility. Whoever the victim may be, to successfully conclude this adventure some of the investigators must enter the tunnels.

## The Sacrifice

The ceremony continues while investigators are underground looking for a way to reach the serpent queen. Hopefully they leave one or two of the party above ground in order to stop the sacrifice of Cassy. If they do not, she may well die unless Reverend Hilson or Sheriff Trucks shows up in force. The two Charleston policeman might try to put a stop to it but they number only two and it is quite likely that the cultists would turn on them, literally tearing them to pieces before horrified investigator eyes (lose 1/1D4 SAN).

If the cultists go unchecked, the unfortunate Cassy is carried through the crowd. If no one has contacted little Joe by this point in the adventure, and he has not been killed and turned into a zombie, he ambushes the guards in the midst of the swamp, bringing down two of them before he is killed in front of his screaming sister. Any investigators observing this tragedy without taking action to halt it lose 1 SAN.

If Cassy is quietly rescued, without disturbing the ceremony, then another sacrificial victim will be prepared and killed after only a short delay. The net result will be the same. However, the investigators gain 1D4 SAN for rescuing Joe's sister as they probably promised they would do.

The new sacrificial victim more than likely is a semi-willing cultist and investigators will lose minimum or no SAN when the insane worshipper goes to meet a much deserved fate.

If no one makes the rescue, poor Cassy is placed on the altar, to the cheering of the crowd. As the terrified girl is prepared for the sacrifice, Caleb and the serpent man speak certain passwords and make horrifying secret gestures. Elly holds her snakes high above her head. Assuming there are no interruptions, Caleb raises the cutlass, then brings it down viciously. The crowd roars, and player characters present must lose 1/1D6 SAN for witnessing and permitting the sacrifice of an innocent human being.

---

## THE LAIR OF THE

# Serpent Queen

In order for the investigators to find the sorceress's lair they must follow one of the homunculi's tunnels (or be grabbed and dragged off). This can occur either while exploring the swamp or during the ceremony to Yig.

The beaked homunculi of S'ssruxxa are expert burrowers. They attack their victims by tunneling up beneath them, seizing them by their ankles, and then pulling them down into the muddy ground, feet first. The homunculi are swift but a character so grabbed can jump away with a successful **Dodge** roll. If the roll fails, the victim is quickly pulled beneath the surface and out of sight. With both ankles firmly grasped and pulled along at a brisk rate, there is little they can do to free themselves. The tunnels are so narrow as to allow no possibility of firing a gun down at the unseen assailant. In fact, the character's arms will be drawn up over his head and useless. Not until a victim is dragged into the underground temple complex is he or she able to take action against such an assailant. The victim has 1D6 rounds in which to kill and escape from the attacker before the rest of the homunculi set upon the captive. These homunculi wait in the central chamber.

If someone attempts to follow a victim into one of the hell holes, they must crawl into the muddy burrow headfirst, wriggling their way down into the bowels of the earth toward an unknown destination.

The going is uncomfortable but the slippery mud makes it easier to accomplish. After 3D10 minutes of crawling and sweating, the tunnel opens up into a larger space. Hopefully the investigators have brought light sources with them.

## The Hall of the Serpent Queen

If the investigators have spoken with the serpent man or in some other way learned of the serpent queen's existence they understand they now stand in one of the eight spoke like galleries that radiate out from the sorceress's great central chamber. A barrel vaulted roof, supported by massive columns, arches overhead, most of its features obliterated by the layers of limestone that have formed over the countless millions of years since the structure was first built. The columns themselves are near completely concealed by the drippings. The place so closely resembles a cave interior that only the abnormal symmetry belies its artificial architecture. The reptilian stench is unmistakable.

What the investigators first find down here depends on whether they have followed a recently kidnapped victim or entered a hell hole that has been open an hour or so. Whether the Gist ceremony to Yig is in progress or not will also define the situation in the serpent queen's lair.

※ If it is prior to the Yig ritual and the investigators have followed a victim down here, they hear screams issuing from the central chamber some 200 yards away. This is the sound of the recently taken victim being attacked by the homunculi.

※ If they have come down a hell hole that has been open for some time, that victim will by now be dead and devoured, and the hall will be silent.

※ If the investigators have come here while the ceremony is in progress there probably is more than one victim suffering the attentions of the homunculi and the screams of more than one person will likely be heard. In any case, the investigators will be able to approach the central chamber unmolested.

If the investigators are in pursuit of a recently kidnapped captive, they hear horrible shrieks coming from the direction of the central chamber. There the investigators find the victim pinned to the floor by the homunculi who take turns pecking at the victim's eyes, ears, nose, and tongue. How many of these organs are already torn away is up to the keeper; each organ lost indicates the victim has taken 2 points of damage. S'ssruxxa herself lies curled up in the center of the hall watching and waiting while her sexless children finish their snack. When they are through she swallows the still-living victim whole. Investigators may attack or make a run for it while there is still time. The homunculi may follow but it is unlikely they will pursue up through the burrows.

If the investigators have crawled down a discovered hell hole that has been open for an hour or so, and have come here before the Yig ceremony has taken place, the serpent queen is aware of their coming and prepares for them. The hall is almost vacant. In the center of the room, seated upon a stone chair atop the circular dais, facing the investigators, is a beautiful woman dressed in a radiant gown. She smiles beneficently upon the investigators and it will seem to them that she is surrounded by a faint, glowing aura. Perhaps she is a goddess?

A voice sounds in the heads of the investigators, the voice of the beautiful woman, although it can be seen that her lips are not moving. The voice beckons to the investigators, asking them to come forward, she wishes to speak with them. If any of the investigators comes within ten feet of her, the serpent queen attacks with her bite and swallow. Even if she successfully attacks and swallows a victim, she maintains the beautiful woman illusion. The investigators see their companion somehow swallowed whole by this strange woman who may actually be smaller than the prey. SAN loss for seeing this is 1/1D6. S'ssruxxa, if undisturbed, continues to maintain her illusion and attempts to persuade other investigators to approach. Only if they open fire on the serpent queen or otherwise attack her, will the illusion disappear, allowing the investigators to see for the first time their adversary. The homunculi, until now hidden behind nearby columns, move forward and attack. The serpent queen remains where she is, using her magic against the intruders.

If the investigators should come here during the calling of Yig, there will probably be several victims (kidnapped cultists) suffering the tortures of the homunculi. S'ssruxxa herself will appear in her gigantic serpent form and will be poised in the center of the room, her head held up, drinking deeply of the magical energies being released by frantic Yig cultists above. Neither S'ssruxxa or her homunculi will notice the investigators' presence and if they act quickly and quietly, the investigators can make one complete round of attacks before either the homunculi or the queen are able to react.

## Dealing with the Queen

S'ssruxxa is a huge specimen of serpent person, weighing in at several tons. Unnaturally large, the result a combination of her great age and of her delvings into evil and potent magicks, the evil serpent queen is now quite mad, the result of her long confinement within this structure. Her limbs, through disuse, are atrophied and hang limply from her sides. What little movement she is still capable of is accomplished by a slow and painful crawl. S'ssruxxa, attended to by her servant homunculi, sometimes remains in the same spot for decades. Her eyes are filmed by cataracts and her vision weakened but her bite is still swift and she has a command of ancient magic perhaps never excelled by the anyone of the serpent race, living or dead.

Unless the party is equipped with powerful explosives (possibly dangerous to themselves in this ancient, cracked and crumbling structure) it is unlikely they will be able to defeat this powerful adversary. Unless the calling of Yig is underway, the best alternative for the party is to run for their lives.

If the calling of Yig is being attempted, then it is only necessary for the investigators to distract the attention of the serpent queen for the space of three rounds. After this period of time the magical energies being released by the above ground ceremony will be utilized by Yig to bring him into this plane of existence. Once called, Yig wastes little time seeking out and punishing the sorceress.

## Yig Appears

Yig enters this plane by occupying the body of whoever is presently leading the Call Yig ceremony. Most likely this is Caleb Gist, Elly, or Albert Gist. The serpent man avoids this role at almost any cost. To be possessed by Yig is a painful and mind shattering experience. Although most survive the possession, the individual loses 1D20 points of SAN and loses 2D6 hit points, assessed against the character after Yig has left the body.

An investigator who remains above the surface and witnesses the possession sees Caleb (or whoever is leading the ceremony) begin to breathe rapidly and the color drains from his face. As Yig pours into this plane the recipient starts to change, swelling and growing to accommodate the form of the Great Old One. All during this time thousands of snakes pour out from beneath the altar, covering the ground. Images of Yig's reptilian head fade in and out, alternating with the terrified visage of the one he has possessed. Clearly seeing the Great Old One is particularly difficult and his face and form continually shift and shimmer. The SAN loss is 0/1D8.

Yig immediately heads for the underground temple, magically transporting his form through the ground to appear in the Queen's lair. Investigators locked in battle with the serpent woman are first made aware of Yig's coming when, a round before the Great Old One appears, the floor of the underground temple is suddenly covered with a writhing carpet of living snakes. These snakes will not harm the investigators unless the investigators attack them. Anyone who does attack them is immediately bitten dozens of times and within the space of a round or two is completely covered with squirming, venomous snakes that bite their victim repeatedly. Death comes in a minute or two. SAN loss for the carpet of snakes is only 1/1D3

but any character who goes insane when the snakes are present is quite likely to attack them, thereby forfeiting his life.

Yig appears during the next round, his form still shimmering, shifting first from the image of the unfortunate host to the Yig form, and then to the form of a gigantic snake every bit as large as the bloated sorceress. SAN loss is O/1D8. S'ssruxxa, spying the approaching Yig, stops attacking the investigators and turns her attention to this awesome enemy. Her homunculi leap forward to engage the new invader.

They are swept aside and killed immediately. Yig is unaffected by any magic attacks made against him by the sorceress. Yig closes and grapples with the great queen, leaving the investigators to witness the titanic struggle between the two monstrous serpent beings. The investigators may flee at this point, escaping to the surface through one of the mud burrows, or stay and watch the fight. Those who choose to stay are shocked when after a couple of rounds it becomes plainly obvious Yig intends not to kill the sorceress but instead intends to mate with her!

Viewing this horrifying scene forces a loss of 1/1D4 SAN points. Plus, regardless of the SAN roll, each investigator finds himself feeling faint, and soon collapses into a dream state.

### The Dream

The investigators find themselves sharing a common dream wherein they all stand about, observing the coupling between the two monstrous serpents, chanting softly a long-forgotten ritual of the serpent people. The dreamers are dressed in long, dark robes and hold before them candles that glow with an unearthly light. They maintain the chant until the coupling is complete, then watch in amazement as Yig, a few moments later, slashes open the belly of the sorceress and withdraws from it a single glowing egg nearly three feet long. Yig turns to the group and, without speaking a word, begins to distribute his blessing.

Yig speaks to the dreaming investigators telepathically, and the investigators may respond. Any investigator who willingly did what Yig expected of him without complaint or vacillation receives the favor of the Great Old One. This investigator is given 1 point of POW and taught the spells Summon/Bind Child of Yig and Call/Dismiss Yig. Cultists call him a Son of Yig and he now carries the Mark of Yig — the white crescent, similar to a faded birthmark, underneath his left arm. A Son of Yig is invulnerable to any and all normal snake venom and has the ability to communicate with blessed snakes, the Children of Yig, including those sent against him by an enemy. As long as the marked investigator does not actively work against Yig's desires, this ability

*The Serpent Sorceress*

to communicate with the blessed snakes make him effectively immune to attacks by these creatures.

Lesser favored investigators receive the additional POW point but nothing else. Recalcitrant servants of the Great Old One receive nothing. The worst is saved for those investigators who did not want to help Yig but now, after it is all over, throw themselves at the Great Old One, trying to suck up. Mighty Yig is undeceived. These characters receive the "supreme blessing". Yig transforms them into blessed snakes, Children of Yig that crawl off into the tunnels to never be seen again. They remain the permanent servants of Yig and do his bidding. After the distribution of blessings, Yig and the glowing egg fade from view as the investigators regain true consciousness.

They awake on the floor of the cave, the slowly expiring sorceress lying nearby, dying from the gaping wound in her belly. The investigators may dispatch her or, if convinced she is bound to die anyway, abandon her to her fate. In either case the investigators gain an award of 1D10+4 points of SAN plus an increase of 1D6 points in **Cthulhu Mythos** (if they took part in the dreamlike mating ritual). If they hurry, they will be able to crawl out of this place before the narrow mud tunnels begin to collapse in upon them. There is an additional SAN award of 1D8 points if they helped to save Cassy. If the girl was saved without any help from the investigators, they still receive 1D4 points of SAN to learn she was not lost.

### Little Joe, fugitive from evil

| STR 08 | CON 13 | SIZ 07 | INT 13 | POW 13 |
| DEX 15 | APP 11 | EDU 04 | SAN 62 | HP 10 |

**Damage Bonus:** −1D4

**Weapons:** Fist/Punch 65%, damage 1D3

**Skills:** Climb 75%, Conceal 30%, Dodge 65%, Hide 85%, Listen 80%, Sneak 70%

### Professor Albert Gist, student of the unusual

| STR 09 | CON 12 | SIZ 10 | INT 16 | POW 16 |
| DEX 08 | APP 10 | EDU 20 | SAN 25 | HP 11 |

**Damage Bonus:** none

**Weapons:** Fist 45%, damage 1D3

**Spells:** Contact Ghoul

**Skills:** Anthropology 50%, Archaeology 50%, Cthulhu Mythos 6%, Hide 45%, Library Use 90%, Occult 85%, Psychology 75%

**Languages:** Latin 65%

### Rafe Bodeen, evil overseer

| STR 15 | CON 15 | SIZ 16 | INT 09 | POW 08 |
| DEX 11 | APP 08 | EDU 05 | | HP 16 |

**Damage Bonus:** +1D4

**Weapons:** Fist 80%, damage 1D3
    Kick 70%, damage 1D6

Head Butt 90%, damage 1D4
    .38 Revolver 55%, damage 1D8
    Whip 75%, damage 1D3 plus entangle

**Skills:** Cthulhu Mythos 3%, Drive Automobile 55%, Hide 60%, Sneak 45%, Spot Hidden 60%, Track 75%

### Ten Terrible Cultists

| | STR | CON | SIZ | POW | DEX | HP |
|---|---|---|---|---|---|---|
| 1 | 14 | 11 | 12 | 09 | 11 | 12 |
| 2 | 10 | 13 | 15 | 11 | 10 | 14 |
| 3 | 07 | 12 | 11 | 09 | 15 | 12 |
| 4 | 15 | 14 | 16 | 09 | 11 | 15 |
| 5 | 11 | 10 | 12 | 11 | 10 | 11 |
| 6 | 13 | 12 | 11 | 13 | 09 | 12 |
| 7 | 09 | 15 | 14 | 10 | 10 | 15 |
| 8 | 16 | 15 | 17 | 12 | 13 | 16 |
| 9 | 11 | 16 | 12 | 11 | 14 | 14 |
| 10 | 10 | 12 | 15 | 10 | 11 | 14 |

**Damage Bonus:** 1D2 for everyone, or ignore

**Weapons:** Fist/Punch 55%, damage 1D3+db
    Kick 30%, damage 1D6+db
    Head Butt 45%, damage 1D4+db
    Club 35%, damage 1D6+db
    .38 Revolver 30%, damage 1D10
    16-Gauge Shotgun 40%, damage 2D6+2/1D6+1/1D4

### The Zombie

| STR 16 | CON 15 | SIZ 14 | POW 01 | DEX 08 |
| Move 6 | | | | HP 15 |

**Damage Bonus:** +1D4

**Weapons:** Grapple 65%, damage 1D6 plus hurl out window
    Maul 40%, damage 2D8+1D6

**Armor:** none, but impaling weapons do only 1 point of damage

**Sanity Cost:** 0/1D6

### Elihu C. Winsworthy, dilettante

| STR 07 | CON 09 | SIZ 11 | INT 11 | POW 09 |
| DEX 08 | APP 15 | EDU 13 | | HP 10 |

**Damage Bonus:** none

**Weapons:** Walking Stick or Cudgel 35%, damage 1D6

**Skills:** Credit Rating 50%, Drive Automobile 55%, English 65%.

### Virgil Trucks, Colleton County Sheriff

| STR 15 | CON 14 | SIZ 15 | INT 11 | POW 10 |
| DEX 11 | APP 10 | EDU 08 | SAN 77 | HP 15 |

**Damage Bonus:** +1D4

**Weapons:** .38 Revolver 65%, damage 1D8
    12 gauge Shotgun 85%, damage 4D6
    Fist/Punch 75%, damage 1D3
    Kick 80%, damage 1D6
    Head Butt 80%, damage 1D4

**Skills:** Accounting 25%, Conceal 55%, First Aid 55%, Law 65%, Listen 55%, Psychology 65%, Spot Hidden 60%, Track 75%, Treat Snakebite Lore 65%.

### Isaac Hilson, preacher

| STR 17 | CON 15 | 51Z 16 | INT 15 | POW 19 |
|---|---|---|---|---|
| DEX 14 | APP 11 | EDU 15 | SAN 90 | HP 16 |

**Damage Bonus:** +1D6

**Weapons:** Fist/Punch 80%, damage 1D3+1D6

**Spells:** Hilson has a magical ability, Faith Healing (see earlier boxed text)

**Skills:** Art (Oratory) 91%, Bargain 40%, Baptist Theology 97%, Cthulhu Mythos 5%, Fast Talk 40%, First Aid 60%, Forecast Weather 50%, Medicine 40%, Occult 90%, Persuade 65%, Ride Mule 40%, Sing Bass 75%, Swamp Lore 40%

### Caleb Gist, plantation owner

| STR 12 | CON 13 | SIZ 12 | INT 14 | POW 18 |
|---|---|---|---|---|
| DEX 13 | APP 14 | EDU 14 | SAN 0 | HP 13 |

**Damage Bonus:** +1D4

**Weapons:** .38 Revolver 70%, damage 1D10
Saber 70%, damage 1D8+1+1D4

**Spells:** Call Yig, Charm Snake, Create Zombie, Curse of Azathoth

**Skills:** Cthulhu Mythos 13%, Listen 50%, Sneak 50%, Spot Hidden 50%, Swamp Lore 40%, Treat Snakebite Lore 30%

**Languages:** English 70%, Spanish 60%

### Elly, high priestess of Yig

| STR 10 | CON 10 | SIZ 09 | INT 14 | POW 19 |
|---|---|---|---|---|
| DEX 12 | APP 17 | EDU 05 | SAN 00 | HP 10 |

**Damage Bonus:** none

**Weapons:** Straight Razor 85%, damage 1D3+db

**Spells:** Shriveling, Charm Snake

**Skills:** Brew Poisons 50%, Cthulhu Mythos 11%, First Aid 50%, Listen 85%, Occult 60%, Sneak 75%, Spot Hidden 90%, Swamp Lore 35%

### Elly's sacred coral snake

| STR 01 | CON 10 | SIZ 01 | POW 05 | DEX 17 |
|---|---|---|---|---|

**Weapon:** Bite 50%, damage 1 + venom POT 14

**Skills:** Hide 95%, Sneak 90%

### Ben, butler of the mansion

| STR 09 | CON 10 | SIZ 12 | INT 11 | POW 11 |
|---|---|---|---|---|
| DEX 10 | APP 11 | EDU 06 | SAN 20 | HP 11 |

**Damage Bonus:** none

**Weapons:** none

**Skills:** Anticipate Caleb 75%, Courtesy 81%, Formal Demeanor 80%, Serve 77%

### Bess, the housekeeper

| STR 11 | CON 13 | SIZ 14 | INT 12 | POW 12 |
|---|---|---|---|---|
| DEX 12 | APP 12 | EDU 05 | SAN 25 | HP 14 |

**Damage Bonus:** +1D4

**Weapons:** .45 Colt Automatic 55%, damage 1010+2
Iron Skillet 40%, damage 1D8+1D4

**Skills:** Fast Talk 45%, First Aid 65%, Hide 75%, Jump 65%, Listen 50%, Occult 20%, Southern Home Cooking 60%, Sneak 75%, Spot Hidden 55%

### The Serpent Man (Obeah Man)

| STR 12 | CON 16 | SIZ 13 | INT 16 | POW 16 |
|---|---|---|---|---|
| DEX 15 | | | | HP 14 |

**Damage Bonus:** +1D4, hand held weapons only

**Weapons:** Serpent Man Hammer 80%, damage 1D8+2 plus impale
Bite 65%, damage 1D8 damage plus poison POT 16

**Armor:** 2 point scales

**Spells:** Call/Dismiss Yig, Contact Yig, Dread Curse of Azathoth, Summon/Bind Child of Yig, Summon/Bind Byakhee, Summon/Bind Hunting Horror, Summon/Bind Nightgaunt, Shriveling, possibly others

**Sanity Cost:** 0/1D6

### Jeremiah Monroe, undercover police detective

| STR 14 | CON 11 | S1Z 11 | INT 12 | POW 11 |
|---|---|---|---|---|
| DEX 14 | APP 08 | EDU 12 | SAN 66 | HP 11 |

**Damage Bonus:** +1D4

**Weapons:** .45 Colt Automatic 65%, damage 1010+2

**Skills:** Dodge 54%, Fast Talk 65%, First Aid 55%, Hide 80%, Jump 75%, Law 50%, Spot Hidden 75%, Track 65%

### Elias Crawford, undercover police detective

| STR 11 | CON 14 | SIZ 14 | INT 13 | POW 12 |
|---|---|---|---|---|
| DEX 12 | APP 07 | EDU 12 | SAN 70 | HP 14 |

**Damage Bonus:** +1D4

**Weapons:** .45 Colt Automatic, damage 1D10+2

**Skills:** Dodge 44%, Fast Talk, 65%, First Aid 55%, Hide 80%, Jump 75%, Law 50%, Spot Hidden 75%, Track 35%

### S'ssruxxa, the Serpent Sorceress

| STR 42 | CON 45 | SIZ 50 | INT 29 | POW 30 |
|---|---|---|---|---|
| DEX 12 | Move 1 | | | HP 48 |

**Weapon:** Bite and Swallow 90%, swallows whole up to SIZ 20

**Armor:** 12 points of muscle and fat

**Spells:** S'ssruxxa has a working knowledge of almost every spell found in the *Call of Cthulhu* rules

**Sanity Cost:** 1D4/1D20

## The Homunculi

These are man-sized, beaked servants of the serpent queen created of her own flesh and blood. They can dig through the ground at a rate of 5 yards per turn, leaving behind them a tunnel which, due to the nature of the swampy ground, collapses after 1D3 hours. When slithering through an existing tunnel their normal movement rate is 12.

## HOMUNCULI

| | characteristics | average |
|---|---|---|
| STR | 3D6+2 | 12-13 |
| CON | 3D6 | 10-11 |
| SIZ | 3D6 | 10-11 |
| INT | 2D4 | 05 |
| POW | 2D4 | 05 |
| DEX | 3D6 | 10-11 |

**Move:** 6/12 in burrow

**Weapons:** Grapple 75%, damage hold
Peck with Beak 85%, damage 2 points plus the loss of an ear, eye, or tongue

**Armor:** 3 point scales and skin

**Spells:** none

**Sanity Cost:** Seeing a homunculus costs 0/1D6 points.

## THE END!

# SNAKES

Much of the action in this adventure involves the threat of snakes, both natural and magical. The human Yig cultists are no more effective than cultists usually are, but large and poisonous natural snakes, magical snakes, and serpent men of three types are all present to terrorize the investigators. At the conclusion of the adventure, a giant snake or even Yig himself may appear.

## Roleplaying Notes

Knowledgeable investigators initially should be skeptical of the danger presented by snakes in South Carolina. They are probably aware that no snake preys on man, and that snakes normally bite only when threatened or molested. However, the snakes in this adventure are often controlled by malevolent magic. Investigators will soon learn to be cautious of any situation in which a snake could be hidden, such as an ill lit library or a hollow log.

Characters taking severe injury from snakebite, or witnessing magical or unnaturally horrible sights involving snakes, should suffer *Ophiophobia*, fear of snakes. This exposure offers excellent opportunities for roleplaying.

## Fighting Snakes

Snakes are slender, agile targets, difficult to hit with handguns or rifles. Halve such attacks as long as the snake moves at full speed. Shotguns fire at normal damage and normal chance to hit. Melee weapons that depend upon a stabbing attack (like sword canes) also have their chance to hit reduced by half.

The keeper must remember that snakes can only attack at very close range. Thus snakes will attack from ambush, from behind or from the side, when possible.

Once the creatures are spotted, remember to double the characters' chances of hitting at point blank range (their DEX in feet).

## Snakebites

Most common snakes in South Carolina swamps are not poisonous. Luckily for the keeper, several are: coral snakes, copperheads, diamondbacks, and water moccasins or cottonmouths.

The investigators will learn that some snakebites are deadly serious injuries. Although a snakebite may be less immediately harmful than a bullet or knife wound, allowing the bitten character to run around for a while, the ensuing effects are horrifying. We suggest that keepers exploit the snakebite procedures and information below.

### 1) Check for Successful Bite

On the snake's or serpent man's DEX rank, roll for its Bite skill. If it is wrapped around the victim already, or the target is immobile, the snake hits automatically.

If the snake or serpent man is more than a few feet away, it cannot attack this round but must move forward, or wait for its target to move closer, which may occur later in the round.

If the victim is aware of the snake, he or she may Dodge. Parrying a snake's attack simply means that the parrying limb is struck.

Even a small snake's bite is powerful enough to penetrate human skin. However, if the target is wearing heavy clothing or protective garb, the bite may not penetrate. A Luck roll may be in order to see if the clothing saved the victim.

### 2) Check for Resistance

If the snake or serpent man uses its bite attack successfully and penetrates any

boots, clothing, etc, that may be in the way, a Resistance Table roll must be made using the venom's potency (POT) as the active characteristic and the victim's CON as the passive characteristic.

If the venom overcomes the victim's CON, he takes full damage equal to the venom's POT. If the poison fails to overcome the victim's CON, he resists, taking half damage (half POT).

Once resistance is determined, roll secretly for POT. write down the amount of damage (either the full amount rolled, or half) that the victim takes.

### 3) Apply Damage Gradually

Snakebite damage is delayed, and the symptoms are very different from those caused by weapons. Between 5-30 minutes elapse before a snakebite victim feels the effects of the venom, with suffering increasing from then on. The character may continue to take actions once bitten. He may also be unaware that he has been bitten. With luck, even fatally poisoned characters can dictate a will, shoot a last monster, or otherwise act heroically before death occurs.

The keeper may have the effects of snakebite manifest themselves at a dramatic moment. This is the simplest way to handle delayed damage. Simply announce that damage from the snakebite is setting in, and tell the victim to cross off a few hit points. Later in the adventure, ask the victim to lose a few more, and so on till all damage is suffered.

It may be necessary to roll randomly to determine the actual onset of damage. 3D10 minutes gives a realistic range of time for snakebite effects to begin. Alternatively the keeper may assign a percentage chance, say 10%, and check for onset of damage as the adventure progresses. Or a CON roll could be requested. Each subse-

*(continued on next page)*

*(continued from previous page)*

quent roll, or failed CON roll, means the character takes more damage, until the character has taken the entire amount of damage rolled by the keeper (and possibly fallen unconscious or dead).

If a snakebite victim is foolish enough to undertake activity that increases the circulation of blood greatly, such as running or fighting, effects may be felt sooner and lethality may even increase. Such penalties must be handled by the keeper.

## 4: Describe Actual Symptoms (Optional)

Some keepers may wish to accurately describe the strange and gradually worsening symptoms being suffered by a hapless victim, in order to increase the horror of the story. Even tough detective characters, scarred by bullets and knife wounds, may panic as the effects of a coral snake's bite become evident. These symptoms also may limit character actions in game terms.

What are the actual symptoms of snakebite? Of the snakes encountered in this adventure, only the rare coral snake and serpent men produce neurotoxic effects, which cause mental agitation, loss of vision, dizziness, and shortness of breath. Respiratory failure occurs in cases where damage equals or exceeds the victim's hit points. Long-term effects of severe neurotoxic damage on a survivor might involve a permanent loss of INT and/or DEX.

Copperhead, cottonmouth and diamondback bites all produce blood poisoning effects, which manifest as pain, swelling, cramps, and mortification in the areas near the wound. The worse the bite, the further from the wound such effects occur. Death from these bites is unlikely, and is usually caused by various unpleasant complications, such as gangrene, or in the case of a severe bite, by heart failure. These kinds of wounds take as much as a year to heal. During that time the victim will not have the full use of the bitten area of the body.

The severity of such symptoms increase as damage increases in relation to the victim's hit points. Thus a healthy but small woman might resist damage as well as a large man of equal CON, but would suffer more greatly once actually affected by poison damage.

Snakebite damage equal to 2 or 3 hit points or worse ought to inhibit a character's movement rate and reduce skills.

## Magical Snakebites

The bite of Yig or any of Yig's sacred snakes means certain death. Allow no resistance or POT rolls.

# Snake Statistics

Here we give general information and statistics for the four types of snakes that the investigators encounter during the adventure. Serpent men statistics are given elsewhere.

Player characters with knowledge of snakes would be aware of the following facts. Note that this knowledge will make the vicious behavior of the enchanted snakes in the adventure all the more frightening.

Note that two aspects of snakebite lethality, toxicity and quantity injected, are combined in terms of POT for the statistics below. Also remember that snakebites, while not always lethal, can knock characters unconscious or make them ineffective combatants.

## Copperhead

These common, aggressive snakes are responsible for most of the reported bite incidents that occur in North America. Neither large or unusually venomous, their bites are rarely lethal. But they can be a serious annoyance.

STR 1D4   CON 2D6   SIZ 1D3   POW 1D6
DEX 3D6   Move: 7
**Weapon:** Bite 50%, venom POT 1D10
**Skills:** Hide 80%, Sneak 90%

## Eastern Coral Snake

Unlike the other poisonous snakes of the area, the Eastern coral snake injects neurotoxic venom similar to that of the king cobra, death adder, and other dreaded snakes. Luckily, the eastern coral snake is one of the least dangerous of the cobra family. It has little tendency to bite, and its bite can be survivable. There is roughly a 10% fatality rate once a victim has been bitten. On the other hand, most victims are off their feet for several days. Antivenin for coral snakes bites is not easily obtained in the Charleston area during the 1920's.

Perhaps the most diabolical feature of neurotoxic snakebite in *Call of Cthulhu* terms is that the bite wound may not be visible or even painful, and there are normally no local effects. So in the heat of action during the adventure, a bite from a coral snake may not be noticed until too late.

Coral snake venom acts quickly. The keeper should reduce the delay between bite and damage, compared to the other snakes in this adventure.

STR 1D3   CON 2D6   SIZ 1D2   POW 1D6
DEX 3D6   Move 6
**Weapon:** Bite 30%, venom POT 2D8
**Skills:** Hide 80%. Sneak 90%

## Water Moccasin or Cottonmouth

A large, dangerous looking snake, its venom is actually comparatively weak and its bites are rarely lethal. The cottonmouth swims well, and it especially loves the swamp. It is often seen basking on branches and logs along the sluggish streams. Usually it retreats if disturbed, but it may stand its ground, holding its mouth wide open in a threatening gesture. The inside of its mouth is white, hence the name.

STR 1D8   CON 2D6   SIZ 1D6   POW 1D3
DEX 3D6   Move: 6/4 swim
**Weapon:** Bite 40%, venom POT 2D6
**Skills:** Hide 70%, Sneak 80%

## Eastern Diamondback Rattlesnake

The eastern diamondback is the largest of all rattlesnakes, and aggressive. Lengths up to nine feet are possible. Bites are often lethal — the amount of venom injected can be massive. Luckily for the people of the South, it is very rare.

STR 2D6   CON 2D6   SIZ 2D4   POW 1D8
DEX 3D6   Move 7
**Weapon:** Bite 50%, 1D2+venom POT 3D6
**Skills:** Hide 70%, Sneak 80%

## Dealing With Snakebite

**First Aid:** If done successfully, before the poison takes effect, First Aid reduces rolled damage by 1D3. Snakebite first aid involves pressing or sucking out envenomed blood, applying a tourniquet if possible, and getting the victim into a relaxed posture and situation. First aid of snakebite during a combat situation is thus less effective than under peaceful circumstances.

**Medicine, Pharmacy, and similar skills:** If done successfully before the venom takes full effect (see above), and only if antivenin is available, the skill purges the victim's system of 2D6 damage.

Using such skills with no antivenin available is useless. Antivenins first became available around 1896, and antivenins to each of the snakes common in the area of the adventure are available in the city of Charleston. General antivenin for viper bites (diamondbacks, cottonmouths, copperheads) is available locally, but only neutralizes 1D8 points of damage.

A previously prepared snakebite kit containing antivenin adds 20 percentiles to the chance of success, in addition to permitting the venom to be neutralized. ✵

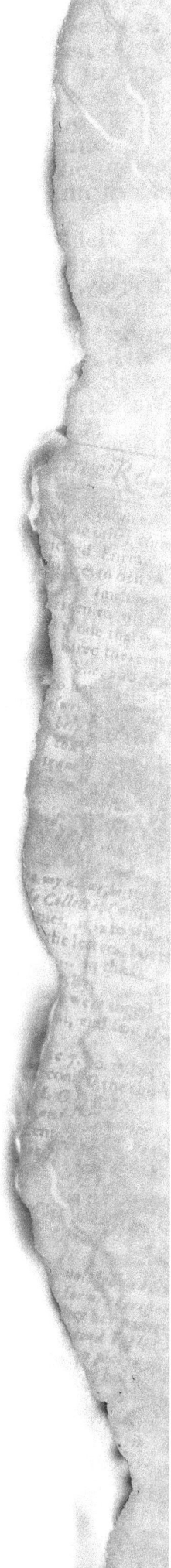

# The Crack'd and Crook'd Manse

*In which the investigators explore the usual sinister house,
only to find a distinctly unusual resident.*

### The Fitzgerald Manse — Sixty Years Ago

*Johnny came marching home, hurrah, marching home from the war. He'd been out there protecting the family honor. His brother Billy didn't come marching home though, Confederate grapeshot hit him in the guts at Bull Run and that was the end of him. Not that Johnny got off scot-free, he copped a bullet in the head at Appomattox: didn't bring him down but it sure messed him up. Most folks reckon that's why he came home, cleaned his rifle, shot his family and then himself. Hurrah.*

### The Fitzgerald Manse — Thirty Years Ago

*It crouched in the dark, comforted by the nearness of that which it cradled in its arms. Murmuring happily, it traced a finger along the blade still slick. Absently it put its finger in its mouth and licked. Spat. Made sightless by the darkened room, it paused to listen, head cocked to one side like an animal. No sounds. They had gone at last. It chuckled. It did not think they would find it, not in here.*

*It could still remember the gasps when they discovered its handiwork in the kitchen . . . and the dining room . . . and the bedroom . . . on the walls, and over the furniture, and on the ceiling . . . it chuckled again. Serves them right, trying to trick it with that woman, and those children . . . little brats. How they squealed. Another chuckle, a hollow sound in its parched throat.*

*Time to go. It stood up, stretched, listened again. Nothing. It felt for the panel, searching for the crack. It should be here, just here. Where was it? Where was the gap? The false wall behind the fireplace, it should be here . . . Gone! They'd taken it away! No! It was trapped no food, no water, no light, no no no no. It swung the weapon, splinters flew. Trapped, no no no no, it wildly swung the axe again, the handle was slick with brains, it flew off into the darkness. Must get out . . . must use hands . . . no no no no . . . after all they had done to it, now this . . . must . . . dig . . . out. . . .*

*Oblivious to the splinters driving in under its fingernails, it howled as it scrabbled at the walls.*

### The Fitzgerald Manse — One Month Ago

*The man flung the bedroom door open and rushed in, his dressing gown flapping crazily, his slippers slapping on the wooden floors. Hurriedly he knelt down and emptied his pockets, the shotgun cartridges tumbling out onto the hearth. Quickly he started scooping them out. The solution was finally within his grasp. For the first time in months, he was truly happy; soon he would be free. He whistled as he worked at emptying the shells, sitting on the bricks of the cold fireplace. He was so engrossed he did not hear the soft gurgling behind him until it was too late.*

## The Fitzgerald Manse — Today

*The house is now dark and quiet, except for the occasional creak and twinge as the plaster loosens and drifts to the floor. For the moment, no people live there. The house is dark and quiet, and waiting.*

"The Crack'd and Crook'd Manse" was originally used as a tournament module at Phantastacon '84 in Melbourne, Australia, and was then published in *Multiverse* issue 3 (1984). It has been substantially revised for this appearance.

The scenario is nominally set in February, 1925 (this can be changed, although 1925 ties chronologically with previous events in the area in 1895 and 1865). The setting is Gamwell, a fictitious Massachusetts town. It lies west of Boston, about halfway between Boston and Albany.

## Keeper's Introduction

Outside of Gamwell stands the Fitzgerald Manse. Two previous tragedies stain its history; the third is in progress.

The house was built in 1805. The original owners and builders were the wealthy Fitzgerald family; their time here finished abruptly in 1865 when young John Fitzgerald, returning home from the Civil War bitter and psychopathic, killed everyone in a fit of rage, and then committed suicide.

The place was purchased by the Ainsfield family in 1866, who lived there until 1894, when mounting debts forced them to sell out and move.

The next owner was Arthur Curwen, who moved in that year with his young family. Curwen had moved to the countryside from New York after making his fortune there, with the intention of bringing his children up in an idyllic rural setting. However, Curwen adjusted badly to the loneliness and quietness of the place after the bustle of the city, and in 1895 he became first irritable, then paranoid, then schizophrenic, and finally psychotic. He murdered his family and, evading pursuit, concealed himself in a monk-hole on the second floor of the house. He was unable to get out again, and his remains still molder there.

After this the house stood vacant for three years, until in 1898 an elderly couple bought it, the Franklins. Martha Franklin died in 1911, and Henry outlasted her by seven years, dying in 1918.

Arthur Cornthwaite, a brilliant and wealthy archaeologist, purchased the place in 1919. Here he spent many a happy hour researching for what he planned to be his greatest expedition to discover the final secrets of a lost tribe of South America. Once again the cloud that hangs over the house waited, then struck, this time in a strange way that brought the Mythos into the story.

The solution to this adventure doesn't rely on special skills or magical knowledge, so the scenario would be well suited for beginning players. Any number of investigators can tackle the situation.

## The Cornthwaite Mystery

The missing archeologist has met his end at the hands of a strange and cunning creature from the blackest jungles of South America, a creature that still lurks in the walls and foundations of the Fitzgerald mansion, hungrily.

## Investigators' Introduction

Out of the blue, a letter arrives one cold day in early February, 1925. The recipient investigator is ideally a private detective in the New England area. The letter is from an attorney, and included with the letter is an interesting newspaper clipping. See the nearby boxes **The Manse Papers #1, and #2**. Research into the Dodge brothers yields no information of note: the firm is tiny but respectable. Research into the missing Cornthwaite's background reveals that the man was respected in his field, and highly successful, but had an obsession for lost tribes and civilizations that made him something of a recluse.

## The Disastrous Expedition

After extensive preparations, Arthur Cornthwaite departed for the jungles of South America in 1923, fully sane and expectant of great revelations. His expedition traveled deep into the jungle, and set to work searching for the huge stone structure that was the lost tribe's temple. The team was constantly harassed by the present-day natives of the area. Undaunted, Cornthwaite pressed his men on.

They reached their goal. Covered in creepers, ancient, dark, forgotten, the domed temple still stood, silent. Inside, great carvings gave the history of the missing civilization, a people who worshipped the earth with passion and fervor. According to the carvings, they had raised this temple to the earth mother, and their efforts to entice their god to manifest herself and live amongst them were detailed in the glyphs. This apparently came to pass, but here their story abruptly ends. The last chiselings were hasty sigils of unknown meaning, clearly warnings of some sort, ringing the building.

## The Secret of the Lost People

Millennia before the first white men arrived on the continent an impressive culture of great magical force grew and flourished in the deep jungles of the continent. On a dark

*Dodge Brothers*
*Attorneys at Law*
*14 Main Street*
*Gamwell, Connecticut*
*January 30th, 1925*
*Dear Sir:*

*I have been referred to you by a mutual friend. As his attorney, I am very interested in locating the missing Mr. Arthur Cornthwaite and our associate mentioned your name as being one skilled in locating missing people, particularly those of Mr. Cornthwaite's persuasion. Thus I have taken the liberty of contacting you.*

*I am a partner of an established legal firm in Gamwell. Mr. Arthur Cornthwaite is one of our clients, and as his attorneys we hold certain documents in trust for him. It would appear that Mr. Cornthwaite has departed without notifying us of his movements. This leaves us in a quandary as to how to manage his estate in his absence without his authority in such matters. We would like you to locate Mr. Cornthwaite, and obtain from him his wishes in respect of this matter, or better still request that he contact us. If it should, heaven forbid, transpire that Mr. Cornthwaite is no longer with us, then we will need some evidence of same to proceed with his wishes as outlined in his Last Will and Testament. Hopefully this is an unnecessary contingency, but one which we must nevertheless consider in the light of Mr. Cornthwaite's mysterious departure.*

*I hope that you are free to give this matter your immediate attention, and would like to extend an invitation to you to attend an interview at our offices as soon as it is convenient, to discuss both the details of the situation and your professional fees.*

*Anticipating a prompt reply,*
*Yours faithfully,*
*Walter Dodge*

*Encl. article from Gamwell Gazette*

The Manse Papers #1

day the proud shamans of the jungle people attempted to summon the forces of primal nature, in the form of their naive vision of the earth mother. Sadly, this resulted in their calling up Shub-Niggurath, to the horror of all.

Many died or went mad, but the mightiest shamans of the tribe managed to temporarily seal the foul goddess into the bottom of the great temple with potent wardings. Then the tribe fled, dispersing in the jungle never to return.

Unable to chase them, the Black Goat of the Woods eventually dematerialized and departed, leaving behind her foul spoor and waste. This obscene by-product gradually built up its own sentience, and grew in the darkness down through the centuries, feeding on local life, the entire area avoided by the terrified descendents of the accursed tribe.

## Cornthwaite's Fate

Cornthwaite's expedition paid the warnings in the carvings no more heed than one would to any quaint local legend, and ventured deeper into the bowels of the temple where he encountered the spawn of Shub-Niggurath, an unearthly mass of gelid consistency and enormous size, a huge pulsing pool of corpulent organic horror. Strange mouths and black eye-like organs formed and dissolved amidst its squirming bulk.

Some of the expedition were caught by it; some gladly threw themselves into it, preferring death rather than acknowledge the existence of such a thing in a rational world; some escaped to be killed in ambushes laid for them above by the local natives, who were desperate to keep the terrible secret unknown in the world of men; some perished in the trackless jungle. One alone reached civilization again: Arthur Cornthwaite.

He left the horror far behind him, locked his exploring gear away in a chest in the attic, and vowed never again to travel south of Mexico. In time, the memory receded.

The explorer had returned safely, but he had sowed the seeds for his own doom. In his clothing he carried the thing's spores. In the sheltering darkness of the attic its spawn woke, grew stronger and expanded, until a tiny monster crawled into the walls to search for food.

## GAMWELL MILLIONAIRE ABSENT

Gamwell's most prosperous son, Arthur Cornthwaite, will not be seen at church over the next few weeks. Mr. Cornthwaite has apparently left the area for a time, possibly for a vacation, or in relation to his studies.

Some mystery surrounds Mr. Cornthwaite's departure, as it came without notice. However, an inspection of his mansion and grounds by Sheriff Whitford has revealed no cause for alarm. The last person to speak to Mr. Cornthwaite was his attorney, Mr. Walter Dodge, on the 7th of this month. At that time he gave no indication of his imminent departure, but according to Mr. Dodge he did seem quite preoccupied, no doubt with his travel plans.

We all know well that besides being a Gamwell landowner, Mr. Cornthwaite is also a millionaire, a scholar, a philanthropist, and an explorer. He may well be off laying the groundwork for some future exciting expedition, or perhaps just relaxing for a time in New York. Gamwell citizens will no doubt remember fondly Mr. Cornthwaite's numerous generous donations to local charities and to the town library, and join with us in wishing him a safe and happy journey.

*From the Gamwell Gazette, January 17th, 1925*

*The Manse Papers #2*

*Mr. Arthur Cornthwaite*

Soon meat and other foodstuffs went missing from the kitchen. As the thing rapidly grew, insects, rats, and mice were its first kills, graduating to small animals on or near the property. Its size increased again, along with its slow and patient hunger. Soon a local pet was missing. Then the gardener took a nap under a shady tree and was never seen again. It had fed on its first human. After that it stealthily hunted people, striking at night or from ambush.

At first believing that the gardener and the servants' mysterious disappearances had some normal cause, the archeologist quickly realized otherwise when he noticed the strange cracks and areas of moisture and mold appearing all over the house. But warnings came too late: by New Year's Day, 1925, Cornthwaite was the only one left. His failure to protect his people drove him to despair. He dared not leave the house, even briefly, for fear that the creature would escape in the meantime. He dared not enlist aid for fear that more would die because of his actions. He resolved to stay and fight to the end.

He and the thing played cat and mouse, until purely by accident he discovered a weakness in it, an aversion to salt. Before he could exploit this, it ambushed him, snatching him through the fireplace in his bedroom with slimy coils.

All has been still for some time now. The thing, well fed, has grown huge. It lives in the cellar and the wall cavities of the Fitzgerald manse, shifting its noisome bulk around to search for nourishment. The old house is rotting with damp, cracking and listing, gradually being worked asunder by the horror which lurks within.

Any food which entered the house has left while the creature was still flowing up to investigate. The supply of bug, rats, field mice and other small creatures in the area of the house has been used up. Already it has begun venturing further afield when hunger gets the better of its caution (recently it has taken a drowsy horse from a nearby field). It still hopes that food will again appear in its lair. Enter the investigators.

### The Creature

The creature moves slowly but insidiously. It may remain utterly motionless for hours, even days, as needed to stalk its prey. It is cunning, not rash. Make the most of the mystery; spin it out. Let creaking walls and spreading dampness puzzle the investigators until the thing strikes. The material below gives you all you need to present the house, but it is up to you to decide when the slime strikes, and shifts the scenario from brooding unease to gushing horror.

# The Town of Gamwell

Gamwell is out of the way, a place you might stop to buy an ice-cream on your way somewhere else, but that's about all. Large properties sprawl across the landscape in a pleasing rustic vista. The town itself is smallish, and primarily exists to serve the needs of the gentlemen farmers who own most of the land for miles around. Town services include a boarding house, a town hall, a police station, a fire station, an attorney's office, a newspaper office, a town library, and several shops.

## The Boarding House

This neat and scrubbed building is run by a friendly couple, Hank and Edith Haggarty. It is a clean place: no chewing tobacco, no alcohol, no smoking, no unmarried couples, and no nonsense. The investigators can get rooms here, but any nocturnal comings and goings will soon see them asked to leave. The Haggartys are a great source of local information, including people, history, picnic sites, etc. They know Mr. Cornthwaite as a thoughtful and generous gentleman, who has been slightly ill for a time, something he contracted in South America which he can't seem to shake off (this was

Cornthwaite's telling of it: he was not physically ill, but his nerves were shot to hell). They of course know the history of the Fitzgerald place, but don't relish talking about it. An **Oratory or Fast Talk** could be used to appeal to their usual garrulous nature.

## The Dodge Brothers' Office

Reginald, Walter and Herbert Dodge, three respectable gentlemen, are Cornthwaite's representatives. Three washed-out-looking little men in washed-out-looking little grey suits, they are fundamentally timid. They have called the investigators in so they won't have to peer into Cornthwaite's disappearance themselves. That way, if anything is unseemly they can safely wash their hands of the matter and sell the old mansion for a handsome profit. They are anxious to find him, although they're so pathetic they haven't actually set foot inside the house, just stood out front calling "Anybody home?".

*Mr. Walter Dodge*

The Dodge brothers have two goals for the investigation: first, to establish Cornthwaite's current location, or satisfactory evidence of his death; second, to keep damage to Cornthwaite's valuable estate and property at a minimum. Pulling apart the mansion or digging up the grounds extensively in order to find a body is a last resort. It is essential that the investigators meet both these goals in order to be paid.

The Dodges keep Cornthwaite's books, accounts, and will for him. Ethics prevent them from disclosing the contents of the will, but the investigators are free to inspect the ledgers. These detail his income and his outgoing expenditure, both in running his property and organizing his trips abroad.

Looking at income, an **Accounting** roll confirms that Cornthwaite is indeed a wealthy man, and likely to remain so, with many sound investments to bolster up his already healthy financial reserves.

Under outgo, an **Accounting** roll reveals that his last major expedition was to South America in 1923. Entries record the hiring of men and the transport of equipment, but an **Idea** roll will note that passage for only one person was booked coming out of South America.

The ledger for domestic expenses does not include staff; the Dodges will explain, if asked, that Mr. Cornthwaite liked to manage the staff of the estate himself, and they simply made available a payroll which

Cornthwaite distributed himself. He invariably hired people from out of town.

Another interesting fact found in the ledgers, spotted through either an **Accounting or Spot Hidden** roll, is the very last entry: on January 7th Cornthwaite requested that a dump truck full of salt be delivered to his property. The order was not filled (the Dodges were still lining it up when Cornthwaite disappeared). If the investigators ask for the instruction to be carried out, and can convince a Dodge brother with a **Fast Talk or Persuade** roll, the salt will be grudgingly provided. The Dodges point to this request as a sign that their client had become unbalanced, and request that it be hushed up if possible.

They may ask Reginald Dodge about the last meeting with Cornthwaite, but he can't add much more than was in the newspaper. He seemed tense, and stressed; Reginald was too polite to ask why.

The investigators will be given two keys to the Fitzgerald Manse, for the front and back doors. They are welcome to sleep out there. In the meantime, accommodation will be arranged for them (and paid for) in the local boarding house, until they are ready to move out to the mansion. While in residence, they should take care not to do any damage to the house, which is in poor repair but still valuable.

The Dodges are willing to pay the investigators $100 to locate Mr. Cornthwaite, with a $100 bonus if they have the answer within the week. A **Bargain** roll may be used to drive them up in price by up to another $100.

## The Gamwell Gazette

The office of Gamwell's weekly ("Gamwell Gazette: Established 1887") is small and cluttered. The editor is Stan Artemis, a gregarious, overdressed man in his late forties. He is wearing a bright red-and-green check suit and a panama hat. He is a nauseatingly friendly person, and gladly chats with the investigators, while trying to wheedle what tidbits he can out of them for next week's edition.

*Mr. Stan Artemis*

Two people work at the *Gazette*, Stan, who sets the type and puts the newspaper together, and Joe Virelli, who does the reporting and photography. Joe is out gathering material at present.

The investigators are welcome to look through back numbers of the paper these are kept in ratty cardboard boxes. In them are constant references to Cornthwaite, stretching back to his arrival in 1919; opening fetes, attending tea parties, donating to the church, winning at bridge nights, giving books to the library, and so on. If they look back further, though, with reference to the Fitzgerald estate, a **Library Use** roll uncovers a clipping from 1895. See *The Manse Papers #3* nearby.

## Graveyard

Some odd compulsion might lead the investigators out here. All of the house's previous owners are here, so the investigators can walk among the headstones of Elma Fitzgerald (1865), Albert Fitzgerald (1865), Simon Fitzgerald (1865), Grace Fitzgerald (1865), Gloria Curwen (1895), Harold, Sarah and Susan Curwen (1895), Martha Franklin (1911), and Henry Franklin (1911). Fresh flowers are laid on the childrens' grave the year round. Murderer John Fitzgerald is here too, but in an unmarked grave.

## Sheriff's Office

Sheriff Whitford is the man here, a lean old conservative. Some spark went out of him in 1895 when he saw those murdered Curwen children. He does his job, but not in an overly friendly fashion. Folks respect him though. Whitford doesn't like anything to do with the Fitzgerald manse, so he didn't like Cornthwaite, and he doesn't like the investigators. He resents their intrusion on his jurisdiction, and warns them to stay within the law. He has a lot of power to make life difficult for them.

He is gruff and resentful in discussing Cornthwaite, but a **Fast Talk or Credit Rating** may get him to open up. He's had a quick look around in the house, but the fellow obviously isn't there. There's no indication of violent kidnap, or any foul play. The man had fired all his servants one by one in the weeks preceding (all out-of-towners, Whitford sneers); he was obviously planning to take off for a while. He has the money to do such a thing, and he hardly needs to hold his lawyer's

*Sheriff Whitford*

## GAMWELL FAMILY SLAIN IN TERRIBLE ATTACK

### Mother and Three Children Killed

#### Police Seek Missing Father

A tragedy of awful proportions unfolded today in Gamwell when Mrs. Gloria Curwen and her three children (Harold 5, Sarah 3, and Susan 2) were found brutally murdered on their estate north of Gamwell, the well-known Fitzgerald Manse.

Deputy Whitford of the Gamwell County Sheriff's Office made the grisly discovery while making a routine inspection. "I've never seen anything like it," the brave but shaken deputy told this reporter, "They were all dead." The family had indeed been brutally and cowardly slain, struck down by repeated blows from an axe. Not even little Susan was spared from this hideous fate.

No murder weapon has been discovered, and Mr. Arthur Curwen, the children's father, is presently missing. He is wanted by the police for questioning, although fears are also held for his safety.

*Gamwell Gazette, May 17th, 1895*

*The Manse Papers #3*

hand to ask permission. The whole business is ridiculous.

A **Psychology** roll at Whitford reveals the man's distaste for the Fitzgerald Manse. If the investigators ask him about the Curwens, his lips will stretch into a thin line, and he mutters that he hopes that Arthur Curwen is still alive somewhere, because he's looking forward to shooting him down like the dog that he is. Something wild in Whitford's eyes at this point suggests to the investigators that it might be time to go.

During the whole interview he is preoccupied, and is typing up a report when they enter. At some stage he begin to ask them where they were last night, and whether they have witnesses. If pressed on the point, with a **Persuade** roll or similar (he really doesn't like these people), he says that a local farmer, Seb Watkins, lost a horse last night. It was a valuable animal. Whitford knows it was taken sometime in the night, as there was a particularly heavy dew on Watkins' property this morning, lasting well past midday, and any tracks would have been easily seen in it. Watkins and his dogs heard nothing. If the investigators think to ask, they learn that Watkins' property adjoins the Fitzgerald grounds. (The creature took the horse. The "heavy dew" was its trail of moisture.)

## Town Hall

A wooden edifice, here council meetings are held, and records are kept. A **Law** roll will be required to convince the dusty little clerk of their worth, but once they have negotiated him they may have access to any legal documents that might be kept here.

These include birth and death certificates, and the title deed for the Fitzgerald Manse. The latter is resting on a high shelf, tied with a fading red ribbon, and is home to a large but harmless furry spider, which will crawl out to check out any disturbance (down the arm of the investigator who reaches for it). The deed records the house's original owners and builders, the Fitzgeralds, in 1805, and the subsequent transfers: Ainsfield 1866, Curwen 1894, Franklin 1898, Cornthwaite 1919. There is no plan of the house.

## Town Library

A small but crammed wooden building. The librarian is Mrs. Susan Arwell, a fairly helpful person. There's not much in the way of books about Gamwell, although she will modestly say that she had thought of writing one.

The library has a scattering of books on all types, but a disproportionate amount are about anthropology and archaeology. The librarian

*Mrs. Arwell*

explains that these were donated by Mr. Cornthwaite, and represent only a fraction of the books he has given; the rest are in storage, with no room to put them. Oddly enough, he came in and borrowed one of them in November: it's now overdue, but she didn't really consider it diplomatic to mention it to him. The book is *The Missing People*, by Thomas Pratt. An **Anthropology** roll reveals that Pratt is usually on the fringe of accepted science.

A **Library Use** roll does not turn up anything in particular, although there are some penciled notes in the margins of many of Cornthwaite's old books, which infer that he was involved in a complicated search for a "great dome" described in native South American legends.

# The Fitzgerald Estate

After they have followed the leads mentioned above, there's nothing much more they can learn without actually going out to the place. The house is situated ten miles out of Gamwell, in a peaceful but isolated district. The house is surrounded by a tangled garden, which in turn is bordered by a high stone spiked wall. The property covers twenty acres. As they drive towards the house, black and grey clouds scud across the sky, and a chill wind picks up.

## Neighboring Estates

The Fitzgerald estate is located miles from town. Several other large mansions are the nearest neighbors. Inquiries about Cornthwaite at any of these gains no useful information except that he seemed a nice,

intelligent sort of man, though he was looking rather ill since his return from South America.

The only unusual event of late is the disappearance of a horse belonging to one of the less wealthy estate owners. If the investigators spend an afternoon searching the many acres of ground between the two estates, they find several large bones, oddly crushed. A **Zoology** roll identifies them as from a horse.

The iron gate which gives access to the driveway is padlocked; the Dodge brothers neglected to give the investigators the key. They can pick the lock on a **half-chance Mechanical Repair** roll, or they can try to break the STR 30 chain. Failing that, they'll have to park their vehicle outside the property, and move in on foot after a **Climb** roll to get over the gate. Or they can drive back to town and get the key.

A wide driveway leads towards the house, while other ill-defined paths lead off into the rambling garden. A **Spot Hidden** will note the house ahead; **another Spot Hidden** glimpses the roof of a shed through the trees to the right of the drive.

## The Ornamental Garden

The estate includes an extensive garden, with stone benches, planters, and even a fountain. Trees include several exotic varieties such as willows. Untended for months, the garden has become a wild expanse of runaway foliage, overgrown, threatening. A **Cthulhu Mythos** roll might link, for a paranoid investigator, the exuberant growth with the unholy influence of the Black Goat of the Woods. It's a dark place, dank, green, and dripping.

Anything could be concealed in here, so they should mount a search of the garden. Several strange occurrences transpire while they wander around. Someone is tripped up by a tree root, which he swears was not in the way when they put their foot down. Someone is struck in the head by an overhanging branch, for which there seemed to be enough clearance. At one point a huge fungi-encrusted hollow log has fallen across the path in a particularly damp area, over which they'll need to clamber or jump (and probably get their clothes filthy). In another area there is a huge and slippery mud patch, for which a **DEX x3** roll is needed to avoid sprawling full length.

The garden is essentially harmless, but the keeper should make it out to be as menacing and mysterious as possible. At the very least get the investigators good and muddy.

A **Botany or Biology** roll suggests all to be quite natural here, except for a certain number of plants rarely encountered outside the tropics (also see the wood cellar, below). A successful **Idea roll** detects a total absence of bird and animal life, unusual for such circumstances.

## The Sinister Shed

The windowless garden shed is small, wooden, peeling green in color, and the door is slightly ajar. Puzzle and frighten the investigators here: tell them that they sense something sinister, almost evil, about the little building.

Within is darkness, and there is a litter of leaves and detritus on the floor. There are many tools: rakes, a wheelbarrow, shovels, some hedge-clippers, a pick, a saw, and so on. Many have fallen to the floor. All are disused, a little dirty, some a little rusty. There are no axes to be found, although a **Spot Hidden** discerns an empty rack for one.

If searching the crowded tool shed, a person failing a **DEX x5** roll bumps into various tools — they might receive a cut in the shin from a shovel, a slash to the cheek from a rake, stub their toe on a roller. If they panic, they'll only collide with more things. In the poor light, with the wind whistling through the shed, rustling the dead leaves, it will seem almost as if the implements are moving with a murderous life of their own. If a **Spot Hidden** roll on the tools is failed at this point, the viewer must roll SAN or lose 1 point.

## Outside the House

The house is silent, shuttered, brooding; cobwebbed by ivy, masked by trees, caressed by the wind. It is large and well constructed, with high ceilings and thick, substantial windows, walls, and doors. From the outside, a suspicious (or imaginative) observer notes that the entire edifice presents a strange, slightly skewed, or tilted appearance. The foundations seem solid enough when viewed closely, but the house itself is oddly crooked.

The house has two floors, with doors front and back. The front door waits atop a short flight of steps. The door is carved oak, the fine brass knocker cold to the touch. It opens into the hall. The back door is less assuming, and leads into the kitchen. The windows are also points of entry, although they are shuttered. The only other way in is down: a pair of wooden hatches that give access to the wood cellar (see "The Cellars", further below). A **Track** roll discerns wheel marks near this area (trucks would pull up to unload wood and coal). One of the hatches has a hole in it, and a few odd vines protrude through.

# Inside The Fitzgerald Manse

This place is to be the investigators' home while they conduct their search. Encourage them to move some stuff in. When they get here they'll be tired and hungry. They'll also probably be very nervous. Encourage this feeling.

It is best if the investigators sleep here. If they insist on living in town, the creature has little hope of catching them off guard, and may prefer to make more depredations in the neighboring estates. If the investigators camp in the garden, the keeper's job is easier: the thing can sneak quietly across the lawns and surround one or more of them at the climax of the adventure.

## Things That Go Crack

The mansion appears to be in a state of bad, and worsening, disrepair. Entering the house, one can see that large cracks have appeared in the walls, and are slowly widening. Water damage is noticeable in many rooms, although the roof seems to leak very little when it rains that night. Loose plaster, sometimes in chunks, sometimes in drifts, covers the floor at the base of the walls. The wallpaper sags in places; pictures hang at odd angles; the curtain rails do not run parallel with the floor; the floor dips in places; it's a renovator's nightmare.

When the investigators first enter, the downstairs floors do not creak; the upstairs floors do, loudly. (This is because beneath the floorboards of the lower story lurks the creature.) Only an investigator successful in both a **Listen and an Idea** roll will note this peculiar point.

Judging by the evidence, Cornthwaite left suddenly (or is still here), for his personal effects are much in evidence. See the individual room entries for more information.

With all the shutters closed, the house is dark and dingy throughout. A slight moldy, wet smell is noticeable.

## Things That Go Bump

Make this place menacing. The investigators don't know where Cornthwaite is, or why he's vanished. For all they know, the house may be haunted, or cursed, or sentient. Build up as much atmosphere as you can. Some suggestions for spooks and false starts are given in the brief room descriptions below.

## House Calls

The investigators receive several visitors during their explorations of the house. The timing of the introduction of these unexpected guests is left to the keeper.

Sheriff Whitford stops by to make sure that these foreigners aren't misbehaving. He enters the house unannounced, with gun drawn. He hates and loathes this building, but since his interview with the investigators he has become pathologically convinced that they're up to no good. He sneaks up on them to check them out; his sudden appearance makes them jump. (Roll SAN against 0/1.) If he's satisfied that no property damage or theft is taking place, he'll slink away, muttering dire warnings. If not, he'll insist that they leave at once. A **Persuade or Fast Talk** may be needed to convince him otherwise.

Joe Virelli, the lanky local reporter, also drops by. Stan has sent him out here to see what's going down. He's not too happy about this; the place gives him the creeps. He has a look around the garden first, and finds a rusted axe in the bushes — thinking it may be important, he picks it up. (It's not important. Some gardener just left it there.)

*The Reporter, Mr. Virelli*

Eventually he comes creaking up the steps (a **Listen** from within the house will detect this) and nervously pounds on the door, hard enough to rattle it in its frame and shake some plaster loose above it. As an investigator opens the door, a sudden gust of wind blows it wide open and standing outside is a large figure with an axe! (Roll SAN, losing 1 point if missed.) What do they do? Any sudden violent attack is greeted with great dismay by Joe, who falls off the steps in surprise. If they pick him up out of the rose bushes and apologize profusely, he might be persuaded to join them. His further involvement in the events is up to the keeper. A good use is as a first victim to show how the monster works.

One final visitor doesn't come into the house, but is perhaps glimpsed through a window walking in the garden: a figure walking stiffly, wearing a blue uniform, and carrying a rifle. It walks around the side of the house, out of sight. It will not be seen again. If they search the area it walked, a **Track** roll reveals no tracks. Anyone succeeding in a Track roll must also make an **Idea** roll. If the roll is made, then the investigator knows for a fact that there should be tracks here, but there obviously aren't; this costs them 1 SAN point. Johnny Fitzgerald, cold and lonely in his unmarked grave, still comes marching home.

## The Thing That Goes Creak

The investigators are being stalked, very, very slowly. The predator is patient, and oddly cunning; it knows its trap, the house, well; it knows how to hide from its prey, waiting for the right moment. It is an alien abhorrence, part slime mold, part fungal growth, part slug, and an abomination not of this earth. Grown from the spores of the larger version of itself in South America, it has been bred in the bowels of the Fitzgerald Manse, and has adapted well to its environment.

It is enormous, bloated. At its center float the bodies of its most recent prey, horribly liquiscent and slowly digesting, their bones crushed and dissolved into slime, or excreted. It has no nucleus or outer wall. Its mass is moist and wet, and leaves traces of moisture wherever it goes — thus the mysterious water damage that is found in various random areas of the house. Less noticeable is a translucent slime trail that dries quickly, and is not easily noticed.

By nature it is clever but timid. Its intelligence is alien, and its only understandable goal is to feed and grow.

**Habits and Behavior:** When dormant, the creature follows the pull of gravity and pools in the main cellar, filling it entirely, with smaller pseudopods infesting the first floor of the house. But in moving it can stretch itself out, covering an enormous area. It can monitor the entire house if need be, or thinly cover many acres of ground. It prefers not to move outside the house, but of late this has been necessary, and may be again if the investigators do not sleep in the house.

It leaves only at night, oozing slowly and silently out of the basement and across the ground. In this manner it surrounded and caught the horse mentioned above.

It prefers to stay out of rooms, but lurk in the cavities between them. By quietly oozing into the gaps in the walls, and sliding along under the rafters, and flooding itself under the floorboards, and pouring itself into the plumbing, it can access, and if necessary fill, any room in the house.

The creature attacks its victims with powerful pseudopods, allowing it to grab prey even in the middle of rooms.

It can form hideous mouth-like organs as well, mouths that are strangely similar to those of the Dark Young of Shub-Niggurath. If an investigator should see a mouth, a successful **Cthulhu Mythos** roll reveals this odd resemblance — the only clue to the creature's origin. The mouths are simply for display: boneless and soft, like all of the monster, they do no significant damage.

**Evidence and Observations:** Its movement affects the house. Plaster is loosened. Patches of moisture and slime trails accumulate. Doors which were once operable jam shut. Doors previously stuck fast swing freely. Occasionally its passing will knock something over (a **Listen** success will permit an investigator to notice the distant crash).

Anyone in a room it is exploring will sense the walls and ceiling very gradually swelling and shuddering; this

*A Sleeping Victim Awakes, As the Creature Oozes Softly Into His Room*

is a subtle, almost hallucinatory experience, and a SAN roll is required. Failure costs one point.

**Tactics for the Keeper:** The creature moves slowly, but it knows its food. Its food is quick, dangerous, and loud, but always tires eventually. Sooner or later its food's guard relaxes, and that's when it's ready for the kill.

During the investigators' explorations, the creature is sizing them up and will be extremely cautious. There may be many small aural manifestations of it, but no sightings of the main mass of the creature. Should they spot a small portion of its bulk through a crack in the walls or in a room, they will see only an odd film of moisture, or at best, what appears to be an unmoving puddle of slime, not a monster.

They may well suspect the house of hiding some evil, but the keeper should hint at a ghostly presence pervading the house, not at a physical threat. Insist that the various peculiarities of the house itself are caused by settling. Age, rotting wood, mold, and water in the foundations are causing these things, not a monster.

If they actually expose part of the creature, they will undoubtedly take samples and perhaps burn or eradicate the area exposed. At first the cunning creature will accept such indignities and remain unmoving as long as its surface is exposed to light. It can lose much of itself without harm. Analysis of the material removed indicates a plant growth of a kind not easily identified by science. Successful **Biology** rolls indicate that the material is similar to fungus, but in fact is far closer to a slime mold in many ways.

Once the player characters begin looking for moisture and slime in the house, they will find traces everywhere. But the beast initially will retract its body and pseudopods as fast as it can whenever aggressively approached. If the investigators realize where its main body may be and chop down a door it is lurking behind (*e.g.* the cellar), or suddenly punch through a wall it is currently sliding behind, then it will respond by attacking. If the investigators have not prepared for this, and don't know its vulnerability, they will probably be killed, with any luck while separated from each other. Ordinary weapons are of little use against it. Ideally the body will be dragged down the chimney or even down the side of a wall outdoors, so that it will seem that the investigator has vanished. Note that the creature's method of killing does not leave much blood.

Remind the investigators of the value of the mansion: though cracked and sagging, the Dodge brothers still believe it can be repaired and sold for a good price. So removal of walls or other major surgery is not acceptable.

The moment of realization (that the moist areas and masses of slime seen in the house are actually the trail and pseudopods of a gigantic creature) requires each investigator to make a SAN roll against 0/1D4 points.

More details on the creature are found below, in the General Cellar and in the Statistics section.

## Detours to South America

It is possible that the investigators will consider leaving the house immediately and retracing Cornthwaite's tracks in central South America. One solution to this divergence from the adventure is the fact that the Dodge brothers will not accept it. "Surely you gentlemen do not intend to gallivant off to a foreign land and be paid for it?" one of them mutters angrily when informed. "Leave the job and you're fired!" Neither **Art (Oratory) nor Persuade** rolls convince the attorneys that a trip to South America is necessary. If the investigators are willing to lose the job, fine. The sheriff will make sure that they are evicted from the house immediately (he never did trust them). The creature will further afield for its food, slowly growing. Perhaps years will pass before it is discovered.

## The House

Following are room descriptions, keyed to the floor plan. These have been kept to the minimum, where things in the room either add color or relate to the plot; the keeper can extra realistic detail where needed to fill the place out.

The doors of the mansion are very solid, and built with heavy locks of top quality. Decorations and furnishings are extensive.

The investigators will be looking for a hidden body. Although the manse is large, the walls are too thin to hide the body of an adult, unless, of course, it had been dismembered. However, an undismembered body will eventually be found: the *monkhole* (see p. 65) does in fact hide a body, though not Cornthwaite's. The room's presence can be deduced by a competent architect or by means of several hours' careful study and measurement.

Other than the monkhole, the only rooms of special interest are the Master Bedroom where Cornthwaite grabbed, and the preferred home of the creature, the General Cellar, which is large and contains few objects. See page 69.

### Downstairs

**The Hall.** As the investigators step through the door a huge wet chunk of plaster shivers off and gently showers them. The whole ceiling is moist and dark.

**Cloakroom.** There is a huge dark figure with an axe in here — no, it's just an overcoat.

**Kitchen.** There is a series of metal canisters on the shelf above the stove flour, sugar, tea, coffee. It is obvious from a gap in the line that one is missing (the salt; an **Idea** roll might suggest this if the players can't guess it). The door to the cellar (from the kitchen) will not budge — the creature is shored up behind it. A **Track** roll in here detects a line of white crystals (salt) along the base of this door. The taps on the kitchen sink don't work; the pipes are blocked.

**Empty Room.** A large area, devoid of furnishings, with a polished wooden floor. (It's a dance floor.) Water damage is visible on the floor edges.

**Pantry.** A terrible rotting meaty smell comes from in here. This is from food decaying in the icebox.

**Laundry.** Empty disused tubs with odd sediments. There is a linen closet; an investigator opening it is suddenly showered with towels, bedding, etc. Again, the taps in here don't work either. Water damage is present on the ceiling.

**Parlor.** Comfy chairs wait patiently for absent guests.

**Dining Room.** There is a silver service laid out, a table for one. There are thin slivers of broken glass on the floor here, the remnants of a peppershaker. There is no sign of a saltshaker. The walls are cracked and moist.

**Store Room.** Filled with junk, boxes, barrels, crates, and so on. A large area of mold and moisture can be seen in the center of the floor. The patch of weak floor gives way under any inquisitive investigator, dumping them suddenly into the Coal Cellar. Damage is 1D6 for the fall, halved if a **Jump** roll is made. Any light will be extinguished, and the investigator is sprawled in total darkness, possibly with something terrible moving closer, jaws slavering . . . roll SAN, or lose 1 point.

**Study.** Lying open on the roll-top desk is a book, *The Missing People: The Tribe That The Jungle Swallowed*, by Thomas Pratt. The book is in poor condition, the binding is cracked, there are odd stains, and some pages are loose (Cornthwaite read it a little feverishly). It can be skimmed in an hour or so with an **English** roll (missing the roll indicates

imperfect comprehension), or read it thoroughly and carefully in three hours. See *The Manse Papers #4*.

**Library.** This has books on exploring, archaeology, history, anthropology, and more. There are many gaps on the shelves though, and a **Library Use** combined with an **Idea** roll indicates that there are no books whatsoever about the South American continent here

# THE FITZGERALD MANSION

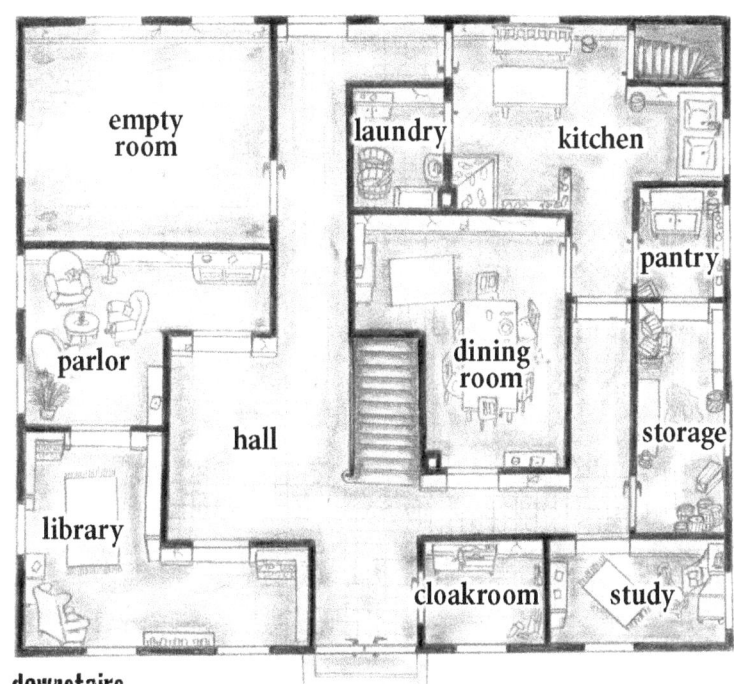

**downstairs**

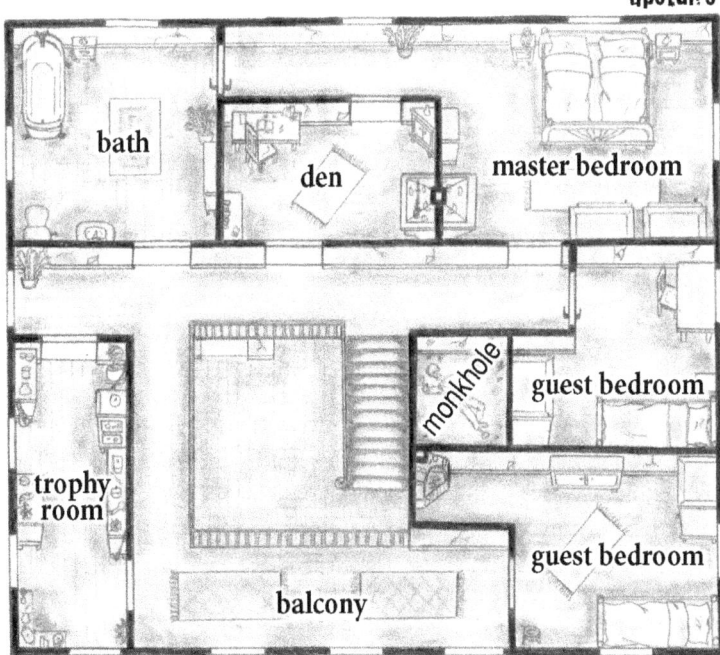

**upstairs**

# THE MISSING PEOPLE

*The Tribe That The Jungle Swallowed*
by Thomas Pratt
Published in 1913, Oxford, England

**Summary:** This book concerns a South American tribe in ancient times, whose existence is testified to by various ruins, but of whose demise nothing is known. The book is based on legends of the tribe and archaeological discoveries. Pratt makes note of the tribe's religious fervor, and conjectures that they may have been wiped out in civil holy war. He mentions in particular a "Great Dome", depicted in carvings and art. He believes that this was an actual stone structure, that it probably still stands, and may well house the last secrets of the missing people. ❈

*The Manse Papers #4*

(Cornthwaite threw them all out or gave them away after his return).

A **Spot Hidden** in the library reveals an oddly bulging knothole in the wood paneling. They can slip this out with a **DEX x3** roll; inside is a tubular hollow into which a yellowed piece of paper is stuffed. The paper is covered on both sides with closely-packed scrawl. It has aged badly, and is almost illegible, except for the signature: A.C.

A **Psychology** roll while investigating the paper detects a severe emotional imbalance in its author. (These paranoid ravings were the work of Curwen.)

Mold and moisture are noticeable among the books, although few have been made unreadable. Water damage is present on the walls and ceiling.

## Upstairs

**Balcony.** A weak rail here might cause trouble to anyone leaning on it.

**Lounge.** Huge windows afford a wide view out over the garden, except that they are shuttered at present. Some moisture is visible at the edges of the walls.

**Guest Bedroom.** The back of the fireplace is false, and can be pushed in to reveal the monkhole.

**Monkhole.** Curled up in here are the pitiful remains of Arthur Curwen. The corpse has no toes, nor fingers on the left hand. An old axe lies in the corner, the dents in the wall signify his attempts to get out. SAN loss for this scene is 1/1D4. The fireplace door is sprung in such a way that once you're in it is impossible to get out. This realization (trapped in the dark with a corpse and the same fate awaiting you) will cost 1/1D3 SAN. The actual means of exit are via a trapdoor in the roof, leading up to the attic. Curwen starved unaware of this, the way to freedom just above his head.

**Bedroom.** Tiny black handprints dot the floor in here. A **Track** roll shows them to lead under the bed. A Listen roll will discern furtive scratching. Underneath the bed is a horrific black beast, two feet long, with red-rimmed eyes and humanlike hands. A SAN roll is needed, costing 1D2 points if missed. If made, they recognize it as a raccoon that obviously fell down the chimney. If the investigators don't rescue it, it will be eaten by the creature sooner or later.

**Trophy Room.** This room is locked at present. Inside, gathering dust, is loot from tombs the world over. Pots, vases, statuettes, carvings, musical instruments, idols, and more. Some leer and snicker at the investigators, seemingly. One or two fall off the shelves for no readily apparent reason. Some have already been smashed into unrecognizable fragments. All stare with painted outrage, flat eyes hostile to the men who removed them from their ancestral homes. The keeper should be able to whip up a feeling of a curse emanating from in here, perhaps something Cornthwaite dug up and brought home, but should have left in the ground. An **Archaeology** roll will identify most of this stuff as South American, many of them funerary artifacts.

**Bathroom.** The investigators will probably be pleased to see this large, luxurious bathroom if they have been out rolling in the garden, but will be disappointed when no water comes from the taps. (The creature blocks the pipes. It may well issue forth from the taps on the washbasin and the bath, from the plugholes, and from the toilet, when the keeper is ready to get tough; preferably after the players have an idea of what they're up against).

As they look at themselves in the mirror, they notice writing across their face traced in the dust of the polished glass. Someone (Cornthwaite) has scrawled a message. Written hastily on the bathroom mirror are the letters: "NaCl" which any person with a smattering of chemistry knows is the formula for salt (make a **Know** roll).

**Den.** A shotgun hangs above the mantelpiece inhere. There is a crumpled piece of paper in the grate (**Spot Hidden** to notice). The investigators can smooth it out if they rescue it. See ***The Manse Papers #5***.

**Master Bedroom.** This expensively-furnished room contains much in the way of clothing and personal effects, but few clues. Several valuable objects, such as a gold-plated cigar case or a diamond tie pin, could be lifted by an unscrupulous investigator.

The ceiling of this room is moist, and water occasionally drips soddenly from the center. The fireplace also shows moisture around the edges.

Scattered near the fireplace are nine partially disassembled shotgun cartridges; the powder and shot has been scooped out, and separated into neat little piles.

*The Creature in Its Cellar Lair*

Directly in front of the fireplace is a pair of fluffy blue men's slippers. A **Spot Hidden** roll in the room will note a line of white crystals (salt) along the bottom of the doors, and across the windowsills — all the points of entry. A **Spot Hidden** on the fireplace reveals a translucent stain. A second **Spot Hidden** near the fireplace makes out a crystal saltshaker under the hearth rug (this was taken from the dining room). Another **Spot Hidden** in the room detects the missing salt bin from the kitchen, empty, tossed under the bed.

## The Attic

This open space contains lots of junk, from each of the families who have lived here. There are old chests, a rocking horse, a broken mirror, a locked wardrobe, a tailor's dummy, odd bits of furniture. There is a small wet area near the south wall, but no significant water damage structurally speaking.

The investigators notice a trunk that has been absolutely flattened outwards, burst as if an explosion had taken place in the interior. Inside are items of jungle clothing, a pith helmet, a compass, a .45 revolver, a machete, etc. A further **Spot Hidden** will show that one pocket of the trousers has been violently split open. Furthermore, everything in the trunk seems a little bit shiny and reflective under torchlight, yet the items are dry to the touch (this is the track of the creature, who traveled to America in Cornthwaite's pants).

If they turn the flat trunk over, the stickers and labels identify it as belonging to Arthur Cornthwaite, and show that it's been to South America and back again.

There is a trapdoor in here, covered with dust (Spot Hidden to see), and weakened with age. If anyone steps on it they crash through the floor, taking 1D6 damage (1D3 with a **Jump** roll) and plummeting into the dead embrace of Arthur Curwen in the monkhole below. Encountering the corpse in this manner costs 1D2/1D6 points of SAN.

## The Cellars

**Coal Cellar.** Full of black coal. The door leading out into the general cellar is locked and will not budge. It can be broken (STR 18). Water damage is noticeable here.

**Wood Cellar.** Access is gained from the outside via wooden hatches. Inside is a great mound of wood and sawdust, on which unusual vines and creepers grow. A **Botany or Biology** roll will reveal these to be South American in origin, and furthermore that they should not be growing in this climate, let alone thriving.

The door leading into the general cellar is locked and cannot be opened. This whole area looks damp: the water damage is extensive (again, the track of the creature).

**General Cellar.** The door to this cellar is not unusually heavy for this house, but is locked, and worse, is normally held shut by the creature. The door has STR 18.

Normally this room is filled with the huge, bloated mass of the alien horror (see the nearby illustration). Assuming it is home, its noxiousness fills the place from wall to wall, a sickening

hidden trap door ⇒ to monk hole

⇐trap door to balcony

attic

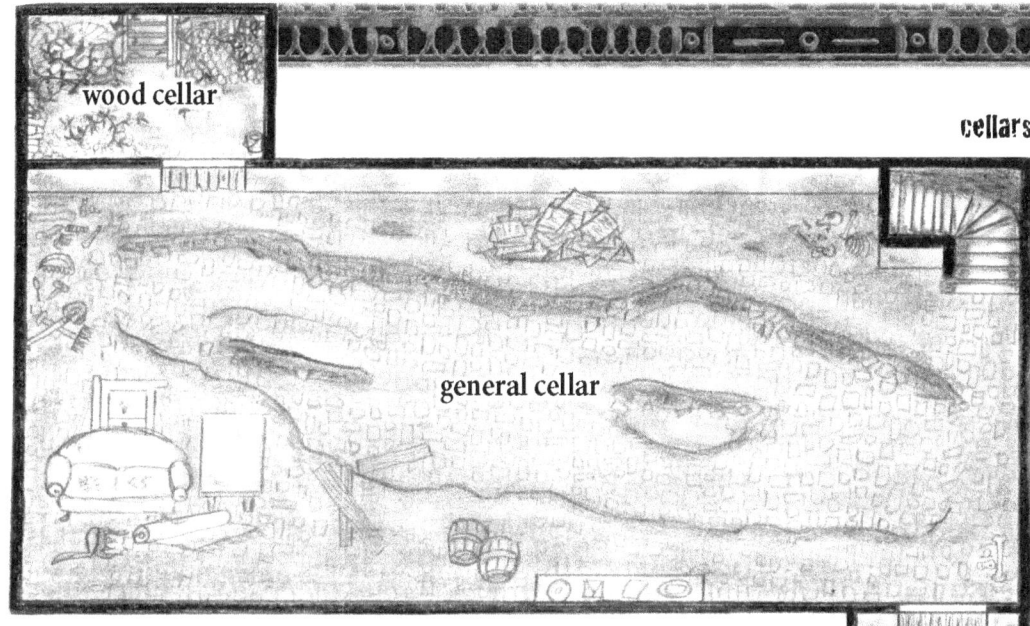

wood cellar

general cellar

coal cellar

Once it has its food, it will close the door again. The best thing for the investigators to do, once they've opened the door and looked in long enough to see the creature, is of course to slam the door shut immediately, which they can easily do on a **DEX x5** roll before the monster oozes itself forward. But if they want a fight, they'll get a fight.

soup of translucent gel in which swirl the liquefied, boneless bodies of its victims: rats, birds, and other animals, the raccoon from upstairs, the horse, the servants, and the late Arthur Cornthwaite, still partly clad in his dressing gown, the look of surprise still discernible on his half-dissolved features.

The cellar door cannot be opened unless the thing wills it. Its mass shores up the door and holds it fast. The door is also locked. Determined investigators can take the door off its hinges or chop through it in several melee rounds (an **Idea** roll will remind them that the Dodge brothers were anxious to avoid any damage to the property).

If the investigators assault the door at the beginning of the adventure, the cautious creature retreats into the walls and foundations immediately, leaving intriguing but not conclusive evidence of its presence behind. In the room are oddly crushed bales of old magazines, severely rusted tools and several valuable-looking pieces of antique furniture, now cracked and waterlogged. There is water damage everywhere. The creature's translucent trail coat the walls, and bones of previous victims may be found in the corners. Remnants of the creature's slime itself can be found with a **Track or Spot Hidden** roll. The entire floor of the cellar has cracked and sagged, obviously due to water damage.

An excavation into the foundations of the mansion might be possible, taking 1D3 hours for a thorough check. Naturally the beast has long since oozed outside or up into the house.

The sheriff is impressed by the strange nature of the damage found in the cellar, and the bones are certainly evidence of foul play. But the murderer has obviously escaped, he says.

Later in the adventure when it is less cautious, the creature can choose to create an air bubble around the door, making it easy to open, and wait poised to flow forwards.

# The Climax

Below is a suggested outcome, which might work if the investigators play into your hands. If not, it should still give you some ideas.

They'll probably search the upper floor after the ground floor, a natural progression. There they should find more of the evidence of the lurking horror, and learn about its peculiar weakness, salt. When all the pieces are in place, a single investigator is quietly ambushed by a pseudopod of the creature. Hopefully the victim will not prevail against the thing, and mysteriously disappears, like Cornthwaite. Joe Virelli is an ideal first victim: "The last time I saw him, he was sitting near the fireplace, writing down notes.")

However, if a vigilant watch is kept, and the thing fails several ambush attempts, it becomes too ravenous for further caution. It constantly pops out at them from cracks, fireplaces, walls, water pipes, vents and so on, often in many places simultaneously. It is probably too much to handle unless they have prepared a major salt attack. Remember that the creature can have simultaneous access to the grounds and to every room of the house!

The investigators may flee rather than fight. If they head downstairs to escape, the scene is set for a truly horrible experience. Expecting downwards movement, the creature has flowed up and now fills the entire ground floor of the house to a height of 4-6 feet.

Investigators missing both their SAN roll and a DEX x5 roll helplessly tumble down the staircase in shock. Splash. The only way out is through the upstairs windows, after smashing open the shutters.

If they try to climb down slowly and carefully, it squeezes out through the ground floor windows and flows up the walls to meet them. The only way down now is to jump. If they made a **Climb** roll, they managed to get a bit closer to the ground, and falling damage is 1D6 (1D3 with a **Jump** roll). If not, they fall the full distance, taking 2D6 damage (1D6 with a successful **Jump**). Anyone smart enough to aim to land in a bush, and making a **DEX x5** roll for targeting, takes halved damage (1D3/1D2, or 1D6/1D3).

It will pursue them across the garden, but slime molds are pretty slow. Naturally no one believes the tale the survivors tell in town, and the cellar will be empty when they and the police return.

If they want to finish the thing off, they'll return very quietly and wait, hopefully with lots and lots and lots of salt close at hand. Eventually, the thing will relax its vigilance and become dormant in the cellar, to digest any victims it has taken — Virelli at least.

The best plan at this point is to suddenly back a dump truck of salt up to the wood cellar doors, blast the door between the wood cellar and the general cellar open, and dump the lot in. Even so there may be a bit of fight left in it.

When the final climactic confrontation takes place, when the investigators rain hails of stinging salt down on the creature, it thrashes and rages. As the titan shakes and surges, huge fissures are rent in the walls, roof tiles fly off, boards are showered outwards, shutters flap and bash wildly, furniture is slung through windows, glass shatters, timbers crack and list. Anyone in the area takes 1D8 damage from flying debris, halved if a **Dodge** roll is made.

If the monster is fatally injured, in its death throes it hurls rubble hundreds of feet into the air, burying any vehicles or slow-moving investigators, and finally the house and the creature collapse inwards as a spray of salt, steam and smoke blossoms outwards.

For locating and defeating the creature, each investigator gains 4D6 SAN. They are unlikely to get the promised fee though, as not only have they apparently blown up the mansion, they can't go to the lawyers and tell them that their client was eaten by a South American fungoid monster. The Dodge brothers will of course attempt to prosecute them with the full weight of the law for their inexcusable vandalism. Sheriff Whitford keeps out of it as much as he can, as he's secretly happy to see the place laid low. With a few shrewd **Law or Persuade** rolls, the investigators might be able to provide a feasible explanation (perhaps faulty gas pipes blew the place up).

By hook or by crook, the surviving player characters hopefully leave it all behind them. But some things never end. Down in South America, under the forgotten ruins, the original creature still lurks. And that spring in Gamwell, the bees find a strange new pollen in the wreckage of the crack'd and crook'd manse.

# Statistics

## WILL WHITFORD, county sheriff

| STR 14 | CON 12 | SIZ 15 | INT 13 | POW 09 |
|--------|--------|--------|--------|--------|
| DEX 11 | APP 12 | EDU 12 | SAN 30 | HP 14 |

**Damage Bonus:** +1D4

Weapons: Fist/Punch 70%, damage 1D3
.45 Revolver 50%, damage 1D10+2

**Skills:** Law 55%, Listen 60%, Sneak 55%, Spot Hidden 70%

## JOE VIRELLI, reporter

| STR 12 | CON 10 | SIZ 18 | INT 11 | POW 11 |
|--------|--------|--------|--------|--------|
| DEX 10 | APP 14 | EDU 14 | SAN 55 | HP 14 |

**Damage Bonus:** +1D4

**Weapons:** Rusty Axe 20%, damage 1D6

**Skills:** Fast Talk 25%, Listen 45%, Photography 20%, Spot Hidden 30%.

## THE CREATURE, an alien slime being

A nightmare pool of abhorrent corruption, a bubbling morass of translucent greenish gel in which swirl air pockets, sickly pus-like matter, and the bobbing, decomposing, boneless cadavers of its recent prey. Ghastly pink mouths and bloated black eye-like organs slowly form and dissolve out of the amorphous mass of the creature (see main illustration and cover painting). The mouths and eyes crudely mimic those of its related horror, Shub-Niggurath. The eyes see the world in an inhuman way, but have some small ability to recognize hidden prey or traps.

**Notes:** Two forms are given below, for the main body and for individual pseudopods. Pseudopods are used when the creature is trying to get at victims in the house, while the main body statistics apply when they are face-to-sludge with the thing's entire mass.

The beast once preyed primarily on small creatures like insects or rats, in which the amount of salt in the corpse was too small to affect it. Large animals like pets, horses, or humans are bad for its digestion, but have proved extraordinarily nourishing, as one can tell by its enormous size. The creature takes weeks to digest such prey, and retreats to a safe place once it has gained even a single such victim for its "larder".

To attack, it first uses its quick-moving pseudopods to locate warm, resting prey. The only warning to the sitter or sleeper is a soft gurgling as the creature slurps itself through cracks in the floor or wall. It first flows its pseudopods or body over a victim, grappling should the victim be active rather than asleep. Contact with the creature is not harmful for several minutes: its digestive acids aren't unusually powerful. But its attack is gruesome nonetheless.

In the first round of being engulfed, the victim must roll **CON x5** to hold his breath as it squirms all over his face. A **STR vs. STR** resistance roll is needed to break free. Investigators cannot combine STR (it's too slippery). It probes into the ears, eyes, nose, and mouth of the victim once it has a good grip. In subsequent rounds the roll is CON x4, then CON x3, etc.

Once the CON roll is missed, the victim weakens or relaxes for a moment, and the thing pulses down the throat and into the body, into which it violently and powerfully expands (much like a root's expansion, vastly accelerated), slowly crushing internal organs and bones, eventually leaving nothing but an oozing sack of skin and flesh ready to be absorbed. Death is slow and agonizing, until the victim goes unconscious due to lack of oxygen. Bones too strong to crush are excreted. The sight of a victim killed in this manner costs any witnesses a SAN roll, losing 1D6 SAN If the roll is failed. Once the prey is still, it pulls back out of the interior of the corpse, and immerses the food entirely in itself. Enzymes slowly go to work in breaking it down and extracting the harmful salt. Feeding takes weeks.

### THE CREATURE, Main Body

| STR 110 | CON 60 | SIZ 120 | INT 13 | POW 15 |
|---------|--------|---------|--------|--------|
| DEX 01 | | | | HP 90 |

**Damage Bonus:** not directly applicable due to the soft, fluid, boneless nature of the creature. However, it is strong: note its pseudopod Grapple attack below

**Move:** 3 (when moving outside, the creature may flatten itself out to a remarkable extent; from a distance it might appear to be only a pool of water. Maximum height without an enclosed area to fill is about 4 feet).

**Main Body Engulf Attack:** 75%, Dodge to avoid, suffocates if not avoided (note the *Call of Cthulhu* drowning rules if a victim is rolled over and smothered by the beast, or falls into its mass).

**Pseudopod Attack:** may form 1D6 pseudopods per round up to a maximum of 10; see below for pseudopod statistics. These may be extruded to a maximum length of 10 yards.

**Armor:** All weapons do minimum damage

The creature dislikes light, and avoids fire if possible. Fire does normal damage if brought into direct contact with the creature, but anything short of a flame-thrower will be quickly extinguished by the creature's moistness. A medium-sized torch would do about 1D6 for one or two rounds before it was damped out. However, lighting tires inside an old but valuable mansion is not the ideal solution here.

The creature is susceptible to salt and fears it. A line of salt may deter its movement. Below are damage results for varying quantities. When slinging salt at the thing from a distance, a **Throw** roll is needed, otherwise it only takes half rolled damage. Of course, a truckload cannot fail to hit, as long as it is set up effectively.

*Pinch:* 1 point
*Salt Shaker:* 1D4
*Handful:* 1D8
*12-Gauge Shotgun loaded with salt cartridges:* 2D6
*Shovelful:* 3D6
*Bucketful:* 6D6
*Truckload:* lethal within minutes

**Skills:** Sense Light and Warmth 95%, Sense Movement 80%, Spot Hidden 30%

**SAN cost:** 1D3/1D20

### Creature's Pseudopod

Description: A flexing, dripping, snaking coil of moist, dripping, darkly translucent gel, forming and reforming with loathsome plasticity.

| STR 18 | CON 20 | SIZ 08 | POW 11 |
|--------|--------|--------|--------|
| DEX 03 | Move 8 | | *HP 14 |

*subtract damage given to a pseudopod from the main body's hit points*

**Damage Bonus:** 1D4, *usable only for constricting and crushing*

**Weapons:** Pseudopod Engulf special (see above), must grapple successfully if victim is active. Suffocates and crushes from the inside out (see above), 1D6+1D4 damage per round plus drowning damage.
Grapple 50%, damage special

**Armor:** All weapons do minimum damage. Fire does normal damage; a medium-sized torch would do about 1D6. Highly susceptible to salt, see above.

**Skills:** Sense Light or Warmth 50%, Sense Movement 50%.

**SAN cost:** 0/1D6

THE END!

# The Sanatorium

*A few days visit with an old friend on an offshore island seems like the ideal way to relax, but not all vacations turn out as one would wish.*

This adventure is set on a small island off the coast of New England, the site of an exclusive sanatorium catering to the rich. The asylum was founded by Dr. Aldous Brewer, a brilliant medical doctor with a reputation for unorthodox theories about human psychology.

Dr. Brewer has invited the investigators to visit the island. There can be a number of reasons for this. If one of the investigators is a medical professional they could be a former classmate or colleague of Dr. Brewer. Possibly one or more of the investigators are journalists or free lance writers and have been invited here by the doctor to do a story on his work. Another possibility is that one of the investigators is simply a friend or relative of Dr. Brewer and has been invited for a vacation on the remote and beautiful island. The other investigators can be guests of the invited party.

*Dr. Tiller*

Although not essential, the skills of Hypnotism, Medicine, Pharmacy, Psychiatry, Psychoanalysis, and Psychology, and can be of some to considerable value in this scenario. If the keeper wishes, the investigators can be accompanied by an non-player-character psychoanalyst: Dr. Henry Tiller has excellent skills in these areas; his statistics appear at the end of this adventure.

## Investigator Information

Give the players the letter of invitation (*The Sanatorium Papers #1*). The investigators know Dr. Brewer has operated the North Island Sanatorium for seven years. Financially, the enterprise has done well. The facility's paying patients are from rich and well known families, most of them placed here in order to keep their ailments — and their sometimes embarrassing behavior — away from the prying eyes of the public and press. The large fees charged allows Brewer to take on several charity cases, on whom he's been testing experimental psychotherapies. The results of these experiments, some of them published in a recent professional journal, have brought him criticism.

One or more of the investigators may have read Brewer's article. Any character who is a medical professional may roll an **EDU x5**; others roll **EDU x1**. With a success, give the players *The Sanatorium Papers #2*, excerpts from Brewer's article. In the article, Brewer talks of the obscure but fascinating myth patterns that emerged from the subconscious of certain patients. Although supported by some, Brewer's article has also received scathing rebuttals.

Having packed for the five day visit, the investigators begin the adventure aboard a small motorboat piloted by Ebenezer Waite, bound for North Island. For it, see "Sailing for the Island" further below.

*Dear*

*So glad to hear you could accept my invitation to visit. I am looking forward to showing you the latest developments in my research.*

*I'm also anxious to bring you up to date on my experiments. There's been several more exciting developments since the publication of my article in the <Journal of the American Psychological Society> a few months back. I trust you've read it. There will be a few surprises, too - you can count on that.*

*My isolation is quite tolerable. The staff and I think of ourselves as a family. Old Ebenezer (you'll meet him on the ride over) is always ready to ferry one of us over to the mainland if we should feel the need to touch base with civilization. This summer we've been blessed with a regular dinner companion in the form of Mr. Shelly, a graduate student from Princeton. He is camped on the north beach of the island, conducting some sort of bird study. You'll find him witty and pleasant.*

*Looking forward to seeing you,*

*Dr. Aldous Brewer*

*The Sanitorium Papers #1–*
*Excerpts from a letter from Dr. Brewer*

## Keeper's Information

The player characters are sailing into a nightmare. Arriving at the island in darkness, Ebenezer points them up the cliff toward the warm lights of the sanatorium while he remains at the dock tying up the boat. The sanatorium looks inviting, but when the investigators knock on the door they are greeted not by the doctor, but by the inmates, one of whom immediately attacks the party. Inside they soon discover that most of the staff, including Dr. Brewer, have been horribly murdered and that all the inmates are roaming free. At the same time Ebenezer is murdered, and the boat, the only way off the island, set adrift and sunk. A homicidal maniac — the only surviving member of the sanatorium staff — roams the island with an axe, searching for sacrificial victims while an embryonic horror grows and plots in an abandoned lighthouse.

## What has Taken Place

Soon after opening North Island Sanatorium, Dr. Brewer began his personal studies in earnest. Several charity patients, culled from state homes and even jails, were brought to the facility and have undergone intensive treatments designed by Dr. Brewer. The mythic traces that have turned up under his therapy are connected with the Cthulhu Mythos, and Brewer eventually obtained an obscure tome, the *Castro Manuscript*, to aid him in his research. His published article revealed only a little of what he suspected. One of Brewer's charity patients, a poet named Allen Harding, was bedeviled by voices that talked to him and was also subject to horrible visitations in his dreams. This patient last night, under the instruction of the voices, used his own blood to construct a Gate on the wall of his cell. Through this Gate came one of the creatures that had been contacting Harding for so long. At the sight of this being, Harding's sanity snapped and he could only

# EXCERPTS FROM DR. BREWER'S ARTICLE

If we accept for a moment the theory that the collective unconsciousness is the source of all myth, we have to ask if it is not possible to consciously tap the source? Experiments with hypnosis, sometimes combined with powerful new drugs, have shown some evidence to support this.

Subject A showed little response to any treatments, but B was quite positive. Not only were unsuspected areas of knowledge revealed during these sessions but at times the subject demonstrated an entirely different personality. This personality, on the few occasions that it was observed to emerge, used archaic, almost biblical syntax, perhaps indicating that a true archetypal form may have been reached. This personality was very powerful and almost compelling, causing one to wonder if phenomena such as this is not the explanation for the possessions of the Middle Ages and, in more recent times, of the voodoo cultists in the Caribbean.

While never reaching the archetypal content of B, subject C was nonetheless of interest. Numerous personality types were brought to the surface, one claiming to have lived during the time of the Egyptian pharaohs. Surprisingly enough, the subject did display a fairly thorough knowledge of the history of that long dead civilization (though later research showed much of it to be pure flights of fancy).

All three showed a certain commonality of mythic form, although admittedly much was difficult to decipher. ☀

*The Sanitorium Papers #2*

# THERAPY

The word *therapy* in this scenario denotes the different treatments the sanatorium's patients receive.

This can take the form of Psychoanalysis or drugs, or a combination of the two. Psychoanalysis may or may not be augmented by hypnotism, a skill described nearby. If the investigators are to take advantage of the clues the inmates can provide, it will be necessary to determine the proper therapy for each patient. Investigators may first use **Psychology** to determine the patient's mental state (delusional, manic/depressive, suicidal, etc.) Sometimes these conditions are the result of a physical problem (senility, alcoholism) and this can be determined with an additional **Medicine or Psychiatry** roll. These facts can also be determined by studying the individual patient's records kept in Brewer's files. ☼

gape and babble as the being flowed and bubbled through the Gate into this world.

The creature emerged as a semi-solid being composed of luminescent bubbles. It wishes to reside on Earth for a short time, feed on the life forms it finds here and then, when it is ready to transform to its next stage of development, take its leave of the planet.

Although capable of feeding directly upon life forms, the creature is very sensitive to the elements of this planet. To hide from sunlight and salt air it prefers that a servant perform ritual sacrifices to it, allowing it to feed directly upon the life force Power of the dying victim. To this end, the creature has possessed a staff attendant named Charles Johnson, and now uses this pitiful wretch to hunt down and sacrifice the humans it desires.

The creature's intended servant, Harding, proved useless, his mind completely broken by the sight of his new god. When Johnson, a huge man possessed of great strength, entered the patient wing to investigate the strange noises he heard, the sight of the creature drove him mad and he became its slave.

Johnson committed the gruesome murders the investigators soon discover. After killing co-workers and nurses Bobby Birch and Catherine Ames, he went upstairs to overpower then sacrifice Dr. Brewer in the prescribed manner, to the satisfaction of the malevolent alien.

The creature had meanwhile crawled out of the basement, looking for a way out of the building. The maid, Melba, terrified and cringing in the laundry area, was accidentally touched by the passing creature. It casually sucked most of the life from her lower body before tearing down the back door and escaping into the night. Outside, the creature moved north to the abandoned lighthouse, a place where it sensed shelter. As it moved, it drew in the escaping life force of the

slowly sacrificed Dr. Brewer, glowing warmly as it fed. It now resides on the second floor of the abandoned lighthouse, awaiting its next meal.

Johnson, after murdering Brewer in his office, released all the patients from their rooms. Then, still wearing his blood spattered hospital whites, he fled the house, taking with him a wood axe stolen from the shed. Johnson now hides in the woods, waiting for darkness to come when, under the command of the monster, he will go forth in search of more victims.

## What Will Happen

The investigators probably soon discover that Ebenezer has been murdered and that the boat, their only way off the island, has been set adrift and scuttled. There is no radio on the island. The investigators are, for the time being, trapped. The Coast Guard eventually shows up, but not for several days.

The night of their arrival, Johnson sacrifices the young bird watcher, Shelly, who is camped on the northeast shore. The investigators probably hear the hoarse chants of the ritual and listen to the death screams of the victim. Johnson then turns his attention to the sanatorium, the only source of victims on the island. The inmates trust Johnson: if the investigators do not stop him, he begins luring them out or forcibly kidnaping them, sacrificing them to the alien creature. Given the opportunity, he attempts to capture an investigator and sacrifice him. He prefers killing strangers to his old charges.

Johnson should prove not too difficult to kill or capture, but then the real horror begins. Fearing the sunlight, but hungering to complete its form, the creature waits until dark before issuing forth from the lighthouse window. Making its way across the island, it devours whatever life forms it finds before surrounding the sanatorium, trapping whoever is inside.

Ways exist to destroy the creature. If it isn't stopped it continues to feed until satisfied, then begins changing into its new form. Survivors on the island will then be in danger of being killed by the violent transformation.

The keeper should use the frequency of the sacrifices to help pace the game; one or two a night should be all that Johnson can reasonably commit. The design intention is that the investigators spend at least three or four days on the island wrestling with the problems presented them before the climatic scenes take place.

## The Inmates

The staff are dead or missing; the inmates wander the sanatorium. Beyond sorting through the various clues and corpses, the investigators need to care for Dr. Brewer's charges. Records in Brewer's office describe the patients' conditions and the treatments prescribed.

Some inmates are dangerous, some are not. Some can provide help, while others need regular medication to keep them out of trouble. All of them, shocked by the violence that has taken place, tend to deny that anything is wrong. Dead people are "sleeping", or working somewhere, or visiting the mainland. Getting them to reveal anything about last night's events is difficult, requiring proper therapy. Besides being the only witnesses to the events that took place inside the building, one of the inmates, the young woman named Darlene, can reveal even deeper secrets. The inmates are a major source of information.

## Sailing for the Island

The investigators are ferried to North Island aboard a small motor launch piloted by Ebenezer Waite. Ebenezer is in his eighties and has spent nearly all his life in and around the sea. In his youth he traveled the globe and has seen many strange things (or so he says). He is semi retired now, the handyman for the sanatorium. He lives on the grounds.

If asked, Ebenezer has nothing but good things to say about Dr. Brewer, the staff, and the hospital. He is well paid and well treated and has no complaints.

Ebenezer hints about strange things he's seen while at sea or in foreign ports. Encouraged, he spins tall tales that start out like Mythos oriented stories but turn out to have uninteresting explanations. Mermaids who start out sounding like they might be deep ones turn out to be real mermaids; a long grueling trek through torturous jungle in search of a "fantastic temple, filled with gold and inhabited by a god" turns to be a simple trader's hut, located in the midst of primitives who believe the trader to be of divine origin. Ebenezer is long winded and easily talks his way through the entire two hour boat ride.

It should be noted that Ebenezer wears, underneath his many shirts, a small Elder Sign (carved from sea shell) suspended from a chain around his neck. Ebenezer knows nothing about its powers; it was a gift from an old sailor friend (see *The Sanatorium Papers #9*, found in Ebenezer's shack). The small charm is in no way noticeable and Ebenezer will not mention it.

## Arriving at the Island

Ebenezer maneuvers the boat up to the dock smoothly and flawlessly. Nimbly springing ashore, he ties the boat up fast enough to be able to help his passengers step up on the dock. It is near dusk and a light fog rolls in, as it does every night this time of the year. The shore rises steeply from the end of the dock and the sanatorium, lights warmly aglow, can be seen high above. From its vantage point atop the southern cliffs of the island, the huge house seems safe from sea and storm.

Ebenezer apologizes for not escorting the party, explaining the boat needs to be placed in the boat house. A flight of stone steps cut into the steep hill lead to the sanatorium. The stonework is recent and makes for a safe, though tiring, climb. Ebenezer offers to carry up the investigator's luggage later if they wish to leave it here for now.

## The Sanatorium

### The Front Door

A knock at the front door elicits a response from inmate Blanche Richmond. "Hold onto your horses, I'm comin', I'm comin'," she cries. As Blanche, gray hair standing out on end, opens the door, Leonard Hawkins,

# HYPNOSIS

The ability to hypnotize the inmates of North Island Sanatorium will be an asset to investigators. If the keeper wishes to allow the use of hypnotism by his investigators, check to see if they have this skill. Any character in the medical profession has a chance equal to EDU x5 of having a Hypnotism skill of 30+1D20. Other characters will have a chance of EDU x1 of having Hypnosis for 15+1+D20.

To successfully hypnotize someone, the target must be willing and the hypnotist must receive a successful Hypnosis roll.

Hypnosis is useful only against a single individual at a time. The target must be physically close to the hypnotist. If a Hypnosis roll fails, the hypnotist is never able to hypnotize that particular subject; if the initial Hypnosis roll succeeds, the hypnotist can hypnotize the particular target whenever the target agrees.

Hypnosis can be used in several ways.

**AS AN AID TO PSYCHOANALYSIS:** if an investigator has 10 or more percentiles of Psychoanalysis, and can first hypnotize a subject, add 25 percentiles to his or her Psychoanalysis skill when treating that patient thereafter.

**AS A POST-HYPNOTIC SUGGESTION:** causes the target to perform a single particular action without apparent volition. The target will not accept a suggestion contrary to his or her normal behavior and desires.

**AS AN AID TO MEMORY:** fragmented or buried memories can sometimes be dredged up through hypnosis. Someone who went temporarily insane from the sight of something moving at the bottom of a dark well will probably not remember what he saw. Hypnosis can bring these memories to light but also (in cases where Sanity was lost) cost the individual additional SAN through reliving the incident.

**TO ALLEVIATE:** hypnosis can ease or temporarily erase the symptom of pain in a patient, but the pain itself makes the target more difficult to hypnotize: require a **POW vs POW** resistance roll as well as a skill roll for success in this case. ☀

# THE PATIENTS

**B**rewer's charges reside on two floors of the sanatorium. The paying patients reside in the ground floor patient wing in comfortable rooms. These patients are of normal behavior, but they suffer from diagnosable disorders. The basement houses the special patients — indigents or hopeless cases on which Brewer tried experimental therapies.

The patients may be played as the keeper sees fit. Anytime the keeper needs more action or complications, an inmate might attempt to flee the sanatorium, attack an investigator or fellow inmate, or even attempt suicide, as befits their individual descriptions.

## Normal Patients

These are housed on the first floor and all are from prominent, moneyed families. If properly treated, these patients usually pose no problem but do require care. If neglected at all, they are quick to let their displeasure be known. As to be expected, most have low SAN. If they actually see the creature, they may be driven mad.

### Blanche Goddard Richmond, pedicide

Blanche is in her early sixties and about five feet tall. Her hair is gray and frizzed, standing out from her head in all directions. She always dresses in a shapeless, faded print shift. Blanche is talkative and friendly. She has rarely caused problems at the sanatorium and for years has been given free run of the house and grounds during the day. If locked up for any length of time she grows angry and vocal, then very quiet.

Blanche is quite paranoid and she may, for no apparent reason, begin to think the investigators are her enemy. She may lie to them or even attempt to kill them. She talks incessantly about her three grown children (two sons and a daughter) and accuses them of "keeping her locked up in here just so they get their greedy hands on my money". In truth, as Blanche's records show, she murdered all three of them on Christmas Eve, 1922.

Found legally insane, she was remanded to the care of Dr. Brewer. Her bills are paid by a trust fund set up by the family's attorneys.

Blanche knows the hospital routine. If she chooses to help the investigators she is

capable of cooking, organizing cleaning crews and, in general, taking care of a lot of chores that would otherwise present additional problems for the investigators. If, however, she feels that the investigators don't listen to her, or treat her improperly, she withdraws to her room and sulks, refusing to help. If left untreated she becomes paranoid and begins to believe the investigators are her adult children in disguise, come to kill her. She will seek to reenact the terrible murders she committed several years ago. Blanche, who has never given Brewer the least cause for worry, is allowed to keep keys to the cabinets and closets that contain cooking and cleaning supplies, including the knives.

Blanche also knows the combination to Dr. Brewer's safe but will not reveal this unless pressed by the most dire of circumstances, or while under the effects of therapy.

**Psychology:** she subconsciously denies the deaths of the staff, and is harboring some darker secret of her past.

**Psychoanalysis:** Blanche witnessed neither the monster or the murders. The first successful treatment with **Psychoanalysis** only makes her realize the staff is dead, not sleeping. Further **Psychoanalysis** brings out the truth about her children's deaths.

*Mrs. Richmond*

*Colonel Billings*

This skill can be used to talk her out of her murderous sulks.

**Physical Condition:** Blanche is healthy as a horse.

### Henry Adam Barber III, heir and sociopath

Henry, 28 years old and heir to the Barber Paper Company fortune, grew to be such a

problem for his father that the elder Barber was forced to have his son committed to Brewer's care. Henry is a manic/depressive transvestite with suicidal tendencies. If this is not enough, Henry exhibits a whole raft of antisocial tendencies. On rare occasions he can be concerned and caring but most of the time he is tightly wrapped up in his own problems and treats everyone as though they were dirt under his feet. He is not, however, dangerous to anyone but himself. If he should lose too much SAN he attempts suicide; either by throwing himself off a cliff or by feeding himself to the creature.

*Mr. Barber III*

**Psychology:** Barber is a manic/depressive with suicidal tendencies.

**Psychoanalysis:** makes him realize the staff has been murdered. It can also be used to bring him out of a suicidal state of mind.

**Physical Condition:** Other than being underweight from bad eating habits, Barber seems healthy.

**Medicine, Pharmacy, Psychiatry, etc.:** mild sedatives are of value but, if he is in a suicidal state, they must be administered every four hours.

### Colonel Crandall Billings, old warhorse

Colonel Billings is 92 and a veteran of the Civil War. The Colonel suffers from advanced senility and has been placed here by his grandchildren. He is not really treatable and in his case the sanatorium provides care similar to that of a nursing home. Colonel Billings poses no problem but must be spoon fed his meals, etc. He can barely walk and, mostly wheelchair bound, almost never leaves his room. He is so senile that seeing the creature has no effect on his SAN.

On occasion the colonel relives Bull Run and comes charging down the hallway in his wheelchair, brandishing a non existent saber and screaming "Death to the rebels!"

**Psychology:** no deep trauma.

**Psychoanalysis:** is of no use.

*(continued on next page)*

**Medical Diagnosis:** the old man suffers from advanced senility. There is no treatment for his condition other than keeping him clean and fed.

### Mrs. Cecil (Carla) Randolph, wealthy socialite

Mrs. Randolph is the 48-year old wife of a well known newspaper tycoon. A long time alcoholic, she suffers from intense hallucinations and is usually kept sedated. If her medication is not administered at the proper times she hallucinates and screams that horrible monsters are crawling around the room, are flying past the windows, are living under the floorboards. After a couple of these episodes the investigators may disbelieve her even if she actually sees the creature.

**Psychology:** she suffers from intense hallucinations brought on by severe paranoia.

**Psychoanalysis:** although of some value, when the session is over she quickly reverts to her normal, hallucinatory state.

**Medicine, Psychiatry:** a victim of severe alcoholism.

**Medicine, Pharmacy, Psychiatry:** needs regular mild sedation, administered every four hours.

## The Special Patients

These patients are the grist for Dr. Brewer's controversial researches. They have been gathered from various state institutions and, in one case, a local jail. Ostensibly they demonstrate Dr. Brewer's charitable side but, as noted, they have also been guinea pigs upon which he could experiment freely. All three suffer from Mythos based delusions and possess definite psychotic tendencies.

### Allen Harding, possessed poet

Harding is a poet, an alcoholic, and a drug abuser. It is this man that has provided Brewer with his most significant findings and the man who opened the Gate. Harding was discovered by Brewer in 1923 and has provided much of the impetus for Brewer's present research. Harding suffers from intense dreams of horrifying aspect and hears

*Mr. Harding*

voices in his head. On several occasions, while actively undergoing therapy, Harding has seemed possessed, taking on odd mannerisms and speaking in a voice distinctly unlike his own. He has also demonstrated violent tendencies while in this state. Harding is completely insane by the time the scenario begins and remains this way.

**Psychology:** Harding is hopelessly deranged.

*Mrs. Cecil Randolph*          *Darlene*

**Psychoanalysis:** although this patient is insane, the skill may be attempted once per day. Each success provides the investigators with one cryptic clue, as follows:

*#1 "1 didn't let it in! I wouldn't do it! I called it, and I made the door but when I saw it I couldn't stand to help it anymore. The other one's helping it now! It's all his fault! Now we'll all die!"*

*#2 "He doesn't want to stay here but he has to feed before he can leave. He wants you, and you, and you, and me!"*

*#3 (if Johnson has been killed) "You think you've stopped him but you're wrong! Now it will be worse worse for all of us!"*

*#4 "He's coming! He's coming!"*

The keeper should use these lines as he sees fit, following the development of the adventure. Feel free to invent clues or attempt answers to Mythos questions using Harding's 22% Cthulhu Mythos skill.

While undergoing **Psychoanalysis** therapy there is a 40% chance Harding will be possessed by the mind of the alien being. It then speaks directly to the investigators, threatening them with certain destruc-

tion, and boasting of its deathless strength. Before leaving Harding's body it demonstrates its power by destroying Harding before the investigators' eyes. The mad poet's skin bubbles and scorches while his abdomen swells. Internal organs, swollen and blackened, burst forth from Harding's body in a shower of gore and blood. Anyone witnessing this loses 2/1D6+1 SAN.

**Medicine or Psychiatry:** Harding suffers from debilitating drug and alcohol use.

**Medicine, Pharmacy, or Psychiatry:** only the strongest of sedatives are effective. When administering these drugs, a succesful **Medicine, Pharmacy, or Psychiatry** roll must be made to avoid accidentally overdosing the patient. Failure could result in the death of the patient, as the keeper wishes.

### Darlene, woman with many pasts

Darlene is an indigent taken off the streets of New York. Her last name is unknown. She appears to be in her late twenties and is reasonably pretty. She actually witnessed the coming of the creature but her mind has blocked the memory. Darlene speaks rarely. Under proper therapy she reveals evidence of having lived former lives. A supposed Egyptian princess is the most interesting of the bunch. This personality (the Princess Annephis) has faced things like the creature before and knows how to defeat it. For further details, see "Contacting Princess Annephis".

**Psychology:** suffers from deep, perhaps irreversible, amnesia.

**Psychoanalysis:** admits the staff is dead and allows her to reveal what she saw in the basement. Treated with the proper drugs, or successfully **Hypnotized**, she regresses through her former personalities, and eventually the Egyptian princess, Annephis, can be reached. The proper drugs, and dosages, can be learned by studying Brewer's notes.

**Medicine:** she's quite healthy.

### Leonard Hawkins, prophet of doom

A former accountant who, after suffering a head injury, began experiencing messianic delusions. He soon lost his job, then his family. On the street, he was eventually arrested for assaulting a police officer and jailed. His wife committed Hawkins to the care of Dr. Brewer. Since then, while experiencing intense psychotic episodes, he has several times threatened to kill his

*Mr. Hawkins*

estranged wife. Leonard is the most violent of all the inmates. Female investigators especially draw his hostility.

He saw the creature as it crept past his cell, an event which has further unhinged his mind. He may turn violent at any time (at least every time he misses a SAN roll) and upon reaching 0 SAN remains dangerous permanently.

**Psychology:** suffers from messianic delusions and is paranoid to the point of violence; his misogyny is readily evident.

**Psychoanalysis:** brings him to understand what has gone on, so that he can reveal what he witnessed from his cell in the basement.

Although this skill can staunch Hawkins' violent tendencies, he reverts to his normal state of mind 2D4 hours after treatment.

**Medicine:** Hawkins' suffers from a weak heart, probably the result of persistent stress. His old head injury also is evident.

**Medicine, Pharmacy:** mild sedatives, administered every four hours, help quell his violent tendencies. ☀

who has been lurking around the north corner of the building, comes running full bore and attempts to **Grapple** one of the investigators — a female if possible. Leonard is a pitiful fighter and if he should succeed in the Grapple, he does no damage before the startled investigators subdue him. If any of the investigators make a successful **Listen** roll, they hear Leonard coming and can take some kind of action against him. Any aggressive act by the investigators stops Leonard in his tracks. If the roll fails, Leonard is not noticed until the last instant and there is little chance of stopping him from tackling one of the party.

Leonard should be easily subdued and Blanche will scold him severely before formally welcoming the group to the house. "Dr. Brewer's taking a nap upstairs. I'm in charge right now," she explains. "You can wait in there." She points to the library, then marches Leonard off toward the patient wing. At the door leading to the patient wing she turns and says: "Please stay out of the living room. I'm afraid we've had a little accident in there." If no one moves to stop her, Blanche then disappears, with Leonard, into the patient wing, shutting the doors behind her.

## The Ground Floor

**The Foyer:** beautifully tiled with a chandelier suspended from the second floor ceiling. Two sweeping staircases wind sinuously up to the second floor in best Federalist style. The walls throughout the house are decorated with high set plaster friezes displaying garlands, festoons, and medallions. The high ceilings and broad mantels are similarly ornamented.

**Dining Room:** formal, with a long table and enough chairs to seat twelve.

**The Kitchen:** facilities large enough to cook for more than a dozen people. All utensils are kept in a locked wooden cabinet (remember, Blanche has a key).

**The Pantry:** lots and lots of food.

**The Library:** numerous books line the walls and it is comfortably furnished. On a couch sits Darlene, engrossed in an illustrated version of Dante's Inferno. If spoken to, she curtly replies: "Shhhh! We're in the library," and refuses to say any more.

**The Living Room:** more nice furnishings. The investigators immediately notice that objects have been knocked from tables. Extending from behind a couch are two white-stockinged legs, toes turned down.

The legs belong to Catherine Ames, whose body lies face-down on the floor. A large puddle of coagulating blood stains the carpet in the area around her head, but the cause of her death is not immediately evident. Only after she is rolled over do the investigators see the shiny scissors handle protruding from her left eye socket. Lose 1/1D3 SAN.

## The First Floor Patient Wing

**Storage:** this is a large walk in closet storing blankets, linens, paper goods, etc.

**Desk Area:** this is a wooden desk and chair used by patients and staff alike. Presently it is occupied by the corpse of Bobby, the male nurse. The body slumps in the chair and the head is twisted around to face backward. It hangs down at an awkward angle. No skill roll is required to recognize a broken neck. Lose 0/1D3 SAN.

**Deep Sink:** cleaning supplies, mops, etc. Located between the Desk and Henry Barber's room. Attached to the inside of the door is a work schedule. All capable patients are expected to pitch in with cleaning and cooking chores.

**Patient Rooms:** these are spacious and comfortable. Each is equipped with its own toilet, sink, and bathtub. Most of the inmates brought their own furnishings, sometimes including works of art, as well as their own clothing. Although allowed the run of the house during

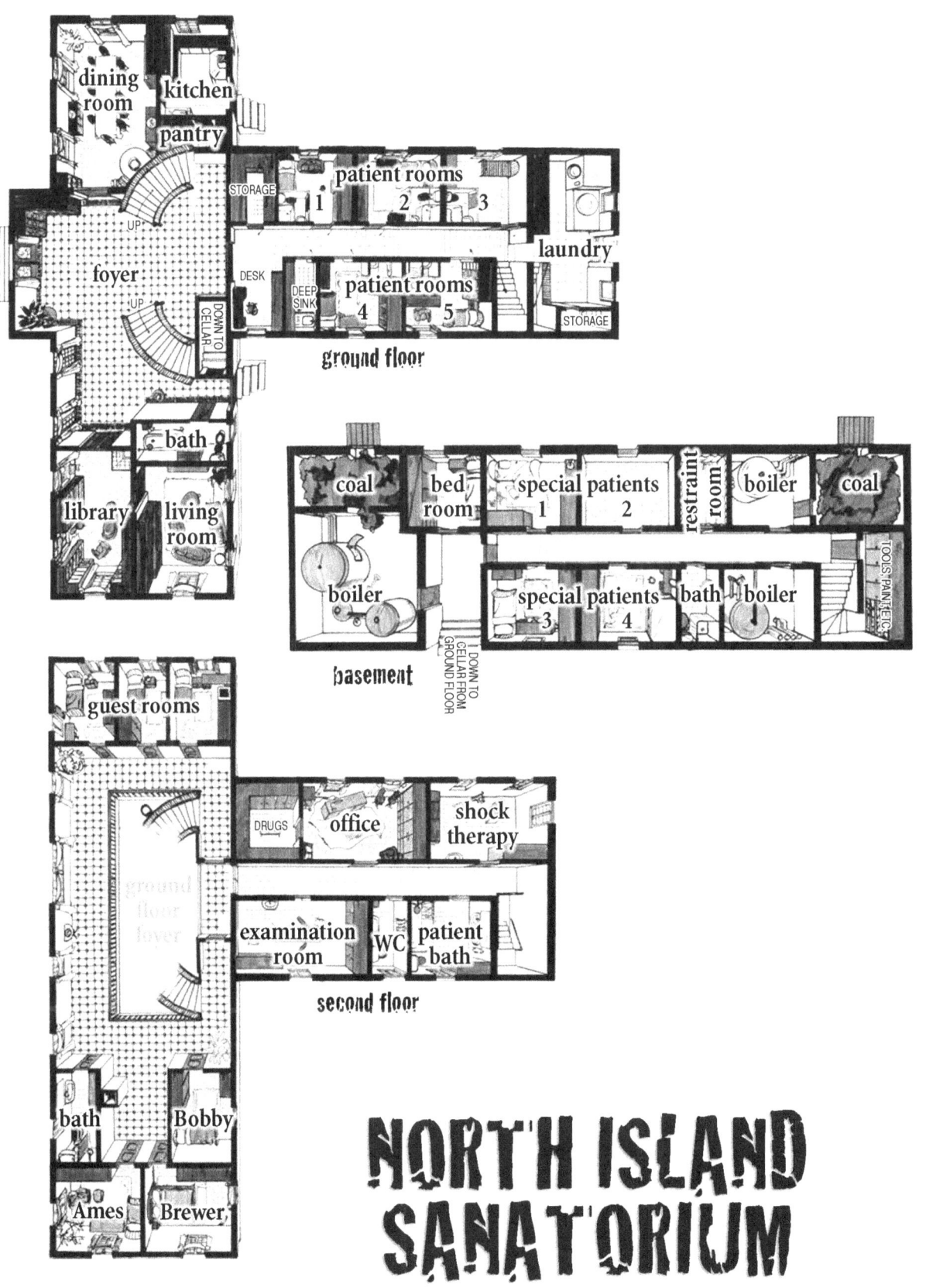

dining room

kitchen

pantry

STORAGE

patient rooms

1  2  3

DESK

laundry

foyer

UP

UP

DEEP SINK

patient rooms

4  5

DOWN TO CELLAR

STORAGE

ground floor

bath

library

living room

coal

bed room

special patients

1  2

restraint room

boiler

coal

boiler

special patients

3  4

bath

boiler

TOOLS, PAINT, ETC.

basement

DOWN TO CELLAR FROM GROUND FLOOR

guest rooms

ground floor foyer

DRUGS

office

shock therapy

examination room

WC

patient bath

second floor

bath

Bobby

Ames

Brewer

# NORTH ISLAND SANATORIUM

the day, the patients were usually locked in their rooms at around 10 PM. The rooms are sealed by heavy doors (STR 22) with large wire-reinforced windows. Each room has a window overlooking the grounds, strengthened by heavy bars (STR 40). If the patients should require something during the night, there are buttons in each of the rooms that will ring a bell in the basement bedroom of attendant Johnson, as well as in Dr. Brewer's bedroom upstairs.

**#1** This is Blanche's room.

**#2** The residence of Colonel Crandall Billings. Mr. Billings rarely, if ever, leaves his room and is here now.

**#3** Vacant.

**#4** This room belongs to Henry Barber. He's presently taking a nap on his bed.

**#5** Mrs. Randolph. She is sitting in an armchair by the window staring out across the sanatorium grounds. Upon seeing the investigators she leaps up and begins babbling to them about bat like creatures flying by her window. She is past due for her medications. She becomes hysterical if not attended to soon.

The doors closing off the patient wing to the foyer and the laundry facilities are of heavy construction and set with strong locks (STR 20). The door closing off the stairs leading to the second floor is of similar design. When the investigators arrive they find the door between the patient wing and the laundry area locked.

**The Laundry:** this room contains a large commercial washer and dryer and a locked storage cabinet (STR 12) containing strait jackets, canvas restraints, and other equipment. The rear door has been blown off its hinges and lies buckled on the ground outside.

Sitting on the floor, propped up against the big washer, is Melba the maid. Her eyes stare blankly, mouth frozen wide-open. Her upper body seems healthy but her feet and legs are withered brown sticks — dried dead limbs split open like old and rotting leather to expose the bones within. There is little or no blood from her injuries, the vessels cauterized shut by the burning action of the creature's attack. Anyone seeing this unprepared for the sight loses 1/1D4+1 points of SAN or, if forewarned, 1/1D2 points. Melba was accidentally injured by the creature as it fled the sanatorium into the night. She will die before morning without uttering a word. If a **Psychoanalysis** roll succeeds, Melba screams incoherently about "It! It!" then dies of cardiac arrest.

Close inspection and **Spot Hidden** rolls reveal a faint trail of scorch marks on the doorway, floor, and stairs, left by the passing of the monster. If the investigators move outside, the grounds and the whole island are discussed a little later.

## The Basement

This floor contains large boilers, storage areas, patient cells, the facilities to care for Dr. Brewer's special patients, and the unoccupied bedroom of the now insane attendant, Charles Johnson.

**The Patient Rooms:** these rooms are not quite as nice as the ones upstairs (they do not have private toilet facilities for one thing) but they are still more than adequate and far better than any state institution.

**#1** The room of Allen Harding, failed poet and madman. Harding was the one who, instructed by his dream voices, made the Gate that opened the way for the creature (and in the process lost his mind). After the creature passed through into this world, Harding defaced much of the Gate, clawing his fingertips to the bone in a frantic effort to close the way. He presently huddles in the corner, streaked with blood from his injured hands as well as from the earlier blood-letting used to construct the Gate. He has lost 4 hit points and needs medical attention. Infection will soon set in.

There are clues in the room. Minute scorch marks made by the creature might be found with **Spot Hidden** rolls. A successful **Cthulhu Mythos or Occult** identifies the remains of the bloody symbol on the wall as some type of Gate. If an investigator has had experience with Gates, he automatically recognizes it.

**#2** This room is vacant.

**#3** The room of Leonard Hawkins. Hawkins, watching from his own cell, witnessed the creature when it appeared in the Gate and watched in terror as it crawled through into this world. After Johnson freed all the inmates, Hawkins escaped out the back door of the sanatorium. He did not roam far but stayed near the grounds until the investigators arrived.

**#4** Darlene's room. From this spot she could not witness the construction of the Gate but she did see the creature when it crawled past her door.

**Restraint Room:** a padded cell for extreme problem patients. There are cobwebs in this room.

**Charles Johnson's Bedroom:** there are no clues here other than Johnson's large-sized clothes and his personal items. This may be the investigators' first hint of Johnson's existence.

## The Second Floor

This floor contains the bedrooms of most of the staff as well as Dr. Brewer's office and examination and treatment rooms.

**Guest Rooms:** these three rooms were intended for the visiting investigators. They have been freshly dusted and the linens changed. Welcome to North Island.

*Dear Editor,*

*In response to the letter from Drs. Hagen and Allen that appeared in your June issue I must say that I would have expected better from two so highly regarded in our profession. Disagreement I take no exception to; my work is highly experimental and any results, as I specified clearly in my article, are, at this time, purely speculative in nature. I make no claims but only observations.*

*Since the time that article was written I have conducted further experiments that seem to uphold my earlier observations. However, I will not again go to print until I have proof positive; proof that will convince even the most fossilized of skeptics. I would not lower myself to*

*The Sanitorium Papers #3–An Unfinished Letter atop Brewer's Desk*

**Nurse Catherine Ames' Bedroom:** there is little of interest here.

**Nurse Bobby Birch's Bedroom:** nothing to be found here.

**Dr. Brewer's Bedroom:** there is nothing of obvious interest but taped under the bottom of the top dresser drawer is a slip of paper with the numbers "32 46 21", the combination of the safe in Brewer's office. Also, with a properly directed **Spot Hidden** roll, the investigators might find a pair of womens' panties crumpled up under the bed. They are the same size as those worn by Nurse Ames.

**Dr. Brewer's Office:** this room contains the mutilated corpse of Dr. Brewer, sacrificed by the attendant, Johnson, to feed the hunger of the creature. The furniture has been pushed back against the walls and Dr. Brewer apparently staked out on the floor hand and foot. An unidentifiable cryptic symbol is painted on his

forehead and it appears his arms and legs were removed one by one with the bloody bone saw now lying on the floor. The doctor has also been disemboweled and a huge pool of blood soaks the expensive oriental rug on the floor. Lose 1/1D6 points of SAN.

Atop Brewer's desk is an unfinished letter, addressed to the editor of the Journal of the American Psychological Society, the magazine that recently published his article (see **The Sanatorium Papers #3**). If the desk is pulled away from the wall and the drawers checked the investigators find Brewer's personal journal in which he reveals his innermost fears and mentions the Mythos tome kept locked in the safe (see **The Sanatorium Papers #4**). In the other drawers can be found a full set of keys for the sanatorium and a loaded .38 revolver with a box of fifty bullets.

There are quite a few books on the shelves. Many are professional works and none bear on the adventure. Investigators who take time to look (and make an **Idea** roll) note a preponderance of volumes dealing with ancient Egypt. None of the books contain any clues themselves but if they are perused, a newspaper clipping will be found. See **The Sanatorium Papers #8**. Among the rest of the books might be found (with a **Spot Hidden**) a slim volume of Allen Harding's poetry. Reading this

# EXCERPTS FROM BREWER'S JOURNAL

If those asses, Hagen and Allen, could hear what I've heard I'm sure it would shake them loose form their high perches. I don't know yet what I'm on to but the sheer power of H's voice while under the effect of that personality is astounding. Jameson in London has found a book — an old one — that he says contains references similar to many of the things mentioned by both H and D. He promises to send it along following his last letter. It is supposed to be a copy of a transcription made by a 15th-century Spanish monk. It contains the ravings of a madman condemned to death by the Inquisition.

The book arrived yesterday and I spent some time with it. Most of it was incomprehensible, seeming nonsense, but Jameson was right. Those pages he was kind enough to mark seemed definitely linked to many of the things referred to by H and D, and, on occasion, Hw as well. Reading those select pages gave me an eerie chill. It was if I was hearing H's voice all over again — a thing that never fails to leave me affected. ❁

*The Sanitorium Papers #4*

## EXCERPTS FROM DARLENE'S FILES

She was initially brought to the state home by the police who had found her wandering naked in a downtown Boston alley. Repeated attempts over the years have failed to identify her and her last name is still unknown. She is now probably in her late twenties.

Traditional therapies seemed incapable of reaching her but under hypnosis, or the influence of the compounded drugs listed below, she seemed to open up. Repeated treatments brought forth what was at first thought to be Darlene but, under questioning, the individual claimed to be a woman named Fanny and said she lived in Ireland. Oddly enough she also claimed that the year was 1862.

Over the course of treatments even more personalities emerged and, at last count, the list numbered twenty seven; although some of these have appeared only once and were never reached again. The oldest, and perhaps most interesting personality is Annephis who is, if she's to be believed, a princess of Egypt who has been dead for over 3000 years. When in this personality Darlene has exhibited a startling knowledge of Egyptian history, including a number of facts that I have been unable to verify by any amount of research. Perhaps most mystifying was Darlene's prediction of the finding of King Tutankhamen's tomb. She made this prediction after reading in the newspaper the expedition's plans to explore the area.

Much of the odd mythology that Annephis speaks of brings to mind the possessions experienced by the patient Harding and seems hinted at in the occasional ravings of Hawkins. This possibly indicates a root mythic form common to all men and would go a long way toward supporting the theory of the collective unconscious mind.

*The Sanatorium Papers #5a*

## EXCERPTS FROM ALLEN HARDING'S FILE

About the time of publication of his first and only book of poetry, Harding dropped out of sight and his whereabouts for the next six months were never established. It is thought that most of this time he spent in a drug and alcohol induced stupor, this being the condition he was found in.

The deteriorated condition of Harding's mind seems to make drug therapy unnecessary, if not useless. He is, however, quite susceptible to hypnosis. He has not revealed the multiple personalities of Darlene but reverts always to the same one. This personality speaks in a deep, intelligent voice; very commanding and quite unlike Harding's own. Sometimes the personality does not speak but the changed face and expression of the subject belie its presence. It almost seems to be observing, contemplating. When finally induced to speak it will usually prefer to not answer any questions but simply makes statements. These statements are usually of the darkest sort, pre-

dictions of doom, and the coming of He Who Waits.

*The Sanatorium Papers #5b*

## EXCERPTS FROM LEONARD HAWKIN'S FILE

Leading a fairly normal and secure life until the sudden breakdown. Hawkins was unconscious for more than a week and upon awakening displayed signs of intense paranoia. He was unable to recognize even his wife for the first few days, although most of his memory seems to have returned over the next two months.

Not long after returning to his job (an accountant with a major firm) he began displaying signs of a religious conversion and before long joined an obscure sect of ultra conservative Baptists. His wife and children were, against their wishes, also compelled to join. Not long after, he was reprimanded by his supervisor; his continued proselytizing on the job was beginning to irritate the other employees. Two weeks later Hawkins quit his church, accusing them of stupidity, and began to preach on the streets. His family was completely alienated and soon after he lost his job. He moved out of the house and several months later was arrested for assaulting several palice officers.

A hatred of his wife, ostensibly stemming from her committing him to North Island, with overt violent tendencies. He will not talk about the source of his knowledge of the "coming of those who wait" but continues to preach his faith in his vision. ※

*The Sanatorium Papers #5c*

---

book costs an investigator 1D3 SAN and adds 3 points to his Cthulhu Mythos score. There are also a large number of issues of the Journal of the American Psychological Society including several copies of the

## EXCERPTS FROM THE PERSONNEL RECORD OF CHARLES JOHNSON

*Dear Dr. Brewer,*

*I can recommend Mr. Johnson whole heartedly. His work at this institution has been exemplary and I'm sure you would find him more than satisfactory. Perhaps his own years spent in an institution developed within him a special sympathy. I have seen him handle even the most violent patients always in a way to minimize injury. Of course, I needn't mention that his size and strength also stand in his favor.* ※

*The Sanitorium Papers #6*

issue containing Dr. Brewer's article. See **The Sanatorium Papers #2.**

A four drawer filing cabinet stands in the corner. In the cabinet can be found the patient records as well as those of the employees. The records are very complete and filled with notes from the patient's sessions. It takes at least three hours to read each patient's file and requires a roll of **INT x5** or less to understand Brewer's scribbled shorthand notes. Medical professionals understand them without a roll. The records of the normal patients tell the investigators very little except to provide them with some background on these non-player characters and, in Mrs. Randolph's case, and to inform the investigators she requires regular doses of sedatives. Those files of the special patients reveal information pertaining directly to the adventure. See **The Sanatorium Papers #5a, 5b, and 5c.**

The employee records represent the staff as competent and professional. An **Accounting** roll shows them to be well paid and the books well kept. Checking the employee records reveal the existence of Charles

# A MARKED PAGE IN THE CASTRO MANUSCRIPT

And it was said when "Those Who Wait" came unto the land of pharaoh they laid waste to the country and were not stopped until faced and destroyed by the priestess Annephis of the Temple of Bast. They moved by night, fearing Ra, and shunned also the rushing water. And the stones were made by her and they, carried by the priest, drove the creatures into the Nile which took them to the sea and there they were destroyed. Annephis died of her injuries and, so it is said, died the secret of the stones. She was buried in a tomb in a place which has yet to be discovered. ☀

*The Sanitorium Papers #7*

Johnson. His file may be of particular interest to them. See *The Sanatorium Papers #6*.

There is also a safe in the corner, locked and probably unopenable (unless the investigators are exceptionally creative). The combination to this safe is found on a piece of paper taped to the bottom of a dresser drawer in Brewer's bedroom. The safe contains legal papers, contracts, investment bonds, and a copy of the *Castro Manuscript*. See *The Sanatorium Papers #7*.

**Drugs:** always locked (STR 18) this room contains drugs, hypodermics, etc.

**Exam Room:** a small surgery with table, scale, etc.

**Shock Therapy:** state of the art equipment renders this technique safe and reliable.

## The Grounds

**Dead Cat:** this is Cicero, a pet of the sanatorium. He was begging to be let in when the creature blew the door off and engulfed the unfortunate feline. His tanned and desiccated body, most of the fur scorched off it, weighs less than two ounces and easily crumbles apart in the hands. A closer inspection of this area might reveal a large number of dead, dried insects and within a couple of days all plant life touched by the creature blackens and withers, clearly showing the path the creature took to the lighthouse.

**Melba's Quarters:** where Melba lived. There is nothing of interest here.

## ANCIENT TEMPLE RUINS FOUND

CAIRO — An unusual archaeological find was reported today by the privately funded Huntsford expedition. Operating some twenty miles west of the Valley of the Kings the expedition has uncovered the ruins of a temple and several colossal statues. It is suspected that this find may answer a number of questions about Egyptian history.

One of the first pieces uncovered was a broken stela originally raised in honor of a Princess Annephis. Unknown until now, Annephis, around 1400 BC, was apparently responsible for the routing of an enemy that then threatened the Egyptian people. The enemy is not identified on the stela but it is speculated that perhaps they were Hyksos raiders or perhaps even the mysterious Sea Peoples mentioned in other records.

Work at the site is expected to continue for at least another two years, or longer.

*The Sanatorium Papers #8—A Newspaper Clipping Found in Brewer's Office*

**Ebenezer's Cabin:** similar to the maid's but smelling of old sweat and tobacco. A tin box contains a dozen or so letters from friends and family. All the letters are old and most useless. One, however, dated some thirty years ago, might be of interest. See *The Sanatorium Papers #9*).

**Maintenance Shed:** lots of tools and equipment to keep the place running. Additionally, twenty-two five gallon cans of gasoline are stored here to supply the generators.

**Generator Shed:** a large gasoline powered generator supplies electricity to the sanatorium, providing light and running water. The generator is due to run out of fuel and will shut down at about 1 AM the first morning after the investigators arrive. It needs to be fueled and restarted. This requires an **Electrical Repair, a Mechanical Repair, or an EDU x1** roll to successfully restart the unit.

**The Trees:** if the creature surrounds the building, an investigator can attempt to leap from an upstairs window to one of these oaks in order to get past the thing. A successful **Jump** roll is required. Failure results in 2D6 damage plus the possibility of falling on top of the creature.

**The Cliffs:** sheer and high. The perfect place for a suicide.

**The Dock:** this is where the investigators arrived. Unknown to them, Charles Johnson watched them from behind some nearby rocks. As soon as the investigators entered the sanatorium and were out of sight, Johnson crept out and bashed in old Ebenezer's head. He left the body lying on the dock, dripping blood

## THE CASTRO MANUSCRIPT

This book is thought to have been written by a 15th century Spanish monk (name unknown) and is the transcript of the ravings of a madman (Castro) condemned to death by the Inquisition. Castro was thought to have been possessed by the demons but was in fact a victim of multiple personality disorders and amnesia, much the same as the patient, Darlene. Much of the book is incoherent but a page has been marked by Dr. Brewer. This page can be read without incurring a SAN loss but if the whole book is read (it has been translated to English from the Latin) it adds 5% to the investigator's Cthulhu Mythos knowledge and costs 1D6 points of SAN. Within its pages are the instructions for constructing an Elder Sign (6 hours plus INT x2 to learn). ☀

# SANATORIUM GROUNDS

mansion—
dock—
Melba's quarters—
Ebenezer's cabin—
dead cat
outhouse
maintenance shed
generator shed
cliff edge

into the water, while he untied the boat and opened the bilges. If the investigators return to the dock they will discover the old sailor's body (lose 1/1D2 SAN) and see the boat awash a couple hundred feet off shore. If the investigators left their belongings aboard, they can probably wave them goodbye.

If the investigators left a guard at the dock, Johnson sneaks up and attacks this character first. Once the investigator is down, Johnson turns his attention to Ebenezer. Although Ebenezer probably dies from his wounds, the lucky investigator suffers only knock-out damage.

## The Rest of the Island

North Island is quite small, hardly more than a mile in length and about a half mile across. The southern and southeastern boundaries of the island are guarded by sheer cliffs, some nearing a hundred feet high. The northeastern coast sports a small sandy beach; the most northern tip is the site of the long abandoned lighthouse.

**The Student's Camp:** this large tent has been here all summer and houses Princeton student Shelly and his ornithological equipment. On the night of the investigators' arrival Johnson attacks and subdues Shelly, then drags him to the sacrificial rock to murder him in the ritual fashion. It is extremely unlikely that the investigators visit Shelly's camp prior to his demise as it is near dark when they arrive and the student dies only a couple hours

October 13, 1896

Dear Ebenezer, I'm leaving this letter with friends at port and I'm sure you'll get it when you return home. I'll probably be gone by then and don't know when I'll see you so I'll wish you good luck now.

In this envelope is a small present. It's a good luck charm given to me by one of those Kanakys we ran into in the islands. I don't know if it's any damn good but I always wore it, especially anytime I was around those islands. It's been said that some of the ships that sailed out of Innsmouth had something similar attached to their bottoms. I don't know what my address will be but after get to Cincinnati I'll write to let you know.

Your friend,
William

*The Sanitorium Papers #9—A Letter Found in Ebenezer's Shed*

later. Arriving after Shelly's murder, they find the tent knocked down and equipment and papers scattered across the beach. Signs of a struggle are evident, as are footprints, along with the marks of something being dragged (noticeable with a successful **Track** roll). **Two more successful Track rolls** allow the investigators to follow the footprints all the way to the sacrificial rock.

Among the ruins of Shelly's camp the investigators may find (with **Spot Hidden** rolls) a loaded .45 automatic and the student's private journal, both partially buried in the sand. A third successful roll turns up a box of 25 bullets. The journal was started in late spring when Shelly first arrived and chronicles his personal time on the island. He mentions the staff at the sanatorium, remarks how friendly they are and describes his explorations of the woods, cliffs, and abandoned lighthouse. He also makes mention of an old shipwreck, partially exposed by the violent spring storms, that lies just a hundred yards east of his campsite.

*Mr. Johnson*

**The Shipwreck:** this is the remains of an old whaler that was run aground by a storm over a hundred years ago. Driven high onto the beach, the ship was abandoned by the owners and eventually partially covered by sand. The exposed portions quickly weathered away leaving only part of the hull and deck planking now pressed flat together by the weight of the sand. A part of the forward keel now protrudes about a foot and a half above the surface of the beach and if the investigators dig down in this spot for a couple of hours they will find an Elder Sign carved on a lead disc. This plate was attached to the

keel below the water line and supposedly helped protect the ship on its voyages.

**The Sacrificial Rock:** an abomination. This flat rock has been chosen by Johnson to use in the ritual to feed the creature. It is over seven feet long and table-like, perfect for the job. It is soaked with blood while various portions of human anatomy litter the scene. Insects, birds, and small mammals have been attracted in great numbers. Seeing this place will cost 1/1D4 points of SAN.

**Johnson's Hideout:** Johnson hides out in the woods in a low spot, dark and dense with pines. He moves only by night and remains here all day. He does not sleep. His mind has been touched by the creature and by the terrible murders he has committed, and is now permanently insane.

Johnson appears dirty and disheveled and still wears his hospital whites, covered with dirt, gore, and spattered blood. Since being touched by the creature he has been imbued with increased attributes including improved night vision and extra sensitive hearing.

**The Lighthouse:** the creature is securely ensconced on the second floor of the lighthouse (the third floor contains the inoperative light itself). A stair on the ground floor leads to a trap door. Anyone trying to open this will find it wedged shut with a resistance of 14. If an investigator manages to force the door up he finds himself confronting the alien creature. If the character does not lose his sanity, give him an opportunity to **Dodge**; if successful, allow him to fall off the narrow stairway,

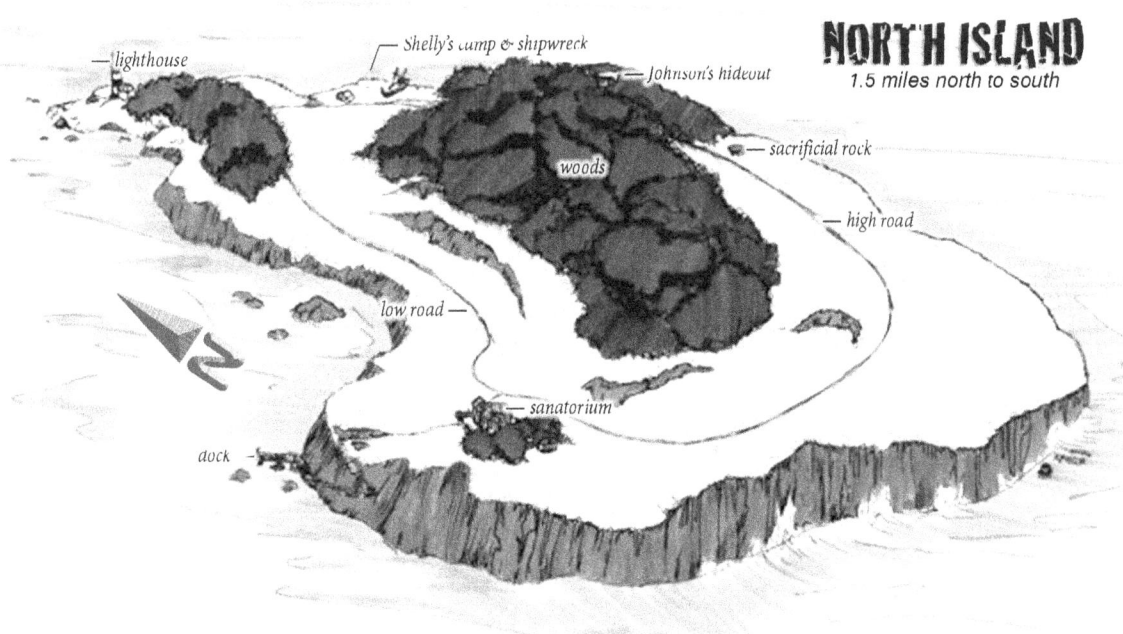

## NORTH ISLAND
1.5 miles north to south

— lighthouse

— Shelly's camp & shipwreck

— Johnson's hideout

woods

— sacrificial rock

— high road

low road —

— sanatorium

dock —

avoiding certain death. He takes 2D6 points of damage, 1D6 if a **Jump** roll is made. If the Dodge roll fails, the creature attacks with a pseudopod to the face. The captured investigator is dragged screaming, legs kicking, up into the aperture. This investigator is lost.

The creature is naturally a liquid/gaseous state, but it can alter its mass and constitution for short periods of time, assuming a granular, blob-like consistency with which it exerts force, reaches out and captures victims, etc. It used this ability to knock down the back door of the sanatorium. It doesn't need to alter its entire body, only that portion needed to accomplish the task.

In daylight, the creature appears as a slowly roiling mass of gassy spheres, nearly transparent but with a shifting, oily iridescence. Prowling by night, the creature is nearly invisible except for small red veins of light that flicker through its mass as it feeds upon the life energies of small insects and animals.

Only semi-material, the being moves by stretching out like a gigantic slug. It is itself silent, but an investigator making a **Listen** roll detects its approach by the slight crackling and popping sounds made as the creature consumes the small life forms in passing. It can assume a hemispherical shape nearly sixty feet across or form almost any other shape, including a ring surrounding the sanatorium.

While still in this embryonic form the creature is susceptible to damage from fire (2D6 points per five gallon can of gasoline), exposure to sunlight (6D6 points for every hour the creature spends in the direct sun), or immersion in seawater (nearly instant death). It is also vulnerable to the Elder Sign and although it suffers no damage from touching it, it avoids coming into contact with such a symbol at all costs.

## A Likely Chain Of Events

Some time during the night of the investigators' arrival (just about the time they have all the inmates nicely settled down and quiet) human screams float over from the eastern edge of the island. It is the beginning of another sacrifice. Accompanying the human screams is Johnson's nearly inhuman voice, intoning the horrible chant that must accompany the ritual. This event lasts approximately ten minutes. Listening to the agonized cries of the innocent victim costs the investigators 1/1D3 points of SAN. If an investigator can make a **Listen** roll followed by a **Cthulhu Mythos** roll, he is able to understand some of the chant and recognize it as a

*The Monster Emerges*

ritual intended to accompany the feeding of something. If a character makes a successful **Spot Hidden** roll while scanning the rest of the island, he or she detects a soft red glow coming from the distant lighthouse. The red glow is a sign that the creature is feeding. It is unlikely they can reach the sacrificial rock before the victim is dead and Johnson long gone.

These sacrifices continue, one or more per night, until the investigators find and stop Johnson. Johnson only moves by night and the investigators may find him more than a match in the dark and fog. Their oil lamps (the sanatorium has plenty) highlight their movements in the dark. Johnson can follow them, launching deadly sneak attacks with his axe. But with any luck, the investigators should be able to track him down in his lair and subdue him. Johnson is sane enough that he surrenders if the situation is hopeless. Upon capture he suffers a complete breakdown and, if returned to the sanatorium, requires restraints to keep him from injuring himself. Stopping Johnson brings a SAN reward of 1D8 points.

During the day, forcing the creature out of the lighthouse can probably be accomplished by setting a huge fire on the first floor. The heat forces the creature to flee through one of the narrow windows to the ground outside. Unless somehow stopped it heads for the nearest dark forest to escape the sunlight.

Once Johnson is subdued, getting the creature out of the lighthouse is easier. As soon as darkness falls, the monster, knowing it has lost its servant, creeps forth. It attacks and drains the life from anyone it meets on its way to the sanatorium. Reaching the sanatorium, it surrounds the building and makes attacks at anyone standing too near a first floor or basement window.

People inside the sanatorium, once they realize the danger, should be able avoid the creature simply by staying away from basement and ground floor apertures. The creature then turns its attention to inmates locked in their rooms, reaching through the windows and killing them in their cells. These individuals are trapped and the creature, once it senses their situation, makes short work of them. Investigators listening to the cries of the victims will lose 1/1D2 points of SAN for each person they allow to be killed in this terrible way.

Other inmates may lose their sanity after seeing the monster and do something stupid like running out a door and prostrating themselves before the creature in a demonstration of submission. The monster, although capable of it, hesitates to enter the building, fearful of becoming trapped inside.

In order for the creature to transform to its next stage, it must consume the life force of 9-12 (keeper's choice) victims, either sacrifices or characters it takes itself. If it cannot obtain its victims easily enough (or if

it chooses to) it may attempt to possess a character (**POW vs. POW** struggle on the resistance table) to act as its agent. This could be one of the inmates or an investigator. The possessed character then attempts to provide food for the monster. How long the creature maintains this possession is at the discretion of the keeper.

### The Creature from Another World

| | | | | |
|---|---|---|---|---|
| STR 40 | CON 40 | SIZ 32 | INT 05 | POW 38 |
| DEX 16 | Move 06 | | | HP 36 |

**Weapon:** *Pseudopod 95%, 108 damage plus 4 points of POW per round

**Armor:** The monster is impervious to all attacks save fire, electricity, sunlight, and seawater. It regenerates 6 hit points per round. Fire causes damage at the following rates: torch 1D2, 5 gallon gas can 2D6. Electricity: 120 volts AC does 4D6 points per round. Sunlight causes 6D6 points per hour. Seawater causes 8D6 points per every round the creature is immersed.

**Spells:** It can possess a character and bend him to its will if it wins a POW vs POW struggle on the resistance table. The possessed person can be used as a servant or as a mouthpiece by which the creature can speak directly to the investigators.

**Skills:** Hide in Dark 90%, Sneak 80%.

**SAN Cost:** 1/2D6

*Once the victim is struck the monster holds on with STR 40 while it sucks the life energies of its victims. The victim quickly blackens and shrivels as bolts of red, electric looking energies flow from the dying investigator into the body of the creature. Witnessing someone die this way for the first time costs the viewer 1/1D6 points of SAN, thereafter 0/1D2.*

## Destroying the Monster

Fire is the investigators' best friend. Although the monster can quickly regenerate most fire damage, it always seeks to escape the flames. It may be difficult to actually destroy the creature with fire but fire may be used to force it out of the lighthouse or the dark woods. If properly trapped, the investigators might use a circle of flame to force it off one of the cliffs into the sea. A burning circle of flame, if maintained, could possibly keep the monster trapped in the sunlight long enough to kill it. Luring it into the sanatorium then setting the building ablaze is another possibility. Seawater is near instant death for the alien creature and the surest way of destroying it. With an **Electrical Repair** roll, an investigator might figure a way to rig an electrical grid powered by the generator. Once on the powered grid the creature begins losing hit points at the rate of 4D6 per round and is unable to move from the grid. A **second Electrical Repair** roll must then be made, failure indicating the grid is overloading and shuts down in 1D6 rounds when the circuit breakers blow. The creature may or may not be destroyed by this time. This failure does not damage the generator and later attempts may be made.

The creature is also vulnerable to the influence of the Elder Sign and can not cross a threshold guarded by such a sign. If a person can hold forth one of these symbols and win a **POW vs. POW** struggle, the creature will be forced to avoid the character. More than one character can join in this row struggle, adding their pow to the contest, but each must be bearing a separate Elder Sign. By using this method, with multiple characters cutting off its avenues of retreat, the creature could be forced into the sea and destroyed.

## Contacting Princess Annephis

One of Darlene's many personalities is the Egyptian princess, Annephis, a priestess of the cult of Bast. Around 1000 BC Annephis was the head priestess of the Temple of Bast. It was Annephis who stood against the mysterious invaders and turned back the horrors that came upon Egypt, that race of beings referred to only as "Those Who Wait". Praying to her goddess, Annephis learned how to destroy the creatures and, with the help of Bast, constructed many Elder Signs with which she and her followers drove the creatures into the mouth of the Nile where they perished.

To contact the princess, Darlene must either be hypnotized or treated with a special combination of drugs. She then regresses through a number of personalities until the princess is finally reached. If unable to hypnotize the woman, the investigators might try the combination of drugs listed in her file. Brewer experimented with several different formulas before hitting upon the right one and the scratchy, often modified notes are difficult to decipher. To successfully understand the drug formula requires either a **Pharmacy or INT x1** score (medical professionals may roll **EDU x3** if they wish). The roll is not made until after the drug has been administered and if it is failed, the patient slips into a coma for 2D4 hours. If failed with a 95-00%, Darlene dies of an overdose.

Annephis, if contacted, is more than willing to help the investigators defeat the creature. She can give them information about its habits, its weaknesses, and she can construct Elder Signs to help defeat it. The personality regression lasts about four hours, just long enough for her to make one Elder Sign. Annephis can only be brought forth once per day.

## Failure to Destroy the Creature

If and when the creature begins its transformation, there is little an investigator can do but flee for his life. The transformation lasts two to three minutes and is very destructive. The air begins to turn a sickly shade of

## THE BLESSING OF BAST

This spell was known to the high priestesses of Bast in the days of dynastic Egypt. The spell costs 4 magic points to cast and simultaneously heals 1D6 hit points and restores 1D6 SAN points. However, the recipient of the spell must successfully pray to Bast. This prayer can be easily learned from Annephis but the would be recipient must roll POW x5 or less to convince the goddess of his or her worthiness. The spell itself is only available to consecrated priestesses of Bast and cannot be learned by investigators. ☀

yellow and, if it is daylight, the sun begins to dim. As the creature begins to swell and solidify, a great dark sphere suddenly forms in the sky above the creature, creating a sonic boom that knocks any character failing a **DEX x5** roll to the ground for 1D2 points of damage. The ground begins to heave and buckle as bits of the creature tear loose, rocketing upward toward the dark sphere. Tree branches snap, flying skyward and huge rents open in the ground. If the metamorphosis takes place near the sanatorium, the building starts to sway and creak ominously. It soon collapses and anyone inside takes 2D6 points of damage if a **Luck** roll is made and 3D6+2 if it is failed. Surviving investigators will suffer additional SAN losses of 1/1D2 for each inmate left trapped in their locked rooms.

As the ground heats up and the earth continues to crack, huge gouts of red light race skyward, accompanied by a horrible smell, and the investigators notice that the air temperature is steadily rising. Anyone fleeing the scene across level ground is subjected to 2D6 points of heat damage when the creature suddenly explodes upward and, in fragments, rockets toward the dark sphere. It appears as a huge red ball of pulsing energy and witnesses suffer an additional 1/1D6 SAN loss. Investigators fleeing down the stairs to the dock suffer only 1D6 points of heat (plus the SAN loss) but the eruption causes the cliff face to crack and fall. If a **Luck** roll is failed a huge section of the cliff face falls toward the character. A successful **Dodge** roll will have to be made or the character will suffer 3D8 points of damage from the hurtling boulder. Anyone attempting to save themselves by diving off the 100-foot-high cliff suffers no heat damage or SAN losses but has to make a successful **Jump** roll to survive the dive and a successful **Swim** roll to avoid being swept out to sea by the current.

## Awards for Success

Destroying the creature before it manages to transform gives the investigators an award of 1D10+4 SAN points. Whether successful or not, any surviving investigator who witnessed the transformation receives 1D6 points added to their Cthulhu Mythos score.

# Statistics

### Blanche Goddard Richmond, loving mother

| STR 08 | CON 11 | SIZ 08 | INT 13 | POW 11 |
|--------|--------|--------|--------|--------|
| DEX 11 | APP 07 | EDU 14 | SAN 25 | HP 10 |

**Damage Bonus:** -1D4

**Skills:** Cook Well Balanced Meal 85%.

### Henry Adam Barber III, rude young man

| STR 12 | CON 13 | 51Z 14 | INT 13 | POW 08 |
|--------|--------|--------|--------|--------|
| DEX 11 | APP 10/6* | EDU 15 | SAN 12 | HP 14 |

*in woman's garb*

**Damage Bonus:** +1D4

**Skills:** Dither 75%, Flounce 75%, Speak in Insulting Tones 85%.

### Colonel Crandall Billings, senile patriot

| STR 05 | CON 06 | SIZ 08 | INT 07 | POW 05 |
|--------|--------|--------|--------|--------|
| DEX 05 | APP 09 | EDU 14 | SAN 11 | HP 07 |

**Damage Bonus:** 1D4

**Skills:** Holler Loudly 95%, Navigate Wheelchair 15%.

### Mrs. Cecil (Carla) Randolph, alcoholic wife

| STR 07 | CON 06 | SIZ 09 | INT 09 | POW 05 |
|--------|--------|--------|--------|--------|
| DEX 1O | APP 07 | EDU 14 | SAN 12 | HP 08 |

Damage Bonus: 1D4

**Skills:** Botany 55%, Make Unreasonable Demand 85%, Sing 20%, Sneak 65%, Snide Complaint 90%, Speak Haughtily 85%.

### Allen Harding, mad poet

| STR 11 | CON 10 | SIZ 14 | INT 15 | POW 13 |
|--------|--------|--------|--------|--------|
| DEX 11 | APP 09 | EDU 14 | SAN 00 | HP 12 |

**Damage Bonus:** +1D4

**Skills:** Cthulhu Mythos 22%, Recite Yeats 95%.

### Darlene, woman of mystery

| STR 10 | CON 12 | SIZ 10 | INT 14 | POW 11 |
|--------|--------|--------|--------|--------|
| DEX 12 | APP 12 | EDU 10 | SAN 35 | HP 11 |

**Damage Bonus:** none

**Skills:** Answer Obliquely 80%.

### Princess Annephis, long dead priestess of Bast

| STR 10 | CON 12 | SIZ 10 | INT 16 | POW 18 |
|--------|--------|--------|--------|--------|
| DEX 12 | APP 14 | EDU 22 | SAN 85 | HP 11 |

**Damage Bonus:** none

**Spells:** Blessing of Bast, Create Elder Sign, Dread Curse of Azathoth, Shriveling, Summon/Bind Nightgaunt.

**Skills:** Anthropology 55%, Archaeology 65%, Art (Oratory) 80%, Astronomy 85%, Cthulhu Mythos 14%, First Aid 65%, Hide 65%, History 65%, Occult 75%, Sneak 85%, Spot Hidden 65%.

### Leonard Hawkins, angry accountant

| STR 14 | CON 15 | SIZ 12 | INT 14 | POW 10 |
|--------|--------|--------|--------|--------|
| DEX 11 | APP 10 | EDU 14 | SAN 19 | HP 14 |

**Damage Bonus:** +1D4

**Skills:** Accounting 90%, Hate Women 90%

### Charles Johnson, insane attendant

| STR 18 | CON 17 | SIZ 18 | INT 07 | POW 09 |
|--------|--------|--------|--------|--------|
| DEX 12 | APP 06 | EDU 06 | SAN 0 | HP 18 |

**Damage Bonus:** +1D6

**Weapons:** Wood Axe 75%, damage 1D8+2+1D6
Fist/Punch 55%, damage 1D3+1D6
Grapple 35%.

**Skills:** Climb 35%, Cthulhu Mythos 3%, Dodge 25%, Hide 65%, Jump 20%, Listen 35%, Pharmacy 15%, See in the Dark 85%, Sneak 80%, Spot Hidden 80%.

### James Shelly, an unlikely encounter

| STR 10 | CON 12 | SIZ 13 | INT 15 | POW 14 |
|--------|--------|--------|--------|--------|
| DEX 12 | APP 13 | EDU 15 | SAN 72 | HP 13 |

**Damage Bonus:** none

**Weapons:** .45 Pistol 45%, damage 1D10+2

**Skills:** Archaeology 20%, Botany 25%, Dodge 40%, Hide 55%, History 50%, Library Use 65%, Spot Hidden 75%, Zoology 75%.

### Dr. Henry Tiller, a useful non player character

| STR 09 | CON 11 | SIZ 11 | INT 15 | POW 13 |
|--------|--------|--------|--------|--------|
| DEX 10 | APP 13 | EDU 20 | SAN 70 | HP 11 |

**Damage Bonus:** none

**Skills:** Chemistry 65%, Credit Rating 85%, First Aid 90%, Hypnosis 50%, Listen 45%, Medicine 80%, Persuade 55%, Pharmacy 80%, Psychoanalysis 80%, Sneak 35%, Spot Hidden 55%.

**Languages:** English 80%, Latin 25%.

THE END!

# Mansion of Madness

*Wherein the investigators visit the house of a wealthy art collector, and find his collection of paintings to be odd but intriguing. Do they offer a hint of things to come?*

The investigators are drawn into this adventure when they are asked to look into the matter of a missing Boston businessman. Andrew Keetling has been kidnapped by his lover, Josephine Garsetti, who holds him captive in her childhood home in Muskrat Rapids, Pennsylvania. She intends to sacrifice him to a strange being from the Dreamlands known as The Thing Hanging in the Void. Meanwhile, Zeke Crater, a Boston gangster, is trying to track down Garsetti. She has a magical object, the Dark Stone, which belongs to him. He wants it back. Unable to achieve this himself, he may prevail upon the investigators to help him, offering them a hefty fee for the return of the object. Both Garsetti and Crater are insane and the investigators probably discover that they don't want the Dark Stone to fall to either party.

This adventure is presented in three parts:

## Part One: The Investigation

This portion of the adventure is set entirely in Boston. Beginning at the Keetling house, the investigators follow a long chain of clues which may require visits to the police station, the Boston Museum of Fine Arts, Boston University, a speakeasy known as the Sailor's Club, and the newspaper files of the Boston Globe. They have a chance to meet with Josephine's ex best friend, Andrea Pentargon, as well as the mysterious gangster, Zeke Crater.

Throughout this portion of the adventure the investigators may several times meet up with a mysterious dream-figure, part ghoul and part human, who alternately helps and hampers the investigation. See the section entitled "The Dream Ghoul".

## Part Two: House of Dreams

Following the clues they find in Boston, the investigators travel to Muskrat Rapids, Pennsylvania, the hometown of artist Josephine Garsetti. With any luck, they rescue Andrew Keetling and either kill or capture the insane Garsetti.

Although they may recover the Dark Stone, they will probably not have it for long. Crater has sent some of his men to the area and they attempt to buy back (forcibly, if necessary) the Dark Stone that their boss so desires. If the investigators somehow get rid of the gangsters and retain possession of the Dark Stone, Crater sends other, more alien, henchmen to obtain his goal.

Worst of all, while in Pennsylvania, the investigators probably stumble upon the Thing Hanging in the Void, which now is dwelling so near the real world that it can be encountered in one of the rooms of the house.

## Part Three: Tracking Down Crater

In this final chapter, the investigators return to Boston to deal with the Boston crime lord, the depraved and insane Zeke Crater. More than likely they wish to retrieve the Stone, or simply attempt to revenge themselves for something that

# THE DARK STONE

The Dark Stone is a six-inch-long lump of polished dark brown crystal carved to vaguely suggest the form of the Thing Hanging in the Void. It was constructed in prehistoric times by a priest of Lemuria whose dreams had been touched by the Thing Hanging in the Void. The Stone, once impregnated with the proper number of human souls, will allow the Thing to draw nearer the real world where it can feed upon the human souls it relishes. Discovering the hideous plan of the priest, the Lemurians murdered him and buried the stone deep in the ground, erasing all records of the object and all records of the priest. This stone lay buried for millennia until late last century when it was accidentally uncovered by an amateur archaeologist and later sold to a collector living in France. Upon the death of the collector the piece, along with a number of other objects, was willed to the Miskatonic University but by accident fell into the hands of Zeke Crater, It is now in the possession of Josephine Garsetti. The Thing Hanging in the Void, after a wait of thousands and thousands of years, is now attempting to finish its plan.

The Dark Stone is filled with POW, very nearly pulsing with the magical energy stored within it. This can be sensed by almost anyone. Because of this, seeing the object for the first time causes a loss of 0/1D2 SAN.

Any investigator making a **Cthulhu Mythos** roll can identify the Dark Stone by name but unless they have read *Kingdom of Shadows* they will know little about it.

## The Dark Stone's Capabilities & Powers

The possessor of the figurine can harness special powers. Exact knowledge of these abilities can only be gained by reading the book *Kingdom of Shadows*, or possibly by experimentation. However, vague ideas about its powers will filter into the possessor's mind within a few hours of picking up the stone.

First, the possessor's POW and his magic points increase by 10 points, whenever the figurine is on his or her person.

Relinquishing the stone becomes difficult after possessing it for a time. A strange feeling of reluctance will come over anyone who tries to put the stone down. Any investigator possessing the stone for more than 24 hours must roll less than his or her POW x(5 minus the number of weeks he has had the stone) to give the object up. If the stone has been possessed for less than 24 hours, an investigator will only feel a mild unwillingness to relinquish it, one which is easily overcome. To break the hold the stone has on a person, the stone must be clearly given away. Simply placing it in a safety deposit box or some such thing does not constitute giving up possession and the stone will continue to work its effect on the person.

Donating the item to Miskatonic University or similar place may be the safest bet.

The stone cannot be destroyed by any science known in the 1920's.

Finally, the holder of the Dark Stone has a certain immunity to the awful gaze of the Thing Hanging in the Void (but at the cost of becoming receptive to its dream sending ability).

Because the Thing Hanging in the Void now dwells so near the real world, an investigator in possession of the Dark Stone is in extreme danger. Within a day or two the Thing will begin making nightly attempts to send dreams to the investigator. These dreams always convey a sense of well being, centering around a conversation with an odd but friendly animal-headed person in a safe, comfortable place such as a quiet forest glen or a well lit sidewalk cafe. The type of animal will be whatever the investigator's innermost preferences indicate to the Thing's insidious mind probing: a tabby cat, a bright eyed deer, a cute little white rabbit. In these conversations the dream being will always urge the investigator to "extend the invitation to the One" (*i.e.*, invite the Thing to take up residence in your home).

Anyone who experiences such a dream can refuse to "make the invitation" by rolling POW x(5 minus the number of weeks the stone has been possessed) or less. Failure to make the roll means the Thing Hanging in the Void appears in the investigators house — in whichever room it chooses.

## The Dark Stone Spells

These spells become known to the possessor of the Stone only by reading *Kingdom of Shadows* or by having intimate contact with the Thing Hanging in the Void. The Thing will only teach an investigator these spells after it has moved into the character's home and driven the character's SAN to zero.

**DRAIN YOUTH:** Cost: 8 MP, 1D6 SAN. This spell allows the caster to permanently remove 2D6 points of CON, STR, or APP (caster's choice) from the spell's target. A successful MP vs. MP resistance struggle must be won in order for the spell to take effect.

**DROWN MIND:** Cost: 4 MP, 1D3 SAN. For each additional 4 magic points spent, an additional target may be attempted. The target of the spell falls unconscious for 1D20 x10 minutes, assuming the caster can win an MP vs MP resistance table roll with the target. The victim of the spell awakes suffering nausea as described below. The effect of the nausea is to temporarily reduce all physically related skills by one half. Each target of the spell can resist separately.

If the target successfully resists the spell, he stays conscious but feels as if he is falling into a bottomless well. He is still afflicted with nausea for 1D4 x15 minutes. ※

---

Crater has earlier done to them. The final secrets and horror await the investigators in Crater's dark and (almost) deserted mansion.

## Three Villains

This scenario revolves around the wants and needs of three different antagonists: Josephine Garsetti, Ezekiel Crater, and the Thing Hanging in the Void.

**Josephine Garsetti:** Born and raised in an isolated house outside of Muskrat Rapids, Pennsylvania, Garsetti, as a young girl, was contacted, then taken over by the hideous Thing in the Void. Swayed by the Thing's

desires, Garsetti eventually moved to Boston, attending art school but at the same time blindly seeking a mysterious powerful object, the Dark Stone, whose existence the Thing could but dimly perceive from its home in the Dreamlands. Garsetti eventually located this object and, with the use of sinister magic, wrested it away from its owner, the gangster Zeke Crater. Garsetti then began a series of human sacrifices, bathing the stone in the blood of her victims. These rites were intended to allow the Thing to draw closer to the real world.

Betrayed by her friend, Andrea Pentargon, Garsetti's cult was broken up by police, who captured or killed almost every member. Garsetti escaped and fled back to her childhood home in Muskrat Rapids, taking along her present lover, the near helpless Andrew Keetling. Very soon Andrew will be sacrificed to the frightful Thing in the Void.

**Zeke "the geek" Crater:** Zeke is a long time Boston gangster and bootlegger who heads a fair sized operation out of a waterfront speakeasy called "The Sailor's Club". Crater, a couple years ago, accidentally took possession of the Dark Stone and discovered at least one of its powers. Although long known as a dapper womanizer, under the influence of the Dark Stone, Crater's appetites noticeably increased and soon it was rumored that he was staging wild orgies in his isolated mansion on the coast.

Josephine Garsetti, subconsciously seeking out the Stone, began attending these parties, gradually maneuvering herself closer to the crime lord. When a private liaison was finally made she used the opportunity to cast a spell upon the gangster which, while it did not kill him, caused a terrible alteration in his physiognomy. Horribly altered, Crater now keeps himself locked away in his now lonely and near deserted mansion, moving only at night, keeping himself hidden as much as possible under the folds of a voluminous cape. He thinks he has discovered a way to reverse his affliction but needs the power of the Dark Stone to effect the transformation. Garsetti keeps herself magically protected from Crater so he will attempt to use the investigators to retrieve the Stone for him.

**The Thing Hanging in the Void:** This strange and malign being is mentioned in few Mythos tomes. A dweller in the Dreamlands, the Thing feasts upon, and in fact is composed of, human souls. The site of the Garsetti house in Muskrat Rapids is the place in the real world nearest to the home of the Thing. The Thing managed to enter into the dreams of the teenaged Josephine Garsetti and, after a time, took possession of her life. This monstrous being has subtly controlled the woman ever since and used her to seek out the Dark Stone. The human sacrifices Garsetti has committed over the stone have brought the Thing much nearer the real world. Soon it will be close enough to enter the dreams of the residents of Muskrat Rapids and touch off a night of madness and murder, a feast of human souls that the Thing would greatly enjoy.

The Stone is now blooded and bound to the Thing. If the Thing wishes, it can follow the Stone anywhere in the real world and appear in its near vicinity. If Crater gains possession of the object, before long the Thing will show up in his house, taking up residence in a spare bedroom and seizing control of the already insane Crater. If an investigator takes possession of the Stone for any length of time, he may himself be the unwilling host to the Thing Hanging in the Void.

## Investigator Information

Andrew Keetling, 28-year-old Boston businessman and patron of the arts, has disappeared. The police have been unable to uncover any leads and his sister, Sarah, fears foul play. She has contacted the investigators in the hope they can find her missing brother.

The investigators might be friends or former classmates of either of the Keetlings, or might be introduced to Sarah by a mutual friend.

The investigators know that Boston's Keetlings have a long standing reputation as a quiet and conservative family. Other than as supporters of local charities and sponsors of civic events, they are rarely mentioned in the society pages.

---

# PART ONE
# The Investigation

## The Keetling Residence

This large townhouse is located in one of the city's finer sections. Formerly the home of Andrew and Sarah's parents, since the death of their father and mother several years ago it has been solely inhabited by the sister and brother. The investigators are met at the door by Sarah (there are no full time servants) who welcomes them in.

Sarah, a somewhat plain woman in her mid thirties, plunges into her narrative without preamble. Andrew, she says, has always been a quiet, responsible individual — at least until lately. A few months ago, he began associating with a group of young artists and before long was spending much more time with them than he was at home. At first, Sarah thought little of it, expecting her younger brother

*Miss Keetling*

would soon lose interest in the bohemians and settle back into his normal lifestyle. However, as time went on, Andrew was more and more away from home and Sarah began to suspect he had fallen in with "a bad crowd."

"I think Andrew's been writing some very large checks, made out to people whom I don't know," says the suspicious Sarah. When she confronted Andrew with this he grew angry and refused to discuss it. "Later he apologized and explained the money had been spent on some paintings with which he intended to decorate his study." When he later brought the three paintings home, Sarah's suspicions grew. They were all by an unknown and certainly did not warrant the amount of money he had spent on them. "The three pieces were quite atrocious," Sarah complains. "Not only were they executed by a complete unknown, the subject matter is simply ghastly. Hardly the type of thing you would want seen hanging in your home, or even in a gallery."

"We had quite an argument about it but Andrew was vehement about their quality. He told me that one day this Garsetti person would be recognized as a modern day master and that the three paintings would be worth a small fortune." A few days later, Andrew went out one evening and never returned. That was two weeks ago.

Sarah has notified the police but they have uncovered nothing regarding Keetling's disappearance. The officer in charge of the investigation is Detective Sergeant Patrick Devlin. Sarah is sure he is not doing a proper job.

She supplies the investigators with a recent photograph of her missing brother. It shows a thin man in his early thirties with regular features and sandy hair.

Sarah will add that she thinks Andrew met the creator of these "works of art" at the Boston Museum of Fine Art, where he is quite well known. She knows nothing more about the paintings or the Boston Museum.

## Andrew's Study

Andrew's small study is dominated by three large, expensively framed paintings. They are clearly the focus of interest. One of the paintings hangs above the desk while another is suspended from the edge of a bookshelf covering most of the books beneath. The third painting hangs on the wall opposite the bookshelf.

Each of the three paintings is identified by a small silver plaque engraved with the title of the work. In the lower right hand corner of any of the paintings the investigators can find the artist's signature, "Garsetti".

**First Painting:** Entitled "The Dweller in the Void", this painting depicts a large humanoid figure suspended in a distorted field of color. The figure is thin, malformed, its features murky. It appears mummified, decayed.

The eye is irresistibly drawn to the hanging figure. As one begins to pick out the details it becomes obvious that the thing is composed of twisted and tortured faces. Unless the person viewing the painting can make a roll of POW x4 or less, he suddenly sees his own visage among the tortured faces composing the figure. An investigator viewing his own face in the painting suffers a 1/1D3 SAN loss.

*(This is a picture of The Thing Hanging in the Void.)*

**Second Painting:** Entitled "Sylvan Night", this painting depicts a beautiful blonde headed woman sprawled nude across a great rough hewn stone. In the dark background can be seen pine trees, silhouetted against the sky. Above the treetops, seemingly forming from the very air, is a dark swirling mass, identity unknown. Something is very disturbing about the woman's sultry expression and a first time viewer loses 0/1 SAN.

*(This is a self portrait of Andrew Keetling's lover, Josephine Garsetti.)*

**Third Painting:** Entitled "The Watching", this painting shows a solitary building, a large mansion on the coast. Anyone viewing the painting notices tiny red points of light in each of the building's numerous windows and cracks. Increasingly, as the viewer continues to look at the painting, these red points become the most significant feature. A roll of **POW x4** or less is required to look away at this point. If this roll is failed, the viewer no longer sees a building, but the multi-orbed visage of some titanic being, each red dot of light another staring, searching eye. Viewing this painting costs an investigator 0/1 SAN.

*(This building is the nearly identical image of Ezekiel Crater's dismal mansion.)*

**Other Items:** Investigation of the bookshelf turns up travel guides, some books on geography, and a few tracts on ship building. There are also many art books; about twenty large volumes containing reproductions of the works of well known masters. There are no occult works to be found.

Investigators examining the bookshelf and making a **Spot Hidden** roll notice a few slips of paper sticking out between the pages of a volume of pre-Raphaelite plates. Pressed between pages 22 and 23 of this book are several letters written in a woman's hand. They are love notes written by Josephine Garsetti (see **The Mansion Papers #1**). None of the letters are dated.

*My darling Andrew, please meet me at the Sailor's Club tonight at eleven. Do not fail. I really must speak to you. An important time for both of us draws near. - Love, J. G.*

*The Mansion Papers #1—Note Hidden in a Book*

# THE DREAM GHOUL

The Dream Ghoul appears in this adventure at the whim of the keeper. It is a semi corporeal dream projection of the kidnapped and temporarily insane Andrew Keetling. A product of the man's subconscious powered by the close proximity of The Thing Hanging in the Void, the Dream Ghoul treads unsteadily between the Dreamlands and the waking world. It shadows the investigators and when Keetling's personality dominates, tries to help them. Later on, when the Thing has taken more control of the Dream, it attacks and tries to kill them. As the adventure wears on, the Thing gains more and more control over the Dream Ghoul and the spirit-like entity becomes progressively more dangerous. Unless the ghoul is attacking, any violence against it on the part of the investigators will cause it to turn transparent, shimmer, and fade from view.

## Encountering the Dream Ghoul

The party, on foot, after dark, becomes aware they are being followed. They notice that whomever is tailing them is preternaturally quiet (an investigator can never hear the shadow, even using Listen) and that the dark figure exercises little or no guile when it comes to hiding from sight. Whenever an investigator turns back, the figure is a block away, half in shadow, half in light. The brim of the person's hat casts a deep shadow over the figure's face, obscuring it. He wears a suit and an expensive looking overcoat.

If a player makes an **Idea** roll, he notices that the shadowy figure seems to vaguely resemble the photograph of Andrew Keetling shown to them by Sarah. Even the clothing is similar. Without an Idea roll they only notice that the shadow's gait is very stooped, and the feet don't look quite right.

If the investigators decide to confront the shadow, they find it can be easily cornered in an alley or doorway. Trapped, the shadow remains silent, except for a periodic snuffling, and stands relatively still. It allows an investigator to approach and remove its hat. Underneath is a wickedly smiling ghoul's face with whiskered, rubbery, gray flesh and smoky lambent pits for eyes (lose 0/1D6 SAN). If, after a moment's examination, they realize that the features are a distorted travesty of Andrew Keetling's face (Idea roll), they lose an additional 1 point of SAN.

After the ghoul is revealed, it giggles insanely, snatches back its hat, and, knocking any intervening investigators aside, runs to a nearby manhole. There it turns into a silvery mist and disappears down through the small vent holes in the cover. Any attacks against it cause it to disappear as described.

## Questioning the Dream Ghoul

The next place the Dream Ghoul appears is on the doorstep of one of the investigators. The first sign of the ghoul's arrival is a penetrating charnel reek emanating from the area of the front door. A knock will follow. If the Dream Ghoul can get inside the house or apartment (and past a party of paranoid investigators) it passes into one of the investigator's rooms, sits down and removes its hat.

If the investigators ask the Dream Ghoul any questions, it answers in a hoarse whisper punctuated by ragged sniffing noises. The Dream Ghoul always speaks in an allusive way. Some typical questions and responses are listed below:

Q: *Who are you?*
A: *"I am the dream of my mistress's lover, part myself, part Keetling thing, and part something greater than us both."*

Q: *What are you doing here?*
A: *"Keetling wants your help; the One in the Void wants your soul; I know not what I want."*

Q: *Who is the One in the Void?*
A: *"The One who waits. The One who hungers ever so long."*

Q: *Where is Andrew Keetling?*
A: *"In the dark, thinking of kisses, thinking of death."*

Q: *Why would you help us?*
A: *It pauses, the creature's eyes roll wildly, and a gurgle emerges from its throat, as if struggling with itself. "Am I a dreaming thing dreaming I am a man, or a man dreaming I am a dreaming thing?"*

Q: *Where is Josephine Garsetti?*
A: *"She is in her true home, obeying the One in the Void, dreaming of the future day."*

Eventually the thing refuses to answer further questions, stands up, and, after turning pale and silvery, drops through the floor.

## Fighting the Dream Ghoul

At some point, probably while the investigators are traveling to Muskrat Rapids, the Dream Ghoul turns hostile. The Dream Ghoul's sudden appearance and attack is unpredictable. If questions are shouted at it the creature wails and clutches at its head, then redoubles its attacks.

If the investigators are traveling by train it attacks them in their sleeping berths. If the investigators choose to travel by car, the Dream Ghoul attacks whenever they stop to rest for the night. If the investigators intend to drive straight through to Pennsylvania, the Dream Ghoul attacks them inside the car, possibly leading to a fatal automobile accident.

During the dream attack the investigators move with a leaden slowness. They melee at half the normal rate while the ghoul fights normally, always getting the first attack in every round.

If "killed", the body of the defeated Dream Ghoul shimmers and fades, grows insubstantial, then flows downward into the ground. As the body fades from sight, Andrew Keetling's agonized voice rises from the spot where the Dream Ghoul disappeared, pleading with the investigator's to release him from the "Thing's" power.

After the ghoul is defeated, wounded investigators find the damage they suffered to be far less than they thought and hit point losses are reduced by one half (round up fractions). Visible wounds quickly fade and disappear, remaining only as tingly patches. Any character knocked unconscious or "killed" awakes with 3 HP. First Aid is not useful for treating the decidedly non normal wounds caused by the Dream Ghoul.

Every few days after this, the attack may be repeated. The attacks do not cease until the investigators find and rescue Andrew Keetling. Once the young man is taken from the Garsetti house, his ghoulish dreams end.

**THE DREAM GHOUL**

| STR 20 | CON 10 | SIZ 14 | INT 11 | POW 11 | DEX 12 |
|--------|--------|--------|--------|--------|--------|
| Move 09 | | | | | HP 12 |

**Armor:** none, but firearms do half damage.

**Weapons:** Claw 30%, damage 1D6+1D4
      Bite 30%, damage 1D6+1D4*

    *Worry — STR vs. STR to break hold. All damage halved after awakening from the attack

**SAN Cost:** 0/1D6 (+1 if recognized as Andrew Keetling).

*The Dream Ghoul*

If Sarah is questioned about the letters, it becomes obvious that she knows nothing and, in fact, is genuinely surprised to learn that Andrew was seeing a woman. Sarah implores the investigators to remember that Andrew is properly retiring and rather shy around members of the opposite sex. She's never heard of the Sailor's Club.

Most of the drawers of Andrew's desk are unlocked; they contain stationery and writing supplies (pens, ink, nibs), but nothing of interest.

The lower right hand drawer, however, is locked (STR 8). Sarah does not have a key but if an investigator makes a **Mechanical Repair** roll at +25%, he can spring the lock without damaging the hardware. The drawer contains Keetling's ledgers and a cursory examination of them reveals that he has most recently been importing Icelandic wool, canned European cuisine, and foreign language books. Further investigation of the ledgers requires the use of **Accounting**. If successful, the investigator finds the books to be in order with the exception of several large checks written to a person named "Josephine Garsetti."

## The Boston Police

The officer in charge of the Keetling case is Detective Sergeant Patrick Devlin, a harried looking officer in his mid-forties. He is a big man with a doughy face and thinning hair, his forehead dotted by small beads of sweat. Devlin usually wears a plain light colored suit one size too small for his bulky frame. A wrapped bandage on his left hand covers a wound he received while recently leading a raid against the Sylvan Night cult.

It is Devlin's opinion that Andrew had finally had enough of life with his domineering sister and ran away from home. "He'll turn up when he wants to," says Devlin. A successful **Psychology** roll indicates Devlin truly believes this.

If questioned about the Sailor's Club, Devlin gives them directions to the establishment located on Boston harbor. The place is well known to police and is protected by payoffs to the department. Devlin feels compelled to warn them the Club is operating an illegal business.

If asked about the raid on the Sylvan Night, Devlin grows noticeably more serious and close mouthed. He hesitates to discuss the details with strangers and merely recounts the story as it was reported in the newspaper. Only if the investigators succeed with a **Debate, Persuade, Art (Oratory), or Law** roll (or otherwise establish a rapport with Devlin) will he reveal the darker details of the cult and the numerous murders they are suspected of. He knows that the leader of the cult, Josephine Garsetti, escaped and he believes she is hiding out somewhere in the Boston area. Unless the investigators inform him of the facts, Devlin has no idea that Garsetti might be involved in the Keetling case.

Devlin possesses grainy photographs and detailed field sketches of each of the six victims in the case; these are not for the faint hearted. Captions detailing the victim's name, where the body was found, and other technical details are noted on the back of each photo or sketch with a black grease pencil. Each lists the cause of death and all read the same: "Dagger wound to throat, followed by post mortem mutilation by human bites."

*Detective Sergeant Devlin*

Devlin also has the assumed name and new address of Andrea Pentargon, the former cultist who turned police informant. She is under police protection and it's unlikely that Devlin, who is responsible for her security, will readily divulge her location.

However, it should not be beyond the abilities of the investigators to eventually acquire this information. If they can convince Devlin that Pentargon's help might locate Keetling, the detective reveals where she now lives and her new name, "Myra Smith."

If asked about Zeke Crater, Devlin can tell them the gangster heads up a big drug and alcohol business, probably headquartered out of the Sailor's Club. Devlin has heard that Crater's taken sick lately and underworld rumors say he is dying. Devlin doesn't know if there is any truth to this rumor or not. He can tell the investigators that Crater's underworld nickname, "the Geek," stems from the wild parties he used to throw at his mansion somewhere up the coast.

Zeke Crater has many policemen on his payroll, not the least of which is Detective Dave Flannigan. Flannigan's desk is quite near Devlin's; close enough to hear almost everything the investigators say. Once they have visited the station, the investigator's interest in the Keetling and/or Sylvan Night cases will soon come to Crater's attention.

*Detective Flannigan*

## The Boston Museum of Fine Arts

This museum is located on the upper part of Huntington avenue in downtown Boston. Founded in 1870, it has occupied the present building since 1909. It displays, as the nucleus of its collection, works formerly found in the Boston Athenaeum. Perhaps its most famous works are the Stuart portraits of George and Martha Washington. Besides paintings, the museum also boasts a large number of statues, busts, and casts; a very noble tapestry museum; a fine collection of oriental pieces; and extensive collections of ceramics and metal work. The museum is free to the public.

The Museum's director, Mr. Bradley Carrier, recognizes Keetling's name but can offer little information. He directs the investigators to Madelaine DuMort, an exhibit director and one of his assistants. She works out of an office near the back of the building.

*Miss DuMort*

Madelaine is an attractive woman of medium height. She has red hair and is usually dressed in a conservative, but stylish manner. She sits behind a desk littered with photographs of paintings, gallery schedules, pen nibs, small objects d'art, and several art magazines. Her Boston Brahmin accent is considerably less pronounced than the Director's.

Madelaine is already aware Andrew is missing and seems quite concerned. She tells the investigators she first met Andrew about a year ago while he was visiting the Museum. She was attracted to him when she found him looking with great appreciation at one of her favorite paintings, an Impressionist piece by Degas. After getting to know one another the two, at least once a week, would lunch together then spend the afternoon strolling through the museum. As far as Madelaine knows, these soirees were the only time Andrew allowed himself away from his work.

A couple of months ago Andrew began seeing a woman named Josephine Garsetti, a local artist who often visited the museum. Madelaine thinks Andrew met Josephine one afternoon when she was late for their regular lunch date. Madelaine discovered the two of them chatting together in the main gallery. After that, Madelaine's meetings with Andrew began to taper off. Madelaine believes Andrew was spending more and more time with Garsetti. (A successful **Psychology** roll informs the investigators that Madelaine is very fond of Andrew and is jealous of the attention he was giving the Garsetti woman.) Madelaine later heard that Andrew and Garsetti had taken to frequenting a disreputable speakeasy known as the Sailor's Club. She does not know where the place is.

Madelaine believes Josephine is a drug addict and has drawn Andrew into the habit. To Madelaine's knowledge, Josephine's paintings have never been shown in Boston and adds that they would never hang in this museum. "They are grotesque and frightening," she complains.

Madelaine can tell the investigators that Josephine studied painting at Boston University, a fact she learned from the artist's resume Garsetti once sent to the museum. If the investigators ask to see the resume, Madelaine tells them she long ago destroyed it.

## Boston University

The admissions office at BU can inform the investigators that Josephine Garsetti enrolled in school two years ago at the age of 18. She is an Art major and her tuition was paid for by a competitive scholarship she won while living in her hometown of Muskrat Rapids, Pennsylvania. If the investigators try to dig a little deeper into her history (and make a **Fast Talk** roll), the admissions clerk reveals a rural route mailing address in Muskrat Rapids, listed as the home of Josephine's parents.

## Newspaper Research

Back issues of the Boston *Globe* can be found at either the offices of the newspaper or in the archives section of the Boston Public Library. In either place a successful **Library Use** roll will turn up a recent article of some interest (see *The Mansion Papers #2*). The event occurred just two weeks ago. The investigators' atten-

### Kidnap Victim Dies During Police Raid on Occult Ceremony

#### Pitched Gun Battle Ends in Multiple Deaths

Earlier today, proceedings of a secretive Boston religious group known as the Sylvan Night were raided by local police. Led by Detective Sergeant Patrick Devlin of the Boston Police Department, the heavily armed force of men surrounded a wooded area several miles north of the city, then closed in. Authorities had been unaware of the cult's existence but were tipped off to their activities by a former member of the group.

When police arrived on the scene, members of the cult were apparently in the process of performing a "black magic ritu-al". This shocking rite apparently was to include the brutal sacrifice of a young girl recently abducted from Boston's Chinatown. The kidnap victim was unfortunately killed during the course of the raid. According to Officer Devlin, who was himself slightly injured in the battle, twelve cult members were killed, two captured, and one believed escaped. The woman who escaped is thought to have been the leader of the cult and is still at large. The public is warned that she may be armed and should be considered dangerous. City Councilman Bradford Tibbins has assured the press that accusations of police brutality will be dealt with dung the inquest scheduled for next week. Police have refused to divulge the identity of the deceased and captured cultists pending further investigation.

*– May 22*

*The Mansion Papers #2*

tion might be drawn to the name Patrick Devlin or the reference to the Sylvan Night.

If, spurred on by this find, the investigators continue to search the recent papers, they find a related story printed a few days later. It reports the deaths of the two captured cultists who died in their cells as the result of a fire. Oddly enough, although the two victims were charred beyond recognition, the bed sheets and blankets were not even scorched.

**Special Information:** If the investigators seek out and talk to the reporter who wrote the Sylvan Night story, (and make a successful **Fast Talk** roll), they are told that during the raid several policeman apparently lost their nerve and panicked, allowing the leader of the cult to escape. If the investigators accuse the reporter of not printing all the facts, he tells the investigators the police have been pressuring him to keep this embarrassing aspect of the raid out of print.

The reporter's notebook lies on his desk. If anyone can make a successful **DEX x2** roll, they may swipe the notebook and sneak it away for later perusal. Its contents reveal the unspeakable nature of the recent spate of murders and mutilations. In every case the faces of the victims were bitten and chewed. Humans apparently inflicted the bites.

### Andrea Pentargon

Andrea Pentargon is a short, dark haired woman in her mid twenties. Her face is finely chiseled and would be beautiful, but when the investigators meet her they see dark circles under her eyes and a look of wild anxiety tightens her otherwise fine features. She also displays a number of unpleasant nervous tics.

Andrea was friends with Josephine for several years and knows of the woman's occult/Cthulhoid dealings. She witnessed many of the human sacrifices conducted by the Sylvan Night and turned informant only after breaking with Josephine and leaving the cult. Although she is under police protection (they have given her a place to live, and a new name), the authorities do not realize the extent of her danger. Andrea is insanely afraid of Josephine, but feels (wrongly) she has little to fear from Zeke Crater.

Andrea Pentargon lives in a run-down section of Boston's waterfront district under the assumed name of Myra Smith (this information can only be provided by detective Devlin). Her apartment can be found at the end of a darkened hallway on the third floor of an aging building. If the investigators knock she opens it only far enough to allow her to peek through the narrow crack. The slack, down hanging loop of a door chain (STR 14) is visible near her hand. Pentargon fears for her life and the investigators must use **Psychology or Fast Talk** to

*Miss Pentargon*

convince her to let them in. Invoking the name of Detective Sergeant Devlin adds 35% to their chances. If the investigators attempt a violent entry, Pentargon attempts to call the police.

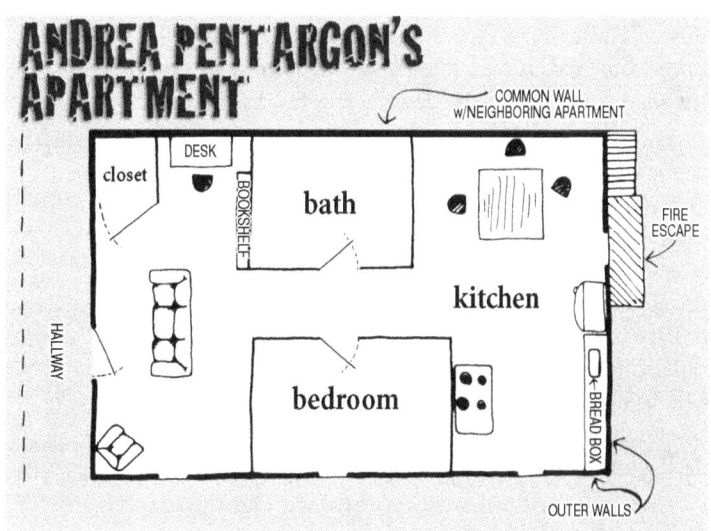

## PASSAGES FROM SCRIPTURES OF THE RIVEN VALLEY

"Many stories of the area seem to have their basis in old Indian legends regarding a being that dwelt somewhere in "the shadow land of the hills." This "god" could contact those it wanted through their dreams and command them. Often, those who would dream of this being would be driven mad. These unfortunates would end up being expelled from their tribes and forced into the wilderness to make their way on their own. The area was taboo to the tribes of the area but occasionally, one seeking wisdom or knowledge would, regardless of the risks, sleep in these dark and forbidding hills.

"An old woman told me a story about a neighbor who once, after suffering a particularly terrible series of nightmares, slew his entire family with an axe before hanging himself in his woodshed. The old woman told me that the man had always been a good husband and father but apparently lost his mind. She remembers her uncle telling her that old Martin Garsetti was a good man until they moved out of town and into the new house he'd built for his family on the slopes of the mountain. This house was built in an area shunned by the local Indians. The house still stands and is presently occupied by other members of the same family, although none of them seem to have been afflicted by any form of madness.

"The Gunderson party was among the first whites to make a home for themselves in the area and, despite the warnings of local Indians, built their first rude settlements among those hills the Indians so assiduously avoided. Although the early settlement seemed to prosper for the first year it was not long before tragedy struck. Apparently during the long winter one of the settlers lost his mind. When they were discovered by visitors from nearby Pittsburgh all the miners and their families were dead, apparently killed by wolves, their faces terribly bitten and chewed. Only one man's death was caused by other means, a single bullet wound to the forehead — an obvious suicide. Oddly enough, the marauding wolves did not see fit to ravage this body as they had the others. ☀

*The Mansion Papers #3*

If asked about Garsetti, Andrea says she has known Josephine for a long time and up until recently they even shared an apartment together. They first met at Boston University where they were fellow art students. Both women shared an interest in the occult and both led what could politely be described as fast living.

One night, while visiting a speakeasy called the Sailor's Club, Andrea and Josephine met a man named Zeke Crater. Crater invited the two women up to his house "for a party and a good time." Soon they began attending Crater's orgies regularly and the two even staged a competition of sorts, both of them attempting to have sexual liaisons with as many of the men as possible. Crater, Andrea says, was a wild man and, at the beginning of the orgies would make a point of killing several chickens and pouring their blood over a small dark stone that he always seemed to keep close to him.

Crater seemed attracted to Josephine and the two began seeing each other away from the regular parties.

Then Crater suddenly dropped out of sight. Josephine told Andrea that she wasn't seeing the gangster anymore and wanted to start her own club. She asked Andrea to join. Andrea claims she declined the opportunity and did not attend the early meetings of the Sylvan Night but Josephine eventually convinced her to "come along and give it a try." She and Josephine, along with about a dozen people from Crater's old group met in a dark wooded area several miles north of the city. Andrea says she was shocked when, at the height of the festivities, Josephine ruthlessly murdered one of the previous cult's members. She then used the victim's blood to wash the same small dark stone that had formerly belonged to Crater. Andrea says all this horrified her and she quit the group and moved out of the apartment she had been sharing with Garsetti. (A successful **Psychology** roll shows this to be a fabrication. If the truth is ever learned, it will be found that Andrea was in on the activities from the beginning and only after several meetings did she grow fearful and go to the police.)

Should the investigators ask Andrea about Josephine's paintings, she gets a wistful, almost enraptured look on her face and says she thinks they are marvelous. "Despite the things that Jodie might have done, I still think they are the most true paintings I have ever seen. They really show things the way they are." If the investigators mention the painting entitled the *Dweller in the Void*, Andrea says quietly, "Jodie told me she painted that one from memory. She claims to have really seen it in a dream. Incredible, isn't it?"

If Andrea grows to trust the investigators she may reveal her deepest fear: "You know I took an oath to die for the Sylvan Night rather then ever betray it. I remember thinking at the time that it was thrilling to say something like that and really be with a group of people who

## SCRIPTURES OF THE RIVEN VALLEY

A copy of this book can be encountered in Andrea Pentargon's apartment and, if missed there, in the Garsetti home.

### SCRIPTURES OF THE RIVEN VALLEY, by Flan O'Leary, first edition 1902. In English.

O'Leary was a well known anthropologist and author of several books. Scriptures is a study of the cultures of the hill people of central Pennsylvania, Virginia, and West Virginia. His last published work, *Scriptures* was an unusual departure from his normal scholarly approach and cost him much in the way of credibility among his colleagues. Of most interest to the investigators is a section that deals with a series of legends, based on old Indian tales, prevalent among the hill peoples around Muskrat Rapids, Pennsylvania. *Sanity loss 0/1D3; Cthulhu Mythos +3 percentiles: average 2 weeks to study and comprehend.* **Spells:** none. ☀

# EXCERPTS FROM A DIARY

This document is found in Andrea's beaded purse. Only those entries with direct interest to the investigation are given here.

### June 30, 1916

*Dear Diary,*

*I don't know how to write about it but my dreams have been so strong the last few nights that I'm actually scared. It seems that I was in a big cave, all filled with glowing lights and then I heard a voice. A big voice, but it made noise only in my head. Like someone else's thoughts were there, racing around inside my skull. I can almost still hear it, whispering to me even as I write this. For some reason I am afraid. But it was, after all, only a dream.*

### August 28, 1916

*Dear Diary,*

*I keep having the dreams about the voice. It says it wants to teach me things but somehow it makes me be afraid. I want to tell mother about it but somehow I feel she wouldn't understand.*

As winter arrives, entries referring to the dream voice become more common; but Josephine remains undecided about listening to the mysterious voice. All her diary entries, however, adopt a darker tone.

### January 28, 1917

*Dear Diary,*

*I tell you I cannot stand this house. The walls are pounding in on me. I cannot get the dreams about the voice out of my head and even now I can see that strange cave. I hate my mother and I wish I could pass from this house into the warm darkness of the ground.*

The entries retain this tone throughout the winter and spring of 1917. Pages at a time are free of words but are covered with intricate, convoluted cross hatchings. At first glance the patterns only show a good sense of texture but at times faces seem to resolve themselves out of the dense layers of crossed lines.

### June 29, 1917

*The teachers at school seem so amazed by the things I draw. Some of them say I have real talent and should go to school somewhere to learn how to draw better. I tried to tell them that I only draw the things I see in my dreams but I don't think they really believed me. Mother says the pictures are no good but I think she's wrong. The voice in my dreams says I could draw better but that I must get away from here. I want to leave this house as soon as I can. Mr. Matthews says there's a contest coming up in Pittsburgh. The winning entrant will be given an art scholarship to Boston University. I'm already starting on a picture I think will win.*

### June 30, 1917

*The voice came again last night while I was dreaming. It told me that if I would listen to it and do as it says that I will have everything I ever wanted out of lift. For the first time I opened my eyes and then I saw the voice and what it was. It was blurry so I couldn't see much but I know that it's awfully big. It showed me something I could draw for the contest and told me that if I did a good job I couldn't help but win. I think the voice really wants me to win and go to Boston. I hope it happens. I can't stand my mother much longer. I swear, she makes me so mad that sometimes I think I'll kill her.* ☀

*The Mansion Papers #4*

all believed in the same kind of things I did. But now I'm just afraid of what it really means. I'm really afraid they're going to somehow make me die."

If Andrea becomes friendly with the investigators, she may accompany them to the Sailor's Club, where she and Josephine (and others) spent many an evening together.

Depending upon Andrea's reaction to the investigators she may or may not divulge the following bits of information:

☀ Josephine was born and raised in Muskrat Rapids, Pennsylvanian. The exact address is found in a tattered pocket address book kept in Andrea's purse.

☀ If questioned about the book, *Scriptures of the Riven Valley* (obtainable in Pentargon's apartment), she says that Josephine lingered over the passages in the book that dealt with secret rituals practiced in the Pennsylvania hills.

## Clues in Andrea's Apartment

On a shelf in the front room is a Boston University yearbook from last year. The book contains portrait photos of both Pentargon and Garsetti as well as a picture of them posing with other members of the Art Club. Andrea shows these to the investigators if they ask for a picture of Josephine.

Among the other books on this shelf is a copy of *Scriptures of the Riven Valley*, by Flan O'Leary. This is a Mythos tome and will only be noticed if an investigator makes a **Cthulhu Mythos** roll or takes the time necessary to plow through thirty or forty books on her shelves. this book details the practices of several rural American religious cults, some of which are said to be in American religious cults, some of which are said to be in areas adjacent to Josephine's home town (see ***The Mansion Papers #3***). For details about the book as a tome, see above.

## Andrea's Purse

In this purse is a dirty and dog-eared address book. Inside is found a mailing address for a Jane Garsetti. This is Josephine's mother. In the event the investigators learn that Josephine has probably returned to her home, this address should come in handy. Also in the purse is the tattered diary written by Josephine when she was a teenager (see ***The Mansion Papers #4***). Andrea stole it from Josephine, along with the copy of *Scriptures of the Riven Valley*, when she moved out of their shared apartment.

The gangster, Zeke Carter, seeks revenge not only against Josephine Garsetti but also Andrea Pentargon, the only other surviving member of the Sylvan Night. If Crater is aware of the investigators actions, some of his thugs follow them to Pentargon's apartment. The first evening that she is left alone, Crater comes to pay her a visit. The next morning her landlady, noticing the woman's door is ajar, discovers Pentargon's mangled body, limbs torn loose from the trunk and internal organs draped around the apartment like gory holiday garlands. The woman's head is missing.

As soon as Devlin learns of Pentargon's death he comes looking for the investigators, perhaps even suspecting them of the murder. It is unlikely that there is enough evidence to bring charges against any of them but Devlin, until he learns better, remains suspicious and apprehensive of the investigators.

## The Sailor's Club

The Sailor's Club is a popular speakeasy located on the shore of Boston Harbor. It is frequented by a wide variety of people from any different social circles. Within its walls an investigator may well find a rum-running underworld type seated right next to a thrill-seeking debutante from uptown.

The dark structure housing the club squats on a muddy bank overlooking the harbor. A nearby run-down wharf is used to receive smuggled alcohol coming in from Europe and the Caribbean. The club opens around 8 PM and closes at 3 AM, seven nights a week.

The bar and stage area is a broad L-shaped room decorated in a seedy nautical style. The bar, seen immediately upon entering the door, is decorated with ancient, torn fishing nets

*Mr. "Wriggles" Pantucci*

draped with cobwebs. A large ship's wheel with several missing pins leans in one corner and the floor is coated with a thick gray-green mulch of beer-soaked sawdust. Alcohol is served in chipped porcelain teacups.

Tending the bar is Randolph Smith, a young man of medium height. He has light brown hair, cold dark eyes, and a brusque manner. If any trouble starts, Smith draws a sawed-off double-barrel 12-gauge shotgun from beneath the bar and, in a loud voice threatens to use it. Smith's skill with the shotgun is 65% (damage 4D6) He has 12 hit points.

Smith has almost absolute control over the muscular club bouncer Albert "Wriggles" Pantucci. Wriggles always asked investigators entering the Club to hand over any weapons they may be carrying. No firearms or knives are permitted within the walls of the club. Pantucci is quiet and stupid. His job is to enforce the strict "no weapons" rule. He comes by his nickname from the pleasure he gathers watching violators of the rule wriggling against the wall while he squeezes the air from their throats. He has become adept at catching victims in a crippling strangle hold (see below).

### Wriggles Pantucci, bouncer at the Sailor's Club

| STR 19 | CON 17 | SIZ 16 | INT 09 | POW 07 |
|--------|--------|--------|--------|--------|
| DEX 10 | APP 08 | EDU 04 | SAN 34 | HP 17 |

**Damage Bonus:** +1D6

**Weapons:** Strangle Hold* 70% (may be dodged or parried)
Fist/Punch 75%, damage 1D3 + db
Kick 55%, damage 1D6
Head Butt 65%, damage 1D4 + db
.38 Revolver 65%, damage 1D10

*\* Lose 2 hit point per round until victim surrenders or loses consciousness. Hit points lost are recovered within 1D3 hours except for one quarter of the points which remain as actual injuries.*

**Skills:** Dodge 31%, Spot Hidden 58%

The keeper may wish to determine whether investigators become intoxicated while at the Club. Beer at the Sailor's Club should be considered to have POT 9, and the gin POT 13. Check these against an investigator's CON. Start making resistance checks after the second drink has been consumed. If a character fails to resist, reduce perceptual and agility-based skills by 10%, and by an additional 10% for every drink thereafter. It takes 1D4+2 hours to shake the worst effects of the alcohol.

### The Band Leader

A lively jazz orchestra performs here Wednesday through Saturday, starting around 10:30 PM. The performance con-

**SAILOR'S CLUB**

~~~~ = SHUTTERED WINDOW
= BOARDED WINDOW
= HEAVY OUTER DOOR

= TABLE
= CHAIR

WRIGGLE'S CHAIR
BAR →
unused kitchen
Crater's office
BAND STAGE
storage
WC
dressing room

*Mr. Candlemar*

tinues, with ten minute breaks every 45 minutes, until 2:30 AM. The orchestra leader is a tall thin black man with graying hair. His name is Zoots Candlemar and he's a sax player.

If approached politely, Zoots is amicable. A successful **Psychology** roll indicates that Zoots is merely a nice guy, and has no ulterior motives.

**Zoots' Clues:** If the investigators ask about Josephine Garsetti, Zoots remembers her from her constant patronage of the club. Zoots says Josephine used to come here with a girl friend and then later used to meet with a certain group of about a dozen people — people with whom she was obviously very friendly. A couple of months ago she started showing up with a young man, whom Zoots describes as tall and sandy-haired, and with an uptown manner (Andrew Keating). If her other friends were in the club at the time they acted as if they didn't know each other.

## The Gangsters

Two men sit at a table near the corner of the bar. They wear dark pinstriped suits and fedoras. Casually studying the room, they alternately drink from chipped tea cups and pick lint from their lapels. The two are members of a rival gang, here just check up on Crater and make sure he does his business by the rules. Gang wars have been infrequent as of late and these two men are here just to make sure Crater's operations are on the up and up. Crater, and members of his gang, recognize the pair and ignore them, knowing why they're here. If the investigators can somehow approach this pair and talk to them, the taller, darker of the two (named Vince) might respond. This guy has blue black hair and a dark rime of five o'clock shadow on his face. The other man at the table is silent and will not respond to direct questions. Vince doesn't volunteer his surly companion's name (Eddy).

**Vince's Clues:** Vince has been in the business for years and knows the full story of Zeke Crater or at least the most common rumors and speculation. "Zeke", he tells the investigators, "was always a party kind of guy. Always dressed to the teeth, usually with a babe on each arm. Zeke would go out almost every night, drinking champagne or just whorin' around. Then, after he got big and went out on his own, he bought that old house up the coast and started throwin' some really wild parties. All kind of shit was supposed to be going on up there and Zeke — well, Zeke was always one to party to

the limit. One guy who went up there said Zeke was roaring like a madman, biting off the heads of chickens and swiggin' expensive champagne right out of the bottle. That's when he got his nickname 'the geek'. Then, a few months ago, Zeke just sort of drops out of sight. Nobody sees him for almost a month. Then he shows back up, not looking too good and sort of hobblin' around. He's still runnin' his business but he don't get out like he used to. Don't hardly ever see him with women anymore either. Some of the boys think that Zeke's real sick and'll probably die soon. Myself," Vince says, "I don't really care one way or the other." Then he laughs.

## The Flappers

*Miss Bobbie*

Seated at a table near the foot of the stage are three young flappers. They are jamming with the orchestra and guzzling gin from coffee mugs. They are easy to approach. One, a tall, lanky girl who calls herself Bobbie, will, if shown his photo, remember Andrew Keetling.

**Bobbie's Clue:** She remembers Andrew but even more remembers his female companion and the way she dressed. "Her clothes were all weird and fancy like she was rich or from Europe or something, you know what I mean, honey?" Bobbie bats her eyelashes.

## A Shabby Individual in a Trench Coat

Roger Cross is a down-on-his-luck private detective hired by the family of one of Josephine's earlier victims. His face is pale and thin, a dark stubble of three-day beard shows in severe contrast to his unhealthy, translucent skin. He usually dresses in a rumpled and dirty light gray trench coat and tan fedora, its wilted brim smudged with grime.

Although skillful in some areas of investigation, Cross is so beset by character flaws he has never achieved any notable success, either as a private investigator or as a man. Cross is an alcoholic and at times he may become completely vacant and inarticulate. He is addicted to cocaine and constantly sniffs while

*Mr. Roger Cross, P.I.*

*Ezekiel Crater in His Office*

holding a crumpled handkerchief under his nose. If the investigators observe his actions, Cross sits quietly until shortly after 11 PM. He then stands up and, crossing the room, says something to the bartender. He waits impatiently while Smith disappears through a door behind the bar. After a moment the bartender reappears and nods to Cross who then steps through the door. After five minutes, Cross emerges from the door and re-seats himself at his table, taking a heavy nasal drag on his handkerchief.

If any of the investigators are also Private Investigators, they will recognize Cross with a **Know** roll of **EDU x5.** Others will recognize him only with a roll of **EDU x1** or less.

If the investigators befriend him, or lend him the ten-spot he says he needs, Cross will share what he knows.

**Cross's Clues:** Crater is the crime lord of the wharf area surrounding the Sailor's Club. Anyone who has ever tried to horn in on his district has quickly and quietly disappeared. All drugs and bootleg liquor sold or distributed within a half mile of the Club pass through Crater's hands. He has been long known as a man with a large appetite for food, drink, and sex, but has for the last couple months been leading a much quieter lifestyle.

Two weeks ago Cross spotted Josephine in here with a sandy haired man dressed in fancy evening clothes. Cross does not remember much more about that night, however, as he got too drunk to really keep an eye on the couple.

Unfortunately, Cross has not been able to make much progress in finding Josephine. He does know that Crater leaves the Club, without fail, every night at 3 AM. He has never followed Crater home.

## Zeke Crater

If the investigators have visited the police station, there is a good chance that Crater already knows of them and what it is they are up to. The investigators will probably be unaware of this and, in an effort to meet with Crater, may attempt some sort of ploy. They can pretend to be drug purchasers, or prospective alcohol wholesalers, or criminals offering to sell Crater some information. The keeper might require they make a **Fast Talk** on Smith before getting in to see the gangster. Crater does not usually check into his office until 11 PM.

If successful in their attempt, the investigators will be escorted through the door behind the bar, through an abandoned kitchen, and into Crater's office. (The abandoned kitchen is used to store crates of smuggled alcohol and other contraband, all kept covered under dusty drop cloths.)

Entering the office the investigators find Crater seated behind a large desk covered with scraps of paper and soiled ledgers — Crater's business receipts. He is reading from a large book and hurriedly scratching down notes with a fountain pen.

He wears a wide brimmed hat shadowing his features and an expensive suit barely visible beneath his flowing black cape. He seems in excellent health, judging by his remarkably smooth, unblemished complexion. An **Idea** roll allows the investigators to wonder why a man Crater's age (supposedly in his forties) would have such a youthful appearance. What can be seen of Crater's features are waxen, and oddly immobile. His eyes are unblinking, large, and mostly inky black pupils. The skin on his hands is pale in color, and, like his face, is also smooth and glossy. His motions are quick, but seem oddly stiff and a bit clumsy. Oddest of all are several unsightly bulges under the crime lord's suit coat, around the area of his ribs. If any of the investigators impolitely ask questions about Crater's strange appearance he tells them that he suffered a number of serious injuries in the Great War and that they never fully healed.

Any investigators who are still suspicious may make a **Spot Hidden** roll (not everyone, just those who state clearly that their investigator is nervous and suspicious). If successful, they must make an **Idea** roll. A failed idea roll suggests that Crater's odd appearance must be due to inferior cosmetic surgery, complicated by a profligate lifestyle spent mainly indoors. The bulges under his suit must be concealed knives or other weapons. However, if the idea roll is successful, the investigator realizes that Crater's skin is actually some kind of rigid, insect like carapace, and that the strange bulges appear to be, not weapons, but body parts of some sort, which occasionally twitch and writhe! The keeper must write a note to the player(s) whose investigators gain this awful knowledge, and instruct them to make a SAN roll against 0/1D3.

Unclothed, Crater resembles nothing ever seen on this Earth. His skin is the shiny, off white carapace of an insect. It turn blows from knives and cudgels, and deflects the main strength of gunshots as well. His chest and back are banded with rib like strips of chitin, with deeply shadowed depressions between. Folded tightly against his sides are four extra appendages much like jointed whips ending in sharp, bony hooks. High on his ribbed back are two small projections, the stumps of the wide, membranous wings which Crater sawed off in order to pass as human. Below, his legs each have an extra joint. His feet have two long flexible toes and clawed heels.

As the investigators enter, Crater closes his book and puts it away in a briefcase on the floor. (Anyone who can make a **Latin** roll at 20 percentiles discerns the title of the book: translated as *Kingdom of the Shadows*. A successful **Cthulhu Mythos** roll identifies it as a 17th century tome of great rarity.) He greets the investigators civilly but warily. Standing up from his desk, Crater bows politely to the group then sits back down. His voice is deep and rich, and his polite style of speaking indicates an intelligent and at least partially educated man. Apparently possessed of great self control, Crater never smiles or frowns, no matter what the investigators say or do.

Crater will not introduce himself, and, at first, only asks what kind of "merchandise" the investigators are interested in procuring (or selling). If the investigators mention Josephine Garsetti he listens carefully to their questions. Crater studies the investigators closely during the interview and gently encourages them to explain everything they have discovered about their quarry thus far. He volunteers nothing himself until they finish.

Crater grows suspicious if any of the investigators volunteer that they recognize his book for what it is. He slyly suggests that they visit his estate some day soon to discuss the rare books and other antiques that they both seem to share an interest in. The investigators may be rightly suspicious of this invitation.

**Crater's Clues:** Once Crater has determined that the investigators are interested in Josephine and not him, or if the investigators reveal an interest in occult items, Crater launches into a story concerning an object that Josephine stole from him. "Yes, I know the woman, and she has stolen something from me that I would very much like to recover," he says. He goes on to say that, for obvious reasons, he prefers to not involve the police. The object in question is a small dark stone about six inches long, carved from a very valuable brown translucent crystal. Crater offers the investigators a reward of $2500 if they will track down the Garsetti woman and recover the object. Once they have it in their possession he would like it shipped to him immediately. This, he says, is for their own comfort, as viewing the stone for any length of time can have an unsettling effect upon the mind. He would rather not subject the investigators to such an experience.

Crater cautions the investigators further by telling them Josephine is an insane murderess, responsible for the ritual slaughter and mutilation of at least a half dozen people. She led the cult known as the Sylvan Night.

Crater says that Josephine is hiding out from the police, trying to rebuild her base of power now that the cult has been broken. He is not sure whether she is even still in Boston and tells the investigators, rather pointedly, that she may have fled back to her hometown of Muskrat Rapids, Pennsylvania.

Crater does not want to seem like he knows too much about Josephine, so he will not volunteer any specifics about her and the cult. He understands enough about the protective magic Garsetti uses to believe that if the investigators go after her while working directly for him, they will probably not be able to get near her. Crater will, however, make every effort to point them in the right direction. If not already known to the investigators, Crater can provide the following leads:

☀ Josephine had a friend, a young lady named Andrea Pentargon, with whom she shared many secrets. The girl seems to have left town, with no forwarding address. Crater believes she may know something of Josephine's whereabouts.

☀ Josephine attended Boston University; perhaps they can uncover some of her background there, if they can avoid making the staff suspicious.

Crater must convince someone to retrieve the Stone for him, as Josephine has erected several powerful Bone Totems (see the following chapters for more information) around her house to prevent him, or any who directly serve him, from entering the area. Given that the investigators want to find Josephine anyway, he feels they will be the perfect tools to realize his plans.

If the investigators should threaten or attack Crater, he cries out, bringing to the rescue the bartender, Randolph Smith, who appears in the doorway after two combat rounds, followed shortly by Wriggles Pantucci. Smith is armed with his 12 gauge, double-barreled sawed off shotgun. He asks the investigators to surrender before firing. If the investigators surrender they are escorted to the door and never permitted within the walls of the Sailor's Club again.

If they actually manage to wound Crater, he flees out the boarded window of his office, which opens on concealed hinges. The only thing that could force him to fight would be the theft of his book.

## Crater's Secrets

It was three years ago that Crater accidentally took possession of the Dark Stone. Found in a shipment of goods intended for Miskatonic University (mistakenly hijacked by some of Crater's men), the Stone was part of a small estate willed to the University by an alumnus who had lived in Europe. Crater at first viewed the crate's contents as useless but after reading the cover letter he found, he explored the items more thoroughly. One book found among the many in the crate was a copy of the *Book of Eibon* (English version). Within its pages Crater found a description of the Dark Stone and hints as to how it could be used. With some experimentation Crater found that if he kept the stone close to his person, his strength and endurance seemed to be increased, particularly his sexual potency. Further experimenting showed that if small animals (usually chickens) were killed in the presence of the stone that these feelings of power were increased even further. Shortly after, Crater began staging weekend orgies in his isolated mansion.

When Josephine showed up on the scene Crater had no idea that she had been led there by some supernatural being and no idea that she was out to take from him his precious Dark Stone. A few months later Crater met with Josephine in their fateful assignation. When Crater was at his weakest moment, Garsetti, aided by the Thing Hanging in the Void, cast a terrible spell upon the gangster, a magical curse that deformed him horribly. The spell would have killed most men but Crater was simply too tough to die. He somehow managed to make it back home and there lay near death for two months, slowly recuperating.

Crater spent much of his recovery time researching the mysterious *Book of Eibon*, looking for some way to change himself back to the man he once was. Although Eibon contained a little information about the Dark Stone, it only hinted at some of its potential. It was in the translator's introduction that he found a reference to an older book called *Kingdom of Shadows* which purportedly contained much information on the Dark Stone. Using his money and criminal contacts, Crater located a copy of the book in New York and arranged to have it stolen from its owner, a private collector. It was not until the book was in his hands that Crater discovered it was written in Latin, a language with which he was quite unfamiliar. Determined to find a way to cure himself, Crater bought text books and began to slowly teach himself to read the ancient text.

He has, up to this time, faultily translated only small portions of the tome but believes himself on the right track. He has already learned considerably more about the Stone than he knew before and feels sure that the object contains the secret of returning him to his former self. He carries the tome, his notes, and his two Latin/English reference books with him wherever he goes. It is possible that the investigators might obtain Crater's book, either here, or later at his mansion (see **The Mansion Papers #5**). The book is in Latin but the following portions have been translated to English. If the investigators obtain the book at the Sailor's Club, only the first excerpt will be found in translated form. To obtain the other clues, the book will have to be read by an investigator with skill in **Latin**. If the investigators get hold of the book at Crater's mansion, all of the following clues will be found in English translation.

## Reading the Tome

*Kingdom of Shadows* requires at least 1D6+2 days and a successful Latin roll. Written in the early 17th century, it increases an investigator's Cthulhu Mythos knowledge by +8 and costs 1D10 SAN to read and comprehend.

## Excerpts from "Kingdom of Shadows"

Using the power of the Dark Stone one can wreak many changes, on both the world and one's self. Great are the promises of the Dark Stone and of The Hanging One, but great also are the dangers. It is said the user can stand transmogrified before the power held captive within, sickness cured and madness dispelled.

. . . The Dark Stone, of fiery Power and promise! The Stone was cleverly crafted in Elder Days by The Secret Messenger With One Thousand Faces (using hands not his own) to burn a hole between daylight and dreams. A passage by which the One Who Hangs in the Void could reach out and touch this world.

. . . Beware lest the Stone take the soul of the impious thief, though it may bring Power beforehand.

. . . Not only power can be obtained through the Dark Stone but other talents can also be learned. Secret are their ways and mysterious the callings, but great are these talents in the hands of the user who would know.

. . . The Stone was made to last forever and no known power on Earth can destroy it. It possesses those who possess it and it rules their lives. ☀

*The Mansion Papers #5*

The book contains intimations of Drain Youth, Drown Mind, and Voorish Sign, but contact with the Thing and consequent insanity is needed before the spells are learned. If Crater's notes are read, it takes a successful **English** roll to decipher his scratchy handwriting.

## Breaking Into Crater's Office

The investigators may want to break into Crater's office. He does not leave, typically, until 3 AM. The reinforced door at the back of the club is especially heavy (STR 22). The well thumbed copy of The *Kingdom of Shadows* is not present. Crater carries the book with him wherever he goes.

## PART TWO
# House of Dreams

Josephine Garsetti, fleeing both the Boston police and gangster Zeke Crater, has returned to the place of her birth, a large isolated house a few miles outside the town of Muskrat Rapids, Pennsylvania. The destruction of her Sylvan Night is the first time in her life she has suffered a real defeat. Distraught and paranoid, she has murdered her mother and presently holds Andrew Keetling prisoner in an upstairs bedroom. The Thing in the Void wants her to complete this final sacrifice (Andrew Keetling) allowing it to institute its plan but Garsetti now hesitates, fearing that to do so might cause her harm. The Thing continues to urge her, by way of her dreams, but still she hesitates. If the investigators visit the property but do not rescue Keetling, Josephine, panicked, will probably commit the sacrifice that very night, unleashing the Thing upon the innocent dreamers of Muskrat Rapids.

Zeke Crater's two stooges are in town, sent here by the gangster to try and retrieve the Dark Stone. Garsetti (with the aid of the Thing in the Void) has magically protected herself against Crater and his minions and they cannot draw near the house unless the bone totems are disturbed or Garsetti killed. Once this has happened they will be free to move in and attempt to take the Dark Stone away from the investigators. If the gangsters fail their mission (or if the keeper wishes) one of Crater's insectile children will show up and attempt to steal the object. In either case, the investigators will probably wish to track down Crater and recover the Dark Stone.

## Muskrat Rapids, Pennsylvania

Muskrat Rapids, founded in the first years of the nineteenth century, is a small community now growing rapidly due to the ever-expanding Pittsburgh steel industry. Most of the town consists of small, slapped together houses intended for mill workers and their families. These houses are built haphazardly up and down the steep hills rising up either side of the Muskrat River. During the week the streets are filled with women and children on errands but on weekend evenings the men take over the town, crowding into the Pelt Trapper's Tavern, an illegal but gleefully patronized establishment.

A general store and a three story boarding house are also located on Main Street as well as a doctor's office. A dull shingle, hung on a leaning post, reads "Anthony Pritchard, MD". His medical abilities are at least average and he can tend to normal injuries the investigators might suffer. The investigators may also want to bring Andrew Keetling here, should they successfully rescue him.

## The Law

The County Sheriff's office, located next to the Pelt Trapper's Tavern, is manned by Sheriff Anson Varley and his five deputies. The steel industry has been attracting workers from all areas of the country. Pay is good, and times are fast. The sheriff's office can sometimes get pretty busy.

Sheriff Varley's primary concern is pleasing the owners of the local mills, not aiding a group of outsiders against a local girl who may or may not be a criminal. Unless the investigators can convince Varley something is definitely amiss up at the old Garsetti place, it is unlikely he will respond favorably to their demands for help (**Credit Rating, Law, or Fast Talk** rolls are at 20%).

The sheriff becomes involved if he witnesses a criminal act committed by Josephine, or if the investigators can show him evidence of foul play, such as a body. In such a case, Varley will help, but also wants to keep "mysterious doings" under wraps.

Inquiries in the Muskrat Rapids area soon turns up the location of the old Garsetti house. However, after giving directions, the face of whomever the investigators are talking to suddenly clouds with concern. "By the way, Mrs. Garsetti hasn't been seen in town for almost two weeks now, stranger. Do you know anything about the old lady that the Sheriff ought to hear?". They glance suspiciously at the investigator. Further inquiries into Mrs. Garsetti's mysterious absence reveal only that no one in town has gone up and checked at the house. Privacy is a valued commodity here.

One old man might tell a rambling story about less recent goings on: "That pretty young Josephine was always a strange one — you could tell by lookin' at her she was just plain wicked. She lit out of here after finishing high school and after foolin' around with just about all the menfolk in town. She caused a bit of trouble with some of the wilder local boys when she got to be a young woman. Most folks around here were real glad she went off to Boston or wherever it was she went. She just wasn't like the rest of the folks from around here."

## The Strangers

Crater has already sent two of his men down here to try and retrieve the Dark Stone, a task they failed due to Garsetti's magical bone totems. The duo are now under orders to hang around town and wait for the player characters to show up. Both hoods, dressed in pin striped suits, overcoats, and fedoras, stand out like sore thumbs among the semi rural blue-collar locals. If the investigators spend any amount of time in town, they are sure to notice this pair.

The two gangsters have already visited the Garsetti home, but when they tried to approach the place they were beset by an unreasoning fear and ran away. Chagrined, they phoned the boss and lied to him, telling him that they been out to the place and found nothing, neither the woman nor the stone. The angry, frustrated Crater, betting the investigators would show up there sooner or later, told the two gunsels to stay put and to keep an eye out for the player characters. The pair are under orders to not interfere with the investigators until they possess the Dark Stone. Once the investigators get their hands on the stone, the two gangsters are supposed to relieve the characters of it, and whisk the stone back to Boston.

The two goons follow the investigators out to the house and observe their actions from a safe distance. If the investigators uproot even one of the bone totems, the field of protection is broken. The gangsters realize this, suddenly noticing that they are no longer fearful of the house. They may choose to move in closer.

### Chuckie the Rat

| | | | | | |
|---|---|---|---|---|---|
| SIR 13 | CON 14 | SIZ 12 | INT 13 | POW 12 | |
| DEX 15 | APP 12 | EDU 08 | SAN 40 | HP 13 | |

**Damage Bonus:** +1D4

**Weapons:** Fist/Punch 65%, damage 1D3
Kick 35%, damage 1D6
.45 Automatic 75%, damage 1D10+2

**Skills:** Dodge 55%, Drive Automobile 65%, Fast Talk 65%, Hide 75%, Spot Hidden 65%.

### Big Al

| | | | | | |
|---|---|---|---|---|---|
| STR 17 | CON 16 | SIZ 17 | INT 08 | POW 10 | |
| DEX 10 | APP 10 | EDU 06 | SAN 30 | HP 17 | |

**Damage Bonus:** +1D6

**Weapons:** Fist/Punch 55%, damage 1D3
Head Butt 75%, damage 1D4
.38 Revolver 45%, damage 1D10

**Skills:** Dodge 35%, Drive Automobile 45%, Hide 65%, Psychology 35%

## The Garsetti Property

Following the directions learned in town, the investigators find themselves on a narrow, seldom used road screened on both sides by a dense growth of brush, hedges, and trees. Tall unkempt hedges and hoary oaks surround the Garsetti house.

### The Bone Totem Barrier

A **Spot Hidden** at –30% reveals the presence of one of the bone totems hidden in the hedges, carefully camouflaged with leaves and vines. All the totem bases are driven deep into the ground and resist uprooting with STR 18.

There are four of these very powerful objects hidden amidst the hedges and trees surrounding the Garsetti house. They are located at the four cardinal points of the compass. Josephine erected them with knowledge provided her by The Thing Hanging in the Void.

Each of the totems, which resemble small vaguely humanoid figures, is between two and four feet in height and composed of carefully gnawed and shaped human bones. The bones are bound together with various odd materials including sinew, old twine, knotted rags, dried intestines, and an unidentifiable adhesive substance that gives off a nauseating stench. Close examination of a totem leads an investigator to discover these disgusting details and requires a SAN roll against a loss of 0/1.

The field of protection created by the totems is effective only against Crater and his minions. Although the field is invisible, the use of magic such as Powder of Ibn Ghazi reveals the area of protection as a dark zone of shadow.

**The Dry Well:** This old brick well to the south of the house is boarded over with heavy, rotting timbers, STR 8 for purposes of breakage. A quick insertion of the nose will detect an immediate, and overpowering stench of rotting flesh. The body of Josephine Garsetti's mother lies at the bottom. Her throat is cut and what's left of her rotting face still shows signs of the bite marks inflicted by her insane daughter. If someone is lowered down the well and sees the corpse, he loses 1/1D4 SAN.

## Josephine Garsetti

Unless the keeper has other ideas, Josephine hides within the house, slyly watching the investigators from a curtained window. She is a reasonably dangerous opponent but perhaps outmatched by most groups of investigators. She has no real wish for a fatal confrontation with armed investigators and a dogged group should be able to track her down and force an end to her depraved activities. She always keeps the Dark Stone on her person and will never voluntarily surrender it.

*Miss Garsetti*

Josephine Garsetti is slightly more than five feet tall, has strawberry blonde hair, prominent blue eyes, and is possessed of a very slender build. Her clothing is of the latest style, tastefully displaying just a hint of provocative decadence.

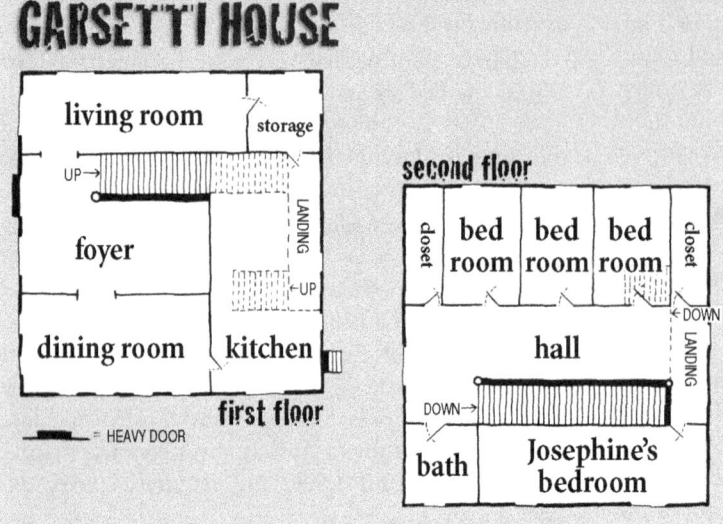

# GARSETTI HOUSE

**first floor**

living room
storage
UP→
LANDING
foyer
UP
dining room
kitchen

▬▬ = HEAVY DOOR

**second floor**

closet
bed room
bed room
bed room
closet
DOWN
LANDING
hall
DOWN→
bath
Josephine's bedroom

**Suggested strategies for Josephine:** She will cast Drown Mind (see the Dark Stone module above) over investigators she discovers in and around the house, then take Andrew and hide in the woods in the vicinity of the house and wait for them to go away. Dragging the nearly unconscious Andrew through the grass leaves a trail of crushed vegetation. A successful **Track** roll allows the investigators to discover and follow this trail into the woods. If followed, Josephine will use more potent spells such as Drain Youth, in an attempt to drive away persistent investigators.

If the investigators find Andrew Keetling and take him from the house without encountering the villainess herself, Josephine hides in the woods until they are gone. Unless the investigators hunt her down and stop her, she will, after a few days, emerge from hiding, kidnap the first available adult male, and complete the Assumption of Night ritual described further below.

The house itself is suffering from long neglect, graying under a peeling coat of paint. The back door is spiked shut with ten-penny nails, giving it STR 22. The front door (STR 12) is kept locked. An investigator making a **Spot Hidden** roll on the back door notices the nails, and also that the wood surrounding the nails is recently scarred, indicating the nails were driven in not long ago.

The front door, if opened, sticks badly, and makes a loud shuddering and creaking sound, unless a successful **Sneak** roll is made. The door opens into a large foyer with several pegs for coats. A woman's coat is hanging on one of the pegs and with a **Spot Hidden** roll a crushed man's hat can be spotted laying in a dark corner.

**Living Room:** Like the rest of the house, a layer of dust coats everything. The house, though nicely furnished, seems lately ill kept.

**Dining Room:** This contains a fine wooden table and six wooden chairs with scrolled arms. A single place at the table has been cleared, and kept very clean.

**Storage:** The storage room contains a few pieces of old furniture, apparently awaiting repair, and several boxes containing old clothes.

**Kitchen:** It is masked by a layer of recent filth including spilled food, half empty cans of vegetables, and piles of unwashed dishes. Several plates have been wiped clean, and nonperishable items of food are stacked on a shelf above the sink.

**Josephine's Bedroom:** The only room in the house that shows much sign of upkeep. The bed appears to be slept in, and has been left unmade. There are some fresh apples in a paper bag on the floor. A shallow closet contains attractive and stylish womens' clothing.

Hidden beneath the pillow of the bed is a copy of *Scriptures of the Riven Valley* (described earlier).

**Guest Bedrooms:** The bedrooms on the north side are usually unoccupied but right now Josephine is entertaining guests. The east and west guest rooms are both tenanted while the center room is furnished but vacant.

**West Bedroom:** Andrew Keetling's cell. Unless Josephine has sacrificed him in the Assumption of Night ritual, this is where the investigators find him. He is bound, gagged, humiliated, and very hungry. For the last two weeks Andrew has been lying in his own filth, and has been fed sparingly and infrequently. His hit points are reduced by 6 and he suffers from a temporary insanity, leaving him weak and irrational.

*Mr. Keetling*

**East Guest Room:** it seems at first to be vacant but within seconds after the door is opened the ceiling begins to silently quiver and buckle in a wholly unnatural fashion.

An unearthly light spills down into the room. Any investigator who looks up witnesses a mind wrenching sight. The apparently solid ceiling splits open to reveal a field of shifting colors within which a single tiny point can be seen, moving closer and closer to the investigators. Flickering lavender and green witch fire dances

*The Thing Hanging in the Void*

upon the surface of the moving thing, obscuring its nature, and its shape.

Any investigator who looks up must make a SAN roll. If the roll fails, the investigator stands dumfounded, unable to move, and watches the slow advance of the Thing Hanging in the Void. Once it has approached to a point where it can be seen clearly (this takes three rounds), charge watching investigators a SAN loss of 1D6/1D20 depending upon whether or not they made their previous SAN rolls. An investigator who is holding the Dark Stone is relatively unaffected (at least on the surface), and can gaze calmly at the advancing shape with no apparent ill effects.

Wise investigators act now. The Thing does not manifest any physical attack, but it exudes menace. Any who are not stupefied before the advancing shape can flee, attempting to overpower and carry away less fortunate comrades. As an alternative, any spell which creates an opaque magical wall or barrier might save the investigators from the scrutiny of the Thing Hanging in the Void. The final effectiveness of such spells is up to the keeper.

If the investigators fail to act, those who are stupefied find they are unable to look away. The field of colors stretches out in all directions, enfolding the investigators until they appear to be standing on the bare rocky summit of a jutting tor. Dimly swirling below are huddled noisome shadows; above, only chaos and the Thing.

Hanging over the investigators is a vaguely humanoid shape, dark in color but wrapped in light. The lower the initial sanity of the investigator, the more horrifying and immediate the sight seems. To those of rigid sanity it seems a simple lifeless mass of stone or crystal. To those of less strength of mind it is much like a mummified body. To even less sane individuals the shape may appear almost appealing, remote and innocent as a newborn baby, hanging curled and fetal in the rippling colors. To those with the least sanity the form will be immediate and maddening; it is a blending, twisting cacophony of mewling faces barely inches from the horrified eyes of the investigator.

Investigators stupefied by the sight of the Thing are in great danger. If the Thing Hanging in the Void can overcome their magic points with its own on the resistance table, the soul of that investigator will be drawn upward to join the twisting mass of screaming faces, and be lost forever. Each resistance table encounter costs the Thing Hanging in the Void five magic points. It continues to absorb souls until no stupefied investigators are left, or until it runs out of five point blocks of magic points.

The Thing Hanging in the Void will suck up the souls of all stupefied and immobile investigators. This process seems to unaffected investigators to take about ten seconds. Then the Thing withdraws. Investigators

ignored by the Thing can wait until it is gone, at which time the real world reforms around them.

## The Fate of the Dark Stone

If the investigators remove the Stone from the area protected by the totems, or kill Garsetti, Crater's two goons show up on the scene. They tell the investigators they are there to collect the Boss's Stone and offer the characters their $2500 in cash, brought with them for just this purpose. If the investigators refuse, the gangsters attempt to take the object by force. they really want no trouble in this backwoods place so they hesitate to use more violence that necessary. They will tie up the investigators rather than kill them, notifying the local authorities of their whereabouts a few hours later. Regardless of how they obtain the Stone, the gangsters give the investigators the $2500 promised them.

If the investigators foil the two hoods and leave Pennsylvania with the Stone in their possession, Crater sends one of his bug-like children to retrieve the item. This monster strikes at the moment it deems most likely to bring it success; at night, probably along some deserted stretch of road. It has no compunction against killing the investigators but once it has an opportunity to escape with the Stone it will flee. If unsuccessful in this attempt, Crater sends more of these creatures to harass the party. They shun the daylight and will usually only be encountered at night or in dark places.

**Crater's Child (Adult):** This tall, manlike creature resembles Crater but the head is narrow and insectile, with a cluster of large curved mandibles protruding from the snout. Bands of small bulb-like eyes run from front to back all along the upper surface of the head. The shintar has wide delicate-looking wings reminiscent of those found on bats. The membranes are translucent, milky in color, and supported by long "finger bones" that emerge from the membrane in fine, curved points.

### An Adult Crater Child

| STR 17 | CON 17 | SIZ 2O | INT 07 | POW 11 |
|--------|--------|--------|--------|--------|
| DEX 15 | Move 9/25 flying | | | HP 19 |

**Weapons:** Whip Claws 70%, damage 2D6, 2 attacks per round

Mandibles 55%, damage 2D6+4

**Armor:** Carapace deflects 10 points of damage per hit

**SAN cost:** 1/1D6

Chances are Crater does not trust his two goons to bring him the Stone, so he sends a monstrous offspring to retrieve it from them. The gangsters defend themselves admirably but the encounter will end with the gangsters dead and the Child winging its way back to Boston. The investigators, while returning to Boston, may stumble upon the gangsters' abandoned car and discover the mutilated corpses (0/1D3 SAN).

## The Assumption of Night

If the investigators fail to retrieve the Dark Stone from Josephine Garsetti, she will make all haste to complete this magic ritual. A single sacrifice is needed to complete it, which was begun months ago with the first sacrifice committed by the Sylvan Night. If Andrew Keetling is still Garsetti's captive, he will be the victim. If rescued by the investigators, Josephine will lure one of the Muskrat Rapids locals out to the house and sacrifice him. The sacrifice must be made at night. Once completed, the Thing Hanging in the Void will begin to invade the dreams of sleepers in Muskrat Rapids.

Over a hundred sensitive people will be affected by the Thing in the Void and, driven mad by their dreams, embark upon a night of terror. The insane individuals begin by murdering their families in their beds, then pour out into the streets to randomly slay innocent victims. The Thing Hanging in the Void feasts upon these slain souls.

The investigators, if they happen to be in the area, are unaffected by the madness, but have to live through a night of mayhem. They are attacked by madman in their rooms, on the streets, or in their cars. Living through the night of terror costs each investigator 1D6 SAN, charged to them in the morning after most of the horror is over. If the player characters are out of town by this time, the bloodbath makes headlines everywhere. They read about it in the papers and lose 1D3 SAN when they realize they are at least partially at fault.

Josephine Garsetti will be one of the murderous maniacs soon gunned down by the Sheriff's stalwart deputies. If she dies in this manner she has left the Stone in her house, or possibly thrown down the well. Will Crater retrieve it before the investigators?

The effects of the ritual last only for the one night. To effect this again requires that 100 POW again be given to the Stone by means of human sacrifice.

---

## PART THREE

# Tracking Down Crater

Chances are by this time Crater has regained possession of the Stone. If he has the Stone, then the Thing has paid him a dream visit and has since moved into an upstairs bedroom in Crater's mansion. The Thing now directs Crater to begin another series of human sacrifices similar to Garsetti's. It wants to enjoy the feast of The Assumption of Night again, this time feasting on Boston souls. Even if the investigators have possession of the Stone they probably want to visit Crater's house for reasons of curiosity, or possibly revenge. They may want Crater's copy of the *Kingdoms of Shadows* in order to learn more about the Dark Stone. If none of these reasons apply, see the next section.

## Another Missing Person

Upon returning to Boston the investigators are approached by Bobbie, a flapper they saw and may have talked to at the Sailor's Club. She says that one of her friends, Millie, has disappeared — the keeper should tell the investigators that they remember Bobbie's friend from their visit to the club. Bobbie says that that Millie, on a dare, went into the back room of the speakeasy but she never came out. They questioned the bartender about it but he claimed to have never seen the missing girl and told Bobbie and her friends to get lost. They think something horrible has happened to their friend. The police have been unable to help.

## Finding Crater

Learning the location of Crater's mansion should not prove difficult. His address is known to the police and to the press. Randolph Smith, the bartender at Sailor's, will clue in the investigators for a C-note bribe, more if he can get it. Following Crater home from the club is another possibility.

### Crater's Mansion

Crater's house is located on the Massachusetts coast, several miles north of Boston; it is a crumbling two story house on a hill overlooking the sea. The grounds have been left unattended for some time and the hedges and gardens have run wild. Thick dark vines climb the outside of the house. An observant investigator notices that one room in the front of the second floor has its windows boarded up.

### The First Floor

**Hallway:** The front door is left unlocked at all times. If Crater is home at the time of the investigators' visit, his voluminous cape is seen hanging on a hook to the left of the door. The inside of the house is in worse condition than the exterior. Furniture is overturned and smashed, paintings ripped, curtains torn and stained. Crater in the last few months has neared losing his mind. The condition of his home, as well as his actions, reflect this.

If Crater becomes aware that the investigators are invading his house, he sends one of his brood to wait in

# CRATER'S HOUSE

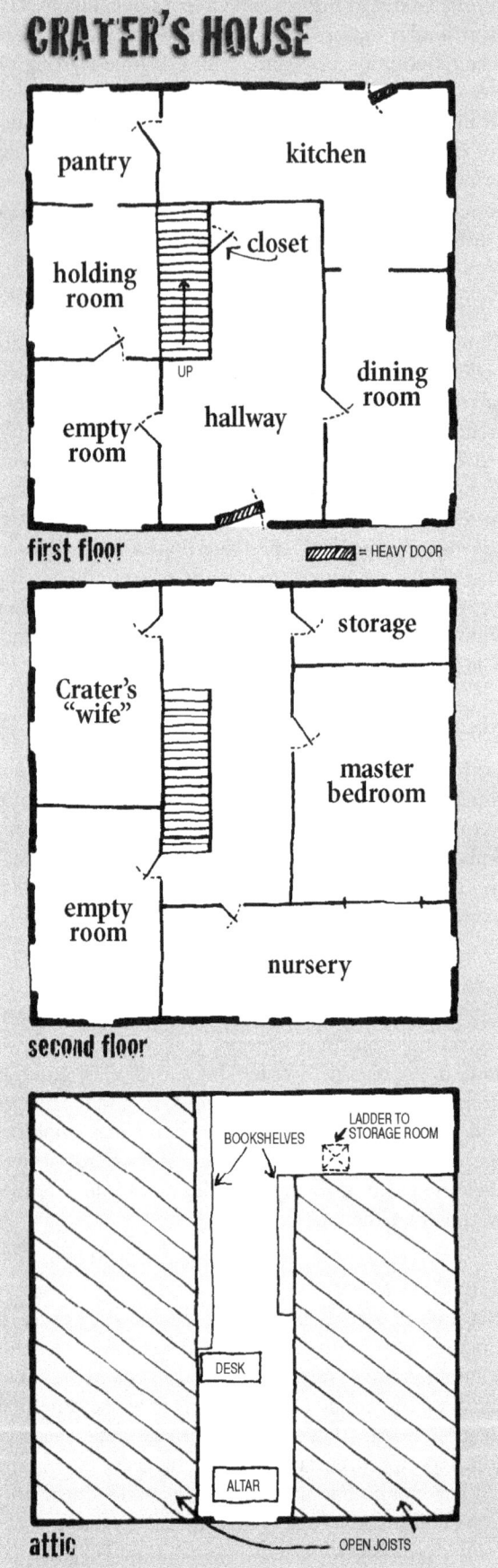

**first floor**

▨▨▨ = HEAVY DOOR

**second floor**

LADDER TO
STORAGE ROOM

BOOKSHELVES

DESK

ALTAR

**attic**
OPEN JOISTS

this area and greet them. The creature immediately attacks anyone who enters through the front door. If the investigators sneak in by another entrance the monstrous child finds them within ten minutes. If the party of investigators is large or pathetically clumsy (and the keeper so desires), Crater may send more than one of his adult children.

### Another Adult CRATER CHILD

| STR 17 | CON 17 | SIZ 2O | INT 07 | POW 11 |
|--------|--------|--------|--------|--------|
| DEX 15 | Move 9/25 flying | | | HP 19 |

**Weapons:** Whip Claws 70%, damage 2D6, 2 attacks per round
   Mandibles 55%, damage 2D6+4

**Armor:** Carapace deflects 10 points of damage per hit

**SAN cost:** 1/1D6

**Dining Room:** This room contains a long wooden table collapsed at one end. Several frames without paintings hang crookedly on the walls. If anyone disturbs the table in the slightest, the still supported end of the table collapses and falls to the floor with a resounding crash, alerting Crater.

**Kitchen:** Upon entering this room the investigator are assailed with a terrible odor. Rotten food lies scattered about and a strange fecal matter, unidentifiable to the investigators, squelches under their feet.

**Pantry:** The door is locked with a padlock and hasp. It can be opened at normal percentage using **Mechanical Repair**, assuming the presence of adequate tools. The locked door has STR 16. The windows are boarded over in a haphazardly, leaving many gaps. During daylight hours random beams of dusty sunlight vector into the room. One of Crater's brood is curled up on the floor in a fetal position in the southeast corner of the room. It requires a **Spot Hidden** roll to identify it as an animate creature. If investigators enter the room, the Child responds to their presence and attacks after about two combat rounds. Its statistics are the same as the ones described before.

**Holding Room:** The west door of this room is shut with a large padlock and hasp. Bolted across each of the windows are stout iron bars. Several sets of manacles have been attached through holes in the plaster to the joists in the wall. The padlock on the door can be opened using **Mechanical Repair or Locksmith** at normal percentage. If the investigators choose to force the door, it has a STR of 18. The iron manacles within the room have an integral STR of 28, but can easily be opened using **Mechanical Repair at +15% or Locksmith at +30%.** Any investigator who might have been kidnapped by Crater is found chained up in this room. Each hour a prisoner is under the care of Crater and his creatures, 1 point is subtracted from his INT until it reaches 2, at which point the investigator begins to lose

POW. Once POW reaches 2 the investigator is reduced to a mindless, soulless husk which no amount of medical or psychiatric care can restore to humanity. Examining the prisoner reveals numerous patches perforated by thousands of tiny bloodless pin holes. These perforated areas are totally numb and cannot be used for 1D6 months after rescue.

Until an investigator reaches the point of no return — POW drops to zero, CON drops to zero, etc. — characteristic points lost in this way may be recovered at a rate of 1D3 for each month spent in total convalescence at a medical institution. Affected characteristics can be restored to their original scores.

## The Second Floor

**Storage Area:** The main contents of this room appear to be broken and empty crates. The ladder to the attic is recessed between two joists near the back of the room. A careful search or a **Spot Hidden** roll reveals the presence of the ladder.

If the investigators spend any time searching through the mostly empty crates they find one with a shipping label indicating that it was originally intended for Miskatonic University. The label states that the shipment originated in France (this is the crate that held the Dark Stone).

**Empty Room:** This appears to have once been a guest room but is now mostly unfurnished. If Crater has invited the Thing Hanging in the Void into his home, it will be encountered here in the same manner described earlier at Garsetti's.

**Crater's Wife's Room:** This well appointed but dingy bedroom is where Crater has been keeping the women he has lately been luring to his home; healthy young women kidnapped by the insane gangster and used for his own horrible purposes. His present mate lies on the bed, securely bound and gagged. Her hands and feet have been amputated to keep her from escaping and the stumps neatly cauterized (lose 1/1D2 SAN). The investigators notice that the woman appears pregnant.

This is Bobbie's friend, Millie, the girl the investigators may have been asked to find. She has gone completely insane. If the investigators untie her and remove the gag, she merely screams, drools, and moans incessantly. She has no information.

This poor young woman has been impregnated by Crater and is about to give birth to a horde of his brood. In fact, the excitement of being rescued by the investigators will bring on her first labor pains. The young woman suddenly begins to shudder and choke, then falls to the floor, writhing in agony. As the investigators watch, her belly starts to heave and quake. Then, with a scream, she gives birth to a dozen or more of the gang-ster's offspring; little bug like Crater things, that chew and bloodily scramble their way out of the womb to scuttle across the floor and disappear into cracks and crevices. Witnesses lose 1/1D8 SAN.

**The Nursery:** The door to this room is heavier than the rest on this floor and is shut with a large padlock. The door has STR 18. This room is where Crater tries to keep and raise some of the distorted travesties born of his unfortunate wives. If the investigators force the door, six scuttling shapes the size of dogs retreat into the shadowed corners. If the investigators enter the room, they attack, following the party into the hallway, even to the first floor and out onto the grounds until they or the investigators are dead.

These are the immature form of Crater's adult monster, the Child, that the investigators may already have met. They have the general appearance of infants but upon closer examination it is noticed that their bodies are bone white and have gleaming chitinous areas on the back and chest. Their faces are merely chitinous shells with ridges and bumps that resemble human features. For every five points of STR, assume the creature has an extra whip-like appendage that ends in a sharp bony hook, and provides the creature with extra attacks (note the differing multiple attacks listed with the creature's statistics above).

An observation window of thick glass is set into one of the walls. Through it the investigators can see a wooden armchair and beyond it, the interior of the master bedroom.

### Five Immature Crater's Children

|         | 1    | 2    | 3    | 4    | 5    |
|---------|------|------|------|------|------|
| STR     | 12   | 10   | 15   | 11   | 15   |
| CON     | 15   | 08   | 15   | 10   | 13   |
| SIZ     | 06   | 08   | 07   | 06   | 05   |
| INT     | 05   | 06   | 06   | 04   | 07   |
| POW     | 10   | 17   | 17   | 16   | 16   |
| DEX     | 14   | 11   | 15   | 10   | 06   |
| APP     | 05   | 04   | 03   | 01   | 03   |
| HP      | 11   | 08   | 12   | 08   | 09   |
| **Armor:** | 4 | 4 | 4 | 5 | 5 |
| **Attack:** | 50% | 50% | 50% | 50% | 50% |
| **Damage:** | 1D4x2 | 1D4x3 | 1D4x2 | 1D4x2 | 1D4x3 |

**Move** 4

**SAN Cost:** 1/1D8

**The Master Bedroom:** This is a normal bedroom except for the thick observation window in the western end of the room.

## The Attic

**Bookshelves:** These contain many books, most of them ledgers pertaining to Crater's illicit businesses. From them could be compiled a list of Crater's customers which the police would be pleased to possess. There are also many occult books, most of them useless frummery but a few are significant.

The first is *Musings of the White Witch* by Olga Hatcher. It increases Occult knowledge +6 percentiles, if studied for two weeks. Another book, *New World Rituals*, offers a +2% Occult knowledge increase with only an overnight perusal needed to read it.

Also on this shelf is *Nameless Cults*, (Golden Goblin Press edition, in English.) Held together with wheat paste and strips of plaster tape, this decrepit copy has many loose pages, and many may be missing. *Sanity cost 1/1D4: Cthulhu Mythos +3%; average of 8 weeks to study and comprehend what little seems whole.* **Spells:** no spells.

**The Desk:** Crater does the bulk of his studying at this desk. Here the investigators find Crater's translated notes from *Kingdom of Shadows* (see **The Mansion Papers #5**). Also in this drawer is the inventory list from the crate of goods intended for Miskatonic University. This lists the *Dark Stone*, and the *Book of Eibon* and several other books and items of lesser interest. These other items can be found by scouring Crater's mansion.

The most hideous discovery is a log book of the breeding experiments Crater has been conducting downstairs the last few weeks. Included in this record are average gestation periods (two days), rate of fertility (over 90%), growth rate (reach full size within 8-10 days) and the average life span for one of his unholy offspring (less than two weeks). The log book also contains diagrams and records of dissections performed both on his offspring and on the hapless wives. Studying this book in detail for a week or so, adds to an investigator +5 percentiles Cthulhu Mythos skill, and chips 1D6 points from his SAN.

If Crater is at home, the Dark Stone is in a drawer.

**Altar:** The sole window in the attic looks out on the sea, and a crude stone altar, Crater's imperfect attempt to reconstruct something described in a book, is placed before it. The altar is darkened by blood stains. If Andrea Pentargon has been murdered, the woman's missing head will be found atop the altar, mounted on an iron spike, rotting and infested with maggots (lose 1/1D4 SAN). Mounded at the altar's base are dried heaps of offal, bones of various descriptions, strips of flesh, and various severed body parts. These are the remains of Crater's wives, sacrificed by the mad mobster in futile attempts to return himself to normal.

**Strategies for Crater:** Crater will not let intruders go unpunished. Upon discovering investigators in his home, Crater is 50% likely to attack immediately, first using spells until all his magic points are gone, then wading in with his claws. If the keeper prefers, Crater lets the investigators escape, then sends a sufficient numbers of his adult Children to attack them in their homes.

# Consequences & Rewards

If the investigators rescue Andrew Keetling, award 2D6 Sanity points: if they also kill Josephine or otherwise prevent her from enacting the Assumption of Night rituals, it costs each investigator 2D4 Sanity points.

The investigators may wish to capture Josephine with the intention of curing her insanity. She proves incurable and will be plagued by dreams sent to her by the Thing Hanging in the Void. The attempt is still worth 1D3 Sanity points if they capture her alive.

If the investigators eliminate Zeke Crater, award them 1D10 Sanity points.

If the items that belong to Miskatonic University are gathered up and handed over to the school, the investigators receive no money but small plaques bearing all their names will be mounted over the items chosen to be displayed in the University's Exhibit Museum. Increase all of their Credit Ratings by 1 point.

If the investigators rescue Keetling he is likely (80% chance), to reward the investigators handsomely for their efforts, $1000 each. If the investigators pursue further information about Keetling, about six weeks after his rescue they see an announcement in the Boston *Globe* regarding his engagement to Madelaine DuMort.

# Statistics

**ANDREA PENTARGON, police informant**

| STR 06 | SIZ 07 | CON 10 | INT 13 | POW 09 |
|---|---|---|---|---|
| DEX 15 | *APP 16(10) | EDU 14 | SAN 30 | HP 11 |

**Damage Bonus:** 1D4

*16 as she was, 10 as she is*

**Weapons:** none

**Skills:** Cthulhu Mythos 6%, Draw 75%, Drive Automobile 30%, Fast Talk 65%, Library Use 40%, Occult 35%, Seduce 65%.

**ROGER CROSS, alcoholic private eye**

| STR 13 | CON 15(9) | *SIZ 14 | INT 14 | POW 11 |
|---|---|---|---|---|
| DEX 14 | APP 07 | EDU 12 | SAN 40 | HP 15 (13)* |

*higher number as he could be, lower number as he is. Perhaps the investigators can keep him from using cocaine for a few weeks, and also dry him out.*

**Damage Bonus:** +1D4

**Weapons:** .38 Revolver, damage 1D10 (*but his gun is pawned*)
Fist/Punch 80%, damage 1D3+1D4
Kick 60%, damage 1D6+1D4

**Skills:** Police Connections 65%, Law 8%, Library Use 40%,
Fast Talk 65%, Pick Pocket 60%, Psychology 50%, Sneak
45%, Spot Hidden 65%.

## EZEKIEL CRATER, waterfront kingpin

| STR 18 | CON 24 | SIZ 15 | INT 14 | POW 14 |
|--------|--------|--------|--------|--------|
| DEX 12 | APP 07 | SAN 0 | EDU 13 | HP 20 |

Move 7

**Weapons:** .45 Revolver 50%, damage 1D10+2
Whip Claws 70%, damage 2D6, 2 attacks per round

**Armor:** Carapace (skin) deflects 8 points of damage per
strike.

**Spells:** Drain Youth, Drown Mind, Shriveling, Voorish Sign

**Skills:** Accounting 75%, Cthulhu Mythos 8%, Drive
Automobile 65%, Fast Talk 55%, Hide 75%, Latin 25%,
Law 40%, Listen 40%, Notoriety 65%, Occult 33%,
Pharmacy 45%, Psychology 50%, Spot Hidden 65%,
Sneak 67%

## SHERIFF ANSON VARLEY, disinterested sheriff

| STR 16 | CON 14 | SIZ 16 | INT 13 | POW 10 |
|--------|--------|--------|--------|--------|
| DEX 11 | APP 09 | SAN 50 | EDU 12 | HP 15 |

**Damage Bonus:** +1D4

**Weapons:** .38 Revolver 65%, damage 1D10
12 Gauge Shotgun (semi-auto) 85%, damage
4D6/2D6/1D6

**Skills:** Bargain 55%, Chew Tobacco 85%, Drive Auto 65%,
Law 65%, Persuade 57%, Psychology 56%, Sneak 55%,
Spot Hidden 45%, Track 75%.

## Stalwart Deputies (five or more)

| STR 14 | CON 13 | S1Z 12 | INT 11 | POW 10 |
|--------|--------|--------|--------|--------|
| DEX 11 | APP 11 | SAN 55 | EDU 08 | HP 13 |

**Damage Bonus:** +1D4

**Weapons:** Fist/Punch 60%, damage 1D3 + 1D4
.38 Revolver 40%, damage 1D10
12-Gauge (pump) Shotgun 65%, damage 4D6/2D6/1D6

**Skills:** Climb 44%, Dodge 60%, Drive Auto 50%, First Aid
50%, Jump 45%, Sneak 30%, Spot Hidden 45%, Track
35%.

## Josephine Garsetti, artist and cult leader

| STR 10 | CON 08 | SIZ 07 | INT 17 | POW 16 (26)* |
|--------|--------|--------|--------|--------|
| DEX 12 | APP 17 | EDU 16 | SAN 05 | HP 08 |

**Damage Bonus:** none

*Score in parentheses indicates POW, MP when the
Dark Stone is on her person*

**Weapons:** Small Knife 60%, damage 1D4

**Spells:** Create Gate, Drain Youth, Drown Mind, Lace
Curtains of Hish (DL), Maws of Pandemonium (DL),
Voorish Sign

**Skills:** Art (Draw) 90%, Cthulhu Mythos 15%, Fast Talk
65%, Library Use 45%, Listen 39%, Occult 70%, Sneak
60%, Spot Hidden 50%.

## Andrew Keetling, Boston businessman

| SIR 13 | CON 14 | SIZ 10 | INT 15 | POW 07 |
|--------|--------|--------|--------|--------|
| DEX 11 | APP 14 | SAN 35 | EDU 15 | HP 12 |

**Damage Bonus:** +1D4

**Weapons:** 9mm Italian Automatic 25%, damage 1D10
Cane 45%, damage 1D4.

**Skills:** Accounting 85%, Bargain 75%, Credit Rating 85%,
Cthulhu Mythos 2%, Drive Automobile 60%, Library
Use 50%.

## The Thing Hanging in the Void, living nightmare

| STR 25 | CON 29 | SIZ varies | INT 21 | POW 22 |
|--------|--------|--------|--------|--------|
| DEX 31 | Move: n/a | | | HP 29 |

**Armor:** none, but physical weapons cannot harm it

**Attacks:** Soul Drain

**SAN Cost:** 1D6/1D20

## Crater Child (Adult), awful offspring

Between eight and ten feet in height, this creature is vaguely
insectile. It has four primary limbs, and four secondary, whip
like appendages ending in bony hooked blades (whip claws).
The two primary limbs located near the narrow head are
equipped with fifteen jointed hook like fingers. The lower-
most legs support most of the weight of the creature and end
in splayed claws. The head is banded with gleaming rows of
bulb shaped eyes and it has large curved mandibles endowed
with great strength. It has wide, delicate looking wings that
account for much of its size: the wings are reminiscent of a
bat's, but the membranes are translucent and milky in color.
The creature carries itself upright, like a man, but occasionally leans on its lower set of whip claws for additional support.

### Average Adult Crater Child

| | characteristics | average |
|-----|-----|-----|
| STR | 4D6+3 | 17 |
| CON | 3D6+4 | 14-16 |
| SIZ | 4D6+3 | 17 |
| INT | 2D6 | 07-08 |
| POW | 2D6+6 | 11 |
| DEX | 3D6+4 | 14-16 |
| HP 17 | | |

**Move:** 9/25 flying

**Armor:** Carapace deflects 10 points of damage per hit

**Weapons:** Whip-Claws or Claws 70%, damage 2D6
Bite 55%, damage 2D6+4

**SAN cost:** 1/1D6

## THE END!

# The Old Damned House

*The investigators are hired to recover the famous Hazard Pearls.*
*Were they really stolen, or are there more sinister truths to be discovered?*

Objects of great value often are cursed. In this scenario the investigators are hired to find such an object: the famous Hazard Pearls. They are valuable beyond imagination, famous throughout New England, and cursed with a sinister and terrible legacy.

The Hazard family, of Connecticut, made a fortune in fishing, whaling, and through wise investment in merchant ships. About two hundred years ago the Pearls came into the family. Ever since their wealth has deteriorated, they have all but ceased to breed, and have became ever more reclusive and secretive. The Hazard curse emanates from none other than the Great Old One, Tsathoggua.

"The Old Damned House" is ideal for introducing new investigators to the horrors of the Cthulhu Mythos, although it is more suited to players with prior experience in the game. Expect an average of three nights play.

The scenario begins with a straightforward investigation, complicated only by the strangeness of the family itself. By the time the investigators conduct their initial research, the mood of the game should begin to reflect the increasing strangeness of the situation. As they learn more of the family the characters should feel a gathering doom, a feeling that will peak when they are forced to battle the demented Wilfred, the ageless head of the Hazard family. The encounters should be painted in an almost surreal palette, as the horrific influence of Tsathoggua finally affects the investigators' world. By the end the mood should be dark and deadly.

The inspirations for "The Old Damned House" have been many. There are obvious relationships to *The Old Dark House* the 1932 film based on the story *Benighted* written by J.B. Priestly in the late 1920s. Hopefully the works of H.P. Lovecraft himself will be somewhat in evidence in this volume as well, particularly in the form of "The Mound", a story he wrote (or more accurately re-wrote) with Zealia Bishop. This story has been used as something of a foundation, and it is highly recommended that keepers find a copy and read it. The scenario was written to capture the mood and

## Format of the Scenario

This adventure is divided into three sections to organize information for the keeper.

**SECTION ONE: THE PAST** introduces the characters and a simple history of the situation, and indicates how the scenario is intended to be played.

**SECTION TWO: THE FUTURE** provides the bulk of the information about the Hazard family and the house. In this section is detailed history of the family, descriptions of the family members, a description of the house, and the sources of information about the family which the investigators might discover when they are completing their investigation.

**SECTION THREE: THE STORY** outlines a likely order of events, indicates what is supposed to happen in what order, and provides information that does not fit into the rest of the chapter. It is intended as a general guide to the scenario, rather than a strict plan for the keeper to follow. ☀

atmosphere of the detective fiction of the time, creating in this scenario a mystery not unlike those of the period.

The town of Mystic, referred to in this scenario, is inspired in only the most distant way by the real town in Connecticut. People who travel there will find that the material we have provided is almost entirely fictional. We have made little attempt to correct our interpretation of the town to ensure that it matches the real world because, after all, this is just a story.

# THE PAST

The following sections explain the nature of the Hazard family and particulars on their situation and the mansion in which they live. The storyline for the adventure follows on page 137ff.

## A Mansion in Mystic

Atop the low cliffs just outside the town of Mystic, Connecticut, is perched an aged mansion. Built by a family of French colonists, the house has grown since the end of the 17th century. In the 1920s the descendants of that same French family, the Hazards, inhabit it.

The town of Mystic has risen and fallen with the prospects of the region: from the early days of fishermen, though years of profitable trade, and finally to its current near-abandoned state. The Hazard house has grown with the town — initially it was a single-room hut occupied by two lovers. Over the years it has expanded and now it is home to the surviving, disenchanted, and unbalanced members of a once-proud family.

The tired walls of the Hazard mansion are the silent observers of a family plagued by misfortune, and worse. Since 1760 the family has suffered under the influence of a most dire curse.

## Wilfred and the Curse

Two hundred years ago, Wilfred Hazard joined an ill-fated expedition to search for the fabled city of Quivira. The expedition was successful in finding the ancient subterranean city, but was quite unprepared for also what was found there, and in the vast caverns of N'Kai below it. Wilfred finally returned to Mystic in 1759 — the only survivor.

Although Wilfred was spared the horrors that consumed his companions, he did not emerge from the mysteries of Quivira untouched. Frantically wandering the fearful caverns of N'Kai far below the city, Wilfred stumbled upon an odd string of pearls. He later understood that he had come upon an item tied to the essence of Tsathoggua, a horrific and powerful creature worshipped by formless things that stalked the expedition through the subterranean world. The token protected Wilfred while those around him were torn asunder. Tsathoggua was unable to harm him. Such was the frustration of the creature that it cursed Wilfred, infecting him with a living piece of its blasphemous being.

Wilfred still carries inside him a sliver of that dread creature. During the centuries since his infection Wilfred's body has decayed into an obscene parody of a toadlike thing. As his body has been twisted so has his mind. Since his return to the Mystic mansion Wilfred's relatives have cared for him, protected him from prying eyes, and have kept him confined.

But Wilfred's curse has affected the whole family as well. For generations they have participated in heinous activities under Wilfred's insane guidance. Broken and twisted under the baleful influence of the Tsathoggua's malevolence, the family survives by the force of its own depravity — a hideous beast eternally sustained only by devouring itself.

## The Pearls

The Hazard Pearls are said to have arrived in Mystic on board a merchant sloop in 1759. They have been passed down through the family from that time, despite rumors that they have been responsible for the bad luck that has dogged the family's fortunes.

A matched string of thirteen of the finest black pearls in the world, the Hazard Pearls are well known. Although their curious luster has beguiled more than one wealthy collector, no offers have ever been accepted. Although most of the rest of the family's three hundred year history has been quietly sold to counter the effects of failed businesses and bad investments, the pearls have remained: part of the family in the same way as is Wilfred.

Wilfred realized the importance of the pearls before his mind had been entirely warped, and bequeathed them to the family in the hopes that they would protect the ones he loved from the foul god's nameless retribution. Instead, the pearls have affected them, gradually twisting their bodies and souls.

## The Accursed Cat Burglar

Legends say that objects of great value carry with them a great price. Such objects often are believed to be cursed; misfortune befalling their owners attributed to such curses. It is from such legends that the Accursed Cat Burglar received his name: his reputation made by stealing some of the most valuable (and purportedly cursed) jewelry in the United States.

Over the course of eighteen months the burglar has baffled police nationwide by pilfering some of the most

# TIMELINE & DISCUSSION

**1348:** The Black Plague infects Paris killing many, including most of the family of the Sire de Hazard. Girard, a distant nephew, is the sole member of the family to survive the plague inherits the title. The inheritance is disputed — some claim that sorcery was involved.

**1393:** The *bal des ardents* (dance of the burning ones): one of the Queen's ladies-in-waiting is said to have suggested a wild dance, to honor the memory of her grandfather, who is rumored to have enlisted the aid of demons to curse his family with a plague, in order to take the family title for himself. The dance was initially called "the dance of the savages", but the pitch-soaked costumes of the dancers caught fire and all but two of them perished, hence the dance's infamous name. The maiden's name was Celestine de Hazard.

**1432:** Isabeau de Hazard is charged with consorting with demons, and swearing allegiance to the Devil. She is burned at the stake.

**1575:** Simon de Hazard, the youngest son of the Sire, is charged with lycanthropy. He is accused of breaking the neck of a young girl and eating her flesh. It is also alleged that he had dug up fresh graves to obtain corpses. Simon claims that a demon appeared to him and instructed him to do these things. The influence of the Hazard family enables Simon to escape the gallows. Instead, he is sent to live out the rest of his life in a lonely castle.

**1656:** Renewed outbreaks of plague deal the deathblow to the Hazard family. The sole surviving son, Jean de Hazard, a bastard who could not legally inherit, flees to the Americas to escape persecution. He settles in the French colonies, and fathers two sons.

**1692:** In Mystic, Connecticut, nineteen-year-old Mary Gallows escapes hanging for witchcraft. She is sent away by her parents, who fear for her safety, should she stay. She marries Jean Hazard, a French-Canadian, who, on their return to Mystic several years later, makes a modest livelihood as a fisherman. Jean Hazard claims to be the son of 1759 Jean de Hazard, who fled France in 1656. He continues to sympathize with the French cause, and still has relatives on Franco-American soil. The Gallows and Hazard families inter-marry many times in the ensuing centuries. Fishing turns to whaling, and then to investment in merchant ships. The Hazard family prospers. Jean and Mary turn the original one room cottage into a two-storey house. The Hazard house begins to grow. Ephraim, the only son among nine daughters, is succeeded by Simon, who is succeeded by his sons, Enguerrand and Nathanial.

**1750:** Mystic prospers. The Hazard name is linked to many sound investments. The family has large numbers of sturdy children. Great success with East Indian sloops allows the family to again enlarge their house. Uproar is caused by allegations of poltergeist activity around the building site. Speculation that the house is haunted is fueled by the disappearance of a worker. The family dismisses such claims. The patriarch, Ellery Hazard, is known for the half-dozen mantraps he buys and conceals around the house to discourage so-called poltergeists.

**1754-63:** The French and Indian War. Trade continues with the West Indies, despite the danger of privateer French corsairs, who capture a number of Mystic's ships. The Hazard fortune continues to grow in this atmosphere of conflict. Aggressive profit-seeking Mystic families (including the Hazards) supply both the British and the French with war materials. The Mystic merchant families join the war of Independence after indiscriminate seizures carried out by British troops. The Hazard house is ruled during this period by Elijah Hazard.

**1759:** Wilfred Hazard manages to make his way to Mystic. He is the only surviving member of a French expedition to locate the leg-

*(continued on next page)*

precious and well-known items in history. With uncanny precision the burglar has gained access to the most precious jewelry in the world. He is a skilled safecracker, and has been able to easily make off with the valuable stones and cash kept with them.

None of the stolen jewelry has surfaced again: none has been sold in criminal circles; nor have offers been made to unscrupulous collectors would move heaven and earth to acquire them. The jewelry has been carefully stolen and just as carefully hidden.

Unfortunately, those curses caught up to the burglar. While stealing the Hazard Pearls he encountered Wilfred Hazard. It is the burglary and the burglar's murder that the characters find themselves investigating in this tale. Such investigations surely will lead to more serious horrors.

# SECTION TWO
# The Future

The elements of the adventure that wise investigators must consider.

## The Case

While it is not intended that all gaming groups who play this scenario will complete it in the same way, it is possible to provide a fairly simple outline of the events that are likely to characterize the story they will experience. This outline is not meant to dictate the course of events, but rather to indicate the initially intended plot.

The insurance company, Rimant & Knowles, in Hartford, which insured the Hazards, is dismayed to find that the Hazard Pearls themselves have been stolen. Their first reaction is to make sure that they have indeed been stolen; it is common knowledge that the Hazard family has been suffering a gradual financial decline, and collecting the insurance on the pearls could go some way towards easing that problem. It is for this reason that Rimant & Knowles hires the investigators to investigate the missing jewelry, intending that they will either prove that the pearls have been stolen, or will be able to retrieve them for the family.

Ultimately, the investigators will find themselves uncovering family secrets that have been hidden for centuries. Whether in self-defense, or for other reasons, the investigators will be forced to kill the ancient Wilfred,

*(continued from previous page)*

endary city of Quivira. His condition deteriorates from the time he arrives. The Indians who accompany him draw much comment from the local populace, as they are considered brutish and over-bearing. They are suspected of having murderous intentions, and soon depart.

**1760:** Saphronia Hazard, the woman of the house, displays an incredible string of perfect black pearls. When questioned, she claims that they were brought back from the Orient on board one of the Hazards' many trading vessels.

**1765:** There is a spectacular falling-out between the Hazard and Gallows families. All relations between the two families are severed. Neither family ever divulges the cause of the quarrel, although it is speculated that an important trade deal went wrong. Many people say that the black pearls have caused this bad luck.

**1778-83:** Elijah Hazard is succeeded by his sole surviving child Prime, who is succeeded by his son Girard, who in turn is succeeded by a single son Ezekiel. The family continues to prosper, despite the effects of Wilfred's malevolent pearls.

**1812:** Renewed hostilities between the British and French makes shipping both unsafe and expensive which leads to an eventual decline in the family's wealth.

**1827:** Extensions to the house are completed in the early months of this year. The building is troubled by renewed claims of poltergeist activity. Several workers claim to have seen Indian ghosts around the building. One workman is killed in an accidental fall from the roof of the house. Cousin Wilfred escapes in the confusion and upheaval of the rebuilding. His humanity has been bleeding away over the years, and he devotes his freedom to stalking and devouring innocents, regurgitating their remains as castings. The wave of disappearances is noted and causes much alarm, although no one connects it to the Hazard family. A casting is found, but is believed to be a mummified Indian infant. The casting causes quite a stir, but is soon forgotten when the disappearances cease. The strange object is sold to a traveling freak show. Eventually the Hazards manage to corner and return Cousin Wilfred to his attic, this time securely chaining him, and allowing him loose only for the ceremonies that are now family tradition.

**1830s:** The family's luck hits rock bottom. Their ventures no longer return them the huge profits of the early years. The Hazard Pearls still shine around the necks of the Hazard women, but the women are shy, single and reclusive. Marriages with other merchant families cease, and the Hazard "bad luck" becomes legendary. Rumors of incest

circulate to explain the survival of the line despite the Hazards being shunned by the other merchant families.

**1860:** The Hazard fortune declines. While many of their contemporaries desert Mystic to pursue new ventures, the Hazard family remains. They are unable to bolster their fortunes with new enterprises, and for the next three quarters of a century, the family continues to decline. They are trapped, tied to the house and to Cousin Wilfred's blasphemous rites.

**1893:** Lighting strikes the Hazard house, causing a small fire and sparking gossip. The damage to the house necessitates extensive repairs to the upper storey. Cousin Wilfred escapes a second time, causing another ruckus. Once again, he is trapped and returned to the attic by his family. He is not to escape again for another 31 years, by which time the only human thing left in him is the wish to die to be rid of his intolerable life. Again castings are found. No printed link is made to the earlier wave of disappearances although gossip is rife. The casting that is turned up this time is eventually rescued by the Mystic Historical Society.

**1920s:** The Accursed Cat Burglar attempts to steal the Hazard Pearls. Cousin Wilfred prepares to escape a third, and final time. ✷

and finally, to face the residual effects of the curse which has gripped the Hazard family for generations. Whether they succeed in the end will depend as much upon their bravery as upon their investigative prowess.

## The House

The Hazard family has suffered for generations under the effects of Wilfred's horrific curse.

The family has fully embraced Wilfred's dementia, taking it on as their own. They practice depraved rites, sacrificing their deformed offspring to sustain the

ancient, undying, Wilfred. The few children born whole and healthy are brought up as part of this close-knit family and are introduced to the truth of the family legacy on the eve of their twenty-first birthday. The youths are given a lengthy document, written by Wilfred before he completely lost his mind, which explains what has happened to him. Some are not able to accept what the document indicates, and so are sacrificed to Wilfred; the others are accepted fully into the Hazard family.

Though once a proud and prosperous family the curse and their obsession with Wilfred have caused the Hazard family to deteriorate. While they still live in an

## INVESTIGATING ELIJAH JAMES RYAN

The Accursed Cat Burglar, Elijah James Ryan, pretended to the world that he was an accountant with an office in a brownstone building in Newport, Rhode Island. Obtaining his address will be a simple matter for the investigators to accomplish.

He hasn't been in lately. His mail has been piling up in the little box built into his door and is beginning to overflow out into the hall-

way. His room is tidy and unremarkable except for two things – his framed Practicing Certificate for Accountancy is hung crooked (**Psychology** roll indicates this is unheard of for a real accountant), and his wall safe is filled with Accursed jewelry (but not the Hazard Pearls), and press cuttings of all the exploits of the Accursed Cat Burglar. In there is also a reasonably detailed floor plan of the ground floor of the Hazard house with the burglar's window of entry and the position of the safe carefully circled. The floor plan has been stamped as the property of Rimant & Knowles.

Resourceful investigators might be able to trace the floor plan of the Hazard mansion to a disgruntled ex-employee of the insurance firm. The results of such investigations are left to the keeper. ✷

expansive mansion overlooking the sea, the Hazard family is gradually consuming itself — one by one the heirlooms have been sold off to put food on the table, as the house falls further into disrepair.

In the past few days, the Hazard Pearls have been stolen, and with them, the document that describes the curse. The two youngest members of the Hazard family are twins, and will turn twenty-one at the end of the week. The family is desperate to retrieve both the pearls and the document. As fate would have it, their insurance company, Rimant & Knowles, has hired the investigators to determine the validity of the insurance claim the Hazards have filed for the pearls.

Although a burglar did steal both the pearls and the document, he was startled by a few of the deformed Hazard children who took the pearls from him and, while trying to retrieve them, the burglar had a fatal encounter with Wilfred Hazard.

Wilfred now has the document with him. Unable to think clearly, he is prepared to take whatever advantage he can of his new freedom. In some corner of his mind he seeks a way to finally end his life of agony, but he needs to find a way to rid the family of the curse. Although he does not yet know it, the investigators will help him reach his goal, and as a result they will find themselves face to face with the same horror that has destroyed the Hazard family.

## The Family

The older members all address each other as "Cousin" and the youngsters address the older family members as "Uncle" or "Aunt". Family members resist discussing their genealogy. None of the family members are directly related.

While occasionally there is some hostility between them, the surviving Hazards care for each other deeply. Their love is based upon the fact that they are different from the outside world but it surpasses simple isolationism — the bonds of familial loyalty and love are capable of leading the Hazards to act with a total disregard for their own safety.

Statistics for all the Hazards is included at the conclusion of the scenario.

## Wilfred Hazard

Cousin Wilfred sits chained in his wheel chair in his damp, dark attic, and broods on the bottomless gulfs of despair spawned by the lightless caverns of N'kai.

Wilfred is now an eldritch, immortal toad-thing with unnatural lusts for human flesh and sexual congress with blood relatives. His presence blights the family, who has cared for him as best they could over the centuries, and has kept him from disrupting the local populace. The family believes, rightly, that if he dies, the

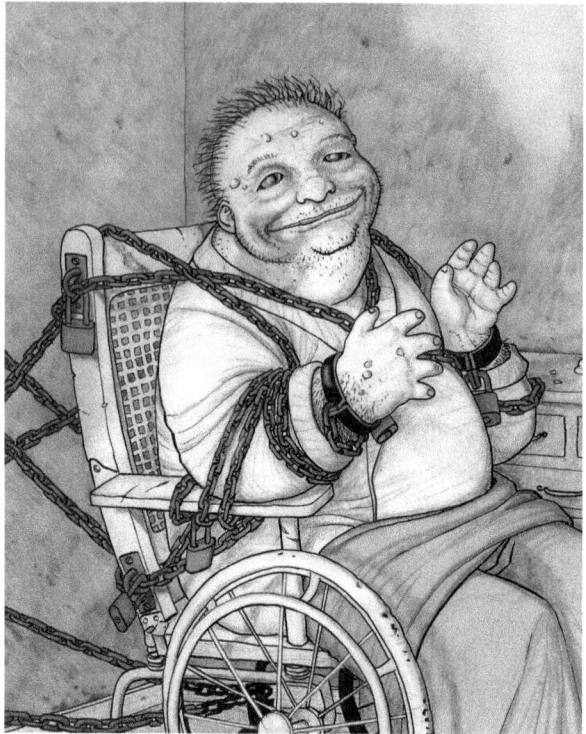

*Mr. Wilfred Hazard*

curse of Tsathoggua will simply infect another member of the family.

At first glance Wilfred looks like a fat man with very pale skin. A molded birthmark discolors his face and all other exposed flesh. He sweats heavily, despite the dampness of the room, and gulps his breaths in slow, even hisses. His large, goggling eyes are blood-shot, and mostly pupil. Light is painful to him. He is normally chained to his wheelchair that, in turn, is attached to the wall with strong, heavy links.

Closer scrutiny is difficult in the perpetual dusk of his attic, but his unduly wide mouth can be discerned with a **Spot Hidden** roll. Such a roll alerts the investigator that Wilfred's chains are no longer secure. *Wilfred's Testament* is concealed in the frame of his wheelchair, where he secreted it after devouring the Accursed Cat Burglar (see the **Old Damned House Papers #1** later in the scenario).

Cousin Wilfred is sly, sardonic and lazy. He pretends to be asleep at first, and slowly "wakes up" to converse with his visitors, opening one long, narrow slit of an eye. He attempts to lure the investigators close with protestations of his own harmlessness (rattling his chains to show that he can do nothing) and may hint that he knows what is going on.

## Prime Hazard

At 83 years of age Prime Hazard is silver-haired, and is always clean-shaven and immaculately presented, although his clothes are old and have been carefully

*Mr. Prime Hazard*

repaired many times. He wears black coats and waistcoats with white shirts, which combined give him a priestly air.

Prime is a Puritan scholar without any religion other than his books; he is deliberate, stern, and dispassionate. His sanity was long ago deeply shaken by reading *Wilfred's Testament*. His reaction to that trauma has been to defend the family honor, and its secret, vigorously. Prime will not tell a lie but he is capable of omitting to tell the whole truth when it suits him.

Prime plays the bass viol most beautifully and can often be heard accompanying Saphronia as she sings. He alone winds the eight-day clock, the key to which he keeps in his breast pocket.

## Saphronia Hazard

Saphronia is a lovely, proud, fragile, elderly woman of 71 years of age in her second childhood. She dresses in the fashions of her girlhood, and is very proper and stately. Her long while hair is carefully coiled up on her head, and each night in the kitchen she lets it down and Caleb brushes it, carefully, one hundred times.

*Mrs. Saphrona Hazard*

She sings sweetly to Prime's viol playing. She lives in a world of her own: a world of fifty years ago, when she had many lovers, and a myriad nephews and nieces, all of whom mutated, except Ellery and Isabeau's mother, and were fed to Cousin Wilfred. The investigators will hear ghastly things if they take the trouble to listen to her sweet whispers.

Saphronia dotes on the crystal bats that she says live in the attic. She takes them scraps, which she forages from the garbage, in the evenings ("there cannot be the sun, or any light at all," she says, "or they are frightened away"). The rest of her family pay little heed to her activities, other than to gently agree with her ramblings.

## Caleb Hazard

Caleb is a colorless, almost characterless little wizened balding man, 66 years old, with a pushed-in face. He

# THE CRYSTAL BATS

Two or three nights a week, Saphronia feeds her "crystal bats" in the attic. The rest of the family thinks she is just confused, and allows her to gather tasty scraps from the garbage. She puts the scraps out in the sun to attract flies, and then takes them upstairs to the attic at dusk.

She is quite willing to let the investigators accompany her on one of these trips, but they must promise to keep quiet and not to use any lights. "The bats are very shy, they only come out at night, on moonless nights," she explains.

Sweet singing is heard, at first faintly, but gradually becoming clearer single notes. A **Listen** roll indicates that the music is coming from outside the room. Hypnotic, luminescent blue shadows begin to flicker amongst the rafters. The shadows are captivating, and Saphronia calls them "crystal bats."

As the singing grows louder, a horrible stench becomes noticeable, wafting into the room in sickening gusts in time with the music. Saphronia fails to notice the smell.

Unseen shapes flutter against the investigators, licking their faces. The "crystal bats" avoid any other contact with the investigators, unless they create a bright light.

If the room is bathed in light, the investigators discover that the blue shadows are not bats, as Saphronia has believed, but rather are caused by five near-human creatures. The creatures are mutated Hazard children, who have been fooling Saphronia for some time. They are described more fully in the Other Hazards section, below.

If the truth is revealed to Saphronia, she is shocked that she has been duped, and takes to her bed. Within a few days she becomes sick, and soon dies. The children come down to her bedside at night. They stroke her hair and hands, and lick her face, weeping, but she refuses to forgive them. ☼

echoes whatever his sisters say, but makes little other effort in conversation. He does many of the household chores, keeps the women company playing card games, and helps in the kitchen.

The one way to animate Caleb is to discuss his hobby: collecting prosthetics. Caleb's face lights up as he lifts the glass eyes from their cases and talks about their individual "water" and striations. Investigators who listen to Caleb talk about his hobby, and endure the hours of

*Mr. Caleb Hazard*

being shown his collection, gain a life-long friend.

Caleb knows of Cousin Wilfred and the rituals, and might caution any friend who seems to be learning too much. He knows Cousin Wilfred is dangerous to those outside the family, or those inside who drop their guard. Nevertheless, like

# WILFRED'S TESTAMENT

This document is actually found within the Hazard house, in the remains of Wilfred's wheelchair when he has been killed.

The testament is a lengthy document in which Wilfred does his best to explain what has happened to him.

It is clearly quite old — the writing is fading, and in parts the yellowed paper has torn away, taking words with it. Throughout the manuscript there are marginal notes in a variety of hands, the import of which is noted at the end of this handout.

The text itself is written in English, although, it would seem it is not the author's native language. *Sanity Loss 1D2 / 2D2, +2 percentiles Cthulhu Mythos, 6 hours to study and comprehend. No spells.*

*My name is Wilfred Hazard, and this is my tale. I relate it now, while I am still able to write and think clearly, so that you, my family, will understand what has happened to me and what I am becoming, that you may avoid the traps into which I have fallen.*

*In the summer of 1723 I embarked upon the greatest adventure of my life...*

Wilfred tells of a French expedition to search for the fabled underground city of Quivira, a city made of gold. The expedition struck out to the West, and with Indians from local tribes as their guides, managed to find a path to the subterranean land where Quivira lay. They found Quivira, he relates, and other cities that surpassed it both in beauty and in riches....

*...The towering golden spires of Quivira paled when compared to those of this new place: gigantic structures reaching out to the cavern roof impossibly high above us. All around us the lanterns caught the twinkle of gold – every surface, every structure, it seemed was constructed of the metal. Surely here were riches enough to make us all kings!*

*If only we had taken what we could and turned back then, but we did not, because we knew that beyond this place there must be another which was richer still....*

Wilfred explains that the sheer value of all that surrounded them drove some of the expedition mad with greed, and the others were forced to kill them before the whole group was endangered. Despite such things, they explored further, until they began to discern the signs of habitation....

*...At first we argued over whether we should proceed, for who could say what manner of creature might make its home in so deep and forgotten a land, however we soon decided that as long as the creatures left us alone, we need not worry about them.*

*It was clear that whatever lived there was not human, although there might once have been some similarities. The ancient carvings that we found depicted bizarre beasts with the shapes of lizards and worse; the lizard creatures seemed to have lived in those great cities, making idols and altars to enormous, blasphemous gods. Many a night we slept with the horrendous images from the shrines we had found haunting our nightmares, and many a morning one or another of us would awake screaming and wreathed in terror at what we had seen. We chose to ignore such warnings, however, until we found the wraiths....*

Odd wraith-like forms beset the expedition. Wilfred describes the forms as little more than a collection of floating blue lights, and yet it is clear from his narrative that they disturbed the entire exploration team. While he does not indicate that the wraiths directly harmed the expedition in any way, they chose to turn around and head for the surface a short time after they first encountered them.

*...it was decided that we would head back to the surface and outfit another, larger expedition. By this time we all had a great deal of gold with us, but that was not all: I had discovered a strange token made of a substance we were quite unfamiliar with. At first I believed it to be a string of dark, lustrous pearls, but since that time I have doubled that assessment, for they are unlike any pearls I have ever seen, and they are far too large. It was this token, I think, that spared me from what we were next to encounter....*

Shortly after they started for the surface, the expedition suffered a catastrophe. With no warning whatsoever, the ground spilt asunder and many of the team were lost. Wilfred speculates that it was almost as if there was a conscious intellect below them, reaching up to prevent them from leaving. They had to retrace their steps several times, as simi-

*(continued on next page)*

*The Old Damned House Papers #1*

all his family, he is reluctant to discuss Cousin Wilfred with outsiders.

## Guillaume Hazard

Guillaume is a sturdy elderly man of 58 years. He has Prime's silver hair and Caleb's pushed-in face. He wears altered overalls and shirts, and changes them for others as equally ill-repaired only when his sisters manage to persuade him to do so. He wears a jaunty, ancient Union cap and a red bandanna around his deeply seamed neck.

Guillaume spends most of his time studying the books of witchcraft that he has managed to locate. Often he reads well into the night, catching up on his sleep during the day. He can be lazy and hard to rouse, responding to all but the most determined attempts with nothing more than muttered French obscenities. When awake, Guillaume is garrulous and constantly searching for amusement. His sense of humor is cynical, sly, black and coarse. He constantly teases the other members of the family: Prime for being too serious, Caleb for being a nothing, Ellery and Isabeau for being young and flighty. He accompanies these sallies with hoarse, genuinely amused, bellows of laughter.

Guillaume fancies a good drop of alcohol, and keeps a stash of illicit liquor hidden in his room.

*Mr. Guillaume Hazard*

## Lucille Hazard

Lucy was once comely, but now she is plump, grey-haired, 50 years old, sprightly and ferocious, especially with regard to

*(continued from previous page)*

lar chasms barred their passage, until they found themselves straying into vast, dark caverns filled with shifting shadows....

> ...even as we clambered over the debris, we could tell that there was something watching us: a cold baleful presence. We moved as fast as we were able, resting for only a few hours when we were too exhausted to continue....

Several times the surviving explorers were attacked by shapes and shadows they could only dimly make out. Tentacles reached out from the darkness dragging screaming men off to their doom. The survivors fled into the dark, time after time, until only a handful remained. Then, when they seemed to be only a day's journey from the surface, they encountered a dreadful creature, which the other formless monsters seemed to follow as a leader. It bore the likeness of a great toad, oozing and fetid. Wilfred describes the encounter as a massacre.

> ...This I know, to my most bitter sorrow, that I alone of the thirty men survived this encounter. I shudder still as I think back and see its gaping maw envelop those I had traveled so far with.

> Many a night have I wondered how I, of all of them, could have survived, and indeed remained unscathed as the carnage went on around me. It is my belief that it was the token that protected me that day – the dark string of pearls I had found. I could feel that nameless creature's desire for the object, and its frustration – for I believe it could not harm me while I possessed the token. It is only through its power, I am sure, that I

escaped the attention of the wraiths and formless things that so blighted that Necropolis. And yet I did not escape unmarked, for even as I fled in terror, I felt a moist presence at my back, and for a single moment knew a boundless pain as something thrust itself within me. To this day I have been unable to say exactly what it was that found its way inside me then, but even now I can feel it within me contorting both my body and, God help me, my soul.

> While my mind and body are being deformed by whatever it is that caught me that day, I feel now that it is the token that holds the key to this dreadful curse I have brought upon us. I can feel, still, the desire burning in that loathsome beast – a desire that cannot rest until the token is returned to those nameless caverns, where it belongs. I can discover no way to destroy the token, nor have I been able to in any way free myself from the bond that I can feel has been created between me and that foul creature.

> I have come to see that the token is somehow part of the soul of that blasphemous toad-god, and that by possessing it I am bound in some way to the beast. It presents me, this token: that venture is now sixty years gone, and still I show no signs of aging; instead my undying body warps and I am prey to hungers and terrible urges that are not my own. And further, I am unable to even take my own life — some part of me, or of the baleful creature to which I am now linked, will not allow me to harm myself in any way.

> I must make haste to finish this document whilst my mind is still my own, and I

beseech you, my great-nephew, to keep it in your hands and pass it to the fittest of your sons when he reaches his maturity, as you have already promised, for the great love of family that fills you. And keep the pearls safely, for it is only by their power that we are able to keep it at bay; I know that should we lose the token, that thing will surely come for us. To these oaths I bind you – you and your descendants to the last generation – on peril of the most fearful consequences. If my condition becomes known I will surely be destroyed and this curse will infect another of you, the best and brightest and fairest. Of this I am sure.

> I beseech you again; keep this thing, this foul carcass, hidden, though I should forget all thought and due care; to tell no one; to attempt no trespass further where once I have trod, at the peril of your immortal soul, for man was not meant to go there, and return whole....

> I pray daily for death and it does not come. I know that I have passed from God's grace. But if He will not spare me, perhaps He will attend you, who are blameless in this. Therefore I pray in God's grace, that He may bless you and keep you in this year of our Lord, 1785

> Wilfred Hazard, a most unhappy soldier.

Notations cover the manuscript attesting to its veracity. Some fragments detail rituals of sacrifice to be enacted upon children of the family who are born deformed. The evidence of the notes suggests that Wilfred is directly responsible for most of the children, and that almost all are born mutated and killed soon after. ✳

---

table manners. She is the youngest and strongest of the older generation, bar Guillaume who is too lazy to help, so she does most of the heavy work: the laundry, the mending, the cooking, etc. She muddles through the family finances in any way she can, which recently has meant the furtive sale of old family treasures. She is the only one of the older generation who is in regular contact with the outside world.

*Miss Lucy*

Lucy dotes on Ellery and Isabeau seeing in them the last glory of the Hazards. She is sewing a long white dress for Isabeau, not a wedding dress, but a shroud. It

is stitched with intricate figures from the *Danse Macabre*.

## Ellery and Isabeau Hazard

Nearing their twenty-first birthdays, the twins are self-centered and glamorous, but are capable of deep affection — as is evidenced by their behavior to one other. They are extremely close, and have yet to meet those who could claim their affections. Rumor has it that they are *too* close, but the gossip is not specific.

Both Ellery and Isabeau are ashamed of their family, and regard Cousin Wilfred as nothing more than an embarrassment. They are quite unaware what he is capable of and might even take curious investigators to meet him.

Every now and then, when Lucy manages to sell something particularly valuable, the twins escape to Hartford for a few days. Despite their desire to leave

Mystic once and for all, the twins are tied to the rest of the family in ways they cannot understand. If they should ever remain away from the house for more than a few weeks, both will become quite distressed.

Ellery attempts to keep Isabeau isolated from the rest of the world. He is very protective, and will do everything in his power to preserve her innocence. Isabeau allows herself to be confined by Ellen, because she loves him so.

If Ellery reads *Wilfred's Testament* and learns of the family curse, he is horrified at the terrible taint in his blood, and yet he cannot help but accept his own sense of doom.

If Isabeau learns the contents of *Wilfred's Testament*, she falls into a catatonic state. She can move and speak, but is incapable of initiative, and simply does as others tell her.

## Other Hazards

A number of the mutated Hazard children managed to escape death at Wilfred's hands. They lurk around the house, rummaging through cupboards, and causing all manner of disturbances. The rest of the family are unaware of their existence, and believe that the house is infested with rats. While they appear to be quite young, the children are all at least forty years old.

All of the children look pretty loathsome. The Sanity loss for seeing all of them at once is 1D3/1D8. The Sanity loss for seeing each one individually is included in their statistics at the scenario's conclusion.

*Miss Isabeau and Mr. Ellery*

The children are responsible for the various poltergeist manifestations throughout the house. They attempt to trick non-family visitors whenever possible, however they would never dream of harming their own family, not even Cousin Wilfred. In many ways the children respect Wilfred, although they are quite afraid of him.

The Hazard children have a strange link with the caverns of N'Kai and are able to find their way to and from that unspeakable place with ease. Jean is the closest to the underground world and when, eventually he ventures there, he will never return.

It should be noted that the children never intend to do serious harm.

### Nathanial

Nathanial appears to be a boy in his early teens (thirteen or fourteen). While his torso and head are normal, his limbs are supple appendages of a glossy black substance that stretches (like hot rubber) allowing him purchase on the walls, floors or ceiling! He tenderly licks people to show his affection, and his tongue is rather long and toad-like.

### Mercy

Mercy seems to be a girl of about ten, with long black hair and large, timorous eyes. Her intestines grow around the outside of her body in slick, pulsating bundles that have taken on a glossy, black, jelly-like consistency. She can speak from orifices in these external body

*Master Nathaniel*

*Miss Mercy*

*Miss Celestine*

*Master Girard*

*Hazard House*

sacs, the piping music that is her only speech. An unpleasant smell is the undesired side effect of this process.

## Celestine and Girard

These two children are younger still in appearance (they seem to be about eight). They have no proper human skin, rather a toad-like, molded, semi-transparent membrane that covers all but their eyes and mouths. Their movements are strangely liquid and inhuman (they are able to turn their joints any way they like), as if within the toad-skin cocoon their human bodies are being gradually liquefied. Celestine and Girard catch flies and tear their wings off, watching the struggling insects with fascination.

## Jean

Jean is the source of the flickering blue light that Saphronia dotes on. He has almost fully mutated into a "Child of Tsath". He is a fluid movement of blackness whose only vestige of humanity is the slowly dissolving face that peers from his form when his interest is aroused. Jean can speak only a little, a gurgling noise of peculiarly alien timbre and pitch. He casts a blue flickering shadow in the darkness, in the same way that normal people cast a dark shadow in the daylight.

*Master Jean*

## Contents

The Hazard house has evolved over several centuries, starting as a one-room cottage, and gradually growing to its present size — a mansion of more than twenty-eight rooms. The layout is confusing to the uninitiated; many parts of the house are inaccessible from adjacent areas. In some cases it is necessary to return to the ground floor to get from one particular room to another.

It is important to note the positioning of the bedrooms; Wilfred's room is in the top, north corner of the house. The eldest members of the family sleep just below him — Prime is able to both keep an eye on gentle Saphronia and make sure that Wilfred does not escape. Ellery and Isabeau have rooms in a portion of the house not easily accessible from Wilfred's room, as they are not yet fully aware of his condition. Lucy's room is near the twins' so that she can keep an eye on them. Caleb sleeps on the top floor, diagonally across the house from Wilfred — he prefers to have a place of his own to retreat to. Guillaume's room is in the basement, where he feels more at home — sheltered from the world, and able to pursue his studies without interruptions.

The house contains many things not listed. Typical 1920s New England furnishings abound, as do stitched samplers framed and hung on the walls displaying Puritan work ethic mottos such as "An hour of idleness is worse than an hour of drunkenness." Display shelves are lined with handsome crockery worn so thin that light can be seen through them. Fine ancient goods from the Orient (silk screens, exotic furniture, and Chinese porcelains), products of the whaling trade (a carved ambergris pipe, scrimshaw and bottled ships on the mantelpieces), and some ornaments and artifacts of French manufacture dating back to the arrival of Cousin Wilfred in the 1750's, all bear testimony to the family's former prosperity. Everything is old.

The house itself is damp and dark. A mist of despair and genteel poverty hangs over the whole place, dulling the colors and weathering the house and its inhabitants. Here and there, toads can be found, moving slowly across the garden and basement, lurking in the bathrooms, and occupying the damp corners of the lower floors. As the scenario proceeds, the toads become more numerous, as they troop up from the ancient caves beneath the house, sensing the drama which is unfolding.

The following is a key to the plans of the house. It is segregated by floor for easy reference. Keepers should

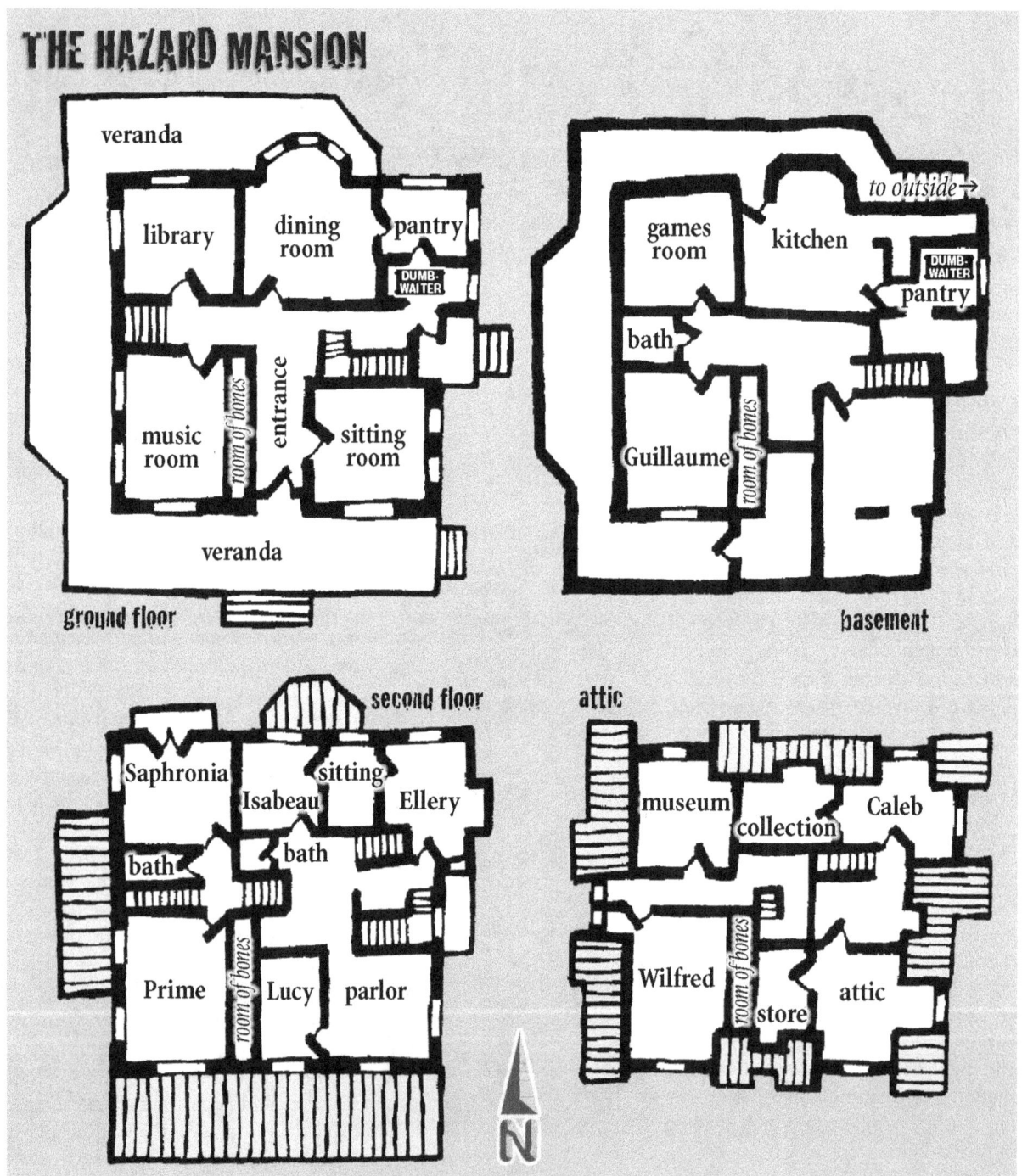

THE HAZARD MANSION

feel free to elaborate on the given information, bearing in mind however, that the building is solid and its contents real — it in no way shifts or changes during the course of the scenario, and players should not be led to think that it does — it is confusing enough without such distractions.

Although the Accursed Cat Burglar was a skilled professional, he has left behind a small number of clues. In certain rooms there is information outlining the things that the investigators might discover. The keeper should feel free to use the material in whatever way seems to best suit the players' styles, although it is recommend not add too many new clues.

## All floors

### Stairs

The stairs on each floor are marble. Keepers should familiarize themselves with the way the stairs link parts of the house, as it can be difficult to determine exactly which areas have access to which others on the spur of the moment.

### Bathrooms

Most of the bathrooms in the house are not described, although they are shown on the floor plans. Each contains a bath and sink. The toilet is outside. Chamber pots are in use instead.

### Closets

None of the house's closets are shown on the floor plans, but they can be found all over the house. The keeper should feel free to place them wherever they are needed. The children have made small holes up high in the walls in most of the closets, through which they are able to climb into the walls and so make their way throughout the house.

### The Room of Bones

An accident of building has led to the creation of a secret cavity in the house, which shall be called the room of bones. It is an empty shaft running from the foundations to the roof. Since his arrival, Wilfred has been discarding the digested remains of his feasting into the Room of Bones, and the shaft is now almost full of the baby-sized pellets. There are a number of holes into the cavity from Wilfred's room, and a few at the back of the cellar, but overall it has remained entirely sealed. Investigators who do discover the room and its contents must make a Sanity roll as they realize how many deaths it represents, with a loss of 1D3/1D6 points.

*The Room of Bones*

## Ground floor

### Porch

Admittance to the Hazard home is gained through a massive porch. The front doors are recessed, with an alcove to shelter the traveler from the elements. The doors are imposing, made from the finest oak and a full 2" inches thick. A sturdy bell-pull alerts the family when visitors come calling. It is up to the keeper to determine which family member answers the door. Wilfred or Saphronia are unlikely to meet the investigator at the door.

### Entrance Hall

The front doors open into the centre of the ground floor. A sizeable hallway connects most of the ground-floor rooms and the various stairways. There are a variety of fine art objects on sideboards and tables in the hall however a successful **Art** roll indicates that none of them are particularly valuable.

There are two sets of stairs that lead to upper floors: the main stairs curve around to a landing near Ellery and Isabeau's rooms, while a smaller set of stairs provide access to Saphronia and Prime's rooms, and ultimately to Wilfred's attic room. Below the main stairs there is a door that leads down a set of stairs to the basement, and Guillaume's room.

### Music Room

This comfortably apportioned room contains a number of musical instruments and a selection of sheet music.

The instruments to be found here include three viola da gambas (a bass, tenor and alto), a harpsichord, and a hammer dulcimer. The viola du gamba is a stringed instrument not unlike a small cello. It is played much the same way as the cello, however it sits on the musician's lap, rather than the floor. The viola da gamba comes in a number of different sizes, but all have a sweeter sound than contemporary violins, although they possess less resonance. On occasion Prime plays the bass viol and Saphronia sings.

The ample collection of sheet music contains a variety of styles. All of the music is over thirty years old, but it has been well preserved. A **Library Use** roll uncovers some music written by the Hazards themselves almost a century ago. While most of the Hazard music is strangely discordant when played, it is competent work.

### Sitting Room

A number of comfortable armchairs have been placed strategically around this room, each with its own lamp and table. Sideboards hold displays of silver and china, as well as vases of attractive flowers (which Lucy proudly acknowledges as her responsibility).

It is through a window in this room that the burglar gained entrance. Any of the family members can point the window out to the investigators.

Underneath the window is a set of clear footprints in the flower garden. A **Track** roll identifies the shoes' wearer as a male of medium build, and indicates that he might be pigeon-toed. A **Know** roll identifies the pattern from the soles of the shoes as that of an expensive brand of shoe. A successful **Spot Hidden** roll notices that a number of the flowers have been stepped upon (the crushed petals stuck to the bottom of the burglar's shoes until he reached the safe).

The windowsill has no clear fingerprints on it, however a **Spot Hidden** roll will reveal a few threads of fabric. A **half Know** roll identifies the thread as having come from an expensive tweed jacket.

Next to the window, there is a small amount of dirt from the burglar's shoes. While most of the dirt comes from the garden outside, a **Spot Hidden** roll indicates that some of the dirt is slightly different. A **Geology** roll reveals that the foreign dirt is heavy gray sand, of the sort that is found on the beach below the Hazard house. It is possible for the investigators to retrace the burglar's tracks. See the section below about the garden and beach.

### Library

Despite the large windows in this room, the library is dark and musty. Bookshelves line the walls from floor to ceiling, and are filled with the evidence of decades of avid study, and a true appreciation of the written word. Most of the books to be found here concern general academic topics, or are about local history. There is a section of fiction, but it is fairly dry, humorless material.

One part of the library contains family documents and history. There are all manner of ships' logs, diaries, family ledgers and business notes from the days when the family was young and prosperous. All of the papers have been bound into leather volumes, each bearing the family crest on its cover. None of the material is indexed in any way and Prime is the only one who knows his way around the volumes . He is glad to allow those with an interest in the history of the area to search through the library however he usually supervises such research to ensure that nothing of a personal nature is accidentally discovered.

There are a number of items of interest that investigators might discover on their own, or search out when Prime is not around.

If an investigator is interested in finding out about the details of the Hazard family tree, a **Know** roll indicates that many Puritan New England families keep such information in the front cover of the family Bible. The Hazards have done just that, and their Bible can be a useful source of information. A cursory glance at the family tree indicates that many names have been erased from it at one time or another. The missing names represent the children who were born deformed and fed to Wilfred. More interestingly an **Idea** roll indicates a noticeable discrepancy between the number of births before and after the 1780's (when Wilfred began to lose control of his urges). Prior to that time, the family had numerous children, often in batches of nine to twelve. After Wilfred's return, however, the numbers of recorded births drop to one or two per couple, and the family decline starts, in numbers as well as in wealth. Those looking for Wilfred Hazard will find no mention of the name, although a **Spot Hidden** roll indicates that one of the early erased names might have been Wilfred's, the date of birth would been early in the eighteenth century.

Investigators searching for any mention of the disappearances that have plagued the family at various times in the past will be disappointed. A **Library Use** roll indicates that the omissions are deliberate, although that impression is impossible to verify.

It is in this room that the Hazard Pearls were kept. There is a safe in the wall behind one of the shelves of books. Only Prime has the key to the safe, and he opens it once every few days to get something out or put something in. When the pearls were stolen, the safe contained about $500 in cash, as well as a number of important family documents (including *Wilfred's Testament*), all of which were taken.

A **Locksmith** roll verifies that only a skilled thief would be able to crack the lock — all attempts to open the lock receive a –40% modifier. If required, an **Idea** roll could indicate to an investigator that the burglar would have to have known exactly where the safe was. This might lead one to suspect help of some sort, possibly from someone within the house.

Nearby the safe, under the lower lip of the bookcase, a **Spot Hidden** roll reveals the crushed remains of one of the flower petals from outside the sitting room window. It stuck to the bottom of the burglar's shoe, coming loose only after he had made his way across the whole ground floor. Another **Spot Hidden** roll reveals that the petal was probably dislodged when the burglar turned around suddenly, as if he was startled. Indeed, the children surprised the burglar, and they managed to grab the pearls from his hands before he knew what was going on. Pursuing the fleeing children up the stairs, he became lost and stumbled into Wilfred's room.

## Dining Room

The dining room is large enough to allow all seven members of the Hazard family to eat comfortably. In the past, up to fourteen family members at a time have eaten here regularly. Sideboards containing the everyday china and silverware fill the available wall-space. An expansive chandelier hangs precariously over the massive mahogany table, and it can be heard creaking in the drafts at night.

An eight-day clock ticks on a sideboard that rests against one wall. Prime has the only key and allows no one else to wind it.

## Pantry

The pantry area is used primarily to ready the food made in the basement kitchen for the table. All manner of simple foods are kept here for convenience, and the kitchen in the basement is only used to prepare the final meal of the day. A small dumb-waiter connects the kitchen and pantry, and is used to hoist the warm food up for serving.

This room is always in a bit of a mess, and the family members may be heard to complain about rats getting into the cupboards. A **Biology** roll indicates that rats would be incapable of getting into most of the containers that are stored in here. Indeed, it is the Hazard children who rummage through the cupboards looking for food.

## First Floor

All the bedrooms in the house are roughly similar: each contains a four-poster bed, a trunk and chest of drawers made from an old, dark wood. The stained teak floors are covered with unassuming, threadbare carpets. The bed linen and blankets have been much patched over the years, but have been well cared for.

### Saphronia's Room

Saphronia's room has a porch of its own, where she has placed a single chair and table, and many an afternoon she can be found sitting there, gazing out over the water.

Also in her room Saphronia keeps the several pieces of needlework on which she is always working.

### Prime's Room

Prime's room contains the materials he uses to bind the family volumes that are in the ground floor library.

Investigators who are explicitly searching for them might be able to find a full set of keys for the house in Prime's room. While he usually keeps the keys on his person, allow a **Luck** roll to determine whether he has left them behind. Finding them also requires a **Spot Hidden** roll, as Prime is careful not to leave such valuable items carelessly strewn about his room. None of the keys in the set are labeled in any way, but one of them does unlock the chains on Wilfred's wheelchair.

## Isabeau's Room

The furniture in Isabeau's room is slightly newer, and in slightly better condition than the furniture in the most of the rest of the house.

Isabeau's room has a balcony overlooking the water, and she sometimes she sits out there with Ellery, late into the night, dreaming about the places they want to see and the things they want to do.

There is a sitting room between Isabeau's and Ellery's rooms, and that is where Isabeau spends most of her time during the day, reading.

## Twins' Sitting Room

Nestled between the twins' rooms is a common sitting room. It is modestly decorated, and contains a few chairs and a low bookshelf of fiction. The twins spend much of their time in this room, and the chances are that at least one of them will be found here at all times.

## Ellery's Room

As in Isabeau's room, the furniture in Ellery's room is slightly newer, and in slightly better condition than the furniture in the most of the rest of the house.

There is a small balcony on the west side of Ellery's room. Ellery has placed a small telescope (which he put together himself) on the balcony. He spends a considerable time gazing out across Mystic and along the coast.

## Parlor

Lucy uses the sizeable parlor on the first floor as a private sitting room. She has placed her favorite paintings, vases, and treasures carefully around the room, and while nothing is particularly valuable, she has managed to create a truly charming atmosphere.

Lucy spends much of her time in this room working on her sewing, and she has dedicated a whole corner to this occupation.

Finally, in another corner of the room, there sits a large desk with a myriad of pigeonholes, where Lucy works out the household accounts and struggles to pay off the bills.

## Lucy's Room

Lucy's room is the smallest bedroom in the house, but she does not mind, as she spends most of her time in the adjoining parlor. Her room is always clean, reflecting many of the virtues extolled in her samplers that decorate the walls.

# Attic floor

## Museum

This room houses years of Hazard family history. It is old, dark, dank and ill lit. The ceiling is low with solid oak beams, and the bare wooden floor sinks underfoot. The room is filled with a musty treasure trove: stitched samplers and gloomy oil paintings cover the walls, and the cabinets and display shelves are filled with curios of the Orient and the whaling trade, and Indian artifacts (brought here by the Indians who came with Cousin Wilfred in 1759). An **Archaeology or Anthropology** roll, coupled with a **History** roll identifies the Indian artifacts as belonging to the Wichita tribe, which was once found in Western Oklahoma, but has been almost wiped out since the middle of the nineteenth century. What little space there is in the room not devoted to storing treasures is filled by tightly packed bookshelves. The books kept in his room are musty and suffer from the ravages of time. While there are a number of topics represented, none of the information to be found within the volumes is of any direct interest to the investigators.

## Wilfred's Room

Wilfred is locked away from the rest of the family, and the world. His room is dank and dusty, and the small amount of furniture he has is cracked and worn. Wilfred does not like intense light and consequently his room is usually dark. While the room contains both a bed and chairs, Wilfred rarely, if ever, uses them. Instead he is confined to his wheelchair, and is content to move around the room as far as his bonds will allow.

The innermost (west) wall of Wilfred's room borders on the room of bones that runs from the basement to the roof of the house. There are several holes along the length of the wall, and Wilfred usually disposes of the remains of his blasphemous meals through them. These holes would not be apparent to the casual observer. A **Spot Hidden** roll is required to notice them unless an investigator is actually walking around the entire room.

The burglar dashed into Wilfred's room while he was trying to locate the children who had grabbed the pearls from his hands. Wilfred took advantage of the situation, convincing the hapless thief to pick the lock on his bonds before he devoured the fellow.

As he was startled when he encountered Wilfred, the burglar dropped one of the white gloves he was wearing. With a successful **Spot Hidden** roll, an investigator will notice the glove caught behind the door. No other sign of the burglar remains in the room (Wilfred is very thorough).

## Caleb's Room

The low, angled ceiling in Caleb's room gives it a cramped feeling, although he actually has quite a bit of space.

Caleb keeps some of his prosthetics collection is his bedroom, rather than the crowded collection room that adjoins it. The wall next to his bed provides the perfect display space for his extensive collection of glass eyes.

## Collection Room

The room was once used as a general attic however Caleb has cleaned it out, and is now using it to house the bulk of his prosthetics collection. He has built an impressive set of racks and cabinets to house the rows of artificial legs and organs that he has collected over the years. A bookcase by the door holds one of the most complete sets of prosthetics catalogues in New England.

Even a somewhat disgusted investigator should be impressed by Caleb's splendid collection — he has spared no expense searching down all manner of replacement limbs and organs, and while the gradually diminishing Hazard finances have forced him to turn to smaller objects (like eyes), his entire collection is quite something to behold.

## Attic

This room is filled with decades of rubbish. Most of the good stuff has been sifted out and sold to maintain the family over the last few years, but the occasional trinket found in here has value. The stuff kept in here does not differ significantly from the things found around the rest of the house (paintings, vases, etc.) except that the stuff here is mainly broken, badly worn, or discarded.

Saphronia has had a careful path cleared through the room so that she can get to the storeroom beyond to feed her "Crystal Bats."

Investigators making a dedicated search of this room might be unlucky enough to stumble on mantraps used by a Hazard over a hundred years ago. Any investigator failing a **Luck** roll while in the room has set off one such rusty trap, and is in danger of being bisected. The great rusted, steel-jawed monsters do 1D8 damage when set off. To open a trap requires a STR roll versus the trap's STR of 15+1D8. Keepers may wish to allow investigators an additional **Luck** roll to determine whether the trap is so old it failed to go off when activated.

## Store Room

This cluttered room is where Saphronia goes to feed the "Crystal Bats" she believes live in the roof. Unbeknownst to her, the Hazard children are leading her on, as described in the section detailing Saphronia above.

The children gain access to the room through a trap door set into the ceiling. The trap door provides access to the roof. A careful examination of the trap door, and a successful **Spot Hidden** roll, will reveal scratch marks all around the opening. The children's deformed limbs cause the marks; a **Biology** roll indicates that no known creature made the marks (and certainly not by bats, rats or the toads that infest the house and grounds).

# Basement level

## Games Room

This is the oldest room in the house. It was the original room in the one-room cottage, built in the late 1690's. Little of the original room remains visible, as the work on the house above has required strengthening the simple walls that were first constructed.

The room is now largely disused, and houses the remnants of ancient games equipment: broken lawn tennis racquets, croquet balls and mallets, a neglected card table, and a ruined pool table, complete with shattered cues and imperfect balls.

Hidden beneath the waste is a handsome sideboard, one of the first in the house. It has long since been forgotten, but any true connoisseur would give his eye teeth to posses such a fine piece.

## Guillaume's Room

Guillaume's room is simpler than the rooms occupied by the rest of the family. It contains a simple bed in one corner, and a desk and chair in another. A hefty chest of drawers lurks at the far side of the room. A low shelf of books lines one wall.

Guillaume's collection of books is somewhat odd, reflecting the shunned studies that he is secretly pursuing.

The only other item of interest is Guillaume's collection of alcohol. It is hidden in the bottom of his chest of drawers. The range is somewhat limited (mainly whiskey and gin), but his taste is good.

## The Kitchen and Pantry

Once staffed by a number of competent cooks, the kitchen is extensive. Recent times have seen the serving staff fired, and now the kitchen is used but once a day to prepare the evening meal. Although under-used, the kitchen is kept clean by those who use it. Occasionally the children get in and out through the pantry, but usually Saphronia and the items they take from the pantry on the ground floor satiate their hungers. A dumb-waiter is used to lift the hot food from the kitchen to the pantry on the ground floor, above.

## FROM THE DIARY OF MISTRESS MERCY STANTON, 1865

It has been a very bad summer indeed, with many of our younger ones taken away by cruel fever n'ague. It has been most sad for the Hazards, with three of their little ones struck down one after the other. They have been most stoic, refusing all offers of aid for fear of spreading the infection, and nursing them themselves most diligently but to no avail. The only result of their labor has been three tiny coffins carried out their front door one after the other. They are most distraught at this loss, little Johnny, eleven, and the heir, Nathanial at eight, and Lucy, only three, "not lost but gone before," as my dear mother would say.

It was at the funeral of little Lucy that one of those carrying the coffin made a most vulgar and coarse joke, causing much comment amongst the crowd of well-wishers gathered to help comfort the bereaved. He said that something was rolling around in the coffin and that it was his opinion that the child's head had come clean off!

This of course excited great outrage and several ladies fainted. Fortunately, being blessed with a sturdy constitution, I was able to witness the man being dismissed from his office immediately, one of the Hazards taking his place. The family was most upset by this grievously unnecessary occurrence.

I heard the man was about the town later, unrepentant and quite drunk, saying that it if it was a child in the coffin it was the strangest load he had ever shouldered, and he was a professional pallbearer and had much practice at such tasks. Notwithstanding the universal condemnation such wild talk received, he continued with his claims for several days, and some of the coarser elements in the town were even taking to buying him drinks, and encouraging him in his hurtful boastfulness.

These people, of course, believe all those stories you hear about the Hazards, about the witch-trials and the peculiar business of the ghost, or the baby, or whatever it was back all those years ago when they were rebuilding the house. Not to mention those pearls. Mere jealousy and spite, and such a trial for my respectable and dear friends. Fortunately after a few days the man moved on, and has since troubled us no more. ☀

*The Old Damned House Papers #2*

## The Cellars

The house has both a coal cellar and a storage cellar. The coal cellar is rarely more than half-full these days. The storage cellar contains mainly refuse.

The children often sleep in the storage cellar, and investigators who search the area carefully easily discover the signs of their habitation. Family members presented with such evidence will mention that vagrants have been known to take up lodgings in the basements of deserted buildings.

## Grounds

The Hazard home sits atop a lonely bluff just to the east of Mystic. From the top of the bluff it is possible to look out across the Long Island Sound and just see Fishers' Island.

The road from Mystic to the Hazard home is steep, but not treacherous. By car the house is not more than a few minutes from the heart (such as it is) of Mystic proper. There are few other houses in this direction from the town, and the environs are quiet.

The number of toads to be found all over the Hazard property may initially surprise new visitors to the house. The little creatures migrate happily all over the garden, falling into the well, infesting the basement of the house and clambering into the exhaust pipe of the investigators' automobile. The toads come up from the caves that riddle the cliff that rises up behind the house.

## Garden

The Hazard garden is well tended in parts, especially near the house itself. The more distant portions of the grounds, however, have been allowed to grow unchecked, and a dense tangle of bushes rings the property.

As mentioned in the section detailing the ground floor sitting room, the Cat Burglar gained entrance to the house through a window on the west side of the building. His footprints by the window are covered in that section.

Investigators who wish to follow the burglar's traces back down to the beach will find their progress barred by the tangle of bushes that surrounds the house. A **Track** roll gives the investigators the general direction the burglar came from, allowing them to locate his trail again on the beach below.

## Beach

The beach at the base of the cliff is covered in heavy gray sand and a scattered coating of dark, ropy seaweed. A hurricane will lash the coast of New England in the 1930s taking with it most of the sand from the beaches all along the coast. Keepers are asked to use the beach sand thoughtfully, while it is still available.

The weather has not been ideal since the burglar crossed the sand, but a **Track** roll can discern just enough of his trail to allow the investigators to wind their way into the trees, retracing his steps.

The trees give way to a small dirt track. Parked at the side of the track is a modest four-door automobile. The burglar left his car here, hidden from the main road, figuring that he would return to collect it.

The registration of the car can be checked and it belongs to a man named Elijah James Ryan, who works in Newport, Rhode Island.

## Further Information

This section outlines a variety of different sources of information that might be of use to the investigators.

It should not be thought of as exhaustive — the keeper should feel free to improvise the results of any research not covered here, although not too much additional information should be made available in this way. The information is presented according to location.

## Mystic Church and Cemetery

The small Mystic church might be the destination of investigators researching the Hazard family tree, or attempting to learn more about the accusations of witchcraft made against the family.

While the Hazard name appears frequently in the church register, and many of their children were baptized there, most of the information to be obtained here is erroneous: the dales of baptism listed in the register all reflect the Hazard policy of waiting to ensure that the newborn children were not deformed, and the current religious leaders know little of the accusations of witchcraft made by their predecessors. A **Persuade or Fast Talk** roll can be used to convince the caretaker to let the investigators into the family crypt.

## Family crypt

The Mystic cemetery is filled with a chaotic scattering of graves and vaults. The sunken, centuries-old graves are marked by cracked, weathered headstones. The Hazard crypt is tucked away at the far end of the cemetery. Although it is amongst the oldest structures in there, it has managed to retain a certain dignity over the years.

Above the stone doors is engraved the following verse:

> *If you are young so once was I*
> *If you are old you soon must die*

Inside, the coffins of almost three hundred years of Mystic Hazards are neatly arranged. The dust is thick, hut there is little sign of rot and the room is strangely free of the stale charnel air usually found in such places.

If the investigators are paranoid enough to prize open any of the coffins, they find that all those from the 1750's through to the present (the most recent is from five years ago — Ellery and Isabeau's mother Elizabeth) contain stones wrapped in rotting cloth (to keep the stones from rolling around when the coffins are shifted). Not a single body can be found amongst the coffins for almost 150 years.

# FROM THE DIARY OF ONE "NAILOR TOM", BOATWRIGHT, FEBRUARY 1759

Night fell early. I had repaired to John Beverly's hostelry and we were making very merry over some hot punch. The day, as I said, had been dark and stormy and no travelers were looked for, so we were made a small party alone in the common room, John, his wife and Isaiah and I. Then a hail came from without.

On going to the door, John found such a strange sight that his exclamation brought us over. A gentleman was there, dressed as a preacher all in black, with a black hat over his eyes. A heavily laden sleigh was behind him, and behind it were two of the most wretched Indians I had ever seen, blue with cold but evil-looking for all that. Murderous thieves, I could tell as soon as I clapped eyes upon them. But it was the man I looked for most sharply for he was uncommon ill looking, very puffy and stark white about the face, with red eyes, from cold or weeping.

Come in come in, says friend John, for in such dirty weather we looked for no traveler or we would have kept a sharper watch out.

I looked again at the sleigh and saw it had no bells upon it, nothing that would carry any sound, even in clear weather. The man just stood there, and his Indians as well, as if carved from the same wood as the sleigh. John would have none of it, especially as the man looked so unwell. Corpse white, and very heavy of breath and red of eye as if in a seizure.

Then the man spoke, in a thick foreign accent, asking for the Hazards. Well, Isaiah and I silently speculated at this, and looked

from the savages to their master, while John told him to go up the road and there would be the Hazard place, a fine, handsome house and well-tended. He would have sent a boy ahead to tell Elijah Hazard of his visitor, but the stranger told him not to mind.

Before you go sir, sez I plucking up the courage at Isaiah's goading, Can you tell us how things fare up in Boston?

I cannot tell you anything of that, sez he.

Oh so you came by sea then, sez I.

No, he sez shortly, I come from Wichita country. Here, he sez, tossing a coin to John. Never let it be said that Wilfred Hazard does not recognize hospitality. I go to see my cousin. Elijah.

He has a bonny family sir, pipes up Isaiah, hoping no doubt for similar favor, and you will find them all in good health.

This seemed to stir him, for his face twisted and he looked most anguished. Then he shook so hard we thought he would fall down and bent forward clutching at his stomach. John stepped forward right smartly to help him up, but one of the Indians came forward instead, and motioned him away, saying something in his guttural tongue. Then the stranger turned without other word, and started to walk up the street very fast, and still doubled up, staggering as though drunk. The Indians followed, leading the sleigh. We saw him go over onto his knees and then get up again and keep walking, but now he was limping very badly, as if his left leg would not hold his weight. We watched until he was out of sight in the dark and snow, fearing another fall.

Well, friend Wilfred will be like to die before the winter is out no doubt, Isaiah says helping himself to the punch, for he looks to me to be on his last legs.

And here he laughs at his own wit. But I said nothing for something about the stranger and his savage companions had troubled me. ☀

*The Old Damned House Papers #3*

## Mystic Historical Society

The Mystic Historical Society contains all manner of local historical information, from the diaries of the first settlers in the area, to collections of clothing and miscellany. Some portion of their collection is always on display, and the friendly staff is eager to assist those who wish to search through the catalogued archive materials. There are four pieces of useful information here for investigators to find: two diary extracts (*Old Damned House Papers #2 and #3*) and a **Library Use** roll is required to locate each one, articles from the newspaper archives requiring a successful **Library Use** roll, and one of Wilfred's castings left over from one of the two times he escaped. This last object requires a **Spot Hidden** made by an investigator who has seen a similar object out at the Hazard house.

## Newspapers

The newspaper archive kept by the society can provide information about strange disappearances in Mystic.

Two spates of disappearances swept over Mystic in recent history: one in 1827 and a second in 1893. In both, a dozen or so people vanished, generally at the rate of one or two a week for the duration of the season. *The Mystic and Beverly Gazette* devoted a good deal of editorial space to both these events, which turned up castings regurgitated by Cousin Wilfred, although no links were made between the two at the time (at least not publicly).

During both outbreaks the Hazards are noted as the most active searchers and the most distraught at news of the disappearances. With a successful **Idea** roll, the investigators observe that on each occasion the Hazards abruptly lost their anxiety and discontinued their part in the search at the end of the spate of disappearances, but well before the end was recognized by others in the community. This led to rumors that still linger in oral tradition.

## Indian Mummified Baby

One of these things is kept in a box in the basement of the Mystic Historical Society. The mummy normally costs 0/1 Sanity points to view. It is the rough size and shape of an infant in swaddling clothes, wrapped in shredded cloth and hair, from atop which a skull peers. Closer examination shows the skull has been completely crushed and reformed, and then has been laid neatly on lop of the other crushed bones, all wrapped neatly in hair and shredded fragments of cloth — clothes that have been through some digestive process. Anyone making a **Zoology** roll recognizes the grotesque similarity to an owl's casting. A successful **Spot Hidden** of the mummy reveals a disturbing incongruity — a crushed fob watch and chain intermingled with the bones.

Clearly, here are the remains of a much larger person — compressed into the size of an infant. It is identical to the disturbing find at the Hazard mansion. Any who realize this lose 0/1D6 Sanity in the knowledge that although separated by a century the finds must be related — and to the Hazards!

## Mystic Oral Tradition

Rumors and gossip are sources of information that some investigators may pursue. Mystic is a slowly dying town, filled with dissatisfied and apathetic people. Anyone asking around is bound to find any number of people willing to gossip about the past. A **Persuade or Fast Talk** roll is all that is required to obtain each piece of information in this section, although a few drinks of one sort or another can never hurt.

## History of the Hazard Family

The Hazards have settled in Mystic since the late seventeenth century. The family house was started, as a small shack, in the 1690s. Over the years the family and the house have grown, and for some time the Hazards were one of the most wealthy and powerful families in the area, as they controlled a sizable proportion of the sea trade.

Most people agree that the Hazards' decline began when they obtained the famous Hazard Pearls. The stories indicate that the pearls came over from the Orient on one of the Hazard merchant ships. Since their arrival, people point out, the family has grown smaller, and the fortune has all but dried up.

Any of the older Mystic inhabitants can tell stories about the Hazard witches. Every couple of decades some of the Hazards were accused of consorting with demons and the like. None of the accusations were ever proven, however people believe that was due more to the size of the Hazard wallets than their virtues.

## Current Hazard Family

The Hazards stay pretty much to themselves, rarely venturing even in Mystic, unless they must. The locals gossip freely about the reclusive family, whispering that they participate in unnatural acts in their lonely mansion, and live a decadent and tarnished life, but they say that sort of thing about most of the old families.

Both Ellery and Isabeau are known in town. People see them as the bright, beautiful sparks who may bring the Hazard family back into the community. Lucy is the only other Hazard who is seen regularly in Mystic. Although no one has any real gossip about her, she is not well liked (probably because she is not part of any of the local social circles, rather than for any other reason).

Someone in the town is bound to comment that there have been no obvious marriages outside the

Hazard family for decades. While it is easy to rationalize that those marriages that have occurred must have been private, those who recognize the situation are sure that the family is entirely inbred (which it is).

## Disappearances

The two sets of disappearances in Mystic (1827 and 1893) are common knowledge. While most locals consider the events to the tragedies, a few are outspoken on the subject, claiming that the Hazards were involved in the mess in some way. The speculations and accusations are not precise, and no one can say for sure what caused the disappearances, but there is a feeling that somehow something in the Hazard house managed to get out. The gossips point out that the first set of disappearances occurred during the chaotic rebuilding at the Hazard house, and the second set followed the lightning strike on the building.

Not much is known about the strange, seemingly mummified babies discovered during the investigations of the disappearances. With a **Luck** roll a local might be aware that one of the objects was found in the cemetery, and was eventually given to the Mystic Historical Society. Very few people would know that the other casting was given to a traveling freak show over 70 years ago; tracking it down would be impossible at this point.

The common belief is that the objects were the mummified remains of centuries old Indian babies, and unrelated to the disappearances. Rumor has it that a professor was brought down from Boston to examine the objects, but the local constabulary rejected his results. It is said that he claimed that they were "the castings of some gigantic owl," and that he was laughed out of the University in Boston. Investigators who check this story can find references to a few scholarly papers on the topic by Hubert Lagrange, a Zoologist from a Boston University, but the papers are impossible to find, and Lagrange died some years ago.

## Jewelers

Most jewelers in both Connecticut and Rhode Island can tell interested investigators a number of useful pieces of information about the Hazard Pearls and the Hazard family itself. Investigators from Arkham will be able to secure the services of jeweler Lazlo Caselius (see page 79 of *H.P. Lovecraft's Arkham*). This information should be easy enough to obtain, perhaps requiring a **Fast Talk or Persuade** skill roll.

## Precious Stones

Great gems are considered by aficionados to have souls. The greater the value of the gem, the more evil the soul. They wish their owners harm. The most famous example is the Hope diamond. The second most is the Hazard pearls, generally considered to have delivered the *coup de grace* to the family fortunes.

## Hazard Assets

With a successful **Luck** roll, the investigators have selected a jeweler who has actually dealt with the Hazards in person. The jeweler is able to confirm that the Hazards have been selling off a lot of their fine jewelry in the last few years. The word is that they have come upon hard times indeed, and that they are gradually getting rid of all they once had. It is Lucy Hazard who has been selling the assets.

Offers have been made on the Hazard Pearls at a number of times, even in the past few months, but the family has shown no interest in selling them, despite their apparent financial difficulties.

## Mystic Library

The library in Mystic is both small and under-staffed, making it difficult to locate material there. While a normal **Library Use** roll is all that is required to locate each of the following items, it takes the best part of a day to complete each piece of research in the library, as the investigator fights his or her way through pile after pile of un-catalogued books to find what he or she is after. The librarians are no help whatsoever; only one is on duty at a time, and must devote all their time to processing all of the un-catalogued material.

Much of the information that can be found in the library is also available in other places in Mystic, as noted below, however, in some cases the books in the library have additional information.

## Local Diary

The diary of a local Mystic woman, Mercy Stanton, is quoted in an obscure treatise tilled "The recorded incidence of malaria in New England." by Dr. P. J. Pettigrew from Harvard University. The treatise was published in 1912 in a small volume of medical articles. Mistress Stanton's extract is used to indicate the social impact malaria had in small communities. Pettigrew comments that the Hazard family must have been exceeding lucky not to have lost a considerably larger number as a result of the illness, with a family of their size living under a single roof. Mercy Stanton's diary can also be located in the offices of the Mystic Historical Society.

## Diary Extract

A collection of anecdotes tantalizingly titled *The Devil Visits Mystic* turns out to contain particularly boring stories from the area. An extract from the diary of Nailor Tom (which can be located in the Mystic Historical Society as well) is used in one section. The author of the volume comments at the end of the piece that he was unable to find any mention of a Wilfred Hazard in the records of the Hazard family, possibly indicating that the story is heretical. Prime Hazard is cited as a source of useful information, and the author makes favorable references to the material in the Hazard library, which he used extensively to compile the book.

## Newspapers

The library is too small to have a newspaper archive of its own, and interested investigators are directed to the Historical Society, which has a fairly complete collection of the local papers stretching to their inception.

## Quivira

Hidden away in a particularly dusty corner of the small library is a tiny book titled *Legends and Folklore of the Plains Indians*. No author or publication date is listed for the book, which contains all manner of Indian tales. The writing is simple and direct. One part of the book tells of a great underground land, and the golden city of Quivira (**Old Damned House Paper #4**).

## Mystic Town Hall

The town hall contains all manner of official records. It is most likely that the investigators will want to check the history of the Hazard family and their house. The keeper will have to handle any other information the investigators expect to find at the town hall.

Desk work in the town hall is pretty dull, and it should be an easy matter to convince any of the clerks there to search through the records for information; any Persuade or Fast Talk roll that is not fumbled sends someone running off into the record vaults, it takes about half a day for a clerk to locate information and collate it in a presentable fashion.

### Births and Deaths

The official dales of birth and death for the members of the Hazard family are incorrect — they have not declared the births of any of the deformed children they have had, and the dates they have given are always at least six months out. However, the dates are not without utility for the investigators: there is a noticeable discrepancy between the number of births before and after the 1780s. Prior to 1780s, the family had numerous children (batches of from nine to twelve are not uncommon), but by the early 1790s the number of recorded births drops to one or two per couple.

### Property Records

The Hazard family has owned the land the house is built upon since soon after the family moved to the area. The original Hazards built a small one-room shack there, to which they have added over the years. While there were disturbances associated with some of the renovations (some claimed that the house was haunted), none of the changes to the house have been particularly controversial.

The records indicate that there is an extensive cave network in the ground below the house, but there has never been any indication that the house or inhabitants, are in any danger.

### Finances

The tax records are particularly sensitive, and any request for information about the finances of the Hazard family must be accompanied by a bribe of some description, offered in an appropriate manner.

There is an indication that the Hazard family has been having trouble making its tax payments. Their declared income has dropped to almost zero, and they would appear to have been selling assets to make ends meet. An investigator making a successful **Accounting** roll is fairly certain that the Hazards will have to make some pretty drastic changes or face absolute poverty in the near future.

If the investigators gain unrestricted access to the financial records of the town, they might be able to locate some additional information. A **Library Use and Accounting** roll are required to discover indications that the Hazards used a considerable portion of their earnings to bribe town officials, and possibly legal officials. It would take a great deal longer than the investigators have to actually prove such suspicions, even with long-term unlimited access to the town's records.

## Police Records

Detective Garth Wheeler, a heavy-set man with a rough, jovial sense of humor, heads the Mystic constabulary. If he is aware that he is dealing with professional investigators, Detective Wheeler will be most helpful. He will be much less accommodating if he believes that the people he is dealing with are simply amateurs. Statistics for Detective Wheeler are found at the end of the scenario.

### Hazard Family

No members of the Hazard family have criminal records. The Hazard name does not appear in any of the police records, except the ones relating to the missing pearls.

If questioned about the accusations of witchcraft against the Hazards, or possible action taken against them following the disappearances during their building projects, Detective Wheeler will simply shrug: "There simply isn't any record of such things here — maybe charges were never made against them."

Detective Wheeler has no reason to suspect the Hazard family. He sees them as a group of quiet, reclusive people. The alleged financial difficulties do not interest him at all — he is sure the Accursed Cat Burglar stole the pearls.

## Accursed Cat Burglar

Detective Wheeler is well informed about the Accursed Cat Burglar's *modus operandi*. His work is characterized in two ways: he is able to get into the most difficult safes with ease and he has an almost uncanny sense of where the goods are located. The Cat Burglar always takes everything kept with the valuable items he is after, and never takes anything from anywhere else.

Positive identification of the Cat Burglar was achieved by comparing the footprints in the garden with the footprints found near the scene of the last Accursed Cat Burglar crime. The burglar is often quite careless with such clues, and yet he has never been located.

None of the items the Accursed Cat Burglar has stolen have ever come onto the market again. It is clear that he is hoarding the treasures, but there has been no indication as to why. He has stolen well over ten million dollars worth of precious items in the past year, none of which has been seen since.

## Investigation

*Detective Wheeler*

Most of the details of Detective Wheeler's investigation into the missing pearls were included in his report to the insurance company, Rimant & Knowles.

During the course of his investigation Wheeler interviewed all seven members of the family (he knows nothing of Wilfred). There was little, if anything, that they told him that he found at all useful. On the other hand he was impressed by their willingness to help, and was charmed by the twins.

If pressed, Detective Wheeler admits to being unable to determine exactly how the burglar exited the house. He believes that the burglar made a clean getaway, but he was unable to find signs of the departure. If asked why the burglar did not use the window to escape, he will point out that it was likely that the burglar was startled by one of the Hazards and was unable to retrace his steps to the open window.

Detective Wheeler does not feel that the case warrants further investigation as there is no concrete indication that the burglar did not leave the scene of the crime, and all indications are that the job was carried out by the Accursed Cat Burglar. He will stand by his report unless provided with concrete evidence to refute it.

---

# The Story

The following paragraphs have been included to indicate the course of events that was initially intended, but should not be interpreted as a plot line to which the keeper must adhere. While there are certain events that should characterize the three sessions of this adventure, it is difficult to say precisely what investigators will achieve. The keeper is responsible for using this chapter to shape the story that is created as each session unfolds.

## The Story

The scenario opens as the investigators are hired are to work on the Hazard case by Rimant & Knowles. After some initial background research they make the short trip to the Hazard home in Mystic.

By speaking with family members, the investigators learn that an important document was stolen along with the pearls. The document contains secrets that must be passed on to the Hazard twins when they come of age in the next few days. The Hazards may even hire the investigators to retrieve the document and the pearls, either at this point, or after they have completed their report to the insurance company.

The investigation uncovers some of the irregularities in the Hazard family, and the discovery of the radically compressed remains of the burglar indicates to the characters that the family is in some way responsible for the situation.

As the family's strange practices are gradually uncovered, the characters become aware that there is a family member whom they have not been permitted to meet, a strange invalid who is confined to a room in a remote part of the mansion. When they meet Wilfred, the characters find themselves faced with more than they expected, as his hideously cursed form leaps to attack them. In the end, they are forced to destroy him before he destroys them.

The demise of Wilfred, the bearer of Tsathoggua's vile curse, leads to further complications: from his shattered body a small toad-shaped mass emerges, which makes its way inexorably towards the twins. The information in the document that Wilfred took from the burglar indicates that the malevolent Tsathoggua-spawn will enact Wilfred's fate upon the twins unless it can he halted .

As the horrific merging draws closer, the mysterious caverns where the toad-god Tsathoggua dwells begin to manifest themselves, gradually swallowing the protagonists and bringing about a cataclysmic confrontation as the investigators strive to save the twins from their doom.

## Recent Occurrences

Using a floor plan he purchased from a disgruntled ex-employee of the insurance firm Rimant & Knowles, Elijah James Ryan (also known as the "Accursed Cat Burglar") made his way to the Hazard mansion just outside Mystic, Connecticut. Ryan was an accomplished burglar and the map detailed the ground floor, and the location of the safe; he let himself in through a window at the side of the house that was never properly locked.

Inside, Ryan quickly located the family safe that contained the famous Hazard Pearls. Working quickly, he opened the safe and pocketed the strange string of pearls, as well as what money he saw, and some strange documents he found there. As he made his way out, however, Ryan fell prey to the pranks of Jean and the other deformed Hazard children. They grabbed the pearls from the burglar, and dashed off into the maze of rooms and stairs. Ryan was unwilling to let the jewels he has so carefully stolen be taken from him, and so pursued the children quietly through the house.

Ryan soon became lost. Unfortunately, he stumbled into the room occupied by Wilfred Hazard, the demented progenitor of the Hazard family curse. Timid by nature, Ryan was an easy target for Wilfred's scheming mind, and within minutes the burglar had been convinced to release Wilfred from his bonds. So swift was Wilfred's attack that Ryan was never aware that his luck had finally, and fatally, run out.

Wilfred took the document, hiding it safely in the frame of his wheelchair, planning idly to use it as some form of bargaining chip in the future. Alter disposing of the remains of Ryan's digested body, Wilfred returned to his room, content to wait for the right moment to reveal his newfound freedom.

## Part One: Missing Burglar

The initial stages of the adventure should have a very investigative feel to it. The characters should become involved in solving the case of the missing pearls, and possibly working out the identity of the infamous Accursed Cat Burglar. Keepers should choose a tone that suits their style, and make sure that they guide the investigators to the Hazard house and the dead burglar.

## Initial Meeting

It is the autumn. The scenario opens as the investigators are introduced to Mr. George Knowles, one of the partners of Rimant & Knowles, the insurance firm that insured the Hazard Pearls.

*Mr. George Knowles*

Mr. Knowles is a stern gentleman. He truly believes that the Hazard family has attempted to make a false claim against his company, and is disappointed that the police have been unable to demonstrate that fact. He has chosen the investigators because he is aware of their reputation. He is anxious for the investigation to show results quickly, and is willing to pay a hefty fee. Statistics for George Knowles are included at the end of this scenario.

## The Details of the Case

The Hazard Pearls were reported stolen from the Hazard family home in Mystic, Connecticut (an address is provided), the day before yesterday. The theft is presumed to have occurred during the previous night.

The theft was discovered because the ground-floor sitting room window was found open the next morning. A check of the family safe revealed that the pearls, some money, and some family papers, were all missing. The local Mystic constabulary was called in to investigate.

Detective Garth Wheeler conducted the police investigation. He reported that the burglar used the open window as a point of entrance. The investigation indicated that the burglar knew exactly where to find the pearls, and was easily able to open the safe and extract the contents without alerting any members of the Hazard family. In conclusion, Wheeler stated a belief that the crime was the work of the renowned "Accursed Cat Burglar", a thief known for stealing the most valuable jewelry in the country.

The Hazard family has not been doing well financially for some time, and has been forced, on several occasions, to sell family heirlooms to make ends meet. Rimant & Knowles believe that the family has staged the theft of the pearls to claim on the insurance. The fact that the police were unable to determine the point of exit for the supposed burglar, and the strange history of the family itself, has left them very suspicious.

Mr. Knowles wants the investigators to find the missing Hazard Pearls, and prove who stole them. The nature of the insurance contract dictates that they be able to prove that the pearls were not stolen by an intruder – it is not sufficient for them to retrieve the pearls, the identity of the burglar must be obtained as well.

## The Investigation

There are a number of places the investigators are likely to search for clues to help them solve this case. Most of the research locations are covered in the section on the House (after the description of the house itself). If the investigators decide to look in places not covered in that section, it is up to the keeper to determine the success, or otherwise, of their efforts. Use the information provided as a guide.

## Visiting the Hazards

Eventually the investigators must travel to the Hazard mansion in Mystic. Investigation of the scene of the crime should be a top priority for the investigators, as should interviewing the family members themselves. It is important that the characters develop relationships with a number of Hazards. When they arrive, they should be introduced to at least one of the elder members of the family. One of the investigators should develop an attraction to one of the twins. This intimate relationship will become important in the third part of the scenario.

During their time in the Hazard house the investigators will be watched by the deformed children. The children will bother the investigators in any small ways they can. The investigators shouldn't meet the children directly at this point, but they should be aware that there are strange happenings in the Hazard house.

## Locating the Mummy

The investigators discover the remains of the Cat Burglar and realize that the compressed mummy is all that is left of the thief.

The investigators can find the casting in any location around the house and grounds, as the situation dictates — Wilfred was able to get around, and has left the "body" to give the family a scare. The casting appears at first to be a mummified baby. It soon becomes apparent, however, that it is connected with the burglar when the investigators notice that there is a set of beautiful, new lock picks embedded in the casting. An **Idea, or relevant scientific skill**, roll might be used to allow the investigators to make the association, if the players seem to have missed the significance. The Sanity loss for seeing the casting is 1/1D4.

## Part Two: Deadly Creature

The investigators encounter the Hazard children during their further investigation in the Hazard mansion, per-

haps by accompanying Saphronia on one of her evening excursions to feed the "Crystal Bat".

## Further Investigations

Having discovered the remains of the burglar, the investigators should be eager to continue the Hazard case. There is plenty of information about the family, both in the house and in Mystic, and the keeper is encouraged to expand upon what is provided, if required.

## Destroying Wilfred

The investigators eventually encounter Cousin Wilfred. There are a number of ways that this goal can be achieved, depending upon the way they have been conducting their investigation. It is perhaps simplest to have one of the Hazards mention him explicitly, and take the investigators to talk to him. Both the twins and Saphronia are naive enough to mention Wilfred to the investigators without realizing the dangers involved. It might also be possible for Prime (or any other the other family members) to suggest that the characters interview him, as they believe him to be chained. The children's pranks could also be used to lead the investigators to his room, in a pinch. It is much better, obviously, if the investigators decide to see him on their own; by revealing his existence, it should be quite possible to achieve this.

Regardless under what circumstances the investigators encounter Wilfred, the meeting results in a violent confrontation. Wilfred attempts to surprise the investigators when he attacks, but if he feels that they know too much about him, or are likely to leave, he leaps to the attack immediately.

The confrontation with Wilfred should be harrowing — he is possessed by the soul of a powerful Mythos deity, after all. It is up to the keeper exactly how he chooses to attack: toying with his prey, or brutally destroying all he can catch. Regardless what he chooses, the rest of the family (if they are present) attempts to restrain him, and tries to prevent the investigators from killing him. They may go so far as attacking the investigators themselves.

Keepers wishing to redeem Wilfred may allow him to warn the investigators to escape from him. Such entreaties should be interspersed with moments of excessive violence, as his fractured mind fights for control.

Wilfred must die.

As he dies, the piece of Tsathoggua that has infected Wilfred since he fled from the caverns of N'Kai pulls itself from his body. It is no larger than a toad, and that is the shape that it takes, as it makes its way across the floor towards the investigators. They should not have a chance to do anything more that notice it before it escapes. The Sanity loss for the creature is 1/1D4.

In the wreckage of his wheelchair, or nearby his dead body, the investigators spot a rolled sheaf of papers. Opening it they discover the Hazard family document: *Wilfred's Testament* (**Old Damned House Papers #1**).

## Part Three: Horrific Confrontation

The gloves come off as the investigators find themselves pursued by strange creatures and threatened by ancient curses. The climax should be the final part of a gradually building spiral of menace and horror.

### The Toad-Thing

The thing that pulled itself from Wilfred's body is a piece of Tsathoggua itself. The toad-shaped mass will pursue the investigators throughout most of this session. It is virtually impossible to kill, and small enough that it can easily conceal itself in the investigators belongings. Somehow it must get out of the house with them, probably without the investigators being aware of its presence. A full description of the creature is given in the Pursuit section, below.

### The Children Return

When Wilfred finally dies, the malformed Hazard children make their presence known. They have watched Wilfred's last stand with mixed emotions. Some immediately rush to his body to pay their last respects (either by tending to him or by devouring what they can of him). Jean rushes toward the investigators, ranting that they have destroyed the soul of the family. He curses them lividly and, in a moment of fury, spits the pearls out at them. "Take them! You want them! You killed Wilfred — take them as well!"

### Destruction of the House

With Wilfred dead and the pearls no longer in the possession of the family, the Hazard house begins to shudder and shake. No force on earth will be able to prevent the baleful influence of Tsathoggua from destroying the house, as caverns and fissures reach up from the unfathomable depths of N'Kai.

The destruction of the house should cause a chaotic, desperate dash for freedom by the investigators. The walls and floors split and buckle, throwing seemingly sentient obstacles in their path. Encourage all manner of physical skills (and **Luck**) to avoid gaping holes and damage from falling objects.

The Hazard family is almost paralyzed with horror; once they recover their senses, it will be too late for the older ones to make it to safety. The twins have a chance, however.

The investigators may well wish to rescue one or both of the twins. Such a rescue attempt should be suitably heroic, and should result in the escape of at least one of the Hazard twins.

### Pursuit

As the investigators and surviving Hazards make their way to safety they will be menaced by the Tsathoggua-piece. Although mindless, the thing tries to infect the surviving twin or twins. It is also attracted to the pearls, and will attempt to stay near them. While attempting to achieve these two goals, it is sure to menace the investigators.

The creature has no fixed form: it can change its shape in any way imaginable, although it never gets any larger, and it cannot change color. It can move with incredible speed, making it difficult to stop or capture. It can easily get under doors, or hide in unlikely locations. Furthermore, it is possible for it gradually to seep through almost any substance. This takes time, however.

For the purposes of the adventure, it is not possible to destroy the creature. It takes little or no damage from physical weapons, and what damage it does take, it can easily regenerate within a round.

The thing attacks by dissolving itself into the flesh and bone of its victim. It does 1D2 points of damage each round, until it is removed, gradually deforming bones and internal organs. It is a simple enough matter to remove the beast, though it will retreat from alcohol, chemicals and fire, as do Spawn of Tsathoggua. However, it keeps coming back. The creature is also able, if necessary, to cause strange chemical transformations. It can, for example, cause a car to blow up by seeping into the gas tank. Naturally, it easily survives such events.

### The Caverns of N'Kai

Drawn by the pearls and the surviving Hazards, the Caverns of N'Kai eventually takes over the building in which the investigators are based, be it their hotel, office apartment, or their homes.

The arrival of the caverns is heralded by the warping of the building itself — the rooms and corridors all take on a dank, oppressive atmosphere, reminiscent of subterranean caves. The stairs and walls begin to degenerate into rough untamed stone, and a palpable malevolent presence reaches up from the bowels of the earth in the guise of a warm, cloying breath of stale air.

With the caverns come the Hazard children. After the collapse of their family's home, they made their way down to the caves that had haunted their dreams and it soon became clear to them that it was their new home. But there was unfinished business to attend to before they could truly lead their own lives. The pearls have to be returned to their rightful owner.

Although Jean leads the small troupe of outcasts, it is more likely that one of the less transformed children will do most of the talking with the investigators. He or she explains their deeply-rooted feeling that the pearls must be returned to Tsathoggua in his black-litten world beneath the earth, for only in that way will the surviving Hazards, and the investigators, be free of his influence. The children offer to show the way and to protect the investigators from what lies below, but they are insistent that the investigators must return the pearls themselves, or they will be caught in an eternal curse of their own. It should be pointed out to doubtful investigators that the caverns have come to them, and there is no way to escape their malevolence.

To make matters even worse the surviving Hazard twin or twins, having become mentally unhinged, take the first opportunity to dash off down the stairs calling out to the lost Hazards as he or she descends to certain doom. Truly stubborn investigators should be forced to make pretty serious rolls, or be overcome with guilt at the danger to such an innocent and be compelled to follow them into the caverns.

## Descent to the Depths

The investigator's building seems to be sinking into the ground itself, which anyone making an **Idea** roll can perceive (Sanity loss 0/1); there are no direct indications, but the impression is unmistakable.

The stairs lead down, through what once was the basement to the outer extents of the Caverns of N'Kai. The air is thick, and light seems to have little effect. The passages twist and turn, but Jean Hazard knows exactly which way to go, although "all these caves lead to N'Kai, one way or another."

In the near dark, the investigators can make out shifting shapes and shadows — hints of creatures and things better left unseen (should they wish to peer more intently, reward a successful **Spot Hidden** with a gruesome bas-relief wall, or a squamous creature, and a **Sanity** roll). As long as they travel with the children, however, the investigators will not be assaulted (and the character who carries the pearls will not be touched, even without the protection of the children).

After some time the caves open out into an enormous underground cavern. What little light penetrates the eternal darkness provides only dim outlines of the ruins of buildings stretching into the distance. Formless shadows roam those ruins and make their way towards the outsiders.

## Confrontation

The exact sequence of events for the confrontation is left to the keeper, with the following suggestions.

The shifting shapes that inhabit this place are Formless Spawn of Tsathoggua. While the investigators are being guided by the children, the Spawn will be loathe to attack, for they can sense the taint of their progenitor in the group. They will retaliate if attacked, however, and once the pearls are given to Tsathoggua, they will begin to converge upon the hapless investigators. Sample statistics for Formless Spawn are provided at the end of the scenario.

Soon after the investigators arrive so does Tsathoggua. Even though the Sanity loss from the Great Old One is not enormous, it should still he presented as a horrible and malevolent presence. It should not speak directly, although the investigators may feel the overwhelming influence if its desires goading them to action.

Tsathoggua wants the pearls back, but cannot take them, or in any way directly harm the investigator carrying them. While the actions the investigators take are entirely up to them, the creature's desire should be made clear.

Once the pearls are handed over, Tsathoggua will immediately depart — such minor creatures as the investigators are hardly worth its effort to destroy. It may tear one or two of them apart if it is harried, otherwise let it quietly retreat. Allow a 1D8 Sanity reward for returning the pearls and freeing the Hazard family from their curse (what little there is left of the family).

The Spawn may not be so kind. At the keeper's discretion, the Spawn could converge and attempt to massacre the investigators. The Hazard children will not be attacked, however there is little they can do to deter an

# THE CITY OF QUIVIRA

The legends of Quivira are widespread, appearing throughout the Indian tribes. As far south as Mexico the stories are told, but historians believe they originated with the Wichita Indians, who dwell along the Arkansas River, in Baron and Rice counties, in what we now call Kansas, before the Sioux drove them south into Oklahoma.

The stories tell of a fabulous underground land, where the buffalo are plentiful, the plains are rich, and the river is two leagues wide. Within this mysterious land is Quivira, a city built of gold and silver, wherein dwells an ancient and reclusive people who discourage all contact with the outside world. The Wichita tribe speaks of this place with awe and respect, almost as if it was something taboo, but still tell the avid listener of huge stone entranceways leading to the city, hidden at the bases of ravines near their original tribal lands.

Because of the tales of fabulous wealth, many have sought entrance to this fabled land, but none have met with success. The famous Spanish explorer Francisco Vasquez de Coronado undertook the earliest well-documented search attempted by Europeans. His expedition set out in 1540, guided by the Wichita Indian El Turco, and turned back in 1542. ✺

*The Old Damned House Papers #4*

## N' Kai

N'Kai is a dark cavern located beneath the North American continent. A wet and slimy world with tunnels that suggest organic origins, and numerous onyx and basalt statues and bas reliefs depicting the Great Old One who lives here, Tsathoggua the toad-god. The location of N'Kai is said to lie beneath the land of Yoth, but it is probably situated in another dimension altogether, as entrances have been found in Oklahoma, Germany and Connecticut. Amorphous servitors of Tsathoggua, which ooze down stone troughs, worship the toad-god's many idols.

Keepers wishing to learn more about N'Kai should read H.P. Lovecraft and Zealia Bishop's collaboration "The Mound". Similarly *The Tsathoggua Cycle* published by Chaosium Inc. features several tales concerning the Toad-God and his dark abode. ☀

all-out assault. Jean either departs or he becomes caught up in the wild frenzy, attacking all the surface-dwellers (and especially the surviving Hazards). Some of the other children might be able to lend the survivors through the caves and to the surface.

Whether any of the investigators and Hazards survives is up to the keeper. It may be that the entire party is wiped out or that the survivors will wander out into daylight some time later. The exact location is also left to the keeper: the ruins of the Hazard house, or maybe across the country, in Kansas, near the ancient Indian mounds.

# Statistics

### Detective Garth Wheeler, age 36, Mystic Police Investigator

| STR 13 | CON 14 | SIZ 13 | INT 12 | POW 15 |
| DEX 16 | APP 10 | SAN 75 | EDU 11 | HP 14 |

**Damage Bonus:** +1D4

**Weapons:** Fist/Punch 60%, damage 1D3+1D4
Grapple 55%, damage special
.38 Revolver 35%, damage 1D10

**Skills:** Accounting 35%, Fast Talk 40%, Law 40%, Library Use 35%, Listen 65%, Locksmith 40%, Spot Hidden 60%

**Languages:** English 55%

### George Knowles, age 45, Partner at Rimant & Knowles

| STR 10 | CON 10 | SIZ 12 | INT 14 | POW 08 |
| DEX 09 | APP 11 | SAN 40 | EDU 16 | HP 11 |

**Damage Bonus:** none

**Weapons:** Fist /Punch 50%, damage 1D3

**Skills:** Accounting 75%, Bargain 40%, Law 30%, Library Use 40%, Persuade 40%

**Languages:** English 80%, Latin 10%

### Prime Hazard, age 83, Scholarly Uncle

| STR 06 | CON 06 | SIZ 11 | INT 15 | POW 12 |
| DEX 05 | APP 08 | SAN 00 | EDU 16 | HP 09 |

**Damage Bonus:** −1D4

**Weapons:** Grapple 25%, damage special

**Skills:** Art (Play Bass Viol) 85%, Cthulhu Mythos 07%, Library Use 65%, Listen 35%, History 70%, Persuade 50%, Spot Hidden 30%

**Languages:** English 80%, French 70%

### Saphronia Hazard, age 71, Proud Aunt

| STR 05 | CON 05 | SIZ 08 | INT 12 | POW 10 |
| DEX 04 | APP 07 | SAN 00 | EDU 10 | HP 07 |

**Damage Bonus:** −1D6

**Weapons:** none

**Skills:** Art (Sing) 85%, Cthulhu Mythos 02%, Listen 15%, Persuade 20%, Spot Hidden 20%

**Languages:** English 50%, French 40%

### Caleb Hazard, age 66, Dull Uncle

| STR 10 | CON 09 | SIZ 11 | INT 09 | POW 11 |
| DEX 13 | APP 08 | SAN 00 | EDU 12 | HP 10 |

**Damage Bonus:** none

**Weapons:** Fist/Punch 35%, damage 1D3
Grapple 35%, damage special

**Skills:** Craft (Play Cards) 20%, Cthulhu Mythos 01%, Listen 30%, Persuade 20%, Know about Prosthetics 75%, Spot Hidden 30%

**Languages:** English 55%, French 45%

### Guillaume Hazard, age 58, Teasing Uncle

| STR 10 | CON 11 | SIZ 11 | INT 13 | POW 12 |
| DEX 09 | APP 07 | SAN 00 | EDU 15 | HP 11 |

**Damage Bonus:** none

**Weapons:** Fist/Punch 35%, damage 1D3
Grapple 35%, damage special

**Skills:** Cthulhu Mythos 03%, Listen 40%, History 30%, Library Use 60%, Occult 40%, Persuade 35%, Spot Hidden 40%

**Languages:** English 65%, French 55%

### Lucy Hazard, age 58, Sprightly Aunt

| STR 10 | CON 09 | SIZ 14 | INT 12 | POW 09 |
| DEX 12 | APP 09 | SAN 00 | EDU 09 | HP 12 |

**Damage Bonus:** none

**Weapons:** Fist/Punch 25%, damage 1D3
Grapple 25%, damage special

**Skills:** Accounting 25%, Art (Sewing) 75%, Bargain 35%, Cleaning 25%, Cooking 45%, Cthulhu Mythos 01%, Listen 50%, Persuade 45%, Spot Hidden 30%

**Languages:** English 65%, French 55%

*Tsathoggua*

### Ellery Hazard, age 20, Glamorous Twin

| STR 14 | CON 15 | SIZ 12 | INT 13 | POW 14 |
|--------|--------|--------|--------|--------|
| DEX 13 | APP 17 | SAN 35 | EDU 10 | HP 14 |

**Damage Bonus:** +1D4

**Weapons:** Fist/Punch 55%, damage 1D3+1D4
Grapple 55%, damage special

**Skills:** Bargain 30%, Listen 40%, Persuade 60%, Spot Hidden 30%

**Languages:** English 65%, French 65%

### Isabeau Hazard, age 20, Glamorous Twin

| STR 12 | CON 15 | SIZ 09 | INT 13 | POW 14 |
|--------|--------|--------|--------|--------|
| DEX 13 | APP 17 | SAN 39 | EDU 10 | HP 14 |

**Damage Bonus:** none

**Weapons:** Fist/Punch 50%, damage 1D3
Grapple 45%, damage special

**Skills:** Bargain 30%, Listen 30%, Persuade 70%, Spot Hidden 30%

**Languages:** English 75%, French 75%

### Wilfred Hazard, age 200+, Cursed Cousin

| STR 20 | CON 25 | SIZ 18 | INT 14 | POW 16 |
|--------|--------|--------|--------|--------|
| DEX 17 | APP 03 | SAN 00 | EDU 12 | HP 22 |

**Damage Bonus:** +1D6

**Weapons:** Tongue Lash 70%, 1D6+1D4
Tongue Grab 65%, 1D6 *
Crush 70%, 2D6+3 **
Devour 90%, 2D8+2D6 ***

*\* Functions as a Grapple attack*
*\*\* Only used after a leap onto opponent*
*\*\*\* Only on immobilized opponents*

**Armor:** Impaling weapons (including guns) do minimum damage

**Skills:** Cthulhu Mythos 20%, Listen 55%, Natural History 30%, Occult 40%, Spot Hidden 60%

**Languages:** English 70%, French 60%, Spanish 25%, Wichita 35%

**Sanity Loss:** 1D2/1D6 points once Wilfred Hazard's true nature is revealed

### Nathanial Hazard, Monstrous Hazard

| STR 12 | CON 15 | SIZ 10 | INT 08 | POW 13 |
|--------|--------|--------|--------|--------|
| DEX 19 | Move 10 | | | HP 12 |

**Damage Bonus:** none

**Weapons:** Tongue Lash 30%, damage 1D4
Tentacle 35%, damage 1D6

**Armor:** Immune to all physical weapons (all wounds simply snap shut after being opened). Can be affected by fire and chemicals, however, and will shy away from bright lights.

**Sanity Loss:** 0/1D3 points to witness Nathanial

### Mercy Hazard, Monstrous Hazard

| STR 10 | CON 10 | SIZ 08 | INT 11 | POW 14 |
|--------|--------|--------|--------|--------|
| DEX 16 | Move 8 | | | HP 09 |

**Damage Bonus:** none

**Weapons:** Claw 35%, damage 1D3

**Armor:** Immune to all physical weapons (all wounds simply snap shut after being opened). Can be affected by fire and chemicals, however, and will shy away from bright lights

**Sanity Loss:** 1/1D4 points to witness Mercy

### Celestine and Girard Hazard, Monstrous Hazards (Assume both have the identical statistics)

| STR 11 | CON 12 | SIZ 07 | INT 07 | POW 10 |
|--------|--------|--------|--------|--------|
| DEX 18 | Move 09 | | | HP 10 |

**Damage Bonus:** -1D4

**Weapons:** Claw 35%, damage 1D4

**Armor:** Immune to all physical weapons (all wounds simply snap shut after being opened). Can be affected by fire and chemicals, however, and will shy away from bright lights

**Sanity Loss:** 1/1D6 points to witness Celestine and Girard

### Jean Hazard, Monstrous Hazard

| STR 16 | CON 14 | SIZ 09 | INT 12 | POW 13 |
|--------|--------|--------|--------|--------|
| DEX 15 | Move 10 | | | HP 12 |

**Damage Bonus:** +1D4

**Weapons:** Whip 90%, damage 1D6+1D4*
Tentacle 60%, damage 1D6 **
Bite 30%, special ***

*\* May choose to Grapple, rather than do damage Range is SIZ in yards*
*\*\* May strike up to 1D2 opponents per round. May Grapple instead of causing damage Range is SIZ in yards*
*\*\*\* Victim is swallowed, and digested. Damage is 1 point for the first round, 2 for the second, etc. Swallowed victims are immobile until the creature is killed. Jean may swallow up to its own SIZ in prey and in most cases he can only partially swallow a victim, leaving legs to dangle from its mouth while the upper portions dissolve (1D3 hours). While digesting Jean may not move from his location but it may continue to attack anything within reach*

**Armor:** Immune to all physical weapons (all wounds simply snap shut after being opened). Can be affected by fire and chemicals, however, and will shy away from bright lights

**Sanity Loss:** 1D2/2D4 points to witness Jean

### Formless Spawn of Tasthoggua

| | #1 | #2 | #3 | #4 | #5 | #6 |
|--------|------|------|------|------|------|------|
| STR | 30 | 33 | 26 | 28 | 34 | 24 |
| CON | 12 | 13 | 17 | 10 | 13 | 14 |
| SIZ | 30 | 26 | 38 | 29 | 33 | 16 |
| INT | 10 | 13 | 12 | 16 | 13 | 10 |
| POW | 08 | 12 | 11 | 15 | 13 | 15 |
| DEX | 19 | 17 | 15 | 20 | 21 | 18 |
| HP | 21 | 20 | 28 | 20 | 23 | 15 |
| Dmg +/- | +3D6 | +3D6 | +4D6 | +3D6 | +4D6 | +2D6 |

Move 12

**Weapons:** Whip* 90%, damage 1D6

   Tentacle** 60%, damage db

   Bludgeon*** 20%, damage db

   Bite 30%, damage special ****

*\*may seek to Grapple rather than do damage; range is always the monster's SIZ in yards.*

*\*\*may strike at 1D3 opponents in a round, and may seek to Grapple rather than do damage; range equals the monster's SIZ in yards.*

*\*\*\*always a 20% chance, damage equal to 2D6 or actual damage bonus, whichever is higher.*

*\*\*\*\*the victim is instantly swallowed. Each round thereafter the victim takes 1 point of damage from constriction, the damage done per round progressively increasing by 1 point (e.g., on the second round he takes 2 points of damage, and so forth). While swallowed, the victim may take no action whatsoever, though friends may attempt to slay the monster to free him or her. A formless spawn can make one Bite attack per round and can continue to swallow prey until having swallowed its own SIZ in prey. While digesting a victim, a Spawn may continue to fight but may not shift location without disgorging what it has swallowed.*

**Armor:** they are immune to all physical weapons, even enchanted ones, and wounds made by them simply snap closed after being opened. Spells may affect them, as may fire, chemicals, or other forces.

**Spells:** Spawn #6 knows the spells Dread Curse of Azathoth and Shriveling.

**Sanity Loss:** 1/1D10 Sanity points to see a formless spawn.

### Tasthoggua, the Sleeper of N'kai

| STR 50 | CON 120 | SIZ 30 | INT 30 | POW 35 |
|--------|---------|--------|--------|--------|
| DEX 27 | Move 24 |        |        | HP 75  |

**Damage Bonus:** +4D6.

**Weapons:** Tentacle 100%, damage Grapple
   Characteristics Drain 100%, damage 1 point per characteristic per round

**Armor:** regenerates 30 hit points per round from wounds and punctures, but fire, electricity, and other such forces have normal effects on the monstrous god.

**Spells:** broad magical powers, as befits a Great Old One; he is recorded as having taught Create Gate and various Summon/Bind spells to humans

**Sanity Loss:** 0/1D10 Sanity points to see Tsathoggua.

## THE END!

# Investigator Handouts

*Clues for the investigators. A presentation of the most important, though not all, diagrams and plans presented in the scenarios.*

## LOCAL BUSINESSMAN KILLED IN ACCIDENT

It was learned today that Theodore Corbitt, owner of Corbitt Importers of America, is dead, victim of a tragic accident while vacationing in India. Corbitt, while in the company of his son Bernard, died in a fall while the two were traveling through the high mountains of the Punjab.

According to authorities, the two men were on a hiking trip when they were set upon by a group of bandits known to frequent the area. While being pursued down the mountainside the elder Corbitt apparently lost his footing and fell to his death. His son managed to escape, eventually making it to safety. The elder Corbitt's body has not yet been located and authorities fear that it may be lost, possibly consumed by wild dogs that roam the mountain.

Theodore Corbitt is survived by his wife, Elaine, and one son, Bernard. At this time it is not known if Bernard Corbitt will take over management of Corbitt Enterprises.

*(dated 14 years ago)*
*The Corbitt Papers #1 (p. 7)*

## LOCAL MAN ARRESTED IN ANIMAL SLAYINGS

Police today announced that a suspect has been arrested in connection with the recent rash of pet kidnappings in the southwest part of town. Although released later for lack of evidence, Randolph Tomaszewski is considered the prime suspect in the recent disappearances of nearly a dozen dogs and cats from the homes and yards of the neighborhood surrounding Central Hospital. Tomaszewski is employed at the hospital as an orderly.

It will be remembered that many of the missing pets have been discovered later in parks, usually mutilated or partially eaten. Public outcry over the atrocities has been strong and police hope that they have uncovered a lead that will eventually allow them to close this case.

*(dated 3 months ago)*
*The Corbitt Papers #2 (p. 8)*

## CORBITT'S PROPERTY

greenhouse

vegetable garden

Corbitt's house

# CORBITT'S HOUSE

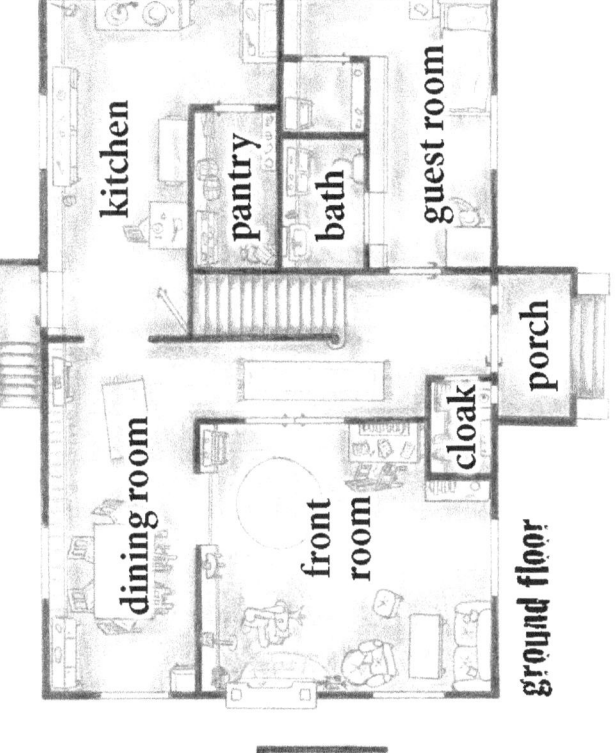

ground floor

- kitchen
- pantry
- bath
- guest room
- dining room
- front room
- cloak
- porch

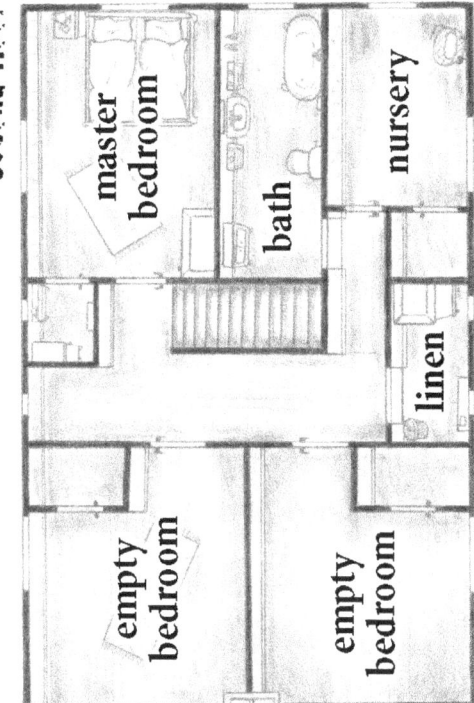

second floor

- master bedroom
- bath
- nursery
- linen
- empty bedroom
- empty bedroom

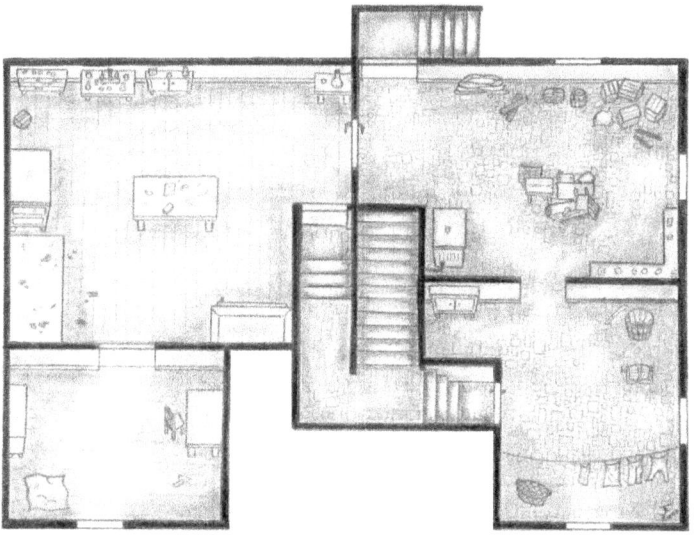

basement

## OBITUARIES

**CORBITT, Lynn Anne Meyers,** aged 22. Died in childbirth, in her home. A graduate of the Pierpoint school, Mrs. Corbitt was married to local businessman, Bernard Corbitt, two years ago. Funeral services for both mother and child will be held Saturday afternoon. Mrs. Corbitt is survived by her parents, Edward and Shirley Meyers, and her husband, Bernard Corbitt, president of Corbitt Importers of America.

### Nurse Hospitalized After Accident In Patient's Home

Professional nurse, Miss Mona Dunlap was admitted to Central Sanitarium yesterday following an accident that took place in a patient's home. Her condition was diagnosed as serious.

Miss Dunlap, hired by Mr. and Mrs. Bernard Corbitt to help with Mrs. Corbitt's confinement, apparently suffered a stroke while attempting to deliver the Corbitt's baby unassisted. Mr. Corbitt returned from his office Wednesday afternoon to find Nurse Dunlap unconscious and his wife and infant son dead due to complications of birth. Doctors at the sanitarium say the woman has yet to regain consciousness and it may be some time before the full extent of her injuries are known.

*(both articles dated 12 years ago)*

*The Corbitt Papers #3 (p. 9)*

## DETECTIVE MURDERED!

The mutilated body of missing Charleston Police Detective Jasper Galloway was discovered early yesterday morning by local fishermen. The body was found under a tangle of cypress roots in the Edisto river just south of the estate of Mr. Caleb Gist. Officer Galloway had been looking into rumors about a Satanist church operating in Charleston. He had been missing for several days. An inquiry by Colleton County Sheriff Virgil Trucks included a search of the Gist land but no evidence regarding the detective's death was discovered. Sheriff Trucks has stated that he believes the detective must have been murdered in Charleston and the body later dumped in the river. Officer Galloway was unmarried and is survived by his father and mother.

*The Plantation Papers #1 (p. 28)*

### Voodoo Rituals Uncovered

A raid led by Captain Pearson of the Charleston town constabulary disrupted a Voodoo Ritual being held in the swamps to the south of Walterboro on property owned by the Gist family. Interrupted was a slave ceremony involving non Christian practices of worship. All participants in the primitive ceremony, escaped into the swamp. Several of Captain Pearson's men were wounded in the assault.

The raiders discovered odd paraphernalia including swords, flags inscribed with undecipherable runes, and human skulls.

*July 6, 1825*

*The Plantation Papers #2 (p. 28)*

# CORBITT'S JOURNALS

Some notable excerpts are listed below; Journal One is from fourteen years ago and Journal Fourteen is for the present year. Entries not listed are very mundane, with statements like "Nothing occurred today," or "Purchased new suit in my afternoon off."

## Journal One

**September 10:** Another embarrassing memory lapse today. This journal should help me deal with the problem.

**September 13:** I have had Mother sign the last of the legal papers that transfer ownership of Corbitt Importers of America from her to myself. She seems to be doing well in the new nursing home and I hope they can give her the treatment and attention she needs. I'm afraid her condition continues to decline rapidly. The death of Father seems to have unhinged her mind. If she knew my role in his death, although I don't in the least feel responsible, I'm sure it would kill her. She would never understand the power of my new lord, Ramasekva. Could she have but experienced those moments on the mountain when HE appeared in all his terrible magnificence! He spoke with me and left his mark upon my breast. Then he took hold of my father and the two became one with each other. Before devouring him, Ramasekva tore my father's head from his shoulders . . . .

**October 29:** Have met a charming young woman at a social gathering, her name is Lynn Meyers. I have arranged to take her to the pictures next week. My lord, I think, would approve of her.

**December 12:** Spent thirty hours in ceremony, have located Ramasekva. He wants a bridge to the world, and needs my help. I have agreed. My studies have shown that Ramasekva is an obscure Asura, an East Indian demon. The Asura are said to be older gods, the ones who ruled before the coming of Shiva. Certain things spoken of in Wenn's book lead me to believe there may be a link to a being called Yog-Sothoth.

## Journal Two

**January 10:** I found myself wanting to make Lynn my wife and have sealed the thought by proposing to her. She accepted and we have set the date of marriage for March 9 of this year. Ramasekva assures me the time is right.

**March 13:** Have returned from our honeymoon. Lynn and I have decided to keep the family place as it is excellent for raising children. In May, all being well, Lynn will accompany me on my trip to Ceylon for a new herbal tea supply. This may be my last trip out of the country for a while. A man who plans a family must be willing to settle down a bit.

**April 1:** Had to send Lynn to visit her mother while I cast the ceremony. I don't believe she is ready to understand yet. Ramasekva has told me he wants a union of flesh. He demands the union be made with my wife. I am to await thirteen days, cast another, easier ceremony, and then wait. Ramasekva is to take my place.

**April 14:** Cast the ceremony in the morning and Ramaseva came. I waited in the basement while he visited Lynn for several hours. She seems to suspect nothing.

**July 19:** Have told my wife to remain in bed throughout the day, as she has taken ill from her pregnancy. I took the day to contact Ramasekva. I am to deliver the child myself, at home. My master has directed me to raise this child as if it were my own.

**November 21:** Horror of horrors! My life is ashes. Poor Lynn went into labor today and in the course of giving birth to the child she expired, despite all I did to save her. Nurse Dunlap blundered into the room at the wrong moment. When she saw the child, she took leave of her senses. In trying to take care of her I may have neglected Lynn at a critical moment. At any rate, she is gone and I blame only myself. A second child, a boy, was born dead. I have turned both bodies over to the funeral home. The child of Ramasekva I have hidden in the basement. The thing is limbless and appears to have trouble breathing. I don't think it can live for long.

**November 25:** The funeral of Lynn and the child was held. Her parents were heartbroken and felt pity for me. I later consoled them and promised to stay in touch.

**November 26:** The ceremony of Ramasekva brought him forth to explain the child. He said the thing would live and that I am to spend the next ten years preparing for a time when it would need me. When the time comes, I am to equip it for life on Earth. It will be given limbs and lungs. I am not to contact Ramasekva until ten years and a day have elapsed.

**December 14:** I have found someone to help me, a man named Randolph Tomaszewski. He works at the local hospital and assures me that he can supply me with the parts necessary to the experiments I need to conduct over the next few years. He is an unsavory type but I need his help. I have agreed to supply him with a small amount of the drugs he desires and he, in return, will try to fill my needs. Perhaps through association with myself, he will find a way to better himself. He seems a particularly irreligious and bitter man. Next week I will make my first trip to the dump and see what my confederate has been able to find for me. The experiments should prove a challenge, but I have every confidence that I can learn, especially with my lord Ramasekva's guidance.

## Journals Three Through Twelve

Nothing of importance to this scenario is included in this time period. The journals cover three trips to the East, acquisitions of unusual orchids and other botanical curiosities, the meeting of several old friends, work-matters and various accounts of mundane purchases and such. Experiments are occasionally mentioned but Corbitt does not elaborate.

## Journal Thirteen

**November 25:** The child grows large, and the time has come. Entered the ceremony with Ramasekva. He told me that when Spring has arrived that I am to search out fresh limbs and organs to be added to the creature — the time of experimenting is over. As the thing is still a child, I will use only the limbs and organs of children. My experiments show that youthful parts adapt much better than older ones. I am directed to feed unusable parts to the child. Ramasekva wants it to develop a taste for such things and says that it is now the time for growing.

## Journal Fourteen

**March 19:** Tomaszewski says I am asking too much of him and claims that he is having difficulty supplying me with parts. The needs of the child increase all the time and I have boosted again the strength of the drug I give the man, hoping that it will entice him to be more cooperative. I fear however that the drug simply exacerbates his derangement.

I must admit to feeling guilt — aiding and abetting his false beliefs somehow seems wrong. However, to try and tell him the truth would, I'm afraid, serve only to further unhinge his mind. I will continue the pretense of believing in his Master. I value the services Tomaszewski renders too much to risk further damage to his grasp on reality.

Most of the child's organs are now in place and a few limbs have been attached. The grafts heal nicely. My years of experimenting are paying off.

**March 28, April 8, April 11, April 19, May 14, May 25:** These dates contain similar statements to those above. The increasing growth rate of the child thing, necessitating increasingly frequent trips to the garbage dump, is a source of surprise (and pleasure) for Corbitt.

## Added Entries

If Corbitt has reason to suspect that the investigators were plotting against him, he will include his thoughts in his journal. If he knows the investigators have followed him to the dump or broken into his home, he will leave an entry that reads: "I am being followed. If I cannot find a way to deal with them myself, in the next ceremony with Ramasekva, I will be forced to ask for their destruction." Another entry mentions the possibility of sending Tomaszewski to deal with the investigators.

*The Corbitt Papers #4 (p. 14)*

# PROFESSOR GIST'S HOUSE

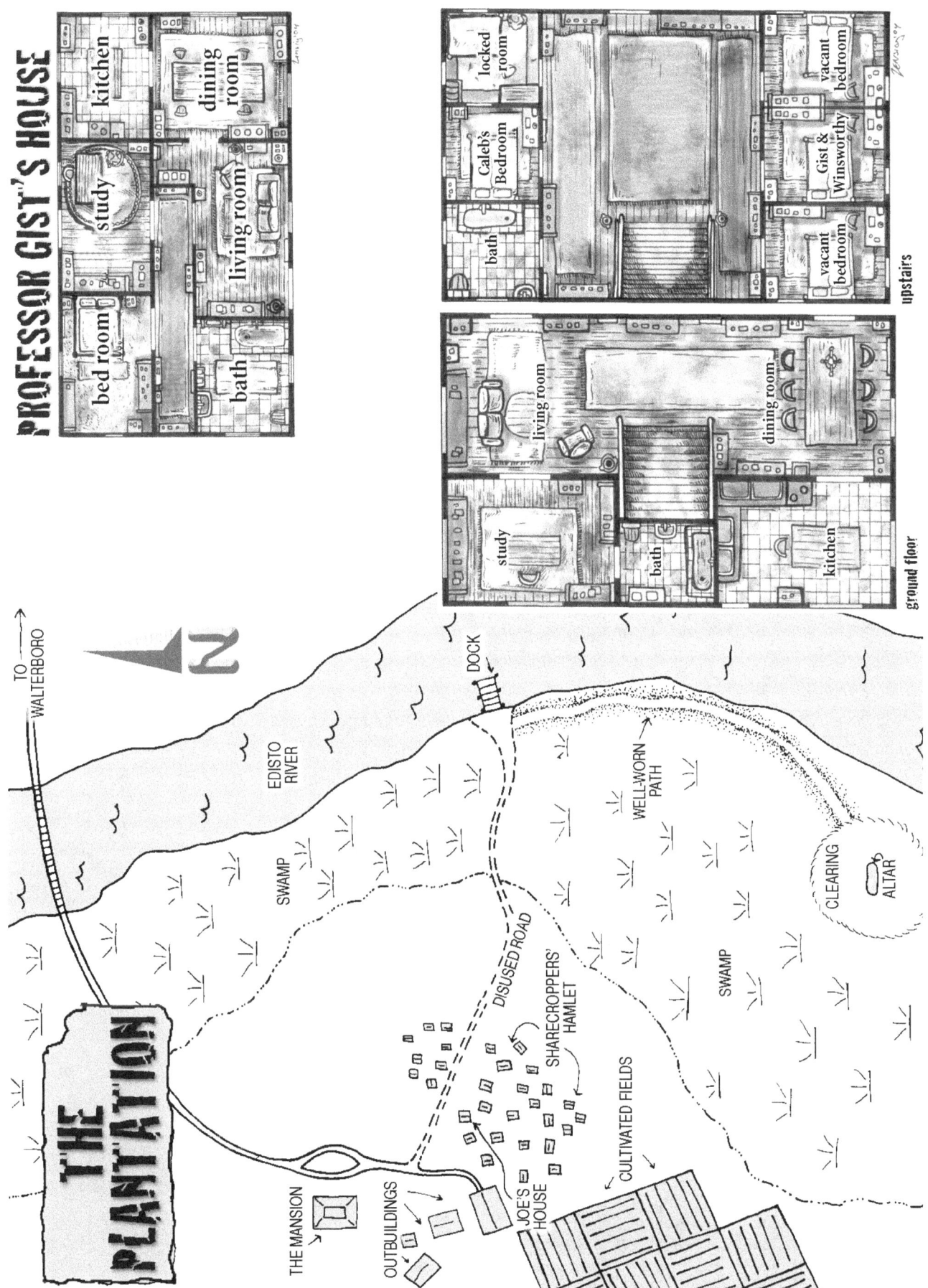

kitchen

dining room

study

living room

bed room

bath

**locked room**

**Caleb's Bedroom**

bath

**vacant bedroom**

**Gist & Winsworthy**

**vacant bedroom**

upstairs

living room

study

dining room

bath

kitchen

ground floor

# THE PLANTATION

TO WALTERBORO

N

EDISTO RIVER

SWAMP

DOCK

WELL-WORN PATH

CLEARING

ALTAR

SWAMP

DISUSED ROAD

SHARECROPPERS' HAMLET

CULTIVATED FIELDS

THE MANSION

OUTBUILDINGS

JOE'S HOUSE

Dodge Brothers

Attorneys at Law

14 Main Street

Gamwell, Connecticut

January 30th, 1925

Dear Sir:

I have been referred to you by a mutual friend. As his attorney, I am very interested in locating the missing Mr. Arthur Cornthwaite and our associate mentioned your name as being one skilled in locating missing people, particularly those of Mr. Cornthwaite's persuasion. Thus I have taken the liberty of contacting you.

I am a partner of an established legal firm in Gamwell. Mr. Arthur Cornthwaite is one of our clients, and as his attorneys we hold certain documents in trust for him. It would appear that Mr. Cornthwaite has departed without notifying us of his movements. This leaves us in a quandary as to how to manage his estate in his absence without his authority in such matters. We would like you to locate Mr. Cornthwaite, and obtain from him his wishes in respect of this matter, or better still request that he contact us. If it should, heaven forbid, transpire that Mr. Cornthwaite is no longer with us, then we will need some evidence of same to proceed with his wishes as outlined in his Last Will and Testament. Hopefully this is an unnecessary contingency, but one which we must nevertheless consider in the light of Mr. Cornthwaite's mysterious departure.

I hope that you are free to give this matter your immediate attention, and would like to extend an invitation to you to attend an interview at our offices as soon as it is convenient, to discuss both the details of the situation and your professional fees.

Anticipating a prompt reply,

Yours faithfully,

Walter Dodge

Encl. article from Gamwell Gazette

*The Manse Papers #1 (p. 56)*

## GAMWELL FAMILY SLAIN IN TERRIBLE ATTACK

### Mother and Three Children Killed

### Police Seek Missing Father

A tragedy of awful proportions unfolded today in Gamwell when Mrs. Gloria Curwen and her three children (Harold 5, Sarah 3, and Susan 2) were found brutally murdered on their estate north of Gamwell, the well-known Fitzgerald Manse.

Deputy Whitford of the Gamwell County Sheriff's Office made the grisly discovery while making a routine inspection. "I've never seen anything like it," the brave but shaken deputy told this reporter, "They were all dead." The family had indeed been brutally and cowardly slain, struck down by repeated blows from an axe. Not even little Susan was spared from this hideous fate.

No murder weapon has been discovered, and Mr. Arthur Curwen, the children's father, is presently missing. He is wanted by the police for questioning, although fears are also held for his safety.

*Gamwell Gazette, May 17th, 1895*

*The Manse Papers #3 (p. 59)*

## GAMWELL MILLIONAIRE ABSENT

Gamwell's most prosperous son, Arthur Cornthwaite, will not be seen at church over the next few weeks. Mr. Cornthwaite has apparently left the area for a time, possibly for a vacation, or in relation to his studies.

Some mystery surrounds Mr. Cornthwaite's departure, as it came without notice. However, an inspection of his mansion and grounds by Sheriff Whitford has revealed no cause for alarm. The last person to speak to Mr. Cornthwaite was his attorney, Mr. Walter Dodge, on the 7th of this month. At that time he gave no indication of his imminent departure, but according to Mr. Dodge he did seem quite preoccupied, no doubt with his travel plans.

We all know well that besides being a Gamwell landowner, Mr. Cornthwaite is also a millionaire, a scholar, a philanthropist, and an explorer. He may well be off laying the groundwork for some future exciting expedition, or perhaps just relaxing for a time in New York. Gamwell citizens will no doubt remember fondly Mr. Cornthwaite's numerous generous donations to local charities and to the town library, and join with us in wishing him a safe and happy journey.

*From the Gamwell Gazette, January 17th, 1925*

*The Manse Papers #2 (p.57)*

# THE FITZGERALD MANSION

downstairs

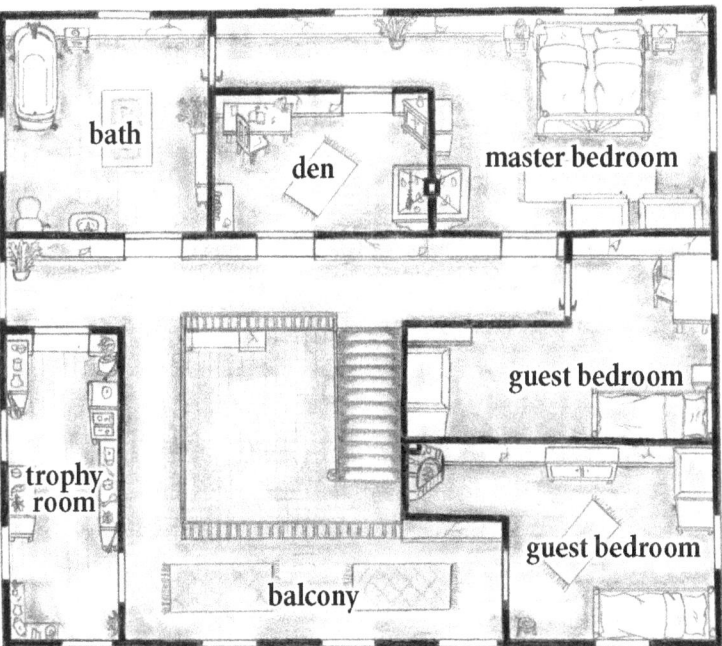

upstairs

*The Fitzgeral Mansion (p.65)*

**KEEPER NOTE: The keeper is provided with diagrams for the basement (p. 68) and attic (p. 69) of the Fitzgerald Mansion. Those diagrams are not provided here—the story is best served through verbal investigation of those areas.**

# THE MISSING PEOPLE

*The Tribe That The Jungle Swallowed*
by Thomas Pratt
Published in 1913, Oxford, England

**Summary:** This book concerns a South American tribe in ancient times, whose existence is testified to by various ruins, but of whose demise nothing is known. The book is based on legends of the tribe and archaeological discoveries. Pratt makes note of the tribe's religious fervor, and conjectures that they may have been wiped out in civil holy war. He mentions in particular a "Great Dome", depicted in carvings and art. He believes that this was an actual stone structure, that it probably still stands, and may well house the last secrets of the missing people.

*The Manse Papers #4 (p. 66)*

**KEEPER NOTE: Some diagrams presented in this Handouts section differ from those offered in the main text. Secret information has sometimes been redacted.**

*To whom it may concern,*

*I am writing this statement in the event of my joining my staff and my expedition members in death. I, Arthur Cornthwaite, being of sound mind and body*

*No time for formality or legalisms. It is the thing I must tell you of. What is sanity, when faced with this? I thought I had fled from it in that foul green place, that accursed temple, yet somehow it has followed me here. I know the signs, there can be no mistake. It is with me. It is a thing so clever, so terrible that*

*MELODRAMA! What's the point! Notes to myself in an empty house! Whoever reads this knows, or will know, of it, but what you must also know is that it has a weakness so simple, so*

*[the note ends here]*

*The Manse Papers #5 (p. 68)*

# EXCERPTS FROM DR. BREWER'S ARTICLE

If we accept for a moment the theory that the collective unconsciousness is the source of all myth, we have to ask if it is not possible to consciously tap the source? Experiments with hypnosis, sometimes combined with powerful new drugs, have shown some evidence to support this.

Subject A showed little response to any treatments, but B was quite positive. Not only were unsuspected areas of knowledge revealed during these sessions but at times the subject demonstrated an entirely different personality. This personality, on the few occasions that it was observed to emerge, used archaic, almost biblical syntax, perhaps indicating that a true archetypal form may have been reached. This personality was very powerful and almost compelling, causing one to wonder if phenomena such as this is not the explanation for the possessions of the Middle Ages and, in more recent times, of the voodoo cultists in the Caribbean.

While never reaching the archetypal content of B, subject C was nonetheless of interest. Numerous personality types were brought to the surface, one claiming to have lived during the time of the Egyptian pharaohs. Surprisingly enough, the subject did display a fairly thorough knowledge of the history of that long dead civilization (though later research showed much of it to be pure flights of fancy).

All three showed a certain commonality of mythic form, although admittedly much was difficult to decipher.

*The Sanitorium Papers #2 (p. 73)*

---

Dear

So glad to hear you could accept my invitation to visit. I am looking forward to showing you the latest developments in my research.

I'm also anxious to bring you up to date on my experiments. There's been several more exciting developments since the publication of my article in the <Journal of the American Psychological Society> a few months back. I trust you've read it. There will be a few surprises, too - you can count on that.

My isolation is quite tolerable. The staff and I think of ourselves as a family. Old Ebenezer (you'll meet him on the ride over) is always ready to ferry one of us over to the mainland if we should feel the need to touch base with civilization. This summer we've been blessed with a regular dinner companion in the form of Mr. Shelly, a graduate student from Princeton. He is camped on the north beach of the island, conducting some sort of bird study. You'll find him witty and pleasant.

Looking forward to seeing you,

Dr. Aldous Brewer

*The Sanitorium Papers #1 (p. 73)*

---

Dear Editor,

In response to the letter from Drs. Hagen and Allen that appeared in your June issue I must say that I would have expected better from two so highly regarded in our profession. Disagreement I take no exception to; my work is highly experimental and any results, as I specified clearly in my article, are, at this time, purely speculative in nature. I make no claims but only observations.

Since the time that article was written I have conducted further experiments that seem to uphold my earlier observations. However, I will not again go to print until I have proof positive; proof that will convince even the most fossilized of skeptics. I would not lower myself to

*The Sanitorium Papers #3 (p. 81)*

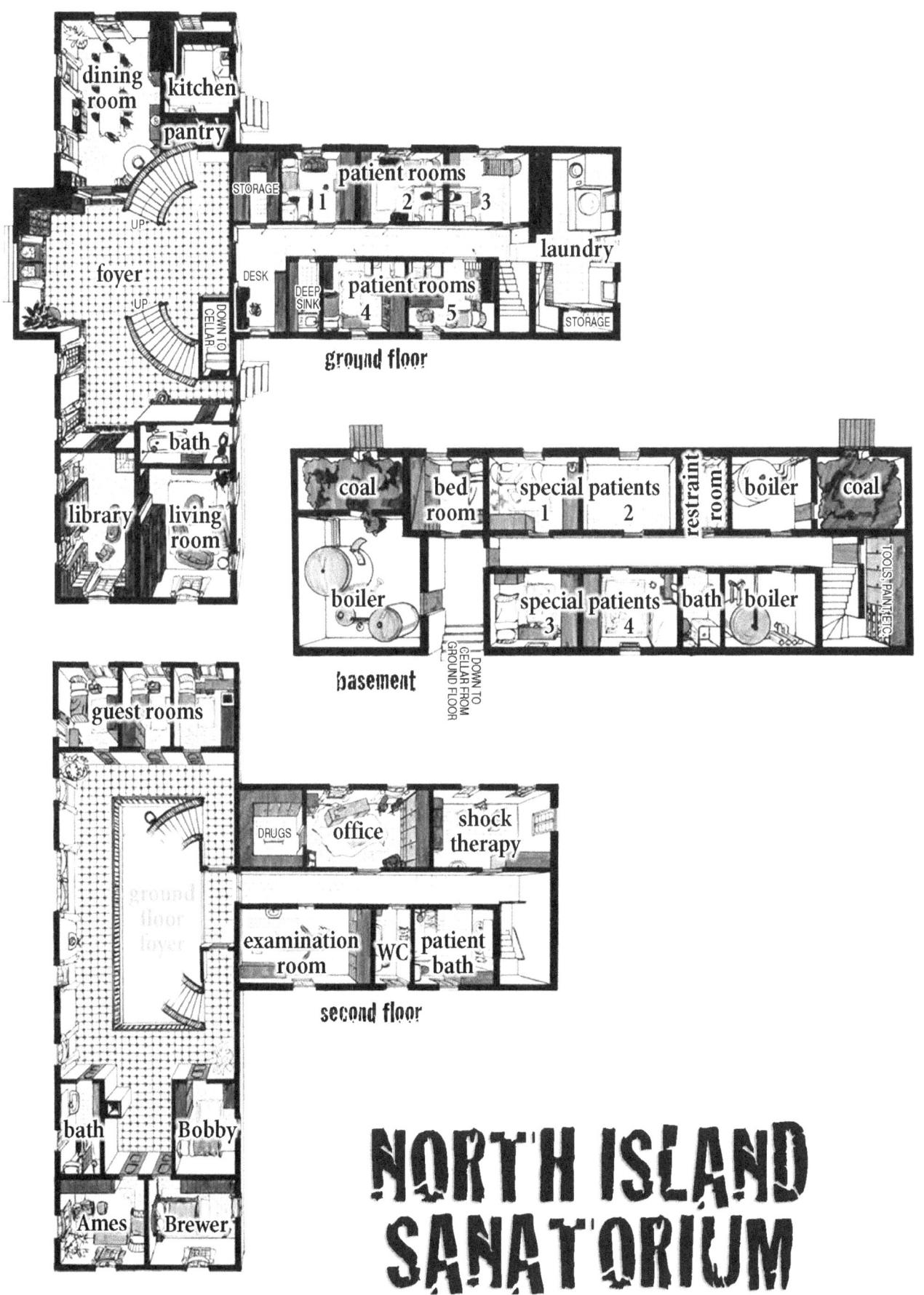

dining room

kitchen

pantry

STORAGE

patient rooms

1  2  3

foyer

UP

UP

DOWN TO CELLAR

DESK

DEEP SINK

laundry

patient rooms

4  5

STORAGE

ground floor

bath

library

living room

coal

bed room

special patients

1  2

restraint room

boiler

coal

boiler

special patients

3  4

bath

boiler

TOOLS, PAINT, ETC.

basement

DOWN TO CELLAR FROM GROUND FLOOR

guest rooms

ground floor foyer

DRUGS

office

shock therapy

examination room

WC

patient bath

second floor

bath

Bobby

Ames

Brewer

# NORTH ISLAND SANATORIUM

# EXCERPTS FROM BREWER'S JOURNAL

If those asses, Hagen and Allen, could hear what I've heard I'm sure it would shake them loose form their high perches. I don't know yet what I'm on to but the sheer power of H's voice while under the effect of that personality is astounding. Jameson in London has found a book — an old one — that he says contains references similar to many of the things mentioned by both H and D. He promises to send it along following his last letter. It is supposed to be a copy of a transcription made by a 15th-century Spanish monk. It contains the ravings of a madman condemned to death by the Inquisition.

The book arrived yesterday and I spent some time with it. Most of it was incomprehensible, seeming nonsense, but Jameson was right. Those pages he was kind enough to mark seemed definitely linked to many of the things referred to by H and D, and, on occasion, Hw as well. Reading those select pages gave me an eerie chill. It was if I was hearing H's voice all over again — a thing that never fails to leave me affected.

*The Sanitorium Papers #4 (p. 81)*

# EXCERPTS FROM THE PERSONNEL RECORD OF CHARLES JOHNSON

*Dear Dr. Brewer,*

*I can recommend Mr. Johnson whole heartedly. His work at this institution has been exemplary and I'm sure you would find him more than satisfactory. Perhaps his own years spent in an institution developed within him a special sympathy. I have seen him handle even the most violent patients always in a way to minimize injury. Of course, I needn't mention that his size and strength also stand in his favor.*

*The Sanitorium Papers #6 (p. 82)*

# A MARKED PAGE IN THE CASTRO MANUSCRIPT

And it was said when "Those Who Wait" came unto the land of pharaoh they laid waste to the country and were not stopped until faced and destroyed by the priestess Annephis of the Temple of Bast. They moved by night, fearing Ra, and shunned also the rushing water. And the stones were made by her and they, carried by the priest, drove the creatures into the Nile which took them to the sea and there they were destroyed. Annephis died of her injuries and, so it is said, died the secret of the stones. She was buried in a tomb in a place which has yet to be discovered.

*The Sanitorium Papers #7 (p. 83)*

## ANCIENT TEMPLE RUINS FOUND

CAIRO — An unusual archaeological find was reported today by the privately funded Huntsford expedition. Operating some twenty miles west of the Valley of the Kings the expedition has uncovered the ruins of a temple and several colossal statues. It is suspected that this find may answer a number of questions about Egyptian history.

One of the first pieces uncovered was a broken stela originally raised in honor of a Princess Annephis. Unknown until now, Annephis, around 1400 BC, was apparently responsible for the routing of an enemy that then threatened the Egyptian people. The enemy is not identified on the stela but it is speculated that perhaps they were Hyksos raiders or perhaps even the mysterious Sea Peoples mentioned in other records.

Work at the site is expected to continue for at least another two years, or longer.

*The Sanitorium Papers #8 (p. 83)*

*My darling Andrew, please meet me at the Sailor's Club tonight at eleven. Do not fail. I really must speak to you. An important time for both of us draws near. -Love, J. G.*

*Mansion Papers #1 (p. 93)*

*October 13, 1896*

*Dear Ebenezer, I'm leaving this letter with friends at port and I'm sure you'll get it when you return home. I'll probably be gone by then and don't know when I'll see you so I'll wish you good luck now.*

*In this envelope is a small present. It's a good luck charm given to me by one of those Kanakys we ran into in the islands. I don't know if it's any damn good but I always wore it, especially anytime I was around those islands. It's been said that some of the ships that sailed out of Innsmouth had something similar attached to their bottoms. I don't know what my address will be but after get to Cincinnati I'll write to let you know.*

*Your friend,*
*William*

*The Sanitorium Papers #9 (p. 84)*

# EXCERPTS FROM DARLENE'S FILES

She was initially brought to the state home by the police who had found her wandering naked in a downtown Boston alley. Repeated attempts over the years have failed to identify her and her last name is still unknown. She is now probably in her late twenties.

Traditional therapies seemed incapable of reaching her but under hypnosis, or the influence of the compounded drugs listed below, she seemed to open up. Repeated treatments brought forth what was at first thought to be Darlene but, under questioning, the individual claimed to be a woman named Fanny and said she lived in Ireland. Oddly enough she also claimed that the year was 1862.

Over the course of treatments even more personalities emerged and, at last count, the list numbered twenty seven; although some of these have appeared only once and were never reached again. The oldest, and perhaps most interesting personality is Annephis who is, if she's to be believed, a princess of Egypt who has been dead for over 3000 years. When in this personality Darlene has exhibited a startling knowledge of Egyptian history, including a number of facts that I have been unable to verify by any amount of research. Perhaps most mystifying was Darlene's prediction of the finding of King Tutankhamen's tomb. She made this prediction after reading in the newspaper the expedition's plans to explore the area.

Much of the odd mythology that Annephis speaks of brings to mind the possessions experienced by the patient Harding and seems hinted at in the occasional ravings of Hawkins. This possibly indicates a root mythic form common to all men and would go a long way toward supporting the theory of the collective unconscious mind.

# EXCERPTS FROM ALLEN HARDING'S FILE

About the time of publication of his first and only book of poetry, Harding dropped out of sight and his whereabouts for the next six months were never established. It is thought that most of this time he spent in a drug and alcohol induced stupor, this being the condition he was found in.

The deteriorated condition of Harding's mind seems to make drug therapy unnecessary, if not useless. He is, however, quite susceptible to hypnosis. He has not revealed the multiple personalities of Darlene but reverts always to the same one. This personality speaks in a deep, intelligent voice; very commanding and quite unlike Harding's own. Sometimes the personality does not speak but the changed face and expression of the subject belie its presence. It almost seems to be observing, contemplating. When finally induced to speak it will usually prefer to not answer any questions but simply makes statements. These statements are usually of the darkest sort, predictions of doom, and the coming of He Who Waits.

# EXCERPTS FROM LEONARD HAWKIN'S FILE

Leading a fairly normal and secure life until the sudden breakdown. Hawkins was unconscious for more than a week and upon awakening displayed signs of intense paranoia. He was unable to recognize even his wife for the first few days, although most of his memory seems to have returned over the next two months.

Not long after returning to his job (an accountant with a major firm) he began displaying signs of a religious conversion and before long joined an obscure sect of ultra conservative Baptists. His wife and children were, against their wishes, also compelled to join. Not long after, he was reprimanded by his supervisor; his continued proselytizing on the job was beginning to irritate the other employees. Two weeks later Hawkins quit his church, accusing them of stupidity, and began to preach on the streets. His family was completely alienated and soon after he lost his job. He moved out of the house and several months later was arrested for assaulting several police officers.

A hatred of his wife, ostensibly stemming from her committing him to North Island, with overt violent tendencies. He will not talk about the source of his knowledge of the "coming of those who wait" but continues to preach his faith in his vision.

*The Sanatorium Papers #5a-c (p. 82)*

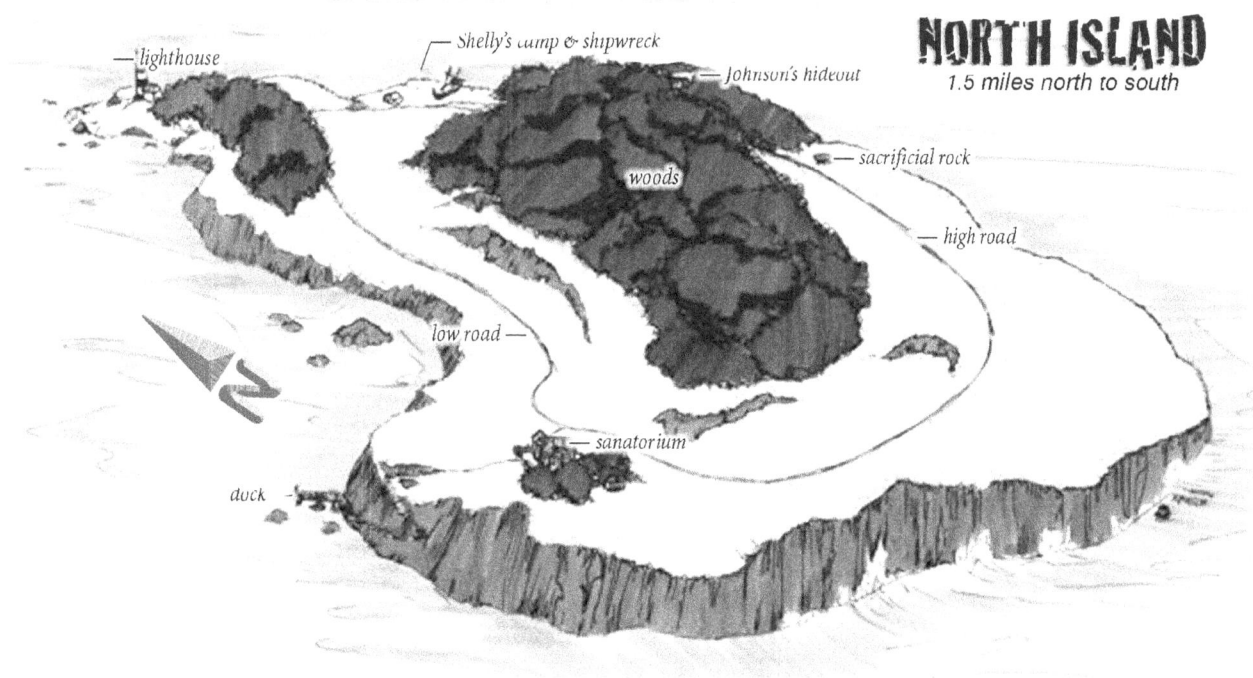

# NORTH ISLAND
*1.5 miles north to south*

— lighthouse

— Shelly's camp & shipwreck

— Johnson's hideout

woods

— sacrificial rock

— high road

low road —

— sanatorium

duck

# SANATORIUM GROUNDS

mansion—
dead cat
outhouse
maintenance shed
Melba's quarters—
Ebenezer's cabin—
generator shed
dock—
cliff edge

## EXCERPTS FROM A DIARY

This document is found in Andrea's beaded purse. Only those entries with direct interest to the investigation are given here.

### June 30, 1916

*Dear Diary,*

*I don't know how to write about it but my dreams have been so strong the last few nights that I'm actually scared. It seems that I was in a big cave, all filled with glowing lights and then I heard a voice. A big voice, but it made noise only in my head. Like someone else's thoughts were there, racing around inside my skull. I can almost still hear it, whispering to me even as I write this. For some reason I am afraid. But it was, after all, only a dream.*

### August 28, 1916

*Dear Diary,*

*I keep having the dreams about the voice. It says it wants to teach me things but somehow it* makes me be afraid. I want to tell mother about it but somehow I feel she wouldn't understand.

As winter arrives, entries referring to the dream voice become more common; but Josephine remains undecided about listening to the mysterious voice. All her diary entries, however, adopt a darker tone.

### January 28, 1917

*Dear Diary,*

*I tell you I cannot stand this house. The walls are pounding in on me. I cannot get the dreams about the voice out of my head and even now I can see that strange cave. I hate my mother and I wish I could pass from this house into the warm darkness of the ground.*

The entries retain this tone throughout the winter and spring of 1917. Pages at a time are free of words but are covered with intricate, convoluted cross hatchings. At first glance the patterns only show a good sense of texture but at times faces seem to resolve themselves out of the dense layers of crossed lines.

### June 29, 1917

*The teachers at school seem so amazed by the things I draw. Some of them say I have real tal-* ent and should go to school somewhere to learn how to draw better. I tried to tell them that I only draw the things I see in my dreams but I don't think they really believed me. Mother says the pictures are no good but I think she's wrong. The voice in my dreams says I could draw better but that I must get away from here. I want to leave this house as soon as I can. Mr. Matthews says there's a contest coming up in Pittsburgh. The winning entrant will be given an art scholarship to Boston University. I'm already starting on a picture I think will win.

### June 30, 1917

*The voice came again last night while I was dreaming. It told me that if I would listen to it and do as it says that I will have everything I ever wanted out of life. For the first time I opened my eyes and then I saw the voice and what it was. It was blurry so I couldn't see much but I know that it's awfully big. It showed me something I could draw for the contest and told me that if I did a good job I couldn't help but win. I think the voice really wants me to win and go to Boston. I hope it happens. I can't stand my mother much longer. I swear, she makes me so mad that sometimes I think I'll kill her.*

*The Mansion Papers #4 (p. 99)*

## Kidnap Victim Dies During Police Raid on Occult Ceremony

### Pitched Gun Battle Ends in Multiple Deaths

Earlier today, proceedings of a secretive Boston religious group known as the Sylvan Night were raided by local police. Led by Detective Sergeant Patrick Devlin of the Boston Police Department, the heavily armed force of men surrounded a wooded area several miles north of the city, then closed in. Authorities had been unaware of the cult's existence but were tipped off to their activities by a former member of the group.

When police arrived on the scene, members of the cult were apparently in the process of performing a "black magic ritual". This shocking rite apparently was to include the brutal sacrifice of a young girl recently abducted from Boston's Chinatown. The kidnap victim was unfortunately killed during the course of the raid. According to Officer Devlin, who was himself slightly injured in the battle, twelve cult members were killed, two captured, and one believed escaped. The woman who escaped is thought to have been the leader of the cult and is still at large. The public is warned that she may be armed and should be considered dangerous. City Councilman Bradford Tibbins has assured the press that accusations of police brutality will be dealt with dung the inquest scheduled for next week. Police have refused to divulge the identity of the deceased and captured cultists pending further investigation.

*– May 22*

## "Kingdom of Shadows"

Using the power of the Dark Stone one can wreak many changes, on both the world and one's self. Great are the promises of the Dark Stone and of The Hanging One, but great also are the dangers. It is said the user can stand transmogrified before the power held captive within, sickness cured and madness dispelled.

. . . *The Dark Stone, of fiery Power and promise! The Stone was cleverly crafted in Elder Days by The Secret Messenger With One Thousand Faces (using hands not his own) to burn a hole between daylight and dreams. A passage by which the One Who Hangs in the Void could reach out and touch this world.*

. . . *Beware lest the Stone take the soul of the impious thief, though it may bring Power beforehand.*

. . . *Not only power can be obtained through the Dark Stone but other talents can also be learned. Secret are their ways and mysterious the callings, but great are these talents in the hands of the user who would know.*

. . . *The Stone was made to last forever and no known power on Earth can destroy it. It possesses those who possess it and it rules their lives.*

## WILFRED'S TESTAMENT

This document is actually found within the Hazard house, in the remains of Wilfred's wheelchair when he has been killed.

The testament is a lengthy document in which Wilfred does his best to explain what has happened to him.

It is clearly quite old — the writing is fading, and in parts the yellowed paper has torn away, taking words with it. Throughout the manuscript there are marginal notes in a variety of hands, the import of which is noted at the end of this handout.

The text itself is written in English, although it would seem it is not the author's native language. *Sanity Loss 1D2 / 2D2, +2 percentiles Cthulhu Mythos, 6 hours to study and comprehend.* No spells.

*My name is Wilfred Hazard, and this is my tale. I relate it now, while I am still able to write and think clearly, so that you, my family, will understand what has happened to me and what I am becoming, that you may avoid the traps into which I have fallen.*

*In the summer of 1723 I embarked upon the greatest adventure of my life...*

Wilfred tells of a French expedition to search for the fabled underground city of Quivira, a city made of gold. The expedition struck out to the West, and with Indians from local tribes as their guides, managed to find a path to the subterranean land where Quivira lay. They found Quivira, he relates, and other cities that surpassed it both in beauty and in riches....

*...The towering golden spires of Quivira paled when compared to those of this new place: gigantic structures reaching out to the cavern roof impossibly high above us. All around us the lanterns caught the twinkle of gold — every surface, every structure, it seemed was constructed of the metal. Surely here were riches enough to make us all kings!*

*If only we had taken what we could and turned back then, but we did not, because we knew that beyond this place there must be another which was richer still....*

Wilfred explains that the sheer value of all that surrounded them drove some of the expedition mad with greed, and the others were forced to kill them before the whole group was endangered. Despite such things, they explored further, until they began to discern the signs of habitation....

*...At first we argued over whether we should proceed, for who could say what manner of creature might make its home in so deep and forgotten a land, however we soon decided that as long as the creatures left us alone, we need not worry about them.*

*It was clear that whatever lived there was not human, although there might once have been some similarities. The ancient carvings that we found depicted bizarre beasts with the shapes of lizards and worse; the lizard creatures seemed to have lived in those great cities, making idols and altars to enormous, blasphemous gods. Many a night we slept with the horrendous images from the shrines we had found haunting our nightmares, and many a morning one or another of us would awake screaming and wreathed in terror at what we had seen. We chose to ignore such warnings, however, until we found the wraiths....*

Odd wraith-like forms beset the expedition. Wilfred describes the forms as little more than a collection of floating blue lights, and yet it is clear from his narrative that they disturbed the entire exploration team. While he does not indicate that the wraiths directly harmed the expedition in any way, they chose to turn around and head for the surface a short time after they first encountered them.

*...it was decided that we would head back to the surface and outfit another, larger expedition. By this time we all had a great deal of gold with us, but that was not all: I had discovered a strange token made of a substance we were quite unfamiliar with. At first I believed it to be a string of dark, lustrous pearls, but since that time I have doubted that assessment, for they are unlike any pearls I have ever seen, and they are far too large. It was this token, I think, that spared me from what we were next to encounter....*

Shortly after they started for the surface, the expedition suffered a catastrophe. With no warning whatsoever, the ground spilt asunder and many of the team were lost. Wilfred speculates that it was almost as if there was a conscious intellect below them, reaching up to prevent them from leaving. They had to retrace their steps several times, as similar chasms barred their passage, until they found them-

*(continued on other side)*

# PASSAGES FROM SCRIPTURES OF THE RIVEN VALLEY

"Many stories of the area seem to have their basis in old Indian legends regarding a being that dwelt somewhere in "the shadow land of the hills." This "god" could contact those it wanted through their dreams and command them. Often, those who would dream of this being would be driven mad. These unfortunates would end up being expelled from their tribes and forced into the wilderness to make their way on their own. The area was taboo to the tribes of the area but occasionally, one seeking wisdom or knowledge would, regardless of the risks, sleep in these dark and forbidding hills.

"An old woman told me a story about a neighbor who once, after suffering a particularly terrible series of nightmares, slew his entire family with an axe before hanging himself in his woodshed. The old woman told me that the man had always been a good husband and father but apparently lost his mind. She remembers her uncle telling her that old Martin Garsetti was a good man until they moved out of town and into the new house he'd built for his family on the slopes of the mountain. This house was built in an area shunned by the local Indians. The house still stands and is presently occupied by other members of the same family, although none of them seem to have been afflicted by any form of madness.

"The Gunderson party was among the first whites to make a home for themselves in the area and, despite the warnings of local Indians, built their first rude settlements among those hills the Indians so assiduously avoided. Although the early settlement seemed to prosper for the first year it was not long before tragedy struck. Apparently during the long winter one of the settlers lost his mind. When they were discovered by visitors from nearby Pittsburgh all the miners and their families were dead, apparently killed by wolves, their faces terribly bitten and chewed. Only one man's death was caused by other means, a single bullet wound to the forehead — an obvious suicide. Oddly enough, the marauding wolves did not see fit to ravage this body as they had the others.

*The Mansion Papers #3 (p. 98)*

---

*(continued from other side)*

selves straying into vast, dark caverns filled with shifting shadows....

*...even as we clambered over the debris, we could tell that there was something watching us: a cold baleful presence. We moved as fast as we were able, resting for only a few hours when we were too exhausted to continue....*

Several times the surviving explorers were attacked by shapes and shadows they could only dimly make out. Tentacles reached out from the darkness dragging screaming men off to their doom. The survivors fled into the dark, time after time, until only a handful remained. Then, when they seemed to be only a day's journey from the surface, they encountered a dreadful creature, which the other formless monsters seemed to follow as a leader. It bore the likeness of a great toad, oozing and fetid. Wilfred describes the encounter as a massacre.

*...This I know, to my most bitter sorrow, that I alone of the thirty men survived this encounter. I shudder still as I think back and see its gaping maw envelop those I had traveled so far with.*

*Many a night have I wondered how I, of all of them, could have survived, and indeed remained unscathed as the carnage went on around me. It is my belief that it was the token that protected me that day – the dark string of pearls I had found. I could feel that nameless creature's desire for the object, and its frustration – for I believe it could not harm me while I possessed the token. It is only through its power, I am sure, that I escaped the attention of the wraiths and*

formless things that so blighted that Necropolis. And yet I did not escape unmarked, for even as I fled in terror, I felt a moist presence at my back, and for a single moment knew a boundless pain as something thrust itself within me. To this day I have been unable to say exactly what it was that found its way inside me then, but even now I can feel it within me contorting both my body and, God help me, my soul.

*While my mind and body are being deformed by whatever it is that caught me that day, I feel now that it is the token that holds the key to this dreadful curse I have brought upon us. I can feel, still, the desire burning in that loathsome beast – a desire that cannot rest until the token is returned to those nameless caverns, where it belongs. I can discover no way to destroy the token, nor have I been able to in any way free myself from the bond that I can feel has been created between me and that foul creature.*

*I have come to see that the token is somehow part of the soul of that blasphemous toad-god, and that by possessing it I am bound in some way to the beast. It presents me, this token: that venture is now sixty years gone, and still I show no signs of aging; instead my undying body warps and I am prey to hungers and terrible urges that are not my own. And further, I am unable to even take my own life — some part of me, or of the baleful creature to which I am now linked, will not allow me to harm myself in any way.*

*I must make haste to finish this document whilst my mind is still my own, and I beseech you, my great-nephew, to keep it in your hands and pass it to the fittest of your sons*

when he reaches his maturity, as you have already promised, for the great love of family that fills you. And keep the pearls safely, for it is only by their power that we are able to keep it at bay; I know that should we lose the token, that thing will surely come for us. To these oaths I bind you – you and your descendants to the last generation – on peril of the most fearful consequences. If my condition becomes known I will surely be destroyed and this curse will infect another of you, the best and brightest and fairest. Of this I am sure.

*I beseech you again; keep this thing, this foul carcass, hidden, though I should forget all thought and due care; to tell no one; to attempt no trespass further where once I have trod, at the peril of your immortal soul, for man was not meant to go there, and return whole....*

*I pray daily for death and it does not come. I know that I have passed from God's grace. But if He will not spare me, perhaps He will attend you, who are blameless in this. Therefore I pray in God's grace, that He may bless you and keep you in this year of our Lord, 1785*

*Wilfred Hazard, a most unhappy soldier.*

Notations cover the manuscript attesting to its veracity. Some fragments detail rituals of sacrifice to be enacted upon children of the family who are born deformed. The evidence of the notes suggests that Wilfred is directly responsible for most of the children, and that almost all are born mutated and killed soon after. ☀

*The Old Damned House Papers #1 (p. 122–123)*

# FROM THE DIARY OF MISTRESS MERCY STANTON, 1865

It has been a very bad summer indeed, with many of our younger ones taken away by cruel fever n'ague. It has been most sad for the Hazards, with three of their little ones struck down one after the other. They have been most stoic, refusing all offers of aid for fear of spreading the infection, and nursing them themselves most diligently but to no avail. The only result of their labor has been three tiny coffins carried out their front door one after the other. They are most distraught at this loss, little Johnny, eleven, and the heir, Nathanial at eight, and Lucy, only three, "not lost but gone before," as my dear mother would say.

It was at the funeral of little Lucy that one of those carrying the coffin made a most vulgar and coarse joke, causing much comment amongst the crowd of well-wishers gathered to help comfort the bereaved. He said that something was rolling around in the coffin and that it was his opinion that the child's head had come clean off! This of course excited great outrage and several ladies fainted. Fortunately, being blessed with a sturdy constitution, I was able to witness the man being dismissed from his office immediately, one of the Hazards taking his place. The family was most upset by this grievously unnecessary occurrence.

I heard the man was about the town later, unrepentant and quite drunk, saying that it if it was a child in the coffin it was the strangest load he had ever shouldered, and he was a professional pallbearer and had much practice at such tasks. Notwithstanding the universal condemnation such wild talk received, he continued with his claims for several days, and some of the coarser elements in the town were even taking to buying him drinks, and encouraging him in his hurtful boastfulness.

These people, of course, believe all those stories you hear about the Hazards, about the witch-trials and the peculiar business of the ghost, or the baby, or whatever it was back all those years ago when they were rebuilding the house. Not to mention those pearls. Mere jealousy and spite, and such a trial for my respectable and dear friends. Fortunately after a few days the man moved on, and has since troubled us no more.

*The Old Damned House Papers #2 (p. 132)*

# FROM THE DIARY OF ONE "NAILOR TOM", BOATWRIGHT, FEBRUARY 1759

*Night fell early. I had repaired to John Beverly's hostelry and we were making very merry over some hot punch. The day, as I said, had been dark and stormy and no travelers were looked for, so we were made a small party alone in the common room, John, his wife and Isaiah and I. Then a hail came from without.*

*On going to the door, John found such a strange sight that his exclamation brought us over. A gentleman was there, dressed as a preacher all in black, with a black hat over his eyes. A heavily laden sleigh was behind him, and behind it were two of the most wretched Indians I had ever seen, blue with cold but evil-looking for all that. Murderous thieves, I could tell as soon as I clapped eyes upon them. But it was the man I looked for most sharply for he was uncommon ill looking, very puffy and stark white about the face, with red eyes, from cold or weeping.*

*Come in come in, says friend John, for in such dirty weather we looked for no traveler or we would have kept a sharper watch out.*

*I looked again at the sleigh and saw it had no bells upon it, nothing that would carry any sound, even in clear weather. The man just stood there, and his Indians as well, as if carved from the same wood as the sleigh. John would have none of it, especially as the man looked so unwell. Corpse white, and very heavy of breath and red of eye as if in a seizure.*

*Then the man spoke, in a thick foreign accent, asking for the Hazards. Well, Isaiah and I silently speculated at this, and looked from the savages to their master, while John told him to go up the road and there would be the Hazard place, a fine, handsome house and well-tended. He would have sent a boy ahead to tell Elijah Hazard of his visitor, but the stranger told him not to mind.*

*Before you go sir, sez I plucking up the courage at Isaiah's goading, Can you tell us how things fare up in Boston?*

*I cannot tell you anything of that, sez he.*

*Oh so you came by sea then, sez I.*

*No, he sez shortly, I come from Wichita country. Here, he sez, tossing a coin to John. Never let it be said that Wilfred Hazard does not recognize hospitality. I go to see my cousin. Elijah.*

*He has a bonny family sir, pipes up Isaiah, hoping no doubt for similar favor, and you will find them all in good health.*

*This seemed to stir him, for his face twisted and he looked most anguished. Then he shook so hard we thought he would fall down and bent forward clutching at his stomach. John stepped forward right smartly to help him up, but one of the Indians came forward instead, and motioned him away, saying something in his guttural tongue. Then the stranger turned without other word, and started to walk up the street very fast, and still doubled up, staggering as though drunk. The Indians followed, leading the sleigh. We saw him go over onto his knees and then get up again and keep walking, but now he was limping very badly, as if his left leg would not hold his weight. We watched until he was out of sight in the dark and snow, fearing another fall.*

*Well, friend Wilfred will be like to die before the winter is out no doubt, Isaiah says helping himself to the punch, for he looks to me to be on his last legs.*

*And here he laughs at his own wit. But I said nothing for something about the stranger and his savage companions had troubled me.*

*The Old Damned House Papers #3 (p. 133)*

# THE HAZARD MANSION

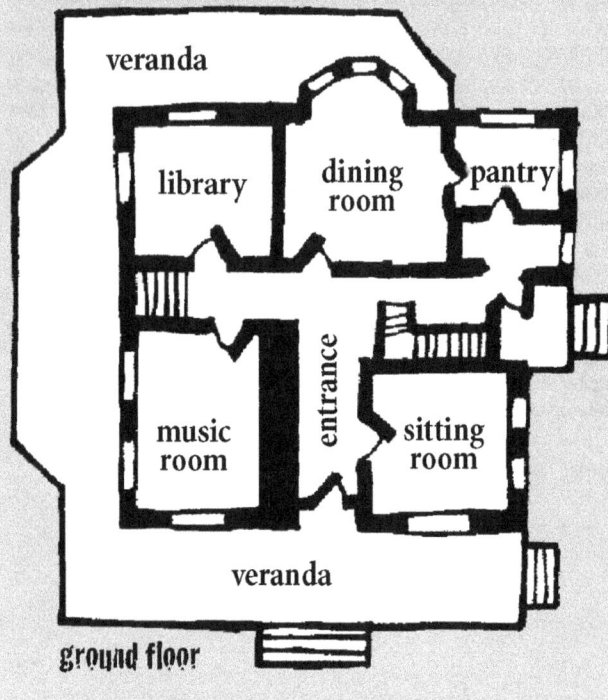

veranda

library

dining room

pantry

entrance

music room

sitting room

veranda

ground floor

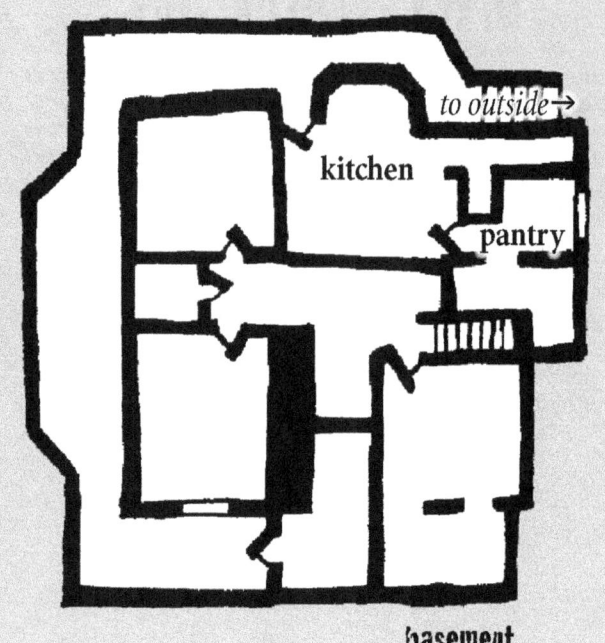

*to outside →*

kitchen

pantry

basement

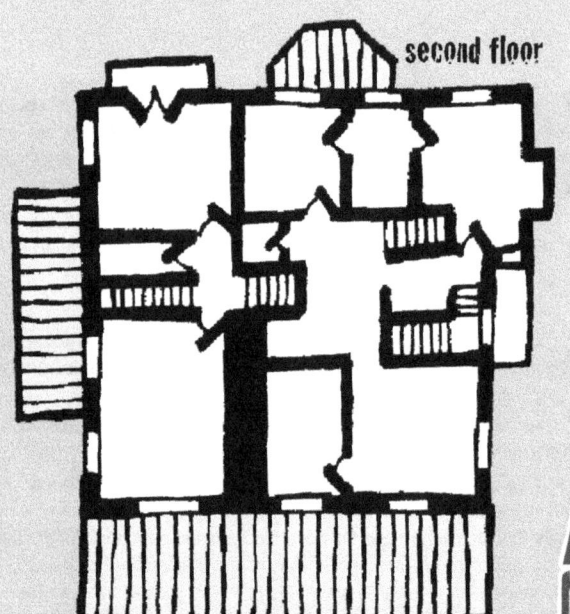

second floor

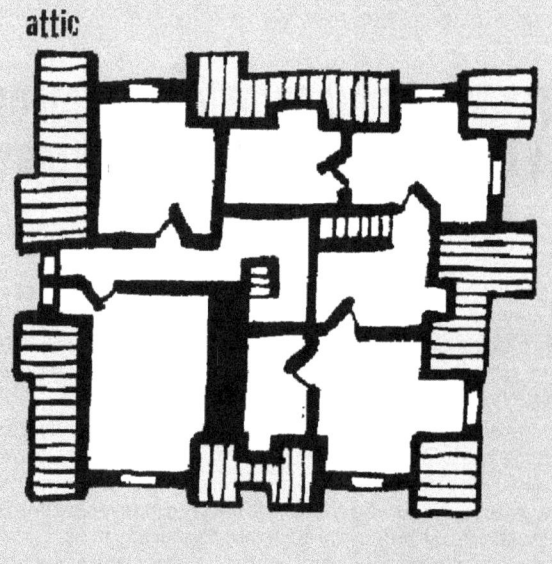

attic

N